Praise for William Martin's first novel

Back Bay

"Well, Wow! Talk about blockbusters. A rip-roaring page-turner, a perfect read that keeps you hanging on till the last paragraph."
—*Boston Globe*

"Don't be fooled by the title; this mystery/adventure is no Beacon Hill tea party, but a Southie-style rouser, starring several generations of Yankee tycoons—the crafty Pratts—and their immigrant-descended allies and enemies. Martin has carefully researched the topography of old Boston and tidily balances his inventive plot with its narrow escapes and stop-watch action. A bracing brew for long cold nights."
—*Kirkus Reviews*

"Martin's first novel is a clever and entertaining blend of history, family saga, and mystery story."—*Publishers Weekly*

"Unlike the traditional first novel, this one is not auto-biographical nor is it a venture into self-discovery. On the contrary, William Martin has given us a story of straight adventure spiced with history and laced with mystery. More-over, its setting is Boston, a city which doesn't figure in fiction as much as it used to do or as often as it deserves to do. Martin has plotted an intricate tale and moves with facility between past and present."
—*John Barkham Reviews*

"Colonial Boston and its modern descendant is the setting for this excellent first novel. Martin has effectively captured the flavor of the past without sentimentality or pedantry. Highly Recommended."
—*Library Journal*

NERVE ENDINGS

NERVE ENDINGS

WILLIAM MARTIN

Crown Publishers, Inc.

New York

Inquiries should be addressed to Crown Publishers, Inc.,
One Park Avenue, New York, New York 10016
Printed in the United States of America
Published simultaneously in Canada by General Publishing Company Limited
Library of Congress Cataloging in Publication Data
ISBN 0-517-55088-1
Book design by Camilla Filancia
10 9 8 7 6 5 4 3 2 1
First Edition

for my parents

ACKNOWLEDGMENTS

This is a work of fiction. However, the best stories are rooted in fact, and I would like to thank several people for helping me to bring a sense of authenticity to this story:

Dr. Sang I. Cho and Dr. Anthony Sahyoun, who permitted me into their operating rooms to observe renal surgery;

Mrs. Janet Delorey, for her moving and perceptive descriptions of a transplant patient's experiences;

Dr. Garner Haupert, who was always willing to answer my questions about the treatment and recovery of a "best-case" transplant patient, such as the character in this book;

Ms. Sondra Madison, who guided me through a dialysis clinic in Boston;

Mr. John Frenning and Professor Eli Noam, who provided opinions and insights into the cable television industry;

And Mr. William F. Kuntz, for his illumination of some of the finer points of corporate law.

I would also like to thank my editor, Pamela Thomas, for her good sense and hard work and my wife, Christine, for her patience and perception.

William Martin
Weston, Massachusetts
June 1983

ONE

SPRING TRANSPLANTS

1

A moment before the sun appeared, its rays struck the top of the television antenna that poked through the center of the island like a spindle. As the sun rose, daylight descended in perfect synchrony onto the island. It traveled down the granite cliffs. It turned the peaks of the Maine pines from black to deep green. It baked into the shingles and chimneys of the lobstermen's houses. And Harry Miller opened his eyes.

He swung his legs out of bed and looked out the window. The sky was clear, the ocean calm, and the thermometer read fifty-nine degrees. On June mornings like this, Harry did not bother to tap the barometer hanging by the window. He had spent seventy-two years on the island, and he knew what to expect from every season and every seachange. He pulled on a pair of khaki work pants and a red wool shirt, he laced on his boots, and he went downstairs.

In the kitchen, he poured a cup of coffee. His son, a Boston attorney, had given him a coffeemaker that automatically started brewing before anyone was out of bed. Harry thought his old percolator made better coffee, and he still brewed it that way on weekends, but his wife liked the convenience of the coffeemaker, and Harry was happy to indulge her. Small thanks, he thought, for all the years that Ellie Miller had stayed with him, loving him, caring for him, nursing him back to health when the sea beat the life out of him, helping him to raise two strong sons, and helping him to mourn when the sea took one of them.

Harry kicked open the screen door and stepped outside. He lived on the edge of the sea. His closest neighbor was half a mile away. Stands of pine grew on the north and east sides of the house, and a vegetable garden was planted on the west. To the south, the land was flat and grassy for twenty feet; then it sloped across a smooth shoulder of granite and down to the water.

Rumrunner's Bulge expanded to the southwest of Harry's

4 house. In the twenties, it had been deserted, a perfect landing for Canadian bootleggers. Now, it was dotted with small summer cottages, but a thick cover of pines secluded them. From Harry's lawn, Rumrunner's Bulge still looked like virgin forest, and that was how he liked it.

Beyond the bulge rose the granite cliffs that were, to Harry Miller, the bedrock and soul of the island. Known as Cutter's Point, the cliffs had been there before the pines and meadows and ponds, before the Indians, before the Boston fishermen who were blown off course and landed on the island one Easter Sunday in the seventeenth century, before the town and the fleet, before the stonecutters who came to chip away at the island's granite skull, before the rich barons of the Gilded Age, who moored their yachts in the deepwater anchorage and built their retreats on the island's north side, before the summer people, who rented cottages in the gentle season between the last spring storm and the first autumn fire. The cliffs and the island, named Easter's Haven by the Boston fishermen, had endured it all. Only the sea and the sky had been there longer.

Harry Miller had spent his life looking at the cliffs, and he had devoted his life to learning the lore of the island. The granite cliffs, the legend went, had been raised by God that Easter morning so that the lost fishermen would see landfall through the storm.

Now, the cliffs protected the home of an islander who was himself a legend, Andrew MacGregor. His family, which owned the southwest quarter of the island, had built its fortune on the granite once quarried on the cliffs. He had expanded it through radio, newspapers, television, and telecommunications, and in 1954, he had erected the antenna that brought television to the island. It was said that Andrew MacGregor was one of the richest men in America, but no one knew for certain because his holdings were private, and for twenty years, he had been a recluse. He traveled secretly to his homes in New York, Palm Beach, and Wyoming. He appeared to the public only on video tape.

Harry Miller was one of the few who visited the MacGregor house, called Brisbane Cottage, and he never divulged what he saw there. A man's privacy, he said, was his birthright, no matter how rich and powerful he was. What mattered to Harry was that MacGregor had loved the island as much as any man, and he had wielded his power to protect it.

On the east side of Harry's house, the Louder's Pond inlet opened to the sea. Twice a day, the tide flowed up the inlet, past Harry's dock, under the bridge, and into the salt pond across the road. Twice a day, it flowed back, leaving barely enough water to support the draft of the *Ellie B.*, Harry's boat. Beyond the inlet was Louder's Point, and beyond that the homes of other lobstermen, the harbor, the ferry slip, and the town of Easter's Landing.

It was slack tide. The water in the inlet was still, the *Ellie B.* was motionless. She was the best lobster boat he'd ever piloted, tight, seaworthy, reliable. She had been hauling his traps for seven seasons, and each winter she had taken him into the Gulf of Maine to drag for northern shrimp. But the *Ellie B.* was getting old, like Harry. He didn't think that either of them could take another winter of rough seas alone.

He flexed the fingers of his right hand and felt the arthritic stiffness. When he was younger, he never thought about winter. Now, he couldn't work the cold out of his joints in June.

He heard the sound of an inboard motor and looked to the southwest. That would be the *Fog Lady,* Izzy Jackson's boat, its wake glistening as it churned away from Andrew MacGregor's dock. Izzy lived by himself on one of the tiny Pentecost Islands, and he kept to himself, except when he did errands and odd jobs for Andrew MacGregor. Most people on Easter's Haven considered him to be a bit strange, but Izzy Jackson was as harmless as a mayfly. On many a morning, Harry had heard Izzy's boat chugging through the thoroughfare, its engine smoking and straining for oil, while Izzy stood at the stern and fed fish heads to the gulls.

There were no birds around Izzy's boat this morning, however. A television producer had come to the island, a man named Roger Darrow, and Izzy was giving him a tour of the islands that surrounded Easter's Haven. While lobstermen like Harry knew every patch of sea bottom in Penobscot Bay, Izzy knew the islands like the tops of his shoes, which he usually studied when he wasn't staring into space.

The day before, Harry had shown the producer around Easter's Haven, and he had answered every question, until the producer had started asking about Andrew MacGregor. Harry liked visitors at his island. He liked the summer people who came for the scenery and the lobster and left with nothing but their memories. He liked writers and painters who came for inspiration. But he did not

ᑕ like strangers who came to probe and question and steal away some piece of the island's magic.

Down the road, another lobsterman sipped coffee and watched Izzy Jackson's boat. Cal Bannister's day, however, had not begun with the arrival of the sun in his room. He had not lived long enough on the island to live now by its rhythms. In fact, he had not been able to sleep at all that night.

In his hand, Cal Bannister held a small, malleable ball of *plastique* explosive, a few wires, and a battery-powered digital alarm clock just powerful enough to work as a detonator. He had received an order to kill the television producer. The request came from Los Angeles and from the past that still demanded Cal Bannister's loyalty. He had killed men before; that was part of the past he had come here to escape. But his time on the island had changed him, because his small bomb was still in his hand and not wired to the gas tanks of Izzy Jackson's boat.

Cal Bannister watched the *Fog Lady* roll on the gentle swell, and he heard the anemic chugging of her engines. She would have been the perfect target for an accident, he thought. In a leaky old tub like that, he could rig an explosion to look like spontaneous combustion. But something had stopped him. He wasn't sure, but he thought it was his conscience, which had not bothered him in many years.

He hefted his little package and told himself he would have other chances before Roger Darrow left the island, if he wanted them.

He looked again at the *Fog Lady*. Izzy Jackson had painted it Day-glow orange, so that people would see him, he explained, in the thickest fog. On a bright morning, the boat stood out like a cooked lobster on a bed of seaweed. Cal could see the bow ropes, the three lobster traps at the stern, and the director's chair Izzy had set out on the deck. He did not see Izzy or the television producer. They were probably in the cabin waiting for the sun to warm the water.

Then he saw a small strand of smoke curl from the engine hold. It was not exhaust.

In the instant it took him to realize that something was wrong, flames leaped from the hold and the *Fog Lady* rose from the water. Her deck flew into pieces. Her windscreen blew out. She remained suspended long enough for the sound of the explosion to reach

the shore and rattle the windows in Cal Bannister's house. Then
she crashed back into the water, split in half, and burst into
flames.

Harry Miller jumped up from the breakfast table and rushed
to the door. He saw the *Fog Lady* flaming in the middle of the
thoroughfare. He turned to his wife and told her to bring the first-
aid kit. Then he hurried for his boat.

Cal Bannister did not move. He watched the tiny figure of a
man, forearms in flames, burst from the cabin of the *FogLady*.
The man spun about in a mad dance of panic and pain, then fell
into the water and disappeared.

The stern of the *Fog Lady* sank a moment after him. The bow
and cabin continued to burn.

Cal's wife appeared at the back door. He told her to call the
Coast Guard, but he did not take his eyes from the wreck. He was
transfixed by the flames.

He saw the *Ellie B.* speeding out toward the *Fog Lady*, and a
feeling of relief came over him. He had not killed the television
producer, nor had he refused the request. The right people would
give Cal Bannister credit.

He tossed the remains of his coffee on the ground and headed
into the house. Then he stopped. He suddenly felt sick to his
stomach. It was the same sickness he had felt when he killed for
the first time in a Vietnamese rice paddy. He did not want credit
for murdering the television producer. Not from the right people,
not from anyone.

2

Just after noon, a helicopter took off from Easter's Haven and swung out over the thoroughfare. The lobstermen below were working their traps, a single sailboat chased the June breeze, and the ferry was rounding Louder's Point. The helicopter passed over the Pentecost Islands and headed for Boston at a hundred miles an hour.

The shipbuilding ports of Maine and New Hampshire appeared on the blue carpet below, places like Monhegan Island and Portsmouth, names that rang with the excitement of the seagoing past. Then, the fishing villages, the artists' colonies, and the yacht clubs of the Massachusetts north shore rolled into view, followed by the manufacturing towns, the wood-frame triple-deckers, and Logan Airport.

The MacGregor Communications Corporation jet was waiting when the helicopter touched down at two-thirty, and the jet was cleared for takeoff fifteen minutes later. At five-thirty, Pacific daylight time, the jet arrived at Los Angeles International Airport.

It was rush hour. The San Diego Freeway looked like a giant, sheet-metal snake sliding all the way from Inglewood to the Sepulveda Pass, and it took nearly forty minutes for the rented Chevrolet to reach Sunset Boulevard. During the drive, the radio played the current hits and told of the Dodger victory in Saint Louis. It gave the news of the latest shootings in East Los Angeles and the San Fernando Valley. It told of heavy traffic on the San Diego Freeway, the Santa Monica Freeway, the Harbor Freeway, the Ventura Freeway, and the Four-Level Interchange. And it predicted the weather, which was seldom a difficult task in southern California. The weather for June: morning low clouds and fog giving way to afternoon sun, with moderate to heavy smog in the inland valleys.

The Chevrolet turned west at Sunset Boulevard. Cypress trees hung low over the road. Rolls-Royces and Jaguars sped past

houses sheltered by evergreens and broad-leafed tropical plants.
Sprinklers pumped rhythmically, and lawns glistened in the spray.

After a few miles, the car turned off Sunset and climbed into the secluded hills of Pacific Palisades. Each turn brought larger homes, greener lawns, more tennis courts, and cleaner air. The car stopped finally in the circular driveway of a Spanish-style home, and a young man got out.

He crossed the lawn and the brick sidewalk, pulled the rope at the front door, and a bell jangled somewhere in the house.

He was tall and slender, with delicate features and blond hair that made him look much younger than he probably was. Had he been at all unkempt, he might have looked like a struggling poet or an assistant professor of English at a small New England college. But his gray suit was unwrinkled, his collar buttoned, and his tie tightly knotted.

A woman's face appeared at the small window in the middle of the door. Then, she opened the door a bit and peered out. "Yes?"

"Are you Mrs. Jeanne Darrow?"

She said yes again and slowly widened the crack in the door, as though she sensed instinctively that something was wrong.

"My name is John Meade," said the young man. "I'm Andrew MacGregor's nephew and personal secretary."

It took a moment before MacGregor's name made its connection in Jeanne Darrow's mind and another moment before her stomach muscles tightened.

"May I come in?" he asked gently.

"Is this about my husband?" The tightness reached her throat. He nodded.

She let him in and closed the door. The foyer was dark and cool, with stucco walls and a red tile floor.

She ran her hands nervously down the front of her white tennis dress. She stood five feet ten in sneakers. Her body was lithe, feminie, athletic. She had just played three hard sets on a neighbor's new clay court. The veins in her right arm were still bulging from exertion, and her hair was plastered to the sides of her face in little ringlets of perspiration.

She had inherited her features and her dark hair from her grandmother, an Irish beauty who came to California to become a star and spent thirty years as a seamstress in the MGM costume department. Jeanne wore her hair in a short layer cut that emphasized the openness and honesty of her face; people could tell what she was feeling simply by looking at her. In a checkered acting career, her most successful role had been as a young mother who discoveres that her brand of bleach does not whiten as well as her neighbor's. At thirty-one, she had the kind of direct attractiveness that advertisers preferred for their image of the average American housewife.

"May we sit down?" asked John Meade.

Jeanne did not move. She spoke softly and slowly and tried to control every word. "What has happened to my husband?"

"There's been an accident."

That much she expected. "How bad?"

"He was touring Penobscot Bay in a fishing boat. The boat exploded."

"How badly is he hurt?" she demanded. She didn't care about details.

"He has second-degree burns on his forearms."

She looked at him for a moment. "You traveled three thousand miles to tell me *that*?"

"I'm afraid not." The young man hesitated. "He's also suffered a massive head injury."

Behind the tan, Jeanne Darrow went pale. Her skin turned yellow.

John Meade had prepared no delicate way of telling her. "Your husband is being kept alive by machines and will die if the machines are turned off."

For a moment, Jeanne Darrow seemed not to comprehend. God was playing a cruel cosmic joke, a nightmare had invaded an afternoon reverie. She stood immobile, her eyes fixed on Meade, her left hand clutching the sweatband at her right wrist. Then, he body began to tremble. She tried to steady herself. Her eyes filled with tears. A cry rose from her throat. She tried to swallow it, but it forced its way out of her.

She ran down the hallway to the kitchen and slammed the door.

John Meade stood in the foyer and listened to Jeanne Darrow's grief. She began to sob slowly, almost rhythmically. The sobs became her husband's name. She repeated it again and again. And then she began to cry. She cried softly for ten minutes or more.

When John Meade heard a crash in the kitchen, he went down

the hallway and opened the door.

The kitchen was filled with sunlight. The west wall was glass," and sliding doors opened onto the patio. Beyond, a swimming pool and tennis court blended into the landscaping. Expensive copper pots hung from the ceiling rack. Ceramic tile covered the cooking island. A jar filled with colorful utensils sat on the island and a Cuisinart beside it. The refrigerator, dark blue to match the tile, murmured politely in the corner. Jeanne Darrow stood in the midst of her kitchen and stared blankly at the jumble of stems and bowls and shards on the floor.

"Can I get you a drink or call your doctor?" asked Meade.

"I broke my sangría glasses," she said. She opened a small closet beside the refrigerator, took out a broom, and methodically swept the shattered glass into a neat pile. Then she swept it into the dustpan and dumped it into the wastebasket. She contemplated the top of the wastebasket for a few minutes, then sat at the cooking island and laughed bitterly. "My husband is all but dead in some hospital on the other side of the country, and I'm sweeping the goddamn floor." She shook her head slowly, and the laugh became a sob. "I guess I could use that drink now."

"I'll make it," said Meade.

She pointed to the liquor cabinet and asked for a gin and tonic. Then, she changed her mind. "Maybe I'll just have a shot of Scotch. Gin and tonic is something you drink when you're having fun."

Meade poured two shots of Scotch and sat beside her. He waited until she had taken a sip before he continued. "Mrs. Darrow, you should know that you're going to have to give permission."

"For what?"

"Permission to turn off the machines that are keeping your husband alive."

"Shit," she whispered softly, almost in defeat. She didn't think she could do it, no matter how badly her husband was hurt. She shook her head violently.

Meade put his hand on hers. "There's really no other choice. That's what the doctors would tell you."

"I'll talk to them myself."

"There's no need for you to go to Maine, Mrs. Darrow. Your husband won't know you. I'm an attorney. You can simply sign the forms I've brought, have a relative witness them, and everything will be taken care of."

Suddenly, she was infuriated. "Just sign on the dotted line, ma'am, is that it? We'll shut off your husband and ship him home to you in a little box and thank you very much . . . Well, no thanks!" She stood and began to pace.

"I would have preferred if someone else had been given this task, Mrs. Darrow. But the lobsterman who pulled your husband's body from the wreckage brought him directly to our dock. He knew that our helicopter was your husband's only hope. We rushed him to the hospital on the mainland, and they did all they could for him."

Jeanne Darrow continued to pace. She wasn't listening.

"Someone had to tell you," continued Meade. "Mr. MacGregor said you should know as soon as possible."

Jeanne stopped pacing and wheeled on Meade. "I'm going to Maine to see him. I want to feel his hand while it's still warm." She paused, fought back another sob, and held onto her composure. "And besides, I'll have to make the identification."

Meade swallowed hard before he spoke. "I'm afraid we'll have to ask you to get his dental records. The medical examiner will need them to make a positive identification."

She shuddered and sat again at the counter. "You mean I can't see his face?"

"The explosion shattered his face, Mrs. Darrow."

She shook her head again, violently, angrily, and she resolved to stay in control. She leaned forward, so that her face was close to Meade's. "I am going to Maine, Mr. Meade. I want to see my husband alive before I allow him to die."

3

You'll *never go wrong if you buy your thongs at Henry Long's.* Scratch it out before someone sees it and thinks you're slipping.

Try again. *Long's, for value in footwear.*

That's a good way to lose the account. Try again.

For footwear, shop Long's, where the footwear you wear . . . The client wants no puns and no wordplaying. Scratch it out and try again.

Go back to your old rules. Think of what you're trying to sell. List its good points. List the reasons why someone might want the product. List the reasons why the competition isn't as good. In the case of this client, that means price. And don't tell them that most of the shoes you buy in Henry Long's Factory Shoe Outlet fall apart after one rainstorm. Then think about the demographics. What kind of population group are you aiming to reach? And then . . . bullshit.

James Whiting fired his pencil at the wall and tore up the sheet of paper in front of him. For the last month, it had become increasingly difficult for him to find the right words, the vivid phrases, the catchy internal rhymes that had once made him one of the top copywriters in Boston. At least, he thought, his creativity had lasted longer than his health. He had been sick for over a year, and he was getting sicker.

He rubbed his eyes. They ached from the strain. He pushed himself away from the desk and walked into the living room.

James Whiting lived on Beacon Hill, in a condominium that had originally been the home of a nineteenth-century merchant. Whiting had bought the place the day he had seen it. He had admired the carefully preserved period detail—the marble mantels, the mahogany doors, the ornate ceiling moldings and medallions—and he had decided that this would be a good place to lead the life of the thirty-three-year-old bachelor. He had furnished the living room in Queen Anne chairs, a Victorian settee trimmed with mahogany, a Peking Oriental rug, and a baby grand piano. The lamps were by Stiffel. The TV was by Sony. The stereo equipment was by Bang and Olufson. It was all very classy, all very elegant, all designed to appeal to the woman who appreciated the finer things, including James Whiting. But life had not worked out according to James Whiting's plan.

He walked to the bay windows and looked out onto Mount Vernon Street, which was lined with trees and gas lamps that glowed in front of red-brick town houses. From his window, which extended over the sidewalk, Whiting could see the State House dome illuminated at the top of the hill and the Charles Street traffic speeding by at the base.

Someplace on the hill, a linden was in bloom, but Whiting didn't notice the aroma. From the windows in the town house across the street rolled the gentle sound of Rachmaninoff's Prelude in D, but Whiting didn't hear it. Once, he had sat by his window for hours to listen to his neighbor, the concert pianist, practice. Now, as the illness deepened, the music became simply another band of static on the spectrum of urban noise.

He looked down at the cars on Charles Street and wondered idly where they all were going, and he noticed a young couple walking up the street. They were taking a long time to climb the hill because they kept lingering in the shadows to embrace and kiss. From the darkness of his window, Whiting felt safe to watch. They stopped under the gas lamp in front of his building.

"C'mon, Jack, give me a kiss," said the woman. She put her hands around his neck, pulled his face to hers, and kissed him.

Whiting heard their breathing, and he thought about dumping a bucket of cold water on them. Someone had done that to him and a girl friend in college.

The young couple broke their embrace but only long enough for the man to pivot the woman out of the light and into the little alley beside Whiting's building. Whiting could no longer see them, but he could still hear them. He stared out at the darkness and listened.

"Hey, Jack, what are you doing?" asked the woman.

"This," came the reply.

The man did something, the woman giggled, and Whiting wondered what he was doing.

"Ooh, Jack, what if somebody comes."

"Somebody's gonna come," Jack snickered.

And the lovers began to laugh. Whiting realized that they were drunk. Then, they stopped laughing. They were probably kissing. The woman inhaled sharply. The man was doing something she liked. Whiting listened and imagined, and then he heard footsteps coming down the hill. The sounds from the alley stopped abruptly. The footsteps passed and continued down the street.

"Let's go, Jack," whispered the woman after a time.

"I like it, Carla . . . right here." He did something that caused her to take another deep breath.

"Oh, Jack, honey, let's go home and finish this right."

"Nobody can see us here," he answered.

"I'm nervous, Jack."

"Give it a chance."

From the sound of things, he was kissing her again, but it didn't last.

"C'mon, Jack, let's go. There's people all around with their windows open."

Jack did whatever he'd been doing. This time, it made her angry.   "Jack, cut it out. Somebody might be listening."

Whiting swallowed a laugh and said, in a very loud voice, "Yeah, Jack, what are you trying to do? Wake up the neighborhood?"

For a moment, there was silence. Then, the woman shouted "Fucking pervert!" And the couple hurried up the street.

Whiting collapsed back into a chair and began to laugh out loud. But he didn't laugh long, because he never laughed long, and the joke hadn't been that funny.

He sat in the silent apartment and looked at the dark. A year earlier, he would have wished them luck on their search for fun in the alley beside his house, and he would have gone back to work. But now, he envied them. They had youth, they had each other, they'd had a few drinks, and from what he could tell, they had their health. People that rich deserved to be envied, and they could afford to be laughed at if it cheered James Whiting.

He was indulging in a moment of self-pity. Usuaully, he resisted the temptation to feel sorry for himself, because it did him no good, and his body needed all the help that his mind could give. Usually, his sickness helped him to maintain his resolve by simplifying his life and focusing his attention on one fact: he was suffering for end-stage renal failure. He knew that if he did not go to the dialysis clinic three times a week and plug himself into the machine that did the work of his kidneys, he would suffer intense headaches, he would develop uremic poisoning, salt deposits would form on his skin, and he would die. Usually, he had no need for self-pity, because he knew that, to survive, he had to confront the illness, treat it as effectively as he could, and try to get on with life.

But dialysis for Whiting was nothing more than a holding action, a way to keep the poisons at bay until someone donated a kidney. And it was an imperfect system, because it could never completely eliminate the poisons in the body, and it rendered many males impotent, including James Whiting.

On nights like this, when he was fighting a losing battle with depression, when his envy for the healthy world caused him to act as he just had, James Whiting would sit in the dark and wonder if somewhere in New England, a young man was driving his car into a telephone pole or suffering a cerebral hemorrhage, or if some teen-ager who'd had too much of life was taking an overdose that would give James Whiting another chance at life.

Whiting always felt uncomfortable with such thoughts. But his doctor had told him not to think about potential donors, because the donors didn't know who they'd be, and Whiting would never know who they were.

He went into the kitchen, which had no windows and no room for his elbows. He popped open the refrigerator, and the light illuminated his face. The strong jaw seemed gaunt, but at the same time, the face looked puffy, especially around the eyes and beneath the jawline. Because his kidneys did not work, his body retained fluid, and the puffiness would not be relieved until after the next dialysis treatment. He had once been handsome, but now, the dark circles behind his horn-rimmed glasses made him look like a student at exam time living on speed and studying all night. His hair, neatly combed and parted on the left, was the only feature that had not changed since the onset of the disease.

The glasses and the hairstyle, along with poplin trousers, Top-siders, tweeds, and Lacoste shirts, were part of the prep-school image he had cultivated at Harvard in the late sixties and still

chose to project. Although he had attended a Boston public school
and his politics leaned toward the left, like that of his classmates,
for whom jeans, work shirts, and general sloppiness had been part
of the political statement, James Whiting had preferred the conservative look. It suited him then and it still did, because James
Whiting was a loner.

He had two or three close friends and a good relationship with
his mother and sister, and he felt no desire to attract attention to
himself, except when he noticed an attractive woman. In a business where self-promotion was as common as competition, James
Whiting had always chosen to let his work speak for him. Until
his illness, it had spoken well, and he had been able to cultivate
his other loves: art, music, good food, the Boston Celtics, cross-
country skiing, and the company of interesting women.

A year earlier, he had been 175 pounds of muscle on a six-foot
frame. He had lifted weights regularly and played racquetball
when he couldn't ski. But he had lost his muscle tone and his
strength along with his potency; fluid retention left him looking
flabby and soft, and sitting at his desk consumed all of his energy.

He cursed at the contents of the refrigerator. He wanted a
Molson's beer and a salami sandwich slathered in Bauer's German
mustard. His renal doctor permitted him a diet that consisted
mostly of cereal, eggs, milk, boiled or broiled meats in small por-
tions, baked fish, fresh fruits and vegetables that did not contain
potassium. Fortunately, he could drink coffee and one beer a day,
but he could consume no more than two liters of liquid in twenty-
four hours. He could have no fried foods, no salted foods, no cakes
or pastries from the local bakery, no mustard, no salami, and no
fun.

He didn't want a chicken sandwich on white bread or a scrambled egg or an apple. He took out a bottle of Molson's, opened it,
and gulped. When he came up for air, half the beer was gone and
he was getting angry . . . at his doctor, at his sickness, and at the
half-empty bottle of beer. He finished the beer in another swallow
and didn't feel angry at the bottle anymore. But he had reached
his fluid limit for the day, and he wanted another Molson's.

He took out a second bottle and held it in his hand. A cool
temptation on a warm June night. He knew he'd feel terrible by
treatment time the following night, but he opened the bottle and
sipped. For a moment, he held the beer in his mouth, letting the

carbonation fizz around his gums. If he was going to break his diet, he wanted to enjoy every last drop.

He sipped again and strolled to the bay window. He heard Chopin now. It flowed smoothly with the beer to soothe him. He listened and stared and wondered if anyone was dying. He hoped so, because he couldn't live like this much longer.

4

In Hollywood, news traveled almost as quickly as rumor. By seven-thirty Pacific time, anyone who had been a friend of Roger Darrow, anyone who had worked closely with him, anyone who considered him a ruthless son of a bitch, anyone who mattered knew that he was lying in a Maine hospital with his skull shattered and his face smashed beyond recognition.

Harriet Sears heard the news first. She was reading a script in the living room of her Santa Monica apartment when the telephone rang.

Jeanne told Harriet what had happened, and Harriet was stunned. She had known Roger Darrow since his early days in television, when he had been a young prodigy writing for programs like "The Defenders." She had performed in the program that won him his first Emmy, and he had written a play for her, a one-woman show about Dorothy Parker. *picky*

"How can I help, dear?" Harriet asked after a few moments. "Do you want me to come over, or should I make the bad phone calls?"

"Both," answered Jeanne.

Harriet finished her vodka and tonic and went into the bedroom to dress. She pulled on an artist's smock and a pair of jeans that looked quite flattering on a woman of sixty. She had not been one of the better-endowed starlets of her day. Her legs, her smile, and the formidable personality she conveyed in her films had been her assets, making her, in the words of one publicist, "the thinking man's Bette Grable."

Her skin had been wrinkled by age and too much time in the sun. Her hair was quickly going gray, and she was wearing it in the pulled-back bun favored by women like Henrietta Redgate, the character she was currently portraying. But she still had the legs and the smile that had made her a fixture on GI footlockers, and her personality, if anything, had grown more formidable with

"Scene eighty-five, take four," said the voice. The hands holding the slate raised the clapstick and dropped it. A grease-pencil X flashed on the screen. The slate was pulled from the shot. The camera was focused on the front door of a southern mansion. "Action."

Henrietta Redgate, a regal woman in a blue silk taffeta dress, walked out the door and across the portico. The camera followed her to the young man standing by one of the pillars. He was wearing the uniform of a Confederate captain.

"I don't pretend to understand this war," she said, "but your father believed that a man had to take a stand someplace. I only wish that . . ." She lowered her head and fought back a sob. "I only wish that"—she sobbed again—"that your brother . . ."

She looked down. She seemed to be fumbling for something to say. "I only wish that your brother . . . wasn't such an asshole."

"Cut."

Harriet Sears and Peter Cross, the actor playing her son, looked at the camera and started to laugh.

"Your exwife must be getting old," said a voice from the darkness in front of the screen. "She's been blowing a lot of lines lately."

"It's too bad she never learned to blow anything else. We might still be married."

For a few seconds, white leader ran through the projector. "Scene eighty-five, take five." Clap. X "Action."

And the telephone rang.

"Shit," said a voice. The receiver was picked up. "Rudermann here."

"Howard, this is Harriet."

"Oh, Harriet, we were just speaking of you, dear."

Someone in the room snickered.

Harriet could hear her own voice playing a scene in the background. "Can you stop the screening for a minute, Howard?"

"I only have an hour to look at dailies, Harriet. This better be good."

"I have some terrible news, Howard. Please stop the screening."

Rudermann pressed the intercom on the console in front of him. He told the projectionist to stop the film and bring up the houselights.

Howard Rudermann was sitting with his director, his editor, and Peter Cross, his star, in a Hollywood relic, one of the executive screening rooms at the Burbank Studios. Twenty-five leather and oak chairs, with high backs and copper ashtrays built into the armrests, were arrayed in tiers like thrones in the College of Cardinals. Whenever Rudermann worked at the Burbank Studios, he screened his dailies in this room because it reminded him of the real Hollywood, the town he'd known over forty years earlier, when Jack Warner watched his films here and barked orders at assistants like Howard Rudermann. Now, for God's sake, a woman was the head of one studio, and most of the Fox lot had been sold to real estate developers.

Rudermann was wearing a cranberry-colored shirt open to the breastbone. His belly oozed over the top of his designer jeans and his hair hugged his face in little hairdresser curls. His teeth were white and capped. His tan was even and deep and looked artificial. It was a sybaritic face. Years of food, drink, sex, and luxury had filled it, rounded it, and caused it now to settle, but in the process had erased the lines of care that marked most men in their sixties.

"How terrible is terrible? He knew that Harriet was not given to exaggeration.

Harriet told him, as slowly and gently as possible. She did not expect that Rudermann would react well. Roger Darrow had been Rudermann's savior, the young man who breathed life into Rudermann Productions when Howard Rudermann couldn't get a show on the air.

Howard Ruderman said nothing as Harriet spoke. When he had heard enough, he simply dropped the receiver and buried his face in his hands.

Word of the accident was now lighting switchboards all over town. At her office on the Sunset Strip, Vicki Rogers, the gossip columnist, was placing a call.

As she waited for an answer, she fingered the onyx brooch pinned to her lapel. Her hair, cut in a short, page-boy style, was as black as the onyx, her lips were bright red to contrast with her hair, and she always wore a pair of large, tinted eyeglasses. At forty-two, she had delicate, almost girlish features, and the eyeglasses, depending on her mood, could give her a hard, professional edge, or they could make her face seem smaller and more vulnerable than it ever had been.

She was calling Vaughn Lawrence, one of America's favorite game-show hosts and talkmasters, one of her best contacts, and an old lover. Something told her that Vaugh Lawrence might know more about Darrow's death than anyone in town.

Lawrence had been a minor east coast radio personality when he came to Hollywood in 1958, during the era when game shows were a prime-time staple. He had hired an agent, who convinced the producers of "Guess My Weight," a new game show, that they needed Vaughn Lawrence, the hot New York disc jockey, to host their program.

"Guess My Weight" had lasted only six weeks, but Vaughn Lawrence had become one of the most popular and durable personalities on television. He had moved from "Guess My Weight" to "Coin Toss" to "Breakfast with Vaughn" and "People and Prices." Along the way, he had made a fortune for himself, a smaller one for Wheeler, and he had, like a dutiful son, had invested most of his money in television.

Lawrence/Sunshine Productions now pumped out six game shows a week into syndication. It owned an independent Los Angeles television station that was beamed onto satellite and picked up by cable services all over America. It produced five popular channels of cable broadcasting, and Vaughn Lawrence had organized the financing for the largest programming venture ever produced directly for cable television, "The Redgates of Virginia."

He was one of the most respected men in Hollywood, because he was one of the most powerful and successful. But no one, not even his agent, trusted him.

Vaughn Lawrence was in bed when the telephone rang, but he was not asleep. Kelly Hammerstein, one of the models who posed beside the prizes on "People and Prices," was sitting on top of him. Her breasts and belly glistened with a thin coating of body oil she had bought in a Beverly Hills boutique. Earlier in the day, at the taping, she had caressed a color television set, a refrigerator freezer, and a beautiful ten-piece mahogany dining room. Now, she was caressing Vaughn Lawrence.

On the secnd ring, she said, "Maybe we better answer it."

"Forget about it," said Lawrence.

"I won't be able to concentrate."

"I'll help." He leaned up on his elbows and took one of her oily breasts in his mouth.

She gently pushed him away.

"Forget the telephone," he growled.

"But it might be my agent."

Vaughn Lawrence went limp.

She answered the phone, and someone asked for Lawrence, who shook his head.

"He's busy right now," said Kelly. "Who's calling, please?"

"Vicki Rogers."

She almost slipped off the bed. "Vicki Rogers the columnist? Ah, yes, hello, Miss Rogers . . . This is Kelly Hammerstein. Can I take a message?"

Lawrence grabbed the receiver. "What is it, Vick?"

"Have you heard the news, Vaughn, dearest?"

"What?"

"Roger Darrow's been in an accident. His boat exploded in Maine."

"How serious?" Lawrence did not sound concerned.

"Quite bad," said Vicki. "He's being kept alive by machine. If he survives, they say he might make a good book end."

"That's a damn shame," said Lawrence. "He was a hell of a talent. If he's done for, this town'll miss him."

"Can I quote you?"

Lawrence did not respond. He was concentrating on Kelly's oiled hands, which were working their way up his thighs.

"What's her name, Vaughn?" asked Vicki.

"Kelly Hammerstein," Lawrence said into the receiver.

Kelly smiled.

"And I really think you ought to meet her. She could use a good plug in your column."

For that, Kelly's hands stopped teasing and immediately rewarded Vaughn Lawrence.

Vicki could hear his breathing change. "Before you get on with things, Vaughn, dear, answer me one question."

Lawrence grunted.

"Who tried to kill him?"

Lawrence laughed. "I thought you said it was an accident."

"I did, but if anyone knows what's really going on among the denizens of this little artists' colony, it's you, dear."

"You're talking ragtime, Vick," said Lawrence, and she was certain that she heard anger buried in his voice. "You go back to your fantasy land and I'll go back to mine."

Vaughn Lawrence hung up and felt Kelly Hammerstein's lips envelope him.

Vicki Rogers looked out across the swimming pools and mansions and palm trees of Beverly Hills. The sun was sliding toward the Pacific, and the sky, which had been yellow at noon, glowed in neon tones of copper and rust. She wondered what Vaughn Lawrence knew and how she could take advantage of it.

When he wasn't in his office overlooking MacArthur Park, Len Haley was usually sitting in the 901. Occasionally, he would stop into Langers, the deli on the corner of Wilshire and Alvorado, eat hot pastrami, and feel like a New Yorker. Sometimes he'd drive up to El Cholo for Mexican. But the 901, in the used-car-lot wasteland on Figueroa, between the USC campus and the L.A. Convention Center, was his regular hangout.

He was forty-four and had the bulk and brawn of a weight lifter who drank too much beer. His nose was red and veined and it had been broken twice by guards in a North Vietnamese prison. He had short black hair, a matching handlebar moustache, and a round, ruddy face.

Most people liked Len Haley from the moment they met him. He offered a firm handshake and a direct gaze, and he could make small talk about almost anything, although baseball and the old days, by which he meant the fifties and early sixties, were his favorite subjects.

People never suspected that as they met, Len Haley was inspecting them from head to foot while imprinting their name, face, and voice on his memory. And few people ever sensed the anger behind Len Haley's facade.

Haley ordered a cheeseburger and looked up at the television above the bar. The Red Sox were playing the Angels. One year, the big bats played for the Sox and killed the Angels. The next year, they played for the Angels and killed the Sox. The team that

payed the most got the best hitters. No loyalty, no tradition. No
wonder he was losing interest in the Grand Old Game.

"Hey, Hank," he called to the bartender. "Put on the news, will
you?"

"I thought you wanted to watch the Angels."

Len Haley wanted to watch the news. He was expecting a story
that the Los Angeles cable news station would probably carry.
"They got it won. Change the station."

"That's Fenway Park they're playin' in, Len. The game's never
over in Fenway until the last out."

Haley laughed. "If the Angels blow an eight-run lead, I don't
want to see it."

The bartender shrugged and changed the channel.

Haley listened for several minutes as the anchorman on the
news program read his script. Then, Roger Darrow's picture appeared on the screen and Haley leaned closer. "Roger Darrow, the
producer of 'Flint,' long one of America's most popular television
detective programs, lies tonight in a Maine hospital and fights for
his life . . ."

Haley listened to the rest of the report, then went back to the
telephone booth at the back of the bar and dialed Vaughn Lawrence's number.

Lawrence answered on the eighth ring.

"It's Haley. My man hit his target. I'll need ten crips C-notes.

"But Darrow's not dead," said Lawrence.

"From the way it sounds, he's not alive, either. Ten C-notes for
my man in Maine." Len Haley hung up.

5

At first, Jeanne Darrow did not look at her husband. She looked instead at the respirator beside him, a plexiglass cylinder sitting atop a console that was covered in buttons, gauges, and lights. Inside the cylinder was a rubber lining folded like an accordion. Each time the lining expanded to fill the cylinder, air rushed through a tube to the patient's mouth and the chest expanded beneath the sheet. As the lining sank back to the bottom of the cylinder, the chest deflated.

Jeanne moved closer to the body. The face was wrapped in bandages. The respirator tube entered one opening in the gauze, the nasal tube another. An intravenous tube dripped water and nutrients into his arm. Electrodes taped to his chest monitored the heartbeat, which was strong and steady. The cardiac monitor beeped like a metronome.

She was standing beside her husband in a white cubicle that reminded her of a sepulcher. John Meade and Dr. Jason Sanderson, head of surgery at John MacGregor Memorial Hospital, were standing at the door, which opened onto the main floor of the hospital's intensive care unit.

In her hand, she held her husband's wedding band. It was engraved "Jeanne to Roger" and, after that, the date of their marriage six years earlier. It seemed so long ago and yet, she thought, they'd had so little time together.

Jeanne touched her husband's shoulder, one of the parts of the body not covered. "With all the bandages, I don't even know if it's him."

"I'm afraid it is," Dr. Jason Sanderson stepped into the cubicle.

Jeanne placed her hand on the bandages that covered her husband's forehead. "Could I see his eyes? I'd feel better if I could see his eyes."

Sandersoon took a deep breath. He was in his late thirties, very young for a chief of surgery, Hollywood handsome, with a deep tan, styled hair, and a three-piece suit, which he accented with the most traditional of medical accessories, the plaid bow tie. Although his reputation was widely known, he looked like an actor auditioning for the role of a doctor on a daytime drama. "I'm afraid that his eyes are . . . they had been . . ."

"He has no eyes left?"

Sanderson shook his head.

Jeanne sat on the folding chair beside the bed. She closed her eyes and gripped the sides of the chair and bowed her head. She had known that his face was crushed, but somehow she had expected that the explosion would have spared his eyes. "Please leave me for a moment," she said without looking up. "I need to be alone with my husband."

For twenty-four hours, she had been fighting her grief. She had shattered the sangría glasses. She had felt the numbing shock that followed. And she had held out the hope that her husband might not be as badly hurt as it first seemed.

When she first arrived at the hospital, she had surprised Sanderson with her understanding of emergency medical procedures and treatments.

"I thought you were an actress," he had said.

She told him that she had retired to become a paramedic with the L.A. County Sheriff's Office.

"That's about as far from acting as you can get."

"Not really," she had responded. "When they lower my team out of a helicopter to save some hiker who's fallen into a ravine, I have to act as though I'm in complete control. It's my best performance."

Sanderson and the hospital neurosurgeon had then shown her X rays of her husband's skull, the front of which had been shattered and splintered into his brain. They had shown her his electroncephalogram, a rolled piece of paper on which was traced a straight line, which meant that there was no electromagnetic activity in her husband's brain, which meant that it had ceased to function, and he had, for all practical purposes, ceased to live.

"Your husband fulfills the Harvard criteria for brain death," Sanderson had explained, then he had begun to enumerate the standards, first agreed upon at the Harvard Medical School.

"I know them," Jeanne had interrupted. "No spontaneous respiration after three minutes without the respirator; no response to intensely painful stimuli; fixed, dilated pupils and the absence of gag, cough, corneal, and deep tendon reflexes; flat encephalograph; and the persistence of these symptoms for forty-eight hours in a patient who hasn't taken drugs and has a body temperature above nine hundred and fifty."

Sanderson had nodded. "Then you know that tomorrow morning, we will officially declare brain death. After that, the decision is yours."

Now, alone in the room with her husband's body, Jeanne Darrow squeezed the sides of the chair, as though trying to muster her strength. Then she stood, stepped to the bed, and looked down at the body.

Six feet two and a 190 pounds, he had been in superb condition before the accident. His body had fought violently to keep itself alive. It might have been better for both of them, she thought, if he had been a little weaker, if his will to live had been less tenacious. She would not be faced now with a decision she did not think she could make.

Slowly, reluctantly, she lowered the sheet covering his chest. There were ugly bruises and lacerations across his pectorals, and she noticed that after a month away from the Beverly Hills Health Club, he had begun to lose muscle tone and weight.

She watched the chest rise and fall, driven by the respirator beside the bed. Except for the few bristles around the nipples, the chest was completely hairless. She reached out and touched it and felt the heart beating artificially beneath it.

"I wouldn't look any further," said Sanderson gently as he stepped into the room again.

She turned.

"You may have a strong stomach, but before you lower the sheet, I have to tell you that he's really been beaten up."

In her work, Jeanne Darrow had seen gunshot wounds, compound fractures, bloody tears, and gashes in human flesh, but she had always been able to detach herself from the immediate horror to confront the problem of emergency treatment. Like most people with medical training, she learned to make patient and wound abstractions.

But not now, not with her husband. She suddenly felt sick.

She pulled the sheet back over his body. She gathered it gently around his neck, just below the bandages swathing his face. She

heard the slow, rhythmic breathing of the respirator and the
steady beep of the cardiac monitor.

She swallowed hard, several times, and told herself she had to accept that this muscular body was good for nothing more than spare parts. There was no hope. He had lost everything that made him human. She decided that she would permit the shutdown of the life-support systems and the removal of the kidneys for transplantation.

Then she had to vomit.

In a healthy person, five hundred gallons of blood are pumped through the kidneys each day. From that volume, the kidneys filter fifty gallons of water, glucose, salt, potassium, calcium, urea, creatinine, uric acid, amino acids, and bicarbonate, and they return all but about two quarts to the system. Those two quarts of filtrate, containing the unwanted chemicals and waste materials of cell metabolism, are gathered in small reservoirs on each kidney. They travel down the ureters to the bladder, and from there, they are voided as urine.

James Whiting had not known the pleasure of emptying a full bladder in four months. For that long, his kidneys had been shut down completely, and he had been living with the machine that cleansed his blood and gave him life in exchange for a small piece of his humanity.

It was eleven-thirty at night, and James Whiting was on his way to dialysis. The clinic was two stories of prefabricated stone and poured concrete near Boston University. Whiting came three nights a week for six hours of treatment.

He liked the late-night shift because it enabled him to sleep through the treatment, and it gave the rest of his life some degree of normalcy. During the day, he tried to follow the routines he had always lived by, but he hated the night. He hated to wake from some dream of health and find that he was alone in his bed, swimming in a pool of sweat that grew cold and clammy as he contemplated the shadows on his ceiling. Better to wake in a place where everyone else faced the same uncertainty, where the walls were white and the fluorescent lights always burned.

The main dialysis clinic was on the first floor: a nurse's desk and forty dialyzing stations, each comprised of a dialyzing unit, a blue vinyl recliner and a television set attached to a gooseneck on the ceiling.

The people who came to the dialysis clinic were about as sick as people could be while they were still walking around. Most were chronically ill. Many, because of age, weakness, or other illness, had no hope of transplant and little hope, despite dialysis, of anything but a long, slow deterioration. Others, like Whiting, waited for the phone call that would mean another chance. But the odds were long and discouraging. Of the forty thousand people on dialysis in the United States, only about a third were considered good candidates for transplant. And each year, only three or four thousand would receive new kidneys.

Some patients responded by withdrawing, becoming passive. They had little to say to the staff, they made no attempt to learn about the dialyzer, and in extreme cases, they pulled blankets over their heads to avoid personal contact during treatment. Others, active, self-reliant people like Whiting, became angry and resentful—about their illness, other people's health, and the machine itself. They knew that their lives depended on the machine, and so it became like an authoritarian parent, hated for the strict regimen it imposed, loved—or at least respected—for the sustenance it brought.

Suzy, his nurse on Thursday nights, greeted him at the desk and sent him to station number five. While she went to get the equipment she would need—needles, dialysate solution, antiseptic—Whiting took off his sneakers and jeans and stood on the scale. He weighed 175 pounds.

"Five pounds in three days?" exclaimed Suzy, who reminded him of his mother, although she was only twenty-four. "You're restricted to two liters of fluid a day, Jim. Dialysis can't remove any more."

Whiting smiled. The two beers the night before had tasted good, cheered him up, and put him to sleep. For that much therapy, he'd suffer.

Suzy put her hand on her hip. "Now, how much fluid have you had today, including Jello?"

"I never eat Jello. I never eat anything that moves on the spoon."

She laughed and told him to sit down.

He stretched out on the recliner and extended his left arm.

"First you chide me, and now you may inflict your torture."

She strapped his arm to the chair.

"But only a little pain, my dear," he continued. "A little pain is good for body and soul and leaves us yearning for more."

"You've been reading that perverted Frenchman again, haven't you?" Suzy located the little knot on his forearm, called the fistula, where the radial artery and the cephalic vein had been surgically joined. She placed her stethoscope on the fistula to make sure that she heard the bruit, the rushing sound made by the blood as it passed directly from artery to vein. Then, she cleaned the arm with antiseptic and tightened the tourniquet.

"We must take advantage of anything that helps us to live with our pain, and thank God for anything that helps us to enjoy it," said Whiting. "The Marquis de Sade developed a philosophy for enjoying pain at just about the time that he sired your great-great-grandmother."

The nurse inserted the needle. Whiting flinched. The needle pierced the fistula and drew arterial blood on the first try. Whiting always declined the local anesthetic because he knew the fistula would last longer without injections of novocaine. He looked away until he heard the rip of the adhesive, meaning that the nurse was taping the needle in place.

A few moments later James Whiting felt the familiar, cool sensation radiating through his arm, and he watched himself flowing down the plastic tube, into the coils of the dialyzer.

After the nurse left, Whiting lay back and listened to the rhythmic beat of the blood pump and the soft hum of the proportioning unit. The sounds had become part of the background noise in his head, distant, indefinable patterns that were always there and became clearer as he slipped away from consciousness. Some people heard the ocean when they fell asleep. Some heard city traffic. Whiting heard the sounds of dialysis, whether he slept in the clinic, in his bed, or at his desk in the office. He tried never to look at the machine until the sounds had relaxed him, however, because they were womb sounds, and it was always a small shock to find that his umbilical cord connected him to stainless steel and plastic tubing instead of flesh and blood.

James Whiting had never been very interested in the physical sciences or in the functioning of machines like the coil dialyzer. He stumbled, unintersted, through science courses in high school and took a single geology course, known as "Rocks for Jocks," to satisfy all of the science requirements he would need for his college degree.

At Harvard, he studied literature and music. He entertained himself by writing limericks. He contributed parodies of famous writers to the *Harvard Lampoon*. And he cowrote a Hasty Pudding show, a spoof of British rock groups called "I Want to Hold Your Gland," which was filled with puns and bad jokes and, because it was a tradition, was enormously successful.

He had not cared about science until his own blood chemistry became an item of daily concern. Now, he tried to learn all that he could about the function of the kidneys, the chemical composition of the blood, and the operation of the hemodialyzer. He knew all of the ways that he could die while on dialysis, from infection at the fistula site to hemorrhage in the dialyzing coil, he knew how infinitesimal the odds were against any of the catastrophes occurring, and he knew exactly how to respond if they did.

He looked at the dialyzer. His blood was flowing from his artery, through the cleansing coils and solution, and back to his vein. Part of his being, his substance, was inside that machine. But he felt secure. He turned off the light above his recliner and went to sleep.

For some reason, he slept soundly that night, as though his body anticipated what was about to happen. Around six o'clock, he awoke, feeling better, if not exactly refreshed.

He took a taxi home, showered, and prepared a breakfast of scrambled eggs laced with Swiss cheese, toast, orange juice, and coffee, all carefully measured to meet his diet requirements. He put his breakfast on his tray and took it back to his bedroom. He sat in the chair beside the bed and turned on the radio, "Morning Pro Musica" with Robert J. Lurtsema. The depression he had been fighting for days had begun to abate, as it always did after dialysis. He could smell the lilacs blooming in the little garden patio below, and the spirit and precision of a Bach Brandenburg Concerto filled him with a sense of order and hope.

As he reached for the orange juice, the telephone rang. His hand stopped in mid-motion. The phone rang again. Whiting glanced at his watch: 7:35. His heart began to race. No one, not even his mother, called him before eight o'clock.

He wiped his hands on the napkin and looked up at the hospital kit, the suitcase he kept packed and ready on a shelf in his closet. It contained pajamas, robe, slippers, shaving cream, razor, toothbrush, and several novels he had always wanted to read. The kit had been sitting there ever since his name and vital statistics had gone onto the computer waiting list at the Organ Founation.

He picked up the receiver. "Hello."

"Jim? This is Doctor Stanton calling."

"And Whiting knew that this was it. His hands began to shake. "What's up?"

"We may have a donor for you."

"A donor?" Whiting's voice cracked. He swallowed and tried to drop it an octave. "A donor?"

"We think so," said Stanton, as though he were talking about the weather.

"When?" said Whiting. "When do we go?"

"Don't get too excited. We haven't even gotten the kidney yet, and when it gets here, we'll have to do a final crossmatch. The donor is in surgery now. However, they knew last night that the kidney was going to be available, so they put the blood type and HLA antigen series into the computer."

"When do we go?" repeated Whiting.

"Relax, Jim. The computer picked out you and three others. You're the highest on the waiting list and the closest geographically," continued Stanton, "so, if the final tissue matches look good, you'll get a new kidney by tomorrow morning, and one works as well as two.

For a moment, James Whiting felt a wave of guilt. Some people waited years for a kidney that their system would accept. Many died before donors could be found. Whiting had waited just four months. But it was all a matter of luck. It was James Whiting's bad luck to have been stricken with a disease called glomerulonephritis, his good luck that someone had died whose system resembled his.

"When was your last dialysis?" asked Stanton.

"Just ended."

"Good. Good. Have you had breakfast?"

"I'm eating it now."

"Make it your last meal."

There was a little laugh at Whiting's end of the line.

"I mean for today, Jim, for today. In a month, you can eat

potato chips and drink beer until you throw up, and I won't give damn as long as your kidney's OK. Now stay by that phone. If there's any problem, I'll call."

"You just get that kidney."

Stanton signed off.

Whiting sat for a moment and watched the steam swirling above the eggs. Then he stood slowly, and he shouted—a single, uncontrollable cry of joy.

6

A t eleven o'clock that morning, two recently harvested kidneys arrived in Boston by private plane. They were stored in a Belzerr perfusion machine, which kept them cool and pumped a steady stream of plasma through them to preserve their vascular structures. They were attended by a medical technician who hurried them through Boston to the New Englad Organ Foundation. There a sample of the donor's white blood cells was mixed with James Whiting's blood serum. If antibodies appeared in the serum, there would be no transplant, because the recipient's immune system would reject the organ immediately. If no antibodies appeared within a few hours, the transplant would proceed.

While the kidneys were arriving in Boston, Dr. Jason Sanderson, as head of the Maine Coast Regional Transplant Team, was stepping before the news media gathered at his hospital in Maine to announce the death of Roger Darrow, producer of the famous television series, "Flint." Although he'd had plenty of time to change into his suit, he had remained in the surgical greens he had worn when removing the kidneys, because he thought the greens made him look more dramatic.

Jeanne Darrow did not meet the press. She waited in another part of the hospital with John Meade. She was wearing the same green-knit dress she'd had on since she left Los Angeles, and there were dark circles under her eyes. John Meade looked fresh and relaxed in a blue blazer and gray slacks.

He suggested that she meet Andrew MacGregor, spend the night at Brisbane Cottage, and return to Los Angeles in the morning. She refused, saying that she wanted to go home as soon as her husband's body had been autopsied and cremated.

She had no reason to remain in Maine any longer than necessary. She knew, in spite of the calm with which she had acted, that she was still in shock. She needed the company of friends and family more than a night's sleep in Andrew MacGregor's guest room. It had been a mistake, she thought, to come alone to Maine. But no one could have made her decision less harrowing.

Sanderson walked into the room, and Jeanne stood.

"The procedure went very well," said Sanderson after a moment of awkward silence. "If there's anything we can do . . ."

"There is," she said firmly. "I'd like to be informed of what happens to the kidneys."

"Certainly. We'll tell you when and where they're transplanted," said Sanderson, "And if you request, we'll tell you how the recipients are doing.

"That's all?" Until now, Jeanne had not thought beyond the surgery. "Are you telling me that what's left of my husband is going be walking around in somebody else, and I won't even know who it is?"

"Kidney transplantation is always a gamble," said Sanderson crisply. "The odds are fifty-fifty that the recipients will reject your husband's kidneys. You wouldn't be very pleased to hear about that if it happened. If you knew who the recipients were, you might direct your anger at them, because they hadn't accepted your husband's gift."

"That's ridiculous," said Jeanne.

"On the other hand," Sanderson continued, "if the transplant is successful, you have someone indebted to you for his life. And you might expect things from him that you wouldn't ask of your best friend."

"Ridiculous," repeated Jeanne.

Sanderson shook his head solemnly. "I'm sorry Mrs. Darrow, but the medical community is of one mind on this issue."

Jeanne looked to Meade for support.

Meade jammed his hands in his pockets and shook his head. "Doctor's orders, Mrs. Darrow. I can't help you."

Jeanne didn't have the strength to continue arguing, and she wasn't sure it mattered anyway. She knew that her sudden attachment to the kidneys was an irrational attempt to keep him alive. But he was gone. That was all that mattered. She walked over to the windows, wrapped her arms around herself, and began to rock back and forth. She wanted to go home.

James Whiting tried to recall a prayer from his days at Saint James Episcopal Sunday School. All he could think of was, "Now I lay me down to sleep." It was prayer enough, and he let it ramble through his head as the gurney glided toward the elevator.

The crossmatch had been negative. James Whiting was going to surgery. Finally.

And he was frightened. No one goes to surgery any other way, no matter how simple the procedure, no matter the the patient's confidence in the surgeon.

James Whiting knew that if all went well, he would have his second chance. But first, he would have to suffer a small death. For three hours, he would lie insensate, dreamless, while men with knives opened his body and probed his insides.

What if they made a mistake? What if they found something they had not expected? What if someone gave him too much gas? He might wake up without a mind. Or he might not wake up at all.

His mother and sister had kissed him before the orderly wheeled him into the hallway. Now, one of the operating room nurses was talking softly to him, trying to assuage the fear he knew she could see in his eyes. But he had never felt as alone.

Beneath the gurney sheet, he was naked, and everyone he passed in the hallway—doctors, nurses, patients, visitors— seemed to be studying him as though he were an exhibit in a medical museum. He wondered briefly if they could see the out-line of his genitals through the sheet.

Then, the stainless-steel doors of the elevator were opening. He was drawing closer. He felt the elevator bounce as the gurney rolled onto it. His stomach sank when the elevator started down. The nurse continued to murmur beside him. The eyes of the other passengers studied him while their faces pretended to ignore him. They were more subtle than the people in the hallways, but all of them, he was sure, were thinking how good it was that he, and not they, were lying on the gurney.

He felt his resentment flash against all of them. This was a hospital, for God's sake. Hadn't they ever seen someone going to surgery before?

Each time the elevator stopped to release a passenger, Whiting's heart stopped with it. Then, as the elevator began again, his heart would race. The ride seemed interminable, and the Demerol shot he had been given in his room had not yet begun to act.

The gurney rolled off the elevator and down a short hallway. Whiting heard the hum of an electric motor that automatically opened a pair of swinging doors. The gurney went through the doors into cool, conditioned, and, it seemed, superoxygenated air.

For a moment, the fear clutching at Whiting's chest released its grip. It could have been the Demerol taking effect or the change in the air, but he felt relieved, almost relaxed. He had reached the inner sanctum: Morton Surgical B. Soon he would know his future.

This was an alien world inhabited by people in green suits, funny hats, masks, and paper-covered shoes. But the Demerol was taking effect now, and Whiting was starting to feel at home in Morton Surgical B. Paper-covered shoes, he thought. Steamed with a little soy sauce, they might make it onto the menu at Hunan.

The gurney stopped in front of a glass both. Inside, a nurse sat at a desk and several others, in surgical dress, read charts or chatted. Whiting's nurse asked the supervisor a question, and Whiting's eyes wandered up to the ceiling. Something was pasted there, directly above him. Whiting squinted.

Smiling down at every patient whose gurney stopped at the nurses' station was the idiot grin of a happy face poster: the yellow circle outlined in black, the two black eyes, the upturned mouth, and, beneath it, the word *Smile.*

"Smile, my ass," grunted Whiting.

His nurse looked down at him. "What did you say, Mr. Whiting?"

"Smile, my ass." And he gestured with his eyes to the ceiling. "Next, you'll be tryin' to tell me that today is the first day of the rest of my life."

"Maybe it is."

Whiting heard a familiar voice and felt Dr. Joseph Stanton's hand on his shoulder. He looked up and saw the friendly face.

Stanton was in his late forties, a big man with oversized hands and a bush of brown hair sheathed in a surgical bonnet. At Yale, where he had played tight end, he had earned a nickname, "the Bear," because he stood six feet four and weighed 210 pounds. Now, he weighed 230, and he always felt hypocritical when he told his patients to lose weight.

But James Whiting liked Stanton's bulk. He would feel secure surrendering himself to the embrace of the Bear.

"You've got a kidney waiting, Jim, so let's get to it."

"All right," said Whiting, "but I won't smile." He was feeling drowsy now, and he wasn't sure that he was making sense.

"No need to smile," said Stanton. He tied on his surgical mask and slaped a big hand on the side of the gurney. "C'mon."

They pushed Whiting through a set of swinging doors into operating room number five. Here it was quiet, peaceful. The silence, thought Whiting, of the grave. He decided he preferred the noise of the nurses' station.

The only textures seemed to be the smoothness of stainless steel and the uniform roughness of concrete block painted light green. Machinery was humming, beeping, and pumping. Indicator lights flashed, oscilloscopes danced, and nurses glided about preparing the room. Some were counting instruments. Others were arranging tables and trays. Others were piling green surgical sheeting on the operating table.

Dominating it all was the light. It looked to Whiting like the impassive eye of some machine-tooled god, an opening of stainless steel and fluorescent tubing that would peer into the darkness inside him. He shut his eyes and thought the prayer again. The sounds in the operating room suddenly seemed distant, harsh, but somehow insignificant, like the wail of a far-off police siron on a summer night.

"Jim, Jim."

Whiting opened his eyes.

Within the circle of the light was Dr. Stanton's face.

"This is Doctor Baum, the anesthesiologist," said Stanton through the mask. "He's going to be putting you to sleep."

Another face appeared between Whiting and the light.

"Is he boring?" muttered Whiting.

Stanton and the anesthesiologist laughed.

"Only to his patients," Stanton chuckled, "and his friends."

"OK, then," Whiting closed his eyes again. "Just tell him to change the oil and rotate the tires." And that was all that Whiting remembered.

After the autopsy, the medical examiner, at the personal request of Andrew MacGregor, had released the body immediately. His preliminary report stated that Roger Darrow's injuries had been sustained as a result of the explosion and he would not call for an inquest.

A hearse had carried the body to the Hanson Mortuary in Rocktown, while Jeanne Darrow and John Meade had ridden in a black limousine. Jeanne had decided to follow her husband's instructions. In the event of his death, he had once said, he wished to be cremated immediately, without fanfare or funeral, and to be remembered in a memorial service when the grief had subsided. Jeanne had seen no reason to transport the battered body across the country, only to cremate it in Los Angeles.

Now, although she found it difficult to believe, the small box containing his ashes was nestled in the bottom of her overnight bag. She tried to put the thought out of her mind as she settled back on the TWA 5:00 P.M. flight from Boston to Los Angeles.

Dinner was being served, and Jeanne had ordered baked halibut. She had eaten almost nothing in two days, and she was hungry. She squeezed a wedge of lemon juice onto her fish and smelled the clean, citrus aroma. Suddenly, her appetite was gone and the tears were welling once more.

On the night before he left, Roger Darrow had cooked one of their favorite meals—grilled mako shark in lemon butter, garnished with fresh-cut lemons. Now, in the cabin of the 747, the smell of the lemons tripped the circuits that took her back to the night a month earlier.

Roger had set the table by the pool, in the deep Pacific twilight. Jeanne had lit candles and made a salad of lettuce and fresh cucumber. Roger had seemed relaxed, at peace with himself, and she had hoped that things between them were beginning to improve.

Calm had settled on their relationship after a year and a half of turmoil. Central to their troubles had been their inability to conceive a child and Roger Darrow's subsequent attraction to a young actress named Miranda Blake. For six months, he had carried on an affair with her, and Jeanne had responded by angrily taking a lover of her own. After Miranda had returned to New York, Roger and Jeanne Darrow had turned back to each other. Jeanne had found excitement and satisfaction in her new job. Roger had begun to develop ideas for a series to replace "Flint," whose ratings had finally faded.

Jeanne had tried to see their spring together as a time of renewal and hope. But she had known that beneath the surface, her husband was restless, frustrated, uncertain of his future. He'd had almost everything, she thought, but he had never learned how to be happy.

On that last night, they had eaten quickly, listening to the sounds of evening in Pacific Palisades and to the tenor sax of Georgie Auld on the tape deck. They had shared a bottle of Chablis from a California vineyard. And then, in the afterglow of the meal, he had announced his odyssey.

He had explained that, for years, he had wanted to cross the country with nothing but his video camera and his ideas for a documentary about America. He said that in the spread of cable television across the land, he had found the perfect topic, and in the elusive figure of Andrew MacGregor, whose cable franchises *hm* spread from one coast to the other, he had found the perfect focus. He said that he needed to change the direction of his career and the direction of his life, and the journey would give him the opportunity to do both.

Then, naïvely, almost stupidly, she thought now, she had offered to go with him. He had responded, without changing the tone of his voice or the expression on his face, that she was one of the reasons he was leaving, and he wasn't sure if he was coming back to her.

In their life together, her husband had been romantic and loving, self-centered and cruel. He had hurt her and she had hurt back. She had told him that night that she didn't care if he came back to her or not. He had left immediately and they had never said good-bye.

She wished now that she could relive that night, that she could relive the years she had spent with him. But he was gone, except on the video tapes he had recorded during the trip. The pain of his leaving would last as long as the pain of his death.

The nurses lifted James Whiting's body onto the operating table. The anesthesiologist inserted an endotracheal tube that would pump oxygen and nitrous oxide into Whiting's lungs. A nurse inserted a Foley catheter into Whiting's penis. Through it, an antibiotic solution would be introduced to cleanse Whiting's bladder.

Jerry Haller, the scrub nurse, finished counting the sponges and instruments he would be handing to Stanton during the operation; when it was over, he would recount the used instruments and bloody sponges to be sure that nothing had been left inside the patient.

In the scrub room beside the OR, Dr. Stanton, an associate, Dr. Richard Hoffman, along with a junior resident, and an intern were covered from elbow to fingertip in antiseptic soap. The intern was about to assist on his first operation, and the resident on his first transplant. Stanton sensed their nervousness. He felt it himself. It was always good to feel nervous before surgery, he thought, like an athlete before a contest.

In the OR, the nurses helped Stanton and the others into their robes and gloves. Dr. Hoffman took a gauze sponge in a pair of scissors, dipped it into an antiseptic solution called Betadine, and painted it onto Whiting's stomach, turning the skin a leather shade of orange. Sterile surgical sheets were draped over Whiting's body and they were ready.

Dr. Stanton stood beside the table, the intern at his right, Jerry Haller and the instruments at this left. Hoffman and the resident were on the other side of the patient. Stanton looked at Haller, who had served four years in a M.A.S.H. unit in Vietnam and three years as Stanton's best scrub nurse. Without saying a word, Stanton held out his hand, and Haller snapped a scalpel into the palm.

The razor-sharp blade traced a semicircle on James Whiting's abdomen, and a thin line of red followed the knife. With a gauze sponge, Dr. Hoffman wiped away the beads of blood that appeared along the incision. Then, Stanton and Hoffman exerted gentle pressure on the sides of the cut, opening it to reveal the thin, yellow layer of fat below.

Stanton called for the electrosurgical knife, an electrical element used for cutting through tissue laywers and cauterizing blood vessels. He touched the knife to one of the larger vessels that was bleeding into the incision. The end of the vessel sizzled and sent up a small puff of smoke. Hoffman pointed out another vessel. Stanton touched it and it sizzled. He squinted a bit, because smoke was rising from the incision and the air now smelled of cooked blood vessels, like the acrid odor of hair singed by a candle.

"We're going for the external iliac vein and the internal iliac artery," he said to his young assistants. "It's going to take us about an hour to get there and prepare the vessels for anastomosis." He touched another blood vessel with the electro-knife, and it sizzled. "We place the kidney in the front of the abdomen, outside the peritoneum, to make it more accessible. If he rejects it and we have to go in and get it, we don't have to go too far."

Stanton glanced at the anesthesiologist. "How's he doing?"

"Fine."

"Good. Just keep him dreaming of a nice, long piss."

There were no dreams for Jeanne Darrow on the TWA flight to Los Angeles. She had picked at her meal, asked for a pillow and blanket, and curled up to sleep. But she did not sleep well on planes. At best, she gained a sort of penumbra, half-alseep and half-awake, lulled by the nomontony but bestirred by the noise of the jet engines. As she squirmed about, she was conscious enough of her thoughts to know that they were not dreams, but they followed one another with the erratic logic of the subconscious. She saw her husband's face that night by the pool. She saw the lemon she had squeezed on the fish. She saw her husband's bandaged head. She saw the man in surgical greens telling her that her husband's life had ended. She saw the form she had signed to permit the removal of his kidneys. She was herself in black.

Then Jeanne Darrow sat up, wide awake. The acceptance of death, of permanent separation, came in small, painful steps. She had just taken one of them. She had seen herself as a widow.

She looked out the window and saw farmland. They were someplace over the Midwest. She wondered if he had found his answers down there in the cornfields and small towns, or if, when he reached the coast of Maine, he was as confused and frustrated as he had been in Los Angeles.

She wondered where his kidneys were at that moment. In a way, they would be his legacy. She thought it would be ironic if the kidneys that were supposed to give two people new lives somehow infected them with the same dissatisfaction that Roger Darrow had found in his.

James Whiting's abdomen had been open now for nearly an hour and a half. The edges of the green surgical sheeting had been tinted red. Instruments lay on his stomach, close by the incision, where the surgeon could reach them quickly. Layers of skin, fat, fascia, and muscle srained against the retractors. The organs below, still sheathed in the glistening white fiber of the peritoneum, looked alive and angry, like a family of animals whose burrow had been invaded.

Dr. Joseph Stanton and his associate had located the internal iliac artery, lifted it from its bed of tissue, clamped it, and severed it at the point where they would connect it to the renal artery. They had prepared the external iliac vein in the same way.

Stanton glanced up at the clock. It seemed to him that only a few minutes had passed. He had been vaguely aware of the questions the young resident and intern had asked, and he had answered them with his second voice, the one that sounded to him as though it belonged to another surgeon, who looked over his shoulder and commented dispassionately on the hands of Joseph Stanton working within the patient's body.

Tchaikovsky's Sixth Symphony, the *Pathetique,* was playing on the radio. Stanton liked music in the operating room because it washed away the other noises, the clanking of instruments as they were moved from table to patient, the whispering of the circulating nurses, the steady beat of the respirator, the comings and goings of med students and other visitors to the OR, and the low-level background hum that seemed to him like the breathing of the hospital itself.

He stepped back from the table. "Now we're ready."

"To conclude this afternoon's Tchaikovsky concert," said the cultured voice on the radio, "we will now hear the *1812 Overture.*"

Stanton looked at the radio. "Not in here, we won't. I've never operated with the sound of cannons firing, and I don't intend to start now." He told the circulating nurse to turn off the radio.

Then he opened the perfusion machine, disconnected the renal blood vessels, and slid his hands under the kidney. He lifted it gently and transferred it to a stainless-steel bowl filled with crushed ice and saline.

"Living tissue, gentlemen," he said over his shoulder. "It may look gray and lifeless, but it is the most complex chemical filtration system known. Even at this point, it's susceptible to bruises and trauma, and if it's mishandled, it may shut down altogether."

He carried the basin back to the operating table, looked at his intern and resident, and said, "Here is where we start earning our money."

The most critical stage of the procedure was about to begin. The time between the removal from the perfusion machine and the introduction of the recipient's blood into the kidney was called the warm ischemic time. While the surgeons worked, the kidney's temperature would be rising and its cells would be without nourishment. The longer the ischemic time, the higher the chance for complication or failure.

"I'll be doing most of the stitching," said Stanton, "most of the time using five-o silk sutures. As I stitch, Dr. Hoffman will hold the blood vessels together, so that the suturing won't put undue pressure on the vascular tissue. We have to work fast, but we have to be careful," he said. And if we're faced with a choice between fast or careful, we compromise and do it both ways, fast *and* careful."

The room fell silent, except for the beating of the respirator and the beep of the cardiac monitor. Stanton made sure that everyone was in place, then he looked at the circulating nurse. "Start the clock."

On the wall opposite Stanton was a large timer, with all three hands set at zero. The nurses threw a switch, and the second hand began to sweep.

"I want to open the clamps in less than thirty minutes," said Stanton.

He reached into the basin, lifted the kidney out of the saline, and wrapped it in a surgical towel. He placed the kidney on Whiting's abdomen, beside the incision.

"Let's begin," he said.

After that, he spoke as little as possible, and usually in single words or short phrases.

Suture. Suction. Five-o silk. Another. Right angle forceps, please. Pass the kidney to me. Five-o. Suture. Five-o. Scissors. Your suture, Doctor. Good. Take the next one. Suction. Five-o Suction. Tie it. Five-o. Another. Five-o. Right angle. Suction. Kidney to you, Doctor. Five-o. Suction. Tie it. Five-o. Suction. Scissors. Good. It was done in twenty-three minutes.

"Good," he repeated after he glanced at the clock.

The arteries and veins had been fully anastomosed. The kidney, pallid and lifeless in contrast to the red tissue around it, rested on top of the incision like a letter about to be slipped into an envelope. The long yellow ureter lay on the surgical sheet beside the kidney.

"We're ready to release the clamps," said Stanton.

There was a shuffling of feet around the operating table. The young doctors holding the retractors were changing their positions, like models preparing for the next pose. The circulating nurses had new tasks to perform. The anesthesiologist injected the contents of three vials into Whiting's IV line. Heparin would clear the clots from the vessels around the kidney. Mannitol would stimulate the blood flow through the kidney. Lasix would accelerate the production and excretion of urine.

After hundreds of transplants, this was still a thrilling moment, thought Stanton. He announced that he was releasing the venous clamp. Everyone, including the nurses, crowded closer to peer over his shoulder.

"What you are about to see," he said, "is a small miracle, the fusion of biology and technology."

Then he removed the hemostat from the Iliac artery. Blood began to flow into the kidney. The gray lump of tissue began to enlarge, to pulse, to fill with life. The gray dissolved into purple. Color suffused the kidney. Color and, with it, new life for the patient on the table.

Stanton released the second hemostat, then looked at the young doctors in training. Ordinarily, they tried to convey the sort of detached, almost nonchalant professionalism that was the manner of most medical people. But above the surgical masks, their eyes were wide. They had been touched.

Stanton reached out and stroked the kidney.

"It's pinking up nicely," said Dr. Hoffman.

Jerry Haller laughed. "That's what the obstetrician says when the baby comes out all blue and gets his first dose of oxygen."

"Precisely," said Stanton. He glanced at intern and resident once more. Both were watching the kidney's color intensify. He let several moments pass, then he said, "All right, we've all been properly impressed. Now, let's get this ureter tied up and get this man onto a bedpan."

He called for saline solution to be released through the catheter into Whiting's bladder. The saline would enlarge the bladder and make it easier to incise. After that, he called for a stabbing knife.

"Hey!" said the intern.

Stanton looked up. "Hey what?"

"Look at the ureter."

A droplet of liquid had collected at the end of the ureter. A periostalitic wave forced the liquid out of the tube, and it soaked into the surgical sheeting beside the incision. Another droplet began to form in its place. Already the kidney was cleansing James Whiting's system.

"Bright clean urine," said Stanton proudly. "Our magic works."

7

One day about a week later, Jeanne Darrow took the box containing her husband's ashes and drove up the Pacific Coast Highway to the place, near Zuma Beach, where the Mulholland Highway reached the sea. She followed the winding road inland for several miles, until she was high in the chaparral-covered mountains that lean against the coast. She drove to a turnoff that she knew well and parked.

The morning sky was clear, a rarity in June, and the sun, just risen above the mountains, cast a knife-sharp shadow that divided the scene into peaks of red-tinted light and arroyos and canyons that still lingered in the night. Across the darkness of the arrayo below her, past a low ridge, was the hard blue backdrop of the Pacific. This had been one of their favorite spots.

Jeanne stared out at the ocean for a time, then took the box and started down the trail to the bottom of the arrayo. A half hour later, she was standing in a small glade of sycamores on the bank of a narrow stream. Above her, the sun had begun to bake the chaparral, but the bottom of the arroyo was still dark and cool and the water in the stream whispered softly as it tumbled toward the sea.

Jeanne Darrow was filled with an ineffable sense of loneliness and loss, and yet, in this deserted glade, she felt at peace, alone for the last time with her husband, safe from the rest of the world, from the prying eyes of Hollywood and the press.

She knelt by the stream and touched the water. It was icy cold. She withdrew her hand, untied the box and opened it. A covering of tissue lay across the ash. She removed it delicately and felt her stomach shiver inside her. She saw coarse gray ash and white lumps that she had not expected. They were fragments of her husband's bones. She looked at them for a moment. She reached out to touch them, but she could not.

She told herself to do it quickly, or she would be sitting there at sunset, still staring into the box.

She had studied the poetry of Browning and Donne and Housman, looking for something tht would be appropriate to the moment, but nothing beyond a simple "I love you" and a silent prayer seemed necessary. She looked at the bone fragments once more, then dumped the contents of the box into the stream. The fragments sank. The ashes floated for a moment on the surface, swirled in the eddy, and then disappeared with the current.

Now, he was gone.

It was a little after seven o'clock. This had always been their time of day, she thought. Most love affairs began at night. Theirs had begun at seven o'clock in the early morning.

He had been the thirty-three-year-old producer of one of the top-rated television programs in America, full of success and full of himself. She had been a twenty-four-year-old undergraduate who had returned to college after two years of struggling as an actress in New York. She had decided, at last, to study premed. She had inherited her father's intelligence and his aptitude, and she had convinced herself that she could follow him into the medical profession. But she had also inherited her grandmother's dreams of becoming an actress, and it was still difficult to deny them, despite her years in New York.

The morning that Jeanne and Roger met, "Flint" had been filming on location at the University of Southern California. Jeanne was hurrying to breakfast at the dining hall. Darrow was strolling across the campus with a cup of coffee in his hands. As they approached, their eyes met. He smiled. She looked away and kept walking. He watched her for a moment, then announced that they were looking for extras to appear in the first shot.

She had been unable to resist the invitation, and in the months that followed, she had been unable to resist anything about him.

People said it was a case of opposites attracting: Roger Darrow, the television producer who had an idea for a new program every day but couldn't do long division; and Jeanne Byrne, a young premed who had cured herself of the acting disease. People said it would be good for Roger Darrow to love someone who had nothing to do with the "industry," someone who was calm, level-headed, rational, and saw the world as something more than a series of good locations.

But the world of Roger Darrow seduced her and she seduced

him. She earned her bachelor's in premed, and then she took up her dream of becoming an actress once more. She married Roger Darrow. She lived a fantasy in Roger Darrow's Pacific Palisades mansion, where she was the envy of half the women in Hollywood, and in her acting classes, where she tried to learn to tap the springs of her own emotion and divert them into other personalities.

She began to appear in local Los Angeles theater. She played bit parts on television programs. Occasionally, with her husband's help, she landed a featured part on a weekly series, and her agent would take an ad in *Variety,* reminding everyone to watch Jeanne Darrow, that fresh new face, as so-and-so on "Lou Grant" or "The Love Boat." For more than five years, she was a fresh new face. But she could not act. She had no presence, no sense of rhythm or timing, no talent.

Although her husband continued to encourage her and offer her roles in "Flint," which she never accepted because she did not want to compromise him, she eventually faced the truth. She told her agent to stop calling. She dropped out of acting class. And she dropped out of sight.

She became the housewife of the Hollywood producer. She studied landscape design three mornings a week. She contributed time in a day-care center each afternoon. She smashed a murderous serve on the court, cooked nouvelle cuisine in the kitchen, and spent a year and a half trying to conceive a child. After she had failed to become pregnant, the bonds between her and her husband began to loosen, and they both turned to other lovers.

People said that after bravely accepting failure as an actress, Jeanne Darrow had no resources left with which to reconstruct her own identity. But Jeanne Darrow was stronger than people thought, and she no longer cared what people thought. She knew that she needed time to reassess her life, and if her life for a time seemed aimless and unfulfilled, that was simply part of the process of growth and change.

She and her husband lived through their affairs. Their marriage, it seemed, survived. When she thought she was ready, she applied to the Los Angeles County Paramedical training program and began a new career.

Now, she was a Class A Emergency Medical Technician. She knew how to splint broken bones, perform CPR, give injections, or rig an IV bottle in the field. She could drop from a helicopter or repel down a rock face with a medical bag on her back. She had earned the respect of her colleagues and, at last, she had regained confidence in herself. Without that confidence, that newfound strength, she did not believe that she could have lived through the weeks since her last meal with her husband.

She peered into the water. She could no longer see the bone fragments and, already, they had mixed into the streambed.

Hollywood is the biggest company town in America, and when someone who works for the industry passes on, it's news. Actors and actresses who have lived their later years in obscurity achieve a final moment of glory when the evening news reports their passing. Cinematographers, editors, and Hollywood craftsmen who have spent their careers in the fine print on the credit roll, became momentary celebrities when the *L.A. Times* carries their photos and filmographies. And the death of an important director or producer is treated in Hollywood like the passing of a senator or congressman.

Three television stations, the all-news radio station, the major Los Angeles newspapers, the *Hollywood Reporter,* and *Variety* covered the death and funeral of Roger Darrow, although no editor bothered to send a reporter to Maine, because official reports indicated that there was nothing there to learn.

Vicki Rogers, however, in "On the Coast," a five-minute gossip segment syndicated to local coffee-time talk shows, had speculated on the reasons for Darrow's trip: "The official story is that he was scouting locations for a documentary, a look at America and her people, from California to Maine. Others think that a rift with longtime producing partner Howard Rudermann caused his departure. Or maybe it was a shaky marriage that sent him off in pursuit of personal adventure on the highways and byways of America. People in the know say he was never the same after he canceled his affair with a certain fresh young face who is no longer on the scene."

At ten o'clock that morning, three hundred people, friends and family, actors and writers, agents and publicists, studio executives, Hollywood technicians, hangers-on, and curiosity-seekers drawn by the Vicki Rogers report, came to Forest Lawn, Burbank, for the memorial service. The church, a replica of Boston's Old North, was the perfect spot for a Hollywood funeral, because it looked like a movie set and overlooked the back lot at Disney Studios.

The service began with music. Jeffrey Davis, a popular studio musician, performed Bach's *"Jesu, Joy of Man's Desiring"*. Later, he played an organ interlude that tried to dignify the theme music from "Flint," making it a dirge instead of the upbeat lead-in to a television detective show. As a recessional that was the most moving part of the ceremony, Davis went to the piano and played "Taint Nobody's Business if I Do," Roger Darrow's favorite song.

There were readings:

"And the Lord said, Lazarus, come forth. [He did it all with special effects thought Howard Rudermann.] Yea, though I walk through the valley of the shadow of death, I shall fear no evil. [For I am the meanest son of a bitch in the valley, thought Vaughn Lawrence.] Observe the lilies of the field, they neither sow nor reap, yet the Lord provides for them. [But not as well as those who look out for number one, thought Len Haley.]"

There were eulogies:

Billy Singer, America's highest-rated television preacher, traveled from Youngstown, Ohio, to speak of Darrow.

"He was a man of dignity and honor in an imperfect world, and he created Jess Flint, one of the enduring fictional characters of the last decade, in that image, an example to our young people, and a ray of hope to the rest of us. Roger Darrow was a man in search of the truth." (An excellent performance even if you couldn't stand him, thought John Meade.)

Peter Cross, the young actor who had gained fame as Jess Flint, spoke for the Hollywood artistic community. "He worked hard and he never compromised; he wanted every show to be as good as the pilot. And we were all willing to work our hearts out for him." (As long as he gave in whenever you threatened to hold out for more money, thought Harriet Sears.)

Howard Rudermann, the last speaker, struggled with his words and emotions. "He was one hell of a man, and we're all going to miss him." (Especially you, you no-talent son of a bitch, thought Vicki Rogers.)

"What the hell is she doing here?" whispered Harriet to How- ard Rudermann.

They were standing in the foyer of Jeanne Darrow's house, and Vicki Rogers was in the living room, in the middle of a circle of people that included Peter Cross and several celebrities. It was two hours later, and the house was filled with mourners whose conversation was becoming, almost in spite of itself, more cheerful as the morning wore on.

"She's a journalist, Harriet. This is a big story." answered Howard.

"A journalist?"

Harriet gave Howard what had been dubbed, during their marriage, as "the look." Whenever Howard said something that Harriet considered unkind, insensitive, or just plain stupid, she would stare at him with her brow furrowed and the corners of her mouth pulled back in an expression that was mingled with annoyance and disappointment. When his lawyer asked him to write down the things about Harriet that were causing him to seek a divorce, "the look" led the list.

"I said journalist." They had been divorced for ten years, and Howard was no longer intimidated by "the look."

"If she's a journalist, you're David O. Selznik," answered Harriet. "She's probably over there trying to rate this gathering like it was a party. 'What a charming brunch at Jeanne Darrow's house the other morning. Peter Cross was there; top-rank agent Frank Wheeler; Laura Keebler, the young screenwriter; Vaughn Lawrence, everybody's favorite talkmaster. John Meade, number-two man at MacGregor Communications is here, lending a touch of East Coast elegance. If you ever need someone to organize a glittering affair after your husband's funeral, call Jeanne Darrow. She gets four stars in my book.' "

Howard tried to give Harriet his version of "the look." "I really think you're getting senile."

Harriet grunted and glanced across the living room, through the haze of cigarette smoke, to Jeanne, who had been standing near the fireplace, receiving guests and condolences, for an hour. Their eyes met, and Jeanne rolled hers toward the ceiling. Harriet stepped down into the living room and elbowed her way through the crowd.

"Are you OK, honey?" Harriet asked when she reached Jeanne.

Jeanne shook her head. Her living room had become close and claustrophobic, despite the cathedral ceilings, white stucco walls, and full-length windows. "I've seen junior executives from every network and studio in town, out-of-work actors and writers whose best meal ticket was Roger Darrow, and half the glad-handers in Hollywood," she whispered." It's starting to get to me."

"Disappear for ten minutes, and I'll do what I can to keep them all occupied."

Jeanne could see Vicki Rogers pushing toward them. "Just keep yourself between me and that bitch until I can get collected again."

Jeanne stepped out the side door and into the hallway that ran from her husband's study to the kitchen. She turned toward the study, but she saw Vaughn Lawrence sitting at her husband's desk, his girl friend sitting on the sofa, and John Meade studying the photos on the wall.

Opposite the living room door was the entrance to the game room. Peter Cross and Jeffrey Jones, a guard for the Lakers, were leaning against the pool table; they were talking about basketball. Several people were sitting at the bridge table sipping drinks. Jeanne continued down the hallway and tried the bathroom door. Locked. No privacy anywhere. She stepped through the swinging doors into the kitchen.

The caterers, four young women who had gained an excellent reputation on the Hollywood party circuit, were going about their work quietly and unobtrusively. Jeanne was pleased with their service and with the menu, which included melon salad, quiche Lorraine, sour-cream coffee cakes, lox and bagels, and muffins. Jeanne had wanted the menu simple but satisfying, with nothing that would seem too elaborate or festive. Perhaps she could sit by the cooking island and watch them for a few minutes. But she did not want to seem like she was supervising.

She pushed through the swinging doors into the butler's pantry. It was the size of a large closet, and it was lined with the original glass cabinets and red tile counter tops, which Jeanne had carefully restored when she remodeled the house.

There, for a few moments, she could be alone. She poured a cup of coffee from the brewer on the counter, sipped, and thought about the mountain glade.

Vaughn Lawrence ordered a tequila sunrise. John Meade said that he would like a dry, ice-cold martini. Kelly Hammerstein went to fetch the drinks, and the two men were alone for the first time.

Roger Darrow's study was paneled in walnut and lined with bookcases. There was a Bokhara on the floor, an expensive print of Winslow Homer's *Fog Warning* above the fireplace, a wall of photographs behind the desk. The drapes had been drawn to keep out the glare, and Lawrence had turned on the desk lamp, as though he did not think he would exist without some form of artificial light bouncing off his face.

He spent seven and a half hours a week under studio lights. On Friday afternoons, he taped five half-hours of "People and Prices," his game show, and they were broadcast the following week. Each morning, from 9:00 to 10:00, he hosted "Breakfast with Vaughn," his talk show.

He came from the first generation of game-show hosts, which was not much different from the second or third, except that most of them were now in their late fifties. His face had been lifted twice, and the wrinkles in his neck would soon need attention. He weighed only two pounds more than he did when he came to Hollywood, however, and he had one feature that many of the younger generation sought to copy—his eyes. They were never open more than halfway, as though he were just waking up, or dropping off to sleep, or deep in some private pleasure. To his fans, the housewives and retirees who watched his programs every day, they were bedroom eyes, somnolent and sexy. To his enemies in the industry, they were the eyes of a snake.

John Meade sat in a leather chair beside the desk. He wore a dark blue suit with gray pinstripes. His tie was neatly knotted and every hair was in place. His close-shaved face seemed to glisten in the light. He looked like an eager young emcee, just arrived from a UHF station in the hinterlands to study at the feet of a master. He wished, however, that he had never crossed Vaughn Lawrence's path.

"It's nice to meet you face-to-face," said Lawrence, "without a battery of lawyers in the way."

"I prefer the lawyers," said Meade.

Lawrence flashed the sadistic smile he reserved for the unemployed engineer who lost the jackpot on the final spin of the wheel. "I prefer a good detective. He can do me more good than my lawyers when the chips are down."

Meade crossed his legs, as though he were nervous.

Vaughn Lawrence could remain motionless for hours if necessary. He had endured as a television personality because he was always cool and controlled, whether moderating a debate on his talk show or standing like a friendly statue while an overjoyed contestant covered him in kisses on "People and Prices."

"Now that we are going to be allies," said Meade, "who is your man on Easter's Haven? Is it Bannister?"

Lawrence shook his head. "I wouldn't know. My man is in L.A., and one of his men is on the island. Even if I did know, I wouldn't tell you until the SEC approves our merger."

"That could take up to six months or more, once they've finished going over the proposal and making adjustments in our corporate structure."

Lawrence nodded. "That's how long you'll have to wait. As I learned when you tried to raid my stock, it's always good to have someone sitting at Andrew MacGregor's front door. You never know what you may find out."

"Or what you may do with your knowledge," answered Meade. "You're an astute businessman, Lawrence. If I'm going to be forced into a merger with anyone, it might as well be you."

Lawrence did not move, but for a moment, his eyes opened wide, as though Meade's remark had pleased him.

"However," said Meade, "I thought it was more than coincidental that Roger Darrow's boat exploded on Easter's Haven."

Lawrence did not blink. "Did you talk to him on the island?"

Meade nodded.

"Did he video-tape you?"

Meade shook his head.

"What was he like?"

"A basket case. No threat to anyone."

"He was a threat," answered Lawrence. "He had crossed the country shooting the video tapes, asking questions about your uncle and his cable systems," Lawrence paused, then added, "He even interviewed Congressman Reuben Merrill about the friendly merger between your company and mine."

"The merger is not friendly," said Meade, without changing the tone of his voice.

"Shhh."

Vaughn Lawrence brought a finger to his lips. "For the good of both of us, I'd keep that to myself, John. Along with your speculation's on Darrow's death."

Meade turned his eyes to the painting above the mantel, as though trying to ignore Lawrence's condescension.

"Remember, John," continued Lawrence, "your secrets are mine, and mine are yours, and for the good of our future together, it should remain that way."

To protect Jeanne Darrow, Harriet Sears had thrown herself into the path of Vicki Rogers.

"Is she all right, Harriet?" Vicki was asking.

"Nothing a few months of crying and a few years of forgetting won't cure."

"How romantic," said Vicki. She was wearing a gray jacket with matching skirt and a white blouse highlighted by her onyx brooch. At the moment, her eyeglasses were making Vicki look vulnerable, as though she were trying to hide her grief behind them. She took both of Harriet's hands in hers. "I'm so sorry, dear. It must be terrible for her."

Harriet barely nodded. She did not like Vicki Rogers. Most people in Hollywood didn't. Harriet was one of the few people who did not mind showing it.

"And you must be crushed." Vicki paused, then added, "Roger wrote some of your best lines."

"He had a wonderful imagination." Harriet smiled. "And so do you."

Vicki's glasses became her only feature. "I report what the public wants to know."

"And the truth be damned," snapped Harriet. "There was no split between Roger and Howard. And what was going on between Roger and Jeannie is none of anybody's damn business."

"An important figure, a national figure, has been killed. Somebody should be speculating on the reasons for his death."

"His boat blew up. That's the reason. And it was an accident. That's what the Coast Guard and the Granite County Sheriff's Office have both said. There's no reason to poke into his private life." Harriet spoke in an angry whisper, just loud enough to be heard above the chatter of conversation in the rest of the house.

"If I think that the reasons for his death are to be found in his private life, that's where I'll look."

"Do your fingers smell?" asked Harriet.

"What?"

"Do your fingers smell? They must if you go around all day picking lint out of people's belly buttons."

Vicki glared at Harriet, and Harriet glared right back. In her youth, Harriet had crossed Hedda Hopper and Louella Parsons. Compared to them, Vicki Rogers was bush league.

"Why do you protect her like a mother?" asked Vicki.

"She's my friend."

In Darrow's study, Howard Rudermann was meeting John Meade.

"Howard was Darrow's partner," said Lawrence. "He's producing 'Redgates of Virginia' and doing a damned fine job of it, even without Darrow. And you can take that to the bank."

Rudermann sat on the edge of the sofa and balanced a plate of coffee cakes on his knee. "You can tell Mr. MacGregor that he'll see every penny he's invested right up there on the screen." Rudermann liked to use the Hollywood jargon with outsiders.

"And the only people who see it have to carry my American Heritage network," said Lawrence.

Rudermann nodded a bit too vigorously. "This kind of programming is a gamble, but Vaughn knows it's the only way to go. Once cable can finance stuff like 'Redgates,' it won't be much longer before we're bigger than the networks."

"Your partner wanted nothing to do with 'Redgates,' said Meade. "Apparently because Mr. Lawrence and my uncle were financing it."

Ruderman shrugged. "Rodge wasn't thinkin' straight that last couple of months. A lot was happening to him.

"Mr. Lawrence tells me that Darrow shot video tapes as he crossed the country."

"Yeah. He wanted to make a series," said Rudermann. "He was going to call it 'One Man's America.' "

"Have you seen any of the footage?" asked Meade.

"No one has, not even Jeanne. She was so mad at him for going off that she kept shoving the tapes into the desk when he mailed them back." Rudermann stuffed a piece of coffee cake into his

mouth. "She's a nice kid, but sometimes she can be damn stubborn."

Lawrence moved slightly so that the light from the desk lamp did not shine in his eyes. "They she hasn't allowed the press to see any of the tapes?"

"No way." Rudermann licked the crumbs off his fingers. "She promised me that I'll be the first outsider to see them and I'll produce the series if it goes."

Lawrence shifted his eyes to Meade. "Wouldn't you love to get a look at Roger Darrow's tapes, just to see what he was doing when he should have been helping Howard finish 'Redgates?' "

Meade did not respond.

Lawrence leaned back and pulled open the middle drawer of Darrow's desk.

"Close the desk," said Rudermann as sharply as he could. "What's in there is none of your business."

"Don't be so honorable, Howard. It's not like you." Lawrence opened two more drawers before he smiled his game-show smile and pulled a pile of video tapes from the desk. He picked one up. "San Francisco. Tape one. May ninth."

"Put it back, Vaughn," said Rudermann.

Lawrence looked at Meade and held up the cassette. "Should we put it back, John?"

"This isn't right, I don't think," said Rudermann.

"C'mon, Howard." Lawrence waved the cassette back and forth in front of Rudermann like a piece of steak. "You could have a major documentary here."

Rudermann began to protest, then fell silent.

The picture tube warmed quickly from green to phosphorescent gray. The stereo speakers connected to the set bagan to hiss. Vaughn Lawrence leaned forward. Howard Rudermann loosened his tie and put his plate on the table. John Meade sipped his drink.

The sound track rumbled. Then it began to pop, as though playing back the sound of tennis balls being smashed against a wall. It was the sound of the wind buffetting the microphone. Then someone on the tape muttered, "Shit."

The men in the room recognized the voice, but no one spoke. Then, an image appeared on the television screen. At first, it was shaky, uncertain. The camera was bouncing about crazily. Then, the tripod was locked down. The image steadied and the picture

We are perched on the hills of Marin County, just above the waters of the Golden Gate. The first wisps of afternoon fog are tumbling in, catching themselves, like pieces of wind-blown tissue paper, on the great orange bridge that spans the screen. In the distance, carefully framed between the towers of the bridge, the city of San Francisco gleams. A man enters the picture with his back to the camera.

The man finds the spot where he wants to stand, turns to the camera, and smiles.

For a moment, no one in the room spike, moved, or breathed. Then Howard Rudermann whispered, "Jesus."

Roger Darrow is tall and ruggedly built. His nose has been broken, notched at the bridge, so that it is dramatically askew. But his smile dominates his face and seems to define his personality. It is honest and spontaneous, and like any good producer, he has built everything else around his best feature. He has carefully chose the location, the hairstyle, the wardrobe, and the timing for his first tape.

There are few places in America where nature's beauty and man's art—the Golden Gate and bridge that crosses it—are more closely linked. On the precipice above the bridge, the wind is blowing, and Darrow has turned his face into it so that it will tousle his hair, giving him an almost Byronic appearance. His clothes— razor-creased khaki trousers, brown leather belt, dress-green shirt with starched open collar, epaulets, and button flaps over the pockets—looks like the uniform of a soldier of fortune. And the sun's rays diffuse through the fog, bathing the hillside, the bridge, and the distant vista in a golden light that is unique to the northern California coast. Roger Darrow is presenting himself as a modern knight-errant about to embark on a quest across an enchanted land.

"It's time to do something different," he announces. "After producing four hundred hours of disposable programming, I want to create something lasting." He pauses to give his opening lines a bit of dramatic rhythm. "This is the beginning.

"What I'm going to be doing on these video tapes is a combination of research and rough draft for a study of American life in

the 1980s. *I want to explore the systems that bind us together and* *the things that make us strong. I'll talk about transportation, food production, politics, religion, the environment. And most of all, I want to talk about television. Because television, whether we like it or not, is the glue that holds this society together. It provides us with our shared communal experiences—rocket launches, elections, assassinations, Super Bowls. And it is the voice around our campfire, telling our tales and creating our myths."*

"It sounds like he was biting off more than he could chew," said John Meade.

"He always did," said Ruderman. "But he always managed to digest it . . . until this time."

"This time," said Lawrence, "he got swallowed up himself."

"And if I'm going to talk about television, I should also talk about one of the most fascinating, elusive, and powerful men in television today, Andrew MacGregor.

"For over thirty years, he has been building a communications empire. He owns VHF stations, radio stations, and he was one of the first men in America to recognize the importance of this. . . ." Darrow holds up a piece of cable that is about an inch thick. An outer wrapping of rubber protects two strands of wire that are wrapped tightly around each other.

"Within the next few years, coaxial cable, carrying up to a hundred channels of information, will connect seventy percent of the homes in this country to entertainment networks, data banks, home security systems, the stock market, churches, hospitals, community centers, city hall, and other homes. We are becoming a wired society, whether we like it or not."

Darrow nods, as though he likes that last phrase. He is enjoying himself. He seems comfortable in front of the camera.

"With coaxial cable and all its connections, we are building a new set of trunk lines for our national nervous system.

"In 1954, Andrew MacGregor established one of the first cable television stations in America, and he has been building them ever since. His franchises reach from coast to coast, and at seventy-eight, he remains on top of his technology."

Darrow holds up a little button-pad for the camera. This is part of his new, two-way interactive system called Respondsible. The viewers push the buttons, talk back to the television, and tell

Andrew MacGregor whatever he wants to know about them. This little system makes Andrew MacGregor an enormously powerful man."

Darrow pauses, like an experienced television reporter, and looks down at the ground. "Nine months ago, Andrew MacGregor decided to gather even more power. He attempted to acquire Lawrence/Sunshine Productions, so that he could control six channels of program software in addition to his delivery hardware."

"It seemed as though he had successfully cornered enough stock to take over the company when he suddenly withdrew his tender offer."

Vaughn Lawrence looked at the others in the room. A little smile crossed his face. They all knew the story of his stand against MacGregor Communications. Only John Meade knew the reasons behind his victory.

"Six months later, MacGregor and Lawrence, as a joint venture, decided to produce 'The Redgates of Virginia,' a property for which my partner and I hold the rights. Then, last week, the cable television industry was shocked when MacGregor Communications refiled Hart-Scott-Rodino papers with the SEC, declaring its intent to merge with Lawrence/Sunshine Productions. Even more surprising, it is a friendly merger, and according to published reports, Vaughn Lawrence will become vice-chairman, under MacGregor, of the new cable delivery and production entity. One of the questions I want to answer is, how did Vaughn Lawrence fight off the take-over and maneuver himself into this position?"

John Meade turned to Vaughn Lawrence. "It's amazing what you can learn in the *Wall Street Journal*."

"You can learn even more by the seat of your pants," answered Lawrence, "just putting one block on top of another and fighting like crazy when someone tries to take what you've built away from you."

Rudermann looked at Meade and waited for a response.

Meade raised his martini glass again. "That's attitude that has won you my uncle's admiration."

On the television screen, Roger Darrow's image continued to speak.

I have always wanted to paint an electronic portrait of this country, the way that Alexis de Tocqueville painted one with&3 *words a hundred and eighty years ago."*

Darrow's face becomes solemn and serious. "For a lot of personal reasons, this is a good time in my life to be taking a trip, and a lot of the places where Andrew MacGregor has stuck his finger are places that have some personal meaning for me.

"Beyond which, the strange mating dance of Andrew Mac-Gregor and Vaughn Lawrence has given me reason to ask some important questions.

"Information is power, and the men who produce and distribute information in our wired society are the most powerful of all. Some men accumulate power for its own sake, some for the money it can provide, and some because they have a vision. I think we should learn what Andrew MacGregor's vision for America is and why he needs a company like Lawrence/Sunshine to help him fulfill it."

After remaining alone in the pantry for several minutes, Jeanne Darrow decided to rejoin the gathering. She pushed through the swinging door into the dining room, which was mobbed. She turned, went back through the kitchen, and down the hallway, where she noticed that the door to her husband's study was closed. It sounded as though people were watching television, which struck her as rather impolite. As she approached the closed door, Jeanne Darrow recognized her husband's voice.

The study door flew open and smashed against the bookcase.

"Goddamn you people!" screamed Jeanne Darrow.

She stopped the video player. The picture disappeared. The cassette popped up. She pulled it out of the machine and pivoted angrily toward the room. "This"—she held the cassette clenched in her fist—"is private. It's none of your goddamn business."

Howard Rudermann jumped up, extending his hands in supplication. "I can explain, Jeannie."

"You'll explain nothing. You had no right to look at this, and no right to go rifling through my husband's desk."

Harriet Sears appeared in the doorway. "What's wrong, Jeannie?"

"They're looking at Roger's tapes." She was trembling with anger.

"We did it because we want to help you," said Rudermann.

"You did it because you're an asshole, Howard," said Harriet.

"*I* haven't even looked at those tapes," shouted Jeanne.

The noise in the study was drawing people from other parts of the house. Vicki Rogers peered in from the hallway. Harriet closed the door in her face.

"I won't look at the tapes until I have the strength to do it," continued Jeanne. "I don't care what's on them. There's no way I can be rational about them right now."

"That's why we want to help," said Rudermann. "We want to know what he was doing."

"All he cared about was figuring out who he was himself." Jeanne said. "That's why the tapes stay private." She opened the door and left the room.

"Jeannie," Harriet called.

"I'll be all right." She pushed her way past Vicki Rogers and headed for the stairs.

Harriet turned back to the men in the study. "What a bunch of jerks."

"Those tapes may be very important," said Rudermann defensively.

"I think you should honor her wishes," responded Harriet.

"We didn't know we were violating them." John Meade offered his apologies.

Harriet studied him, then gestured to the others. "Are you with them?"

"He's Andrew MacGregor's nephew," offered Rudermann.

"I know who he is," answered Harriet. "And he of all people ought to know about respecting people's privacy."

"Good line, Harriet," said Lawrence. "You should think about becoming a writer."

"No. When I hit the skids, I'll become a game-show host." She paused. "So maybe you can tell me what a game-show host wants with Roger Darrow's private tapes."

Lawrence smiled. The eyes seemed hooded and dangerous. "I'm a fan." Then he stalked out. Meade bowed to Harriet and left.

"Sometimes I don't know about Vaughn Lawrence," said Rudermann after a moment.

"So why did you sign a three-picture deal with him?"

Rudermann shrugged. "Business."

Jeanne was standing by the window in her bedroom, with her arms wrapped around her own waist. She was staring out at the empty tennis court and swaying back and forth, as though rocking a baby. Harriet knocked, then stepped in.

"You know, Jeannie," Harriet began softly, "Howard may be right about looking at the tapes."

Jeanne stopped swaying. "Not you, too?"

"For your own good. Until you look Roger in the eye one last time, you're never going to be able to get on with things."

"I just signed his death warrant, Harriet. I just scattered him to the elements. I need some time before I sit down and watch him talking to me on television. Besides, I can't forgive him for running out on me, and that's what he was doing."

Harriet shook her head. "Give him credit for more than that."

"Dammit," said Jeanne. "Give me credit for knowing what I need right now. And what I need is not some morbid reexamination of my husband's last four weeks."

Harriet brought her hand to her throat and nervously stroked the pearl necklace she was wearing with white blouse and black trousers. Most Americans had seen the gesture. She had used it in 1945, when she played an American woman interrogated by the Nazis in *The Wait for D-Day*; in 1958, when she played Salome's mother in an Italian biblical epic; and in "The Redgates of Virginia." When she was upset, nervous, or uncomfortable, her hand went to her throat.

"I'm no shrink," she said, "so I'm not going to try to tell you how to live your life. But don't bury Roger's last project because you and he never patched up. That's not fair to him, or to yourself."

Before Jeanne could respond, Harriet put her hands on Jeanne's shoulders and squeezed hard, as though trying to imprint her words. "That's all I'll have to say on the subject. I promise."

Jeanne took Harriet's hands and held them. "The next few months won't be easy, Harriet. I'll need all the help and advice you've got."

Vaughn Lawrence and John Meade stood together in the corner of the crowded dining room. Lawrence ate melon salad, Meade sipped coffee.

"What do you think Jeanne will do with the video tapes?" asked

"Sit on them," said Lawrence.

"You sound very confident about that."

Lawrence smiled slightly. "She's one-half Irish stoicism, to one-half southern California self-analysis. She has all kinds of feelings screaming for attention, like the therapists say, but the stoical half holds them in check. My bet is that she'll keep the tapes in a safe, look at them some time in the next few months, then put them back and get on with things."

"How can you be sure?"

"I can't, but as long as I own Rudermann, I have a direct line to Harriet Sears, which means that I'll know exactly what Jeanne is thinking. If she starts talk about going public with the tapes, I'll bring the pressure to stop her."

Meade casually stirred his coffee. "I hope it's more subtle than the pressure you put on her husband."

"The tapes may be totally harmless, or they may be dynamite. We don't know. But if Darrow had gotten off of that island, he would have had the evidence to bring everything crashing down on both of us."

"There was no need to kill him." Meade sipped his coffee and replaced the cup on the saucer he held in his left hand.

"You may know how to use the power structure your uncle created, but you haven't learned to protect it. Now that I'm part of it, I'll do whatever I have to to keep it standing." Lawrence popped a piece of melon into his mouth. "Because I don't like you, Meade, and I don't like what you tried to do to me. I don't want to end up buried with you under your uncle's pile of rubble."

Vicki Roger's ambled by and tried to inject herself into the conversation. "Now, tell me, what would two powerful television executives be discussing at Roger Darrow's funeral?"

Lawrence's eyes shifted to Vicki. "Melon balls."

8

We commit his body to the deep that he loved, O Lord, and to the ocean that was his home. We pray that you will watch over the soul of this simple, gentle man." Rev. John Forbison, of the First Congregational Church of Easter's Haven, raised his eyes to the sky and spoke in a voice strong enough to carry across the water, loud enough to be heard above the sound of idling engines. "Into thy hands, we commend his spirit."

The Coast Guardsmen at the stern of the patrol boat lifted the pine coffin, rested it for a moment on the gunwale, then let it slide slowly into the ocean.

Harry Miller, whose boat was bobbing a few feet from the Coast Guardsman, watched the weighted coffin disappear. Then, he reached into his cabin and pulled three long blasts on his horn. Izzy Jackson had always announced his arrival with three long blasts, and among the lobstermen, a superstition had grown. Whenever anyone bought or built a new boat, Izzy had been invited aboard to sound the horn and bring good luck. Now, the air above the grave was split with the shrieking, blaring, and honking of every boat in his funeral flotilla.

Izzy Jackson had left no money, no will, and no relatives. His only possessions had been the *Fog Lady* and the cottage he lived in on a small island owned by Andrew MacGregor. His only abiding wish, one that he had voiced often, was that he be buried at sea.

The service was ended. The patrol boat pulled out of the floating funeral cortege and headed toward land. The others followed.

Cal Bannister, whose boat was the last in the formation, watched Andrew MacGregor step to the stern of his cabin cruiser and throw a wreath of flowers onto the water. MacGregor's boat, the *Communicator,* was followed by the Millers in the *Ellie B*. As they crossed the spot where the coffin had been dropped, Ellie

Miller threw a bunch of roses into the water. Then came the Webb brothers, Samson and McGee, proprietors of the island hotel. McGee tossed a full bottle of beer and it sank among the roses. The Donhegans, all six, were next, and the youngest daughter dropped some wild flowers. As the circle of boats unwound, each boat passed the spot where the coffin had been dropped and left a remembrance.

When Cal Bannister's boat passed, Izzy Jackson's grave looked like a floating garden.

"Everybody threw a flower or somethin'," said Cal's wife, Lanie. "But I didn't bring one."

"Don't worry," grunted Cal. "No one's watching."

"We gotta leave something," she said. She was tall and solid, with wild black hair that seemed permanently unkempt. She was wearing a clean pair of jeans and a white turtleneck sweater that emphasized two of the features that first attracted her husband.

Although she was twenty-seven, the hard lines around her mouth suggested that Lanie Bannister had seen some miles, and not all of them had been smooth. But there was something naïve, almost childish, in her embarrassment that she did not have a flower. "If we don't leave somethin', they'll think we don't like their custom."

"It ain't a custom," said Cal. "He's the first guy in twenty years that got himself buried at sea on purpose."

Lanie looked ahead, at the line of boats led by the Coast Guards' man and MacGregor's cruiser. "Well, I ain't gonna let people think we don't want to belong."

She reached up and grabbed Cal's blue Dodger baseball cap from his head.

"Hey, give me that," demanded Cal.

She flung the hat into the water.

"Goddammit!" shouted Cal. "That hat cost me ten bucks at Dodger Stadium. I ought to smack you."

"I told you when we came here, no more smackin'," she said firmly.

Cal glowered at her for a moment. "I ain't touched you since we got here, have I?"

She stepped closer to him and put her hand on the small of his back. "No, except when it was nice. This place's been good for us, honey. That's why I want to feel a part of it."

"Well, you wasn't born here, and no one knows that I was, so

we'll have to stay for about ten years before the lobstermen figure
we've earned a place."

"I wouldn't mind that," she said.

Neither would Cal. In the bright sunshine, with the cloudless blue horizon all around him, he felt secure, almost relaxed. He had lived his life in jungles, and now his senses were adjusting, remembering. His skin was tanned after years of pallor that came from working at night. And his body no longer threatened the space it occupied. But even on the water, his eyes were constantly shifting, his neck muscles tensing at the slightest shifting in the wind or creaking in the boat.

As a boy, he had loved the island, with its dark forests, its ice-cold quarry pools, its broad, heath-covered meadows, and the boundless ocean that surrounded it. He had wanted to live there forever. But he had been sent away one summer day when he was seven years old. His mother had been called to the home of Andrew MacGregor. Cal had been puzzled because she usually visited Brisbane Cottage on Thursday nights. That night, she had told Cal that they were leaving the island, but Mrs. MacGregor had generously given them the money to find a new home.

Cal never learned what Andrew MacGregor had said to his mother and she had never spoken of him again. When he was older, he suspected that MacGregor had wanted her to leave because he was angry that his Thursday-night mistress had shared her affections with another man, the good Reverend Forbison. The other possibility was that MacGregor had not wished to see a minister's happy family broken apart, and he hadn't cared in the least for Cal's mother.

Cal and his mother began their wanderings. She worked as a cocktail waitress, a secretary, a blackjack dealer, and a hairdresser. She had bad taste in men and a bad taste for alcohol, and Cal spent most evenings alone, in front of the television set, or out on the street of whatever city they were living in that month. The streets were never friendly, but Cal learned from them the way to survive.

When he was fourteen, they were living in Las Vegas, and Cal was talking his way into casinos, where he would pick out players who were winning big and drinking heavily. He and a friend would follow their mark from the casino, and try to relieve him of his winnings in an alley or a parking lot. Then he turned, in a small way, to the drug trade. A friend of his mother supplied him with marijuana, which he sold to his schoolmates first in Las Vegas, and then in Los Angeles, where his mother drifted next. With his Las Vegas drug connections, he became one of the most popular students in his school, despite a personality that one girl described as cranky, dumb, and permanently horny.

While truant officers and local police had never been able to track down Cal Bannister, his draft board found him ten months after he was graduated from high school. He had left his mother, who was drinking herself to death in a Burbank apartment, and he was living with a group of bikers in Venice. Ten months later, he was operating a machine gun on a helicopter gunship in the Mekong Delta and scoring drugs in Saigon.

During a raid against a Viet Cong position on the morning of April 19, 1970, his helicopter was shot down and he was captured. Eventually, after two months of trudging through the jungles, he was brought to a prison near Hanoi. There he met Lieutenant Len Haley, a thirty-year-old officer who ran the camp, stood up to the guards, and infused the men around him with a will to live.

Haley became Cal Bannister's commander, his counselor, and his friend. He nursed Cal back to health after the long jungle march. He spent two weeks in the filth and heat of solitary confinement—eating rancid rice and fending off rats—after intervening when two guards were about to beat Cal Bannister to death. He showed Cal Bannister how to survive.

When the prisoners were released in 1973, Cal and Len Haley promised that they would stay in touch, and they promptly drifted apart.

With good connections in Southeast Asia, Cal Bannister had the opportunity to establish himself as a dope smuggler, but he lacked the attention span to make a success of himself at anything. He brought two big scores into Los Angeles, then lay back to enjoy the rewards of his labor.

He bought the most expensive Harley-Davidson on the market, picked up with a motorcycle gang known as the Vandals, and spent the next few years thundering up and down the freeways of southern California, roaring along mountain roads and through small towns, and cutting new paths across the delicate floor of the Mojave Desert. He picked fights in bars and usually won. He guzzled beer and breathed cocaine and had a new case of venereal disease every month.

To support his habits, he offered his talents to people who
needed personal protection or physical strength. During a southern California drug war, he crossed the Mexican border, tracked
down a group of smugglers, and murdered the leader in his bed.
When the daughter of a Los Angeles textile manufacturer was
raped and the suspect acquitted on a technicality, the father
turned to the underworld connections who supplied his business
with illegal aliens. Cal Bannister was hired to beat the suspect to
a pulp; he beat the suspect to death. And he once rigged a yacht
to explode during a party at Marina del Rey, killing two underworld bosses and a small army of drug pushers. His reputation
spread. His list of clients grew more powerful and prestigious, but
he remained a free-lancer until he met Len Haley once more.

Haley had started a detective agency in Los Angeles, and he
was working on a case that brought him into Cal Bannister's
neighborhood. An old friendship was renewed, and Cal Bannister
went to work for the Haley Detective Agency, providing his special
services to some of Haley's more important clients, including
among them a game-show host named Vaughn Lawrence.

Cal Bannister worked as an enforcer and lived as a biker until
he met Lanie, a waitress in a burrito-and-beer bar in Fresno. She
moved in with him and he began to change. One day, he told
Haley that he was thinking about quitting while he still had the
chance and taking Lanie to the island where he had been born.
Haley said that no one who had seen the action Cal had seen could
ever be happy with a quiet life. And Cal reluctantly agreed.

But six months later Len Haley gave Cal the opportunity. He
said that Vaughn Lawrence was doing business with Andrew
MacGregor, and he did not trust the old man or his associates.
Haley wanted to put someone on MacGregor's island who could
respond if Lawrence needed information or enforcement. In exchange, Cal would receive the money to buy a house and a boat
and a fresh start.

No one on Easter's Haven had recognized Cal Bannister, or
the name, which his mother had changed when they moved from
the island. Because Cal was competition, he and his wife had not
been warmly welcomed by the other lobstermen, except for Harry
Miller, who believed that every man deserved a fair shot if he was
willing to work. And Cal worked. He learned how to pilot a lobster
boat and lay traps. He spent upward of twelve hours a day on the

water. He demonstrated a talent for repairing malfunctioning diesel engines at the town dock. He joined the lobstermen's cooperative and slowly earned respect and friendship.

His only request from Len Haley had been for information: photographs and fingerprints of Andrew MacGregor, not exactly an easy assignment Using a telephoto lens and his knowledge of the island's topography, he had gotten pictures of MacGregor sunbathing in the nude, as was the old man's habit, even in September. When his boat crossed paths with MacGregor's for the first time, and the old man waved to him, Cal pulled up and offered MacGregor a beer—Rolling Rock in a returnable bottle. Tom Dodd, the old man's driver and bodyguard, objected, but MacGregor took the beer anyway. Cal Bannister mailed the bottle back to Len Haley, and for ten months, he heard nothing more from Los Angeles.

Now he feared that the explosion of the *Fog Lady* would mean the end of his tranquil life.

Lanie leaned over the side of the boat and looked up toward MacGregor's cruiser. She saw the old man standing ramrod straight at the stern, with his hands clasped behind his back and a little yachting cap on his head. John Meade was standing nearby, Edgar Lean and his wife, MacGregor's butler and maid for thirty years, were also aboard. And a young woman with blond hair was seated on a deck chair beside MacGregor.

"Folks around here sure like him," said Lanie.

"He's done a lot for most of them," answered Cal. "He's like a grandfather to the place."

"Is that why they don't mind if his girl friend looks like his granddaughter?"

"That's his niece. She commutes between here and New York."

"She looks awful familiar."

At Easter's Landing, the Coast Guard patrol boat veered north and headed for its base on the other side of the island. The *Communicator* turned south toward MacGregor's private dock. The rest of the boats in the flotilla chugged into the small, snug harbor at Easter's Landing, and all the lobstermen and their families went up the street to the Webb House for breakfast and a final toast to Izzy Jackson.

The Webb House was the only hotel on the island and the only restaurant open in the off-season. While tourists filled the Webb House in July and August, it was the center of the island community for the rest of the year. Built at the turn of the century, the hotel now looked a bit frayed at the edges, but the Webb brothers kept it clean and freshly painted. In the dining room, a partition of oak and stained glass separated the bar from a dozen sets of tables and chairs and a row of oak booths. And the bar itself, beautifully carved in oak and topped with marble, had aged like fine wine, which was seldom served there in the off-season.

Samson and McGee Webb were filling pitchers with beer and passing them out to the lobstermen. Island women were running in and out of the kitchen carrying trays of bacon and eggs and steaming pots of coffee. Children were scampering about filling the place with noise. And Cal and Lanie Bannister had taken a table with the Millers.

At the bar, Samson Webb and Harry Miller were talking. Samson had already had three beers too many.

"I still say MacGregor should be here." Samson's name fit his size, his long hair, and his bushy black beard.

"He ain't feelin' too good," said Harry.

Samson leaned an elbow on the bar. "You don't suppose he's plannin' to join Izzy Jackson any time soon?"

Harry stiffened. When he and Samson talked, they usually argued. On occasion, they fought, although Harry was half Webb's size.

"If you was a lobster, Samson, you'd be a cull," said Harry.

Cal Bannister came over to the bar to get a pitcher of beer.

"The newcomer," grunted Samson.

"I been here nine months," answered Cal. "When do I stop bein' a newcomer."

"You'll always be a newcomer," answered Samson, "and newcomers is fools."

"Why's that?"

"Because this island's livin' in the past."

"That's fine with most of us," said Harry.

Samson ignored Harry. He was talking to Cal. He gestured

with his thumb to the window. "And that old man, sittin' up there on his rock, is the cause of it."

McGee Webb came scuttling down to the end of the bar. "Less talk and more beer'd do this place a bit of good," he said to Samson. He was much smaller and several years older than his brother.

Samson waited until his brother had gone back to the tap before he turned again to Cal. "You know a lot about engines. You even worked once or twice on Izzy's boat."

Cal felt his scalp tighten.

"Do you think it blew up the way they say? By accident, I mean."

Cal scowled. "That's what the Coast Guard said. What're you askin' me for?"

Harry sipped his beer and wondered why Cal seemed angry.

Samson was too drunk to notice. "Well, here's this Hollywood guy, come to do a feature on Easter's Haven for national TV. You figure, he's gonna show the place off to all the developers and businessmen back there just itchin' for a place to put their money, which is just what this island needs. This'd be a great place for a cannery or condos out on Saint Bartholomew's Field."

Harry shook his head. He had been battling Samson's development schemes for years, and because of MacGregor, he had always won.

"The next thing you know," continued Samson, "this Hollywood guy's blown to pieces, and we're still sittin' here, livin' like they did in 1906, just like MacGregor wants."

"You're talkin' in circles, Samson. Say what you think," Harry spoke softly.

Samson looked at Harry. "All I'm sayin' is that times are movin' on. This island won't survive much longer on tourists and lobsters and guys paintin' sea gulls on ashtrays. You and MacGregor got to face that."

Harry laughed. It sounded like a grunt.

Samson looked at Cal. "Are you for or against?"

"Against what?"

"The federal gover'ment buyin' Saint John's Island and usin' the granite caves to store nucular waste?"

"We fought that war two years ago, Samson," said Harry. "It's a dead issue."

"Until MacGregor's dead. Then, you won't have nobody callin'

in his chits down in Washington whenever we try to do somethin'
up here. That site would mean jobs for this island, business for
the airstrip, and no danger at all to any of us." He looked at Cal
again. "Are you for or against?"

Cal shrugged. He felt as though he were being tested. "Well,
the country needs places like that, I guess, and Saint John's is five
miles away from anything. But most folks come here to get away
from pollution and live on their own again."

Samson Webb studied Cal for a moment, then turned to Harry.
"Well, I guess that's another one for your side." He jerked his
thumb at Cal. "He sounds like some wishy-washy lawyer who
comes up here for two weeks in August to sail his fiberglass boat."

Cal Bannister's right hand flashed across the bar and grabbed
Samson Webb by the collar. "I say what I mean."

Webb weighed 230 pounds and Cal 190, but Cal almost lifted
him off his feet. Webb's complexion turned red. He grabbed with
both hands at Cal's forearm. Then, quickly, quietly enough so that
no one in the dining area noticed, Cal released Webb, turned, and
strode back to his table.

For a moment, Samson Webb was shocked. Harry Miller was
impressed. Few people stood up to Samson Webb.

"Touchy, ain't he?" said McGee Webb.

"I'm gonna take his head off," Samson started to step around
the bar.

Harry put his hand on Samson's chest. "Wait till folks is finished eatin', Sam. They see a head rollin' around here, they might
lose their appetite."

"Ladies and gentlemen . . ." On the far side of the dining room,
Reverend Forbison was standing. "Now that we've all been served,
let us pray . . ."

An hour later, the meal was over, the community had toasted
the memory of Izzy Jackson, and the families were leaving Webb's.
McGee Webb and Reverend Forbison were shaking hands at the
door. Samson was hulking behind the bar.

"Hey, Bannister," said Samson.

Cal told his wife to go outside, then he approached the bar.
"Yeah?"

Samson Webb reached down and produced two glasses of beer.
He handed one to Cal and smiled. "You move fast for a big man."

After a moment, Cal said, "I just got a short fuse."

76 Samson raised his glass. "Well, come in here good and regular, and we'll make sure it stays too wet to light."

Cal smiled slowly.

Harry Miller approached the bar, and Samson drew another
draft. "Glad to see nobody lost their head," Harry said.

"It ain't worth it," said Cal.

Samson Webb nodded. "Damn right. Me and Harry don't agree
on nothin', but we still take a drink together."

"Island's too small to have it any other way," said Harry.

In his past, Cal would have been fighting by now, out in the
alley, with fists or knives. But Easter's Haven was a special place.
That was why he had come back.

On the way home, he stopped at the post office and Lanie ran
in to pick up the mail. She seldom found more than junk in the
box, but she liked going for the mail because it made her feel a
part of the town. She came out carrying a pile of circulars and
three envelopes. She was studying one of the envelopes, and Cal
was studying her. The beer and the warm sun were making him
feel relaxed, lazy. He was thinking it would be nice to go home
and pull off Lanie's jeans.

"Anything interesting?" he asked.

"Some junk, two bills, and this." She handed him a long white
envelope.

His name and post office box number were written on it. There
was no return address, but it was postmarked from Beverly Hills.
He examined the envelope, then shoved it into his pocket.

"What is it, Cal?" asked Lanie.

"I don't know."

"Open it."

"When we get home."

"I want to see it, Cal," she demanded.

He threw his Ford Bronco in gear and started out. They moved
through the business district, which was only a few blocks long,
past the Webb House, through the small knot of traffic by the
ferry slip, and onto Brisbane Road. In ten minutes, they were
home. Cal pulled the emergency brake and turned off the engine.

"OK, let's see the envelope," said Lanie.

"You'll see shit until I decide otherwise." Cal's eyebrows became a single, unbroken line. His thin upper lip tightened against
his teeth until it all but disappeared. The heavy stubble on his face

seemed to grow blacker. The muscle in his neck and jaw flexed involuntarily.

When Lanie saw the scowl, she always gave her husband wide berth. It was part of the irrational, frightening corner of his personality that had grown smaller and quieter since their arrival on the island. It was more frightening now because she had not seen it in months.

Cal jumped out and went into the house, a one-story cottage with a tiny kitchen, and large living room, and two bedrooms. He went into their bedroom and closed the door. He tore open the envelope. Inside were ten crisp, one-hundred-dollar bills and a note. The bills were so fresh they stuck to one another. The note read, "For services rendered. L. H."

Cal felt the perspiration gathering on his forehead and the muscles tightening in his neck. He was as far from his past as he could get, but not far enough.

He went into the living room. He handed his wife the note and three of the bills. "I towed a guy's yacht into Green Harbor a few weeks ago. I guess he's from the West Coast."

While she read the note, Cal Bannister went out onto his lawn and looked up at the cliffs. Beyond them, Andrew MacGregor's house loomed above the sea. Cal wrapped his left hand around his right forearm. He could kill any man on the island. He could survive by fishing and hunting and cutting his own firewood. He could fix his engine, and help his wife bear their children. But compared to men like Andrew MacGregor or Vaughn Lawrence, Cal Bannister was powerless, and power was all that mattered.

9

Dr. Joseph Stanton dampened a washcloth and placed it around James Whiting's penis. "Just relax."

Whiting lay back, looked up, and counted the holes in the acoustical ceiling panels above his head.

With his left hand, Stanton gently held Whiting's penis. With his right index finger and thumb, he grasped the catheter that entered Whiting's body. With no other preliminary and no other warning, he pulled.

"Jesus Christ!" cried Whiting, but the pain was over in an instant.

"Don't bother him over something like this," said Stanton as he coiled the catheter and threw it away. "Save him for the big problems."

"Like learning how to piss again?"

Stanton stepped to the sink and washed his hands. "No. Pissing is like riding a bicycle. Once you learn . . ."

"Does that go for sex?"

"It has in every other transplant I've ever done. Just give it time."

It was six days after surgery. Whiting was relaxing in a sunny private room overlooking the Riverway. The intravenous tubes had been taken out of his arms, and now, he was free of the catheter. He no longer had to walk up and down the halls with a little bag of urine rolling along beside him.

"Things are looking good," said Stanton.

"How long before I get out of here?"

"Another week, maybe." Stanton sat on the edge of the bed. "That's if all goes well. However, by the eleventh day after surgery, we can expect some kind of rejection episode."

James Whiting knew that his immune system, the product of millions of years of evolution, was trying to destroy his new kidney. To the immune system, the kidney was foreign matter, an invader, like a virus or a splinter of wood. But tissue-matching tests had indicated that the rejection reaction would be a mild one. Whiting was taking two immunosuppressants, Prednisone and Imuran, to combat the reaction, and thus far, his white blood cell count, the barometer of a reaction, had been close to normal. His doctors would monitor the white cell count closely, but with each day, his optimism would grow.

Success, however, did not mean complete or indefinite health. The immunosuppressants could produce discomfiting side effects, from hair loss to increased susceptibility to infection. And with most transplants, the odds were that the body would eventually reject the kidney. But if he could survive the first few months with his new system, James Whiting could be fairly certain of keeping the kidney for at least two years. After that, the odds would begin to slip, so that he had no more than a fifty percent chance of keeping the kidney beyond five years. (Had he received a kidney from a sibling or, better yet, an identical twin, his chances would have been dramatically higher.)

But James Whiting would take the gamble and hope that new treatments and new drugs, like Cyclosporin, would improve his chances in the years ahead.

"Of course," said Stanton, "there's always the possibility that you may not have any kind of rejection episode at all."

"That would be great."

Stanton stood decisively and slapped Whiting on the leg. "What's great is that you've got yourself a good, healthy kidney."

"Hey, Doc . . ."

Stanton stopped in the doorway.

"Who was he?"

"Who?"

"The donor?"

Stanton stepped back into the room. He had expected the question, but not quite this soon. "What makes you so sure it was a 'he'?"

"OK. Who was the person with the good, healthy kidney?"

Stanton sat again on the edge of the bed. "I'll tell you what I tell all my transplant patients, which is just enough to make them feel secure. The donor was a male, around forty years old with no prior history of serious illness. He suffered a massive head injury in an accident, and he was kept alive by machine until he fulfilled the criteria for brain death. He'd signed a donor card, but he didn't expect to die when he did, and he had no idea that James Whiting was going to be the recipient of his posthumous gift." Stanton paused. "That's all I can tell you, because that's all I know."

Whiting waited a few minutes after Staton left, then he pulled out copies of the *Boston Globe* from the last eight days. He wasn't interested in catching up with the opinions of his favorite columnists or with reading the Red Sox box scores. He wanted to look at the obituaries. Regardless of what Stanton told him, or failed to tell him, Whiting was still curious about the donor. He could not fail to wonder about the person with whom he now shared such an intimate biological relationship. It was all as natural as a person's interest in his ancestors, he thought.

The paper for June 7 offered no likely candidates as Whiting's donor. He turned to the June 8 obituary page. At the top of the page were several long obituaries and beneath them, the page was covered with shorter pieces on the passing of less prominent citizens.

Whiting looked first at the headline on the left. JOHN WELCH, RETIRED EXECUTIVE FOR RAYTHEON. Beneath it was a photo of the deceased, a sour-looking man with rimless glasses and a bristle-brush moustache. The photo had been taken in 1949. "John Welch, a retired vice-president at Raytheon, died on June 3 at his Brookline home after a lengthy illness. He was eighty-two." Transplants were not performed with eighty-two-year-old kidneys.

Beneath Mr. Welch was the picture of a young man, a local fashion model who had been involved in a car accident. He looked to be about the right age. Whiting continued reading until he reached the words *killed instantly*. Instant death eliminated the possibility of transplant.

Whiting's eye traveled across to the photograph on the right side of the page. He saw a confident smile, a handsome man wearing a tuxedo and gripping a statuette. Beneath the picture was the caption, "Roger Darrow receives his Emmy for 'Flint,' 1978."

The headline read, ROGER DARROW, TELEVISION PRODUCER, IN MAINE BOATING ACCIDENT. Whiting had not heard of Roger Darrow, and he had seen "Flint" only once in the eight years it was on the air. He did not, as a rule, watch television unless one of his ads was running.

He began to skim through the story, and a phrase in the second
paragraph caught his attention: "life preserved artificially for forty-eight hours."

He went back to the beginning of the paragraph.

After the accident, Darrow was taken to John MacGregor Memorial Hospital, in Rocktown, Maine, where it was found that he was suffering from burns, broken bones, and a massive head injury. The three-time Emmy winner was placed on life-support systems, and his body was artificially preserved until brain death was determined."

Whiting read the next sentence twice. "Before Mr. Darrow was removed from the life-support systems, his organs were taken for transplantation."

This, thought Whiting, could be the guy. He continued to read.

Roger Darrow was born and raised in Iowa, shuttled in and out of foster homes until he moved to Hollywood at the age of eighteen. Within a few years he had established himself as one of television's top writers, winning his first Emmy in 1967 for 'An Iowa Christmas,' a semiautobiographical story of a young boy dreaming of the world beyond his family farm.

In 1975, he and well-known producer Howard Rudermann teamed to create 'Flint,' a handsome private detective who lived in a luxurious San Francisco home, enjoyed the best in life when he wasn't on a case, and each week ended up fighting for someone who needed his help but couldn't pay his fee. The stories revolved around contemporary issues like chemical pollution, urban corruption, or racism, and 'Flint' was one of the most popular programs on television.

At the time of his death, Darrow was concluding a cross-country automobile trip. He had been researching a documentary on American life, and he was in Maine to interview the elusive Andrew MacGregor.

Although the investigation into his death has not yet been completed, all indications are that the explosion was accidental, and the Granite County medical examiner will not ask for an inquest.

A memorial service for Darrow, whose remains are to

Whiting felt a strange little jolt. Not only was Roger Darrow dead. He was now nothing but ash, except for his kidneys.

. . . will be held in Hollywood sometime in the next week.

He is survived by his wife, Jeanne, a former actress.

Whiting looked again at the photograph. Then, he was distracted by an old, familiar feeling, a faint tickling sensation, an awareness of pressure.

He had to urinate.

He swung his legs out of bed and took the plastic measuring bottle from the nightstand. For a week, his urine had been flowing from his bladder, through the catheter, into the plastic bag beside the bed. Now, the last middleman, except for the donor, had been eliminated. Whiting opened his pajamas and held the measuring bottle at a good angle. He felt as excited now as he knew he would feel when he made love for the first time after the transplant. He put his penis into the neck of the bottle. The tension was pleasurable, intense, and he almost wanted to prolong it.

Then, he decided to stand. Men urinated on their feet. The lip of the bottle felt cold, and for a moment, the urine wouldn't flow. Then, it happened. Only someone who hadn't pissed in four months could appreciate what James Whiting felt.

When it was over, he put the bottle, now half-full, on the nightstand. He flopped onto the bed and rang the nurse's bell. When she came into the room, he proudly announced his accomplishment.

"How do you feel?" she asked.

"Great," he answered. "If I smoked, I'd be lighting a cigarette right about now."

James Whiting knew now that his life had been renewed. He stretched out and thought about the women he had met in the last year. He wondered which of them he would call first. He thought about the restaurants he would visit without restriction. He imagined all the accounts he would take on as his strength returned. He even fantasized about opening his own agency.

He told himself that the identity of the donor did not matter, whether the person was a television producer or a teen-age suicide. The best way to repay him was to make full use of his gift. All that really mattered was that James Whiting was getting a second chance.

TWO

THE WINTER SOLSTICE

10

The sun had lost its strength. It rose later and rode lower in the sky each day. Ice had begun to form in the lagoons along the banks of the Charles, and within a few weeks, the river would be frozen.

As he ran past the Boston Sailing Club, James Whiting marked a milestone. "I've been jogging for three weeks, and this is the first time I've made it this far without wanting to throw up."

"I'll make an on the air tonight," said Dave Douglas, who pounded along beside him.

Douglas lived in the condo above Whiting's. He was an all-night disc jockey and one of Whiting's closest friends. Although he was short, thirty pounds overweight, and in worse condition than Whiting, he always pushed himself when they ran, and that was what Whiting wanted in a partner.

Six months after his transplant, James Whiting looked healthy and vigorous once more. The immunosuppressant drugs, which had successfully blocked rejection, had not caused any noticeable side effects. His body's defenses had remained strong enough to protect him from infection. His face had lost its fluid-retention puffiness and, no cushingoid appearance had developed from the drugs. Hair loss had been minimal. He had suffered no mental disorientation or joint pain.

He had enjoyed one of the most successful, complication-free transplants Dr. Joseph Stanton had ever performed, primarily because he had received his kidney before suffering the full ravages of end-stage renal failure and while the rest of his system was still in good health.

Now, he went regularly to the best restaurants. He had season's tickets to the Celtics games. He flew to New York for all the Broadway openings. His copy once more demanded top rates. His doctor had given him permission to begin cross-country skiing again. And he was getting back into condition.

James Whiting and Dave Douglas jogged down the river to the Hatch Memorial Shell, where the Boston Pops played in summer. Then they crossed the Esplanade and ran up the ramp onto the Arthur Fiedler footbridge. Whiting's lungs were burning now and the muscles in his calves were tightening. Three days earlier, this had been as far as he could go. Today, he wanted to reach the corner of Charles and Beacon, another quarter mile, before he stopped. He kicked and picked up speed.

"You're killing me, Whiting!" panted Dave Douglas.

"What doesn't kill me makes me stronger," answered Whiting.

"You're crazy."

"You been through what I have," Whiting gulped for air, "you need lines like that to get from one day to the next."

"Now that it's all behind you, how about finding some new material?"

Whiting spat. His mouth filled with saliva again, as if to douse the burning in his chest. He kept running and did not answer Dave Douglas, because he still needed his aphorisms.

His impotence had persisted. It was not entirely uncommon for dialysis-related impotence to continue a short time after transplant, but not for six months. A few weeks after leaving the hospital, he had tried to make love to one of the dialysis nurses he had been dating. He failed, and over the next few months, a physical problem became a mental problem. A psychologist had counseled that his sexual powers would return, but the right emotional context would be as important as the physical attractiveness of the partner.

Now, deep in December, James Whiting saw his sexual failure as a symptom for a more extensive dissatisfaction with himself. His life was immeasurably brighter than it had been before the transplant, but somehow, not bright enough.

Whiting came off the footbridge, pushed himself as hard as he could, and sprinted for Charles Street. A few minutes later, he stumbled to the intersection. He thought he would collapse. He spat again and sat on a fire hydrant.

"Are you sure you wouldn't like to pop into Rebecca's for chocolate croissants and coffee " asked Dave Douglas as they walked down Charles Street a few minutes later.

Whiting shook his head. "It's the holidays, Dave. You're supposed to watch your waistline."

"Yeah. Watch it expand. Speaking of the holidays, are you coming tonight?"

"I've got the firm's party tonight. I can't get out of it."

Dave Douglas gave a lascicious little laugh, the kind heard usually in locker rooms. "Will Patty Benjamin be there?"

Whiting nodded and smiled. He had never been the sort who discussed his female companions with his male friends. His reticence had once been a source of gentlemanly pride. Now it protected him, since he had permitted no one but his doctors and a few disappointed young women to learn of his impotence.

"Well," said Douglas, "after the other party, bring her over to my place."

"If it's not too late," said Whiting absently.

They turned up the hill and Dave chattered on about the people coming to his party that night. But Whiting wasn't listening. His body had cooled, his sweat was cold, and the sun was too low to break up the chilly shadows that covered Mount Vernon Street.

It was December 21, the shortest day of the year, and the party invitations would be flowing until New Year's. As Douglas talked, Whiting wondered why people had become so intent on celebrating at the winter solstice. It had always been a pagan festival. Then the Hebrews had locked into it with Chanukah, the festival of lights. And sometime in the fourth century the Christians decided that December 25 would be a good day to celebrate Christmas, although most biblical scholars believe that Christ was born at another time of year.

At the winter solstice, the worst still lay ahead. While everyone celebrated, the air grew colder, the snow piled higher, and January drew closer.

What it came down to, thought Whiting as he slipped into a hot shower a half hour later, was that people were never satisfied, because they always expected too much. If they partied like pagans for a week or so at the end of December, they thought they could hold back the depression of a long winter. If they could make another ten thousand dollars a year, they'd be happier than they'd ever been. If they could get another kidney and another chance at life, they would live in absolute bliss and never complain again.

But life seldom worked out that simply, and it hadn't yet for James Whiting. Perhaps Patty Benjamin would help.

"I've decided it's time," said Jeanne Darrow.

"Time for what?" asked Harriet.

"Time to look at the tapes." She stretched her legs and felt the warm sun on her thighs. They were sitting on the patio beside Jeanne's tennis court.

A few days earlier, the rains had begun, and winter had arrived in Los Angeles. The seasons changed subtly in southern California, a bit more heat, a bit more smog in summer, shorter days, and the dry Santa Ana winds to mark the arrival of autumn. But winter came to southern California like spring to New England. The smog dissipated. The temperature reached into the seventies each day, but fell to the forties at night. The birds-of-paradise bloomed. The camellia buds grew as big as robin's eggs. And after the first rain, the air turned clear, crisp, with an invigorating chill. The snow sparkled on the nearby mountains. The pungent smell of the damp eucalyptus trees rolled down the foothills and through the canyons and soaked into the boulevards and parking lots of Los Angeles. And next day, the dried-brown hillsides started to green.

The beginning of winter had reminded Jeanne Darrow of the rhythms of nature, of the cycles that drove the seasons and people's lives, and she had begun to feel that her cycle of loneliness and depression was coming to an end.

She had lived through a bleak summer, gathering strength where she could, from the good sense and good humor that Harriet Sears always radiated; from the knowledge that one day she could look at her husband on video tape, see him as he was in the weeks before his death, and hope to learn, beyond her speculations, what had happened to him in those final days.

Throughout the summer, she had driven herself so that she would have no time to think about her husband. She had worked five and sometimes six days a week riding the ambulance or traveling to accident sites in the helicopter. When she went home at night, she played tennis or swam. She stayed up late and watched television and did not go to the empty bed until she was sure she could sleep.

She would collapse, exhausted, only to awaken before dawn, her mind still spinning with some bizarre dream of Roger Darrow.

Then, she would remember his powerful, naked body, moving toward her in the half-light of early morning. She would recall the gentle touch of his mouth on her breasts, the smoothness of his hands as they moved down her back, the strength of his grip when

she whispered to him to squeeze, to squeeze her tight, and his
hands closed around her bottom and her body surrounded him.

As the sun rose, she would slip back to sleep again, haunted, in those first few months, by the memory of her husband.

On weekends, she gave tennis lessons to her sister's children in Orange County, She redecorated her house, except for Roger's study. And she refused the advances of several men, a few of whom attracted her, because she did not feel ready.

It was as though she had spent the months after his death knitting around the edges of her life, strengthening the fabric, so that when she tried to close the hole at the center, the stitches would hold.

Now, in December, she felt ready. She could face Roger again, for the last time. She would feel the pain, but now, she felt that she could withstand it.

"I've decided to take that last trip with Roger."

Harriet was not surprised. "Alone, I suppose."

Jeanne wiped the perspiration from her face with a turkish towel and draped the towel around her neck. She looked vigorous, atheletic. "There's no other way."

Harriet pulled the cover over her racquet. They had been play-ing several times a week since Roger's death, and Harriet had never mentioned the tapes. "Somehow, probably through Howard, word is going to get out that you've finally decided to look at the tapes. Your phone is going to start ringing like you just signed Margaret Mitchell's ghost to write a sequel to *Gone With The Wind*." Harriet poured two glasses of white wine from the carafe on the table. "You'll have to be strong to resist the networks and the producers and the Vaughn Lawrences."

Jeanne sipped her wine and let the coolness crackle across her tongue. "Don't worry, Harriet. If the footage stinks, or if it's too personal, I'm not going to let anyone see it, not even you."

"That's the only way to do it, honey."

"I thought that would disappoint you. Six months ago, you said to me that I was burying my husband's last piece of work. There's still a good chance that I will."

Harriet put a hand on Jeanne's arm. "You were right. He's gone. Nothing will bring him back. And you can't let anything that he says hurt you now."

"I don't intend to. That's why I've waited this long."

Harriet squeezed Jeanne's arm. "Good. Watching those tapes should be nothing but therapy for Jeanne Darrow, and the rest of the world be damned."

It was three in the afternoon on the Saturday before Christmas, the grandest day of the year on Easter's Haven. All the stores in town, including those closed for the rest of the winter, were decorated with Christmas lights and wreaths. Festive crowds jammed the streets. Carols played from speakers hung on lampposts. People sang along as they moved from shop to shop.

On this day, for more than fifty years, Andrew MacGregor had given his Christmas party, with music, drink, hot food, and fireworks on the front lawn of Brisbane Cottage. Islanders and summer people alike were invited, and Andrew MacGregor made his only annual public appearance.

The summer people returned to check their cottages and buy Christmas gifts. The artists who lived on the island made close to 30 percent of their yearly revenue on this one day. And at the smokehouse by the dock, islanders sold fresh fish and lobsters, smoked herring and salmon, and the crabmeat that their wives spent the winter canning.

Rooms at the Webb House were reserved six months in advance, and the restaurant was packed with people spilling beer and chowder and good cheer. Five people were working the bar, the front windows were steamed over and scrawled with hand-drawn Christmas greetings, people were singing carols by the piano, and even Samson Webb agreed that on the Saturday before Christmas, Andrew MacGregor was good for the island.

The Webb House door swung open, and Harry Miller, Pete Donhegan, and Cal Bannister strode into the bar.

"Merry Christmas, Samson Webb," called Harry.

"God bless all here," shouted Donhegan.

They elbowed up to the bar and Harry called for three boiler-makers, which caused several people around them to applaud.

Samson put three shots and three beers on the bar. "Get yourself good and loose, Harry. Tonight's your big night." He turned to Cal. "And you make sure he stays sober."

"He's as sober as granite," said Cal, without slurring a word.

"And twice as tough," added Harry. Then he threw an arm

around Cal and looked at the others. "Excuse us, boys. Me and
Cal got business to talk."

Harry steered Cal to an empty table at the back of the bar. Cal was puzzled, because he had no business that he knew of with Harry Miller.

Harry took off his checkered cap and rubbed his hands together. The callused palms sounded like two pieces of sandpaper scratching against each other.

Cal held up his shot glass. "Cheers, Harry."

Harry raised his beer. "And Merry Christmas."

Cal swallowed two ounces of whiskey in one gulp. His eyes watered briefly, and he slapped the shot glass down on the table. "So what can I do for you, Harry?"

Harry stared at Cal for a moment before speaking. "I been thinkin' on somethin', Cal, ever since you come here, and it finally hit me last night."

"Yeah?"

"Who you are." Harry smiled. His teeth were yellowed, and there was a brown edge of decay around each of his lowers. It was the only sign of decay on the rock-hard body or the craggy old face.

The beer suddenly felt ice cold in Cal's hand. He looked around to see if anyone was listening.

"Eh-yeh." Harry continued to smile. He did not want to seem threatening. "From the first day I seen you, I said, there's somethin' familiar 'bout that young fella."

Cal straightened in his chair, drawing back from Harry.

"I never forget a face," Harry continued, "and sooner or later, I can put one and one together. I dug back last night and came up with the story of a woman, name of Iris Dunne. She used to dress hair here, 'bout twenty-five years ago."

Cal's face lost all expression.

Harry looked down at his glass. He seemed embarrassed. "She dressed hair and . . . and other things. And—he looked Cal in the eye—"she had a little boy named Calvin. A nice little kid. Used to play with my boy Tommy."

"This ain't somethin' I want the world to know," said Cal coldly.

"That's what I figured."

For an instant, Cal Bannister wondered what this old man planned to do with his knowledge. And if he knew Cal's identity, how much more could he guess at? Cal felt his neck muscles tightening. He saw himself paying extortion money to Harry Miller.

Then Harry said, "And this is as far as it goes."

Cal smiled. His body relaxed. He reminded himself that this was Easter's Haven, not L.A. or Vegas. And this was Harry Miller, not some cheap hustler. Harry Miller was the island's historian, its storyteller. Harry Miller had befriended Cal and Lanie the day they arrived. On this island, people trusted Harry Miller. People trusted one another.

Harry offered his hand and Cal took it.

"This place needs some new blood," said Harry. "It does me good when a young fella moves back after seein' the rest of the world."

Cal raised his beer and drained it in one gulp. "I came back because I love this place. I always did."

"My oldest boy loved it, too," answered Harry. "He loved it too much to be afraid of it."

Harry paused for a moment and looked down at the head on his beer. Cal knew the story of Tommy Miller's death at sea. Harry seldom mentioned it.

"Well, sir," said Harry after a time, "since I lost my boy, I been without a winter partner."

Cal leaned forward and folded his arms on the table.

"It's about time I had one, someone big and strong, someone I can learn what I know, 'bout lobsterin' and winter shrimpin'."

Harry was making an offer, and Cal didn't need to think about it. He smiled at Harry, then called to Samson for two more boilermakers.

Samson brought the drinks, and Cal and Harry toasted. "To new partners," said Harry.

"And to learnin' all you know." Cal touched Harry's shotglass with his and drank.

It was dusk. The sky overhead was a luminous silver gray. A few days before, the town of Easter's Landing had been dark, quiet, frozen by the early winter. Now, it was alive with the excitement of Christmas. The summer people had come back, looking more foreign in their parkas than they did in June. MacGregor was

on the island. And that night, everyone would celebrate the birth
of Christ and the return of the light.

Cal hurried down Main Street, past the general store, the liquor store, the chandlery, Keenan's Hardware, the bank, and he stopped at Sandler's Gallery, open for the first time since October. Mr. Sandler was a painter. Mrs. Sandler made jewelry. She had crafted a beautiful necklace made of tiny, polished, perfectly rounded pieces of clamshell strung on a gold wire. With matching earrings, the set cost eighty-nine dollars. Cal knew that Lanie loved it. He had seen her admiring it through the window. But she had never mentioned it, he knew, because it was too expensive.

Without hesitating, Cal Bannister stepped into the shop, put down one of the hundred-dollar bills that he had been carrying in his wallet for six months, and bought the necklace and earrings.

It was going to be the best Christmas of his life, thought Cal.

11

James Whiting's least-favorite Christmas party of the year, Saturday evening at Brad Henshaw's thirteenth-floor apartment in the Prudential Center: a high-tech aluminum Christmas tree decorated with red plastic ornaments; novelty songs on the tape deck, "Jingle Bell Rock," "Holly Jolly Christmas," "The Chipmunk Song"; mistletoe hanging everywhere, even above the toilet; a hot drink that tasted like Hawaiian Punch spiked with vodka; Kirin beer; platters of hors d'ouevres—baby egg rolls, shrimp puffs, chicken wings—from a Chinese restaurant on Boylston Street; wall-to-wall people in the living room, the kitchen, the dining room; currents of cigarette smoke floating on the hot air; coats piled in the bedroom; at least one couple piled beneath the coats. The kind of party that James Whiting usually avoided, except that this was business.

"Six months later, and you're looking better than ever," Henshaw was saying.

He and Whiting were standing in the corner, near the hors d'ouevres table. Whiting's eyes were following the back of Patty Benjamin's skirt as she moved to the bar. Tonight, Whiting was hoping, would be the night.

"I guess we can stop carrying you," Henshaw continued, "and start loading the work back on."

Whiting kept his eyes on Patty. "There better be a smile on your face," he whispered to Henshaw, "because you never carried me. On my sickest day, I wrote the best copy in your agency."

Henshaw laughed. He was not much older than Whiting, a well-tailored advertising executive with a passion for shoptalk and a head of blown-dry hair. "Well, think of all we'll be expecting of you in the years ahead. We've got some huge accounts out there, just waiting for Whiting."

Whiting laughed. "That's good, good. You should think about writing copy yourself."

Patty Benjamin returned with two bottles of Kirin. She handed one to Whiting. It was their fourth date, and he sensed that she was as interested as he was.

"Did I hear you two talking about a big account?" asked Patty, sipping at her beer. "Jim and I haven't worked together on a big account since he got out of the hospital, and we were the best team in the agency."

"You're right," said Henshaw. "Now, your art makes everyone else's copy read like Whiting's, and Whiting's copy makes everyone else's art look like yours." Then, he smiled. "Besides, we don't like people to work together when they're having an affair. It hurts their work."

From the corner of his eye, Whiting saw Patty's face redden with anger. Before she could say something she might regret, Whiting turned to Henshaw, "If that's the case, then I guess the rumors about you and your secretary aren't true."

For a moment, Henshaw glared at Whiting, then he smiled. "You'd better watch out, Jim. Or you may need a job transplant to go along with your kidney transplant." Then he walked away.

"What an asshole," said Patty.

"If he's going to fire anyone, better me than you." Whiting sipped his beer and cleared his throat. Besides, the word 'affair' implies something illicit. We are two single, normal, healthy red-blooded heterosexual adults."

"That sounds to me like a line," said Patty.

It sounded to Whiting as though he were trying to convince himself of something.

He had been attracted to Patty Benjamin from the day that she came to work at Diehl, Diehl, and Henshaw. She had dark brown eyes and hair that fell to her shoulders. She was shorter than the women who usually appealed to Whiting, but her body was perfectly proportioned to her frame and she had the most gorgeous and shapely ass that James Whiting had ever seen. Although he had been told by other women that his initial response to them should be intellectual or emotional, he always seemed to respond first to the physique. The women who were the most beautiful were not always those whose company he ultimately enjoyed the most, but he found that most women had at least one feature that could captivate him before they had said a word. A smile might do it, or a hairstyle, or a pair of shapely legs, or, in the case of Patty

Benjamin, an apple-round bottom.

However, he had worked for two years with Patty Benjamin, and he believed that professional partners should not become partners in anything else. "Don't dip your pen in company ink" was the Brad Henshaw expression. He had admired Patty's wit, her intelligence, and the energy she brought to her work. On occasion, he had permitted himself a lingering glance at her as she left the room, but he had satisfied himself with becoming nothing more than her friend. After his illness began, he needed friends more than he needed lovers. Six months after his transplant, however, he needed a lover.

An hour later, he was in the living room of Patty Benjamin's Back Bay condominium. Small white bulbs threw a web of light around the Christmas tree. Patty was getting two mugs of wassail. Whiting was touching a match to the kindling already piled in the fireplace. She had prepared everything, he thought. She had even left the punch simmering on the stove.

The flames leaped. The kindling began to burn. Whiting dropped two maple logs onto the fire. A mug of steaming wassail appeared beneath his nose. He smelled apple cider, pineapple, aromatic cloves, vodka, and brandy. He sensed something else.

"Merry Christmas," she whispered.

They sat together on the sofa, sipping the punch and watching the flames wrapping around the logs. A Mozard piano concerto, the antidote to three weeks of Christmas music, played softly in the background. The atmosphere, thought Whiting, was perfect. Patty had seen to every detail, including the touch of Shalimar, which he had not noticed until now.

Without a word, he kissed her. Her mouth was warm and moist and moved in teasing little bites across his cheek to his neck. He ran his hands up the back of her turtleneck. She brought her mouth back to his. They kissed again.

He slid his hand across her armpit and touched her breast. She inhaled sharply.

He laughed. "You like that?"

"Yeah." She kissed him again. "And I'll bet that you do, too."

She slipped her hand under his shirt. She smoothed the palm of her hand across his chest and gently scraped her nails across his nipple. He felt a current nervous energy shoot through him. She scraped her nails again, and the current became more fo-

cused. Then, delicately, she began to rub with her fingertips, and
James Whiting knew that this would be the night. She had found
a pressure point, a switch, and he was responding, at last.

He turned himself against her, as though he wanted her to feel
what was happening. He wished that he had told her how long he
had waited, how long he had been impotent, but he could flatter
her afterward. Now, he wanted to feel his fantasy.

He lay back, and Patty stretched out on top of him. As they
kissed, his hands traveled down her back to the edge of her skirt.
She was wearing boots over heavy wool stockings. He slowly
moved his hands under the hem of her skirt and along the backs
of her thighs. He sensed her body tightening. Then, he reached
the tops of the stockings and was filled with the joy of the season.
Her thighs were warm and soft, and for a moment, he lingered
there, his fingertips rubbing gently. Then, his fingers were inside
the silken panties and he was caressing the flesh he had admired
for so long. He closed his eyes and dreamed, and the words from
some old piece of copy came tumbling out of a lost corner of his
mind. *Cushiony and soft, graceful and firm. Each half fits perfectly in the hand and one size fits all.* He kissed her to keep from
laughing.

Patty kissed him back and pushed herself against him, her
firmness against his. And then, his was gone. Suddenly and completely.

He told himself not to think about it. He kissed her. He caressed her. He tried to focus all his feeling in his fingertips. He
guided her hands back to his chest, but now her touch felt annoy-
ing, almost irritating. The circuits had been broken, in his head
and his body. He pushed her hands away and sat up.

"What's wrong?" she asked. "Did I hurt your kidney?"

He shook his head and explained what had happened. Patty
was gentle and understanding. She said that she was flattered at
whatever success she'd had with him. She suggested they go out
to a movie or go for a walk and try again later. They had all the
time in the world, she said. They didn't have to rush.

But James Whiting wanted to leave. He did not feel like talking, and he did not feel comfortable enough with Patty to sit in
silence and stare at the fire. She said she understood. He kissed
her and told her that he would call.

He walked down Gloucester Street to Marlborough, then down

Marlborough toward the Public Garden. It was eight o'clock. The air was crystal cold. Gas lamps shone like pieces of incandescent ice. In homes all along the street, people were gathering to celebrate Christmas. Live candles shimmered in tall windows. Firelight danced on the ceilings of Back Bay homes. Bulbs twinkled on the branches of fresh-cut evergreens. And people sang carols. But Whiting did not stop to listen.

At Berkeley Street, he approached two young people standing on the corner. They were arm in arm, drunk and happy, and they seemed oblivious to the cold. A Harvard student, thought Whiting, and his Wellesly girl friend, enjoying their last date before the holidays.

The boy looked at Whiting and raised the small silver flask he held in his hand. "Merry Christmas, old man."

"Merry Christmas my ass," said Whiting and he hurried across the street.

"And a bah humbug to you too," shouted the girl.

12

O n video tape, Easter's Haven looked as forbidding to Jeanne Darrow as it had in her nightmares. Viewed from the west, from the deck of the Easter's Haven ferry, it seemed like a fortress with high granite walls and pines that stood like soldiers atop a parapet.

Jeanne Darrow always read magazines from the back to the front, and she could never resist reading the last page of a novel before starting chapter one. When she prepared to look at her husband's tapes, she decided to view the last tape first.

After all, she knew how the story ended. By listening to the conclusions that her husband had drawn, by knowing what he was thinking at the very end, she could better understand the changes as he went through them on the journey, and she could judge for herself if his conclusions had been valid.

It was four-thirty on the afternoon of the shortest day of the year. The sun had gone, and the temperature had started to drop. Jeanne Darrow sat on the leather sofa in her husband's study with her feet tucked under her and a glass of white wine on the coffee table. She did not come into the study often. It remained much as her husband had left it seven months earlier. A small ceramic Christmas tree, which she had given him, sat on his desk, in the spot where he placed it each year.

There were no other Christmas decorations in the house, except for the large, bare tree in the living room. She had bought it a few days earlier, but she could not bring herself to trim it alone. She would wait until her father and her sister's family came for dinner on Christmas Eve.

For the moment, however, it was June, and Jeanne Darrow was riding with her husband on the Easter's Haven ferry.

"The island," says Roger Darrow offscreen, *"is about six miles across, from east to west, and nine miles from north to south.*

There are a few roads and an airstrip service by two small planes to provide a link to the real world. But for most people, a link to the real world is not what they're after when they come to Easter's Haven."

The island is growing larger. The screen goes blank for a moment, then the ferry is in the thoroughfare and the camera is focused on the red roof of Brisbane Cottage. "That's where he lives," says Darrow. The house is partially hidden by the pines. A helicopter sits on the pad beside it. A long wooden stairway leads down the hundred-foot cliff to the water, where a shed and a wharf have been built. "That's Cutter's Cove at the base of the cliff," narrates Darrow. "Sixty years ago Easter's Haven granite was cut from the cliffs and shipped from that wharf by the John MacGregor Quarrying Company. Andrew MacGregor built his electronic house upon those rocks, literally and figuratively."

Cutter's Point, which forms the east side of the cove, sweeps past the camera. Then, the land drops to sea level as Rumrunner's Bulge rolls into view. Darrow's camera zooms toward the center of the island, which is no longer blocked by the cliffs. There, rising out of the pines, is the giant television antenna. Its red lights flash, even in daylight. It is out of scale with everything around it. "A mutation on the landscape," mutters Roger Darrow.

Another few seconds of blank tape run through the cassette. Then, the camera is on the town wharf and it is photographing the empty ferry slip. From the length of the shadows and the deserted parking lot, it seems to be early morning.

Roger Darrow steps in front of the camera. He is wearing jeans, a blue T-shirt, and sneakers. His face seems drawn, despite a tan, and his hair is unkempt, uncombed. He sits on one of the pilings on the wharf and smiles at the camera.

Jeanne turned off the television set. She felt the tears starting again. She hadn't cried in a month, and she wasn't looking at these tapes to start crying again. She walked out of the study, down the hallway to the kitchen. She pushed through the swinging doors into the butler's pantry, then into the dining room, across the foyer to the living room. She walked quickly, with her head down, her heels echoing on the red tile floor. Then, she turned and went back into the study. She flipped on the television, sat on the sofa, and told herself she was not going to cry.

"After all I've seen in the last month," says Darrow, "it's nice to find a little peace and quiet, a place where the world has slowed down." He looks at the harbor and the wharf. "It'll speed up around here next month, when the summer people come, but for now, it belongs to the lobstermen and their families, the people whose lives are bound to the place."

Then, Darrow introduces Harry Miller, the lobsterman who is going to show him around the island. Harry Miller steps before the camera. He does not seem too pleased with where he is. He raises his hand briefly and ducks out of the shot.

"I'm lucky to have him giving me the tour today," says Darrow. "Because, if what I hear is true, no one knows Easter's Haven better than Harry Miller."

In the bright light of an early-June morning, Roger Darrow angles his camera through the windshield of Harry Miller's truck and they travel the deserted streets and roads. They drive through the town of Easter's Landing, past the First, (and, as Harry says, the only) Parish Church, and by the two-story building where students in grades one through eight learn about the outside world.

"A long way from Hollywood High," cracks Darrow.

They pass Saint Bartholomew's Field, acres of grass, scrub brush, and gentle hills dotted with rocks and boulders. They drive up Atlantic Road to Green Harbor, with its oversized summer homes and dry-docked yachts. Then they turn south again, down Midland Road, which cuts through the center of the island.

They pass the airstrip: a single runway cut across a meadow, a two-story building that serves as control tower and waiting room, a Piper Cub and a few cars parked in a dusty lot.

Cut

The camera is perched at the top of a quarry, which descends perhaps twenty feet to a pool of groundwater.

"Used to be, two hundred men worked as cutters on this island, year round," says Harry offscreen. "Our granite built buildings in Boston, New York, Chicago. Now it's all done, but for this."

The camera pans slowly to the right, until Harry Miller is in the shot, looking down into the quarry.

"Was this a MacGregor operation?" asks Darrow offscreen.

"Eh-yeh."

"Can you describe your relationship with Andrew Mac-

Gregor?"

"Nope," says Harry firmly, and he starts to walk away.

"What do you think of the end of the quarrying?" asks Darrow.

Harry keeps walking. "The world moves on."

"And your island got left behind?" Darrow speaks quickly because he is losing Harry.

"If you like it the way it is, that ain't really bad," answers Harry over his shoulder. "Besides, the world don't leave us alone, even when we want."

"You mean, the tourists?"

"Harry stops. "I mean guys like you,"

Cut.

The camera is in the middle of a broad green meadow dotted with boulders and granite outcroppings and dominated by the skeletal legs of the television tower. The camera tilts smoothly and zooms back until the tower fills the shot. Then Roger Darrow steps in front of the camera.

"We've seen the bedrock of Andrew MacGregor's fortune. We've seen beauty that would make any man love this place—meadow, beach, deep pine forest. And we see here the final and perhaps most dramatic symbol of Andrew MacGregor's influence on America. Eight miles out in the Atlantic, at the highest point on Easter's Haven, stands one of the first cable television antennas erected in the United States.

"In 1954, MacGregor wanted to watch the World Series. The nearest transmitter was eighty miles away, and since conventional television signals don't follow the curvature of the earth, you need an antenna to catch them after sixty miles or so. MacGregor constructed the monster behind me, then strung wires carrying the signal to every house on the island."

Darrow pauses for a moment and looks down at the ground, as though separating one thought from another. "While television may have brought something diverting to people who spend their winter nights listening to the wind howl, it also brought the twentieth century, for better or worse, to a place that existed out of time."

Darrow takes a deep breath. "Television can entertain and educate, but no place is safe from it. It unites us . . ." he pauses again and thinks about the next phrase. "It unites us in mediocrity. It gives us all its one-eyed vision of the world, and it tries to

*reduce everything to the simplest terms, so the simplest among us
will hear the message." The anger begins to rise in Roger Darrow's
voice.*

*"I'm talking about cable, too, with its hundred channels of
diverse information and its two-way systems for every customer.
Someone is still making all the programming decisions, except
that when people are pushing button-pads and answering questions every night, they have the misbegotten illusion of being in
control. But the ones who hold the wires run the show, and if
they're not honorable men, we're all in trouble."*

There was something wrong here, thought Jeanne. He was
emphasizing every word as though it were the climax of the story.
His head was snapping forward at the end of every sentence. This
was not casual, relaxed Roger Darrow, the man with the easy
smile. The trip had changed him.

*I have my theories about Andrew MacGregor and Vaughn
Lawrence, about why they've joined forces and what they're plan-
ning to do with the power the thing behind me has given them.
But after three thousand miles of seeing this country, I have just
one question: Do I really give a shit?"*
The screen goes blank.

Jeanne turned off the television, went into the kitchen, and
poured herself another glass of wine. She had waited six months
to learn what his final words to her would be. She had drawn the
time around her like a wall, but his electronic remains had already
begun to batter against it.

She returned, almost reluctantly, to the study. She knew that
the climax to the tape was coming, and with it, the climax to their
lives.

*When he reappears, there is no way of telling how much time
has passed. It could be hours or days. He sits now on the veranda
of someone's house. Behind him, a broad green lawn stretches to
the top of a cliff. Beyond that, the ferry cuts through the waters
of the thoroughfare. He is at Andrew MacGregor's house. And he
no longer looks worn out. He has a fresh sunburn. His nose and
forehead have been cooked red. He is wearing a sweat shirt and a
bathing suit, and his hair is damp. He has been swimming.*
"I have been favorably impressed by the hospitality of Mac-

Gregor's nephew, John Meade and—*he smiles like a little boy who had done something wrong*—"other members of his family. I have not yet been granted an audience with the man himself, but my mind is clearer than it has been in many weeks, and I think that I can draw some conclusions after three thousand miles on the road."

Darrow leans forward, as if to become more intimate with the camera. "I have seen the most complex, sophisticated society in the world. Two hundred and twenty million people, and most of them living better than anyone else on earth, a society supported by hundreds of systems, all wound around one another so that if one of them broke, the rest could unravel in a month and a half. Food, energy, transportation, communication, the environment, it's all interrelated."

He sits back and shakes his head. "But nobody appreciates it, and no one is concerned."

He pauses for a moment and looks out at the ocean. A friendship sloop is cutting through the Easter's Haven Thoroughfare, and the tension is returning to his face.

"We all remember what happened when we ran out of gas back in 1979. What happens if we have two bad harvests and go through our national grain surplus? What happens if the power plants in the Ohio Valley stop working so that we don't have acid rain killing the lakes and ponds of New England? What happens in San Francisco if the acqueduct from the Hetch Hetchy reservoir breaks down? What happens in Los Angeles when the big quake comes and all the overpasses collapse onto all the freeways and all the gas mains rupture? And what happens when somebody in some missile silo finally pushes the button?"

Jeanne Darrow realized that she did not know this man. His thoughts seemed to be spinning without logic or sense. And yet he said that his mind was clear. She realized that she should have watched the tapes from the beginning. She had not been prepared for this.

"Those are things that we should be worried about." *Darrow leans close to the camera, and as he gestures, his hands flash in and out of the shot.* "But nobody cares, and nobody worries, because television tells us that we have everything under control. All across this country, people have given up to the complexity and sold out to the electronic magic show, brought to them by the Vaughn Lawrences, the Andrew MacGregors, and the guys like me, the magicians' fools."

He slumps back in his chair and stares blankly for several moments at the camera, then says softly, "We should be in awe of this country, this continent. We should be amazed that our fragile system is so damn resilient. But we're not. We're numb.

"We've lost our moral fiber. We've lost our capacity for wonder. They've been taken from us. By television. By big corporations like MacGregor Communications, who promise to make our lives easy as long as we pay their price. And by religions that reduce God to the main attraction in some cheap, televised carnival. That's what I saw on this trip, and that's why I'm so damned depressed."

He takes a deep breath. It is more like a sigh. He has reached the climax. He drops his voice to a melodramatic whisper. "The only wonder left to us may be the wonder of a child when it takes its first gulp of air, the wonder of life continuing, of life thriving, the wonder of hope, the hope that we can regain what we've lost.

"And that's why my marriage is done. I loved you, Jeannie. But our love produced no hope, so it has no future. I need that hope. I need a child. I need . . ."

The picture went blank. The tape had run out.

Jeanne Darrow did not know how long she stared at the blank screen. She sat long enough for the pain inside her to grow so intense that she no longer felt it. Then, the wineglass was flying from her hand and smashing against the television and she was screaming, "You crazy son of a bitch, you were sterile!"

13

From a distance, the fireworks on Easter's Haven looked like flowers blooming on a field of black velvet. As a rocket rose and exploded, the thunder rumbled across the thoroughfare, the granite cliffs were illuminated, and Andrew MacGregor's house appeared for a moment beneath the flash. Then, the petals of colored light opened, metamorphosed into new forms, new blossoms, and disappeared into the deep, rich darkness.

The lights of Rocktown left a faint, gray smudge on the horizon. The Christmas lights of Easter's Landing twinkled around the town wharf. The white buoy light flashed at the mouth of the harbor. The red lights on the television tower blinked arhythmically. And every constellation in the December sky stood out in three-dimensional relief.

Brisbane Cottage glowed, with white candles in every window. The house was handsome, the design classical—two stories with a hipped roof, high windows, and a porch that ran the length of the house. Granite had been used for the foundation and for the pillars on the porch. The rest of the house was cedar shingle stained brown with creme-colored trim and dark red shutters that matched the color of the roof.

Although Brisbane Cottage now served as MacGregor's house for over half the year, it still looked like a rich man's August retreat, built in the spirit of the grand wooden hotels and summer houses that once lined the East Coast.

Great bonfires roared in trash cans all across the half acre of lawn. About 250 people had gathered to celebrate—summer people in their winter ski fashions, islanders in jeans, down vests, and wollen jackets, and children scampering everywhere, excited by the fires and the lights. A choir of summer people and islanders was filling the air with carols. Flasks of hot bourbon and cider were moving from hand to hand. Cups of Andrew MacGregor's

fish house punch sent plumes of steam into the cold air. Ham¹⁰⁷
sandwiches, baked beans, brown bread, and Samson Webb's fish
chowder were warming on outdoor cookstoves. And two tables
were covered with cookies and pastries from every state in New
England.

Just outside of the circle of light, pickup trucks, Jeeps, snowmobiles, three Volvos, a Mercedes, and two horse-drawn sleighs
were parked in a friendly jumble, and cross-country skis seemed
to be growing out of the snow like a fiberglass thicket.

Overlooking it all from the top step of the porch was the man
himself. Andrew MacGregor sat in a chair, wrapped in blankets,
with a broad smile on his face and a stocking hat pulled low over
his ears. The old man seemed to be having a wonderful time,
waving to old friends, chatting with children, and sampling his
own punch.

Cal and Lanie Bannister were standing by one of the bonfires
with their arms around each other. They were drinking cups of
fish house punch, a mixture of fruit juices, spices, vodka, triple
sec, and other delights that heated the insides but did nothing for
icy toes. Cal and Lanie did not notice the cold, however; they had
made love all afternoon.

"Hear ye, hear ye!" shouted Rev. Forbison from the top step of
the porch, his voice thickened by good cheer and fish house
punch. The crowd grew quiet, the carolers finished their song.
The children went back to their parents.

Andrew MacGregor rose slowly and ambled to the edge of the
porch. He wore a long, heavy overcoat with his red stocking hat.
His nose and cheeks were bright red from the cold and the punch.
He was stooped and shrunken, and the hat gave him the look of a
lonely old derelict. Cal Bannister found it hard to believe that this
man was the ruler of a communications empire.

"Merry Christmas, Andy," shouted a drunken voice from the
back of the crowd.

"And Merry Christmas to you!" answered MacGregor. "Merry
Christmas to all of you!"

The voice, thought Cal, was more impressive than the appearance, and as the old man spoke, he straightened and seemed to
grow, like a veteran actor returning to the stage. Then, almost as
an afterthought, he pulled off the hat and smoothed his snow-
white hair, and Cal felt the powerful presence of Andrew Mac-

On the porch behind the old man, Cal recognized Edgar and Mary Lean, MacGregor's servants; John Meade; Thomas Dodd, the family's chief bodyguard; and MacGregor's niece, who wore a heavy blue coat over a belly that had recently begun to expand.

"It looks like MacGregor's niece is pregnant," whispered Lanie.

Cal nodded and wondered who the father was.

"Make me pregnant," whispered Lanie.

Nearby, a flashbulb popped. MacGregor shot a glance toward the photographer. Tom Dodd stepped into the crowd and went over to a middle-aged off-islander who was holding a Polaroid camera.

MacGregor smiled at the crowd. "Only one request, folks. No cameras and no pictures. We all know that."

Bannister watched Tom Dodd gently request the photograph. The woman turned over the picture. Dodd wrote down her address and promised to send her a new roll of film.

Then, Andrew MacGregor called to a little girl at the front of the crowd. She jumped up the stairs and into his arms.

"This is Sally Donhegan," announced MacGregor, "and this year, she has the honor of lighting the Christmas tree."

The little girl pressed a button on one of the porch pillars and the forty-foot blue spruce near the edge of the cliff came to life in a display of colored lights as spectacular as any of the fireworks. The lawn in front of MacGregor's house grew bright as day. Everyone cheered, and the carolers began to sing "Joy to the World." Andrew MacGregor picked up the tune, off-key, and then everyone was singing.

Cal Bannister felt a chill. He had never been much for Christmas. In southern California, the holiday season meant Muzak carols in the shopping malls, green trees sprayed with imitation pastel snow, and Santa Clauses in red Bermuda shorts. But this was magical. He began to sing along. "Deck the Halls" followed, and then "Jingles Bells."

"This is the nicest Christmas celebration I've ever seen," Lanie Bannister was saying to Harry Miller. "It brings everyone together like a family."

"Been doin' it for over fifty years," said Harry. "And folks don't seem tired of it yet. Must mean it's a pretty good thing."

They were part of a group that was standing around one of the bonfires in the middle of the lawn. The Donhegans were with them, the Smithfields, a summer family who knew the Millers, the Sandlers, and Samson Webb.

"Tell us the story of how all this began," Mrs. Sandler said after the singing ended.

"Oh," said Ellie Miller, "he tells that every year. Let's hear a new story."

"It's poetry, Dad. Tell it." Harry's son John, the attorney from Boston, was strolling across the snow with his family behind him. He was a head taller than Harry, but he had the same angular jaw and the promise of friendliness behind flinty gray eyes. His two sons, eight and six, were Harry's greatest pride. John handed his father a mug of hot punch.

"Tell it, Dad. We're all just dying to hear it," urged John's wife, who was tall and blonde and looked like one of the summer people.

"Yeah, tell the story," said another man, a burly stranger with a thick black beard.

Cal looked at the stranger, then at Harry Miller, who seemed, for just an instant, to hesitate, as though surprised or frightened to see this man. The stranger was dressed like a lobsterman, in blue watch cap, jeans, suspenders, and a thick woolen shirt over a turtleneck. Cal thought he recognized him.

Harry Miller studied the stranger for a moment, then raised his mug, took a long drink of punch, and launched into his story.

Cal turned his eyes back to Harry Miller.

"It was the winter of 1932," he began, "one of the bleakest, blackest, coldest times any islander could remember. I was twenty years old, and this island was in a bad way. No one had a cent, and I knew by spring, there'd be more 'n one husband turnin' a shotgun on his wife, more 'n one mother boilin' her babes in the bathtub."

"Oh, Harry," said Ellie. "There's children listenin'."

"Truth is truth," said Harry. "Cabin fever is a terrible thing, and there ain't a winter goes by when someone on this island don't come to a bad end."

The group around Harry was beginning to grow. His story was as much a Christmas tradition as the fireworks, and when Harry began to tell it, with the firelight dancing on his face and the crowd forming into a circle around him, every bit of his Down East reserve melted away. He became the storyteller.

"Well, it happens that I was up island one December afternoon, on some of MacGregor's land, cuttin' myself a Christmas tree, when all of a sudden, I look up and who's standing there but Reverend Win Berry, the island minister who is been dead for six months."

"A ghost?" asked Harry's younger grandson.

"In the absolute flesh." Harry crouched down, so that he was on eye level with the little boy. "I stuck out my hand, and it went right through him." Harry reached out and touched his grandson. The little boy jumped back, and people in the crowd began to laugh.

Harry stood and looked around, feigning annoyance, until the laughter had stopped. Then, he continued. "I said, 'Win, we lost you in a squall, back in June. You're dead.' And he said, 'Harry, a shepherd never leaves his flock.' "

"I asked him what he wanted. He brought his face close to me." Harry walked around the perimeter of the circle, looking into the eyes of each listener. "I smelled the dank, dead stink of a ghost's breath. And Win Berry said, 'I'm sad for you, Harry. You've had a bad quarrel with your old friend.' "

Harry stepped back into the center of the circle. Every move had been choreographed, time-honored. "Well, folks. It was true. Andy MacGregor and me, we'd had a fight, just a few days before Win Berry died. MacGregor, he'd layed off a bunch of cutters, includin' my old man and me. I told him what I thought, and we fought . . . with fists. And us two old friends." Harry shook his head. "There's nothin' worse than a hatred between two old friends.

"Then, Win Berry said to me, 'There's new life in Andrew MacGregor's house. A son, born six weeks ago, and here now for his first Christmas on Easter's Haven. It's a good time to make amends.' "

Harry lowered his voice, as though he were ashamed of his answer. "I said, 'Reverend, whether you're real or not, I won't apologize for a fight when I ain't responsible for more than half of it.'

"And right then, I thought, now you've done it." He crouched low, so that he was on eye level with the children, but he knew that the adults were riveted as well. "I'd said somethin' to make the ghost mad. And there's few folks who ever lived to tell what a ghost would do when he got mad."

Harry stood slowly. He took a breath. He played the moment for all its drama. "Win Berry looked at me with a sad face, he shook his head, and he said, 'You're dead for a long time, Harry, a long time.' And with that, he was gone, vanished between the flakes of snow just startin' to flutter down. Right then, I felt the coldest chill that ever cut through me, the chill of the grave it was, a chill to make your scalp freeze and your hair stand on end. And I heard the words again, 'You're dead for a long time.' "

Lanie Bannister was squeezing Cal's arm the way she did when they went to the movies and the suspense became too much for her. Then, suddenly, she released her grip. Something had distracted her. Cal looked at his wife, and she told him to look across the crowd, which had grown now to eighty or ninety people.

On the other side of the circle, Andrew MacGregor's niece was standing beside the bearded stranger.

"I think I know her," whispered Lanie. "Every time I've ever seen her, she's look familiar to me."

Cal was more interested in the stranger with the black beard. But either he'd had too much punch or his sixteen months on Easter's Haven had dulled his senses; he could not place the man. It bothered him. In the past, his survival had depended on his ability to recall a face, a physique, or the way a trail twisted in the jungle.

But here, at Christmas on Easter's Haven, he told himself, it was safe. The stranger's eyes shifted to Cal. For a moment, the two men stared at each other. Then, as if by mutual consent, they both turned their gaze again to Harry Miller.

"I finished cuttin' that Christmas tree, 'bout a seven-footer, I put it on my sled, and rode it right up here. I hadn't been here in six months, and I was surprised to see the house dark at Christmastime. Usually, it was lit up just like it is now, but the only lights on were in the kitchen and the upstairs sittin' room.

"I decided to pound on the door anyway," said Harry, "it bein' only about six o'clock, and after a while, MacGregor opened the door. He was a young man then, young and strong with a head of jet black hair and eyes to cut through all but granite. Before I could sense he was hurtin', I said, 'Merry Christmas. I've brung a tree for you and your wife and your beautiful little son who I'm ashamed I ain't yet seen.' "

Harry dropped his voice again. The crowd moved closer. "He looked at me for a while and I began to think he was gonna close the door in my face. Then, he said, as soft as a whisper, 'He's dead, Harry. My little boy's dead.' "

"Oh, no," cried Lanie Bannister.

Samson Webb sniffled. Ellie Miller was standing beside him. She pulled a small package of tissues from her pocket and offered him one.

" 'My son died ten days ago,' " continued Harry. " 'In New York, of pneumonia. All the doctors and all the money in the world couldn't save him. We buried our boy and came to Easter's Haven. My wife ain't been out of her room since we got here.' "

Harry took a deep breath and a measured pause. "Well, sir, there I was, standin' on the porch, with the snow comin' down and a Christmas tree in my hand, wonderin' what part of the afterlife that ghost was spendin' his time in, that he didn't know the little guy was gone."

People in the crowd laughed nervously.

"And then," Harry continued, "Andy MacGregor looked at the tree and the life seemed to come back into his eyes. He reached out and touched it." Harry reached out as MacGregor had fifty years before. "He said to me, 'It's a nice tree, just the same.' "

"I told him to take it. I said, it might cheer the missus to see it in the big room. Andy MacGregor shook his head and said there'd be no decorations in his house that year. He walked to the top step of the porch and looked up. 'Just after dark's a bad time, Harry,' he said, 'a bad time when you're mourning. It gets black and cold and you never think you'll see the sun again.' I remember them words like it was yesterday."

Harry paused and looked around the crowd, making eye contact with as many people as he could. "Right about then, like somethin' had jolted him, Andy MacGregor grabbed that Christmas tree by the trunk, pulled it out of my hands, and said, 'C'mon.' "

"He ran down onto the lawn, across the snow, to the edge of the cliff, right where that big spruce is growin' now. With all his might, he raised that tree into the air"—Harry raised his arms above his head, then brought them down—"and drove it into the snow. Then, he ran into the house."

Harry turned his body toward the house. He was talking as quickly as he could. The people were mesmerized. "First, the

lights in the foyer came on, then in the living room and the dining
room. Then, one by one, the bedrooms lit up. And I could see his
ma and his aunt runnin' around inside like they didn't know what
was happenin'.

"He came runnin' out," continued Harry, "with a long string
of Christmas lights, an extension cable, and a bottle of Haig and
Haig Pinch Bottle Scotch—Prohibition be damned—stuck under
his arm.

" 'Help me string 'em up,' he shouted." Harry was shouting,
too and gesturing wildly. " 'We'll decorate it outside. We'll drink to
it outside. And we'll shake our fists at the snow and the cold and
the goddamn dark.' "

The people in the crowd began to applaud. Harry dropped his
arms to his sides and waited for quiet.

He lowered his voice. "That's just what we did. And when we
plugged in the lights on that tree and the whole damn lawn lit up,
I swear, I could see Win Berry floatin' in the air, just off the edge
of the cliff, and he was smilin' at me. He knew all along that folks
need their friends when the goin' gets tough."

"Amen to that," said Reverend Forbison from the edge of the
group.

"Damn straight," added Samson Webb.

But Harry had not finished. "I found a firecracker in my
pocket. I pulled it out and lit it and threw it up into the sky. It
banged real loud, and Andy commenced to singin' 'Joy to the
World.' I joined in, and we sang as loud as we could till we forgot
the words. Then we passed the bottle a couple of times, and on the
third pass, Andy stopped and looked up to the porch.

"His mother and his old aunt was peekin' out the window, and
his wife, all wrapped in a shawl, had come outside. After bein' in
her room for so long, she seemed a bit shaky, but she walked out
into the snow, right over to that tree and said, 'I could use a drink.'
After a good slug, she wished me a Merry Christmas, then she
threw her arms around her husband, and I left a happy man."

People began to applaud again, but Harry raised his hands for
quiet. "She's gone now," he said softly. "She died a few years later.
The only woman he ever loved. But we started somethin' that
night that's still goin' on."

"A tradition," said Forbison.

"Merry Christmas, Harry," shouted MacGregor.

Harry Miller reached into his pocket, pulled out a firecracker, lit it, and threw it into the air. "Merry Christmas!" The firecracker exploded, and everyone began to cheer.

Lanie Bannister laughed and cried at the same time. John Miller threw his arms around his father. Samson Webb threw his arms around Harry's wife. Cal glanced across the group to where MacGregor's niece and the stranger had been standing. The man had disappeared into the happy crowd. MacGregor's niece was walking back to the porch.

Lanie blew her nose and wiped her eyes. She looked up at her husband and followed his gaze across the lawn. She watched the young woman walk up the stairs to the porch, where Andrew MacGregor was seated in an armchair, beneath a mountain of blankets. The young woman knelt down, said a few words to him, and kissed him on the forehead.

Lanie brought her lips to her husband's ear. "I know her now. She calls herself Mary MacGregor, but I've seen her on television. She used to be an actress. Her name was Miranda Blake."

14

James Whiting sat in the darkness and gazed at the bare branches on the tree outside his window. The armchair was deep and warm, with wings that kept the cold drafts from his neck. The bottle of Jack Daniels was four shots shorter than it had been an hour earlier. Upstairs Dave Douglas was having his party, and Whiting could hear the sounds of music and laughter.

He was curled into a tight little womb of self-pity, the bourbon was like warm amniotic fluid, and his questions were dividing and multiplying. Why had he failed with a woman he liked, especially after coming so close? Why had he been impotent for so long after dialysis? Why had he been one of the 50 percent who lose their potency because of dialysis? Why had he been forced to endure dialysis at all? Why had his kidneys failed? Why him? He sipped at the bourbon. Why him? He had refused to ask that question when the illness struck.

But tonight, he would allow it. After all, this was Christmas. He sipped and asked the question again. Why him? Why had he been chosen to endure the agony of the last year? And who had done the choosing? Was it God? Was there a God to do the choosing? Why would a rational God do such a thing to James Whiting? And if God had done it, would Whiting find in the next life some special reward for all that he had endured in this one?

Or should he be up on the roof, shaking his fist at the clear black canopy of fate, because there were no reasons beyond the failure of his genes, the weakness of his system, the configuration of the stars at his birth.

He reached for more bourbon. He was drinking too much, but the bourbon had numbed his brain just enough this evening, and tomorrow morning, his head would pound so hard that he would have no energy to devote to self-pity. He tipped the bottle down toward the glass, but the bottle was empty. Reluctantly, he flipped on the light so that he could find the fresh bourbon in the cabinet.

As he stood, he heard the sound of singing rising from the street. He had been hearing it for the last few minutes, but it had not registered until now. He stepped into the bay window and looked out.

Three couples carrying lit candles were singing their way up the street, stopping to carol in front of houses where lights were burning. It was a Beacon Hill tradition that on Christmas Eve, carolers and bell ringers traveled the streets spreading cheer. Whiting looked at his watch to make sure he hadn't been drunk for three days. It was still December 21.

They were singing "Deck the Halls." Their voices were full of laughter. The steam from their breath danced as it rose with their song and disappeared into the air. As they approached his window, Whiting stepped back. He did not want to hear Christmas carols. He had nothing to be cheerful about. He flipped off the light, but the carolers stopped nevertheless, attracted by the light in the apartment above.

"God rest ye merry gentlemen,/Let nothing you dismay . . ." The harmony was precise, delicate. The soprano's voice carried above the rest, gliding through the melody like a sharp skate on fresh ice. "Remember Christ our Savior was born on Christmas day . . ."

Whiting was drawn back to the bay window.

"To save us all from Satan's pow'r/When we were gone astray . . ."

Whiting began to smile.

"Oh, tidings of comfort and joy, comfort and joy!/Oh tidings of comfort and joy!"

From the windows above him, Whiting heard applause, and someone called for "Angels We Have Heard on High."

The group began to sing, and Whiting felt the depression, the self-pity, the numbness of the bourbon draining out of him. He had heard the songs hundreds of times in the weeks before Christmas, but never like this. As the carolers sang the refrain, the soprano's voice rose to the "Gloria," and James Whiting felt a chill at the nape of his neck.

Six strangers had stopped to reach out with their song. They had touched James Whiting. The beauty of their voices had revived him, and they had reminded him again of the simple power of generosity.

As they finished their song, applause and shouts of "Merry Christmas" erupted from the windows above him, and the carolers started to leave.

Whiting couldn't let them go. He pushed at the sash lock, then threw up the window. The cold winter air rushed into the room.

"Hey!" he shouted, and his voice echoed crazily off windows and walls. "Hey! Merry Christmas!"

"Merry Christmas!" answered the carolers.

"Don't stop singing. Ever!"

"Any requests?" asked one of the men.

"The soprano's name and phone number."

The singers laughed.

"The name is Cara Glynn," answered one of the men. "She should be with the Boston Opera!"

"Thanks," answered the soprano.

"And my name's Jack," added the man. I'm her husband."

"Well, Jack and Carla, and all of you, Merry Christmas!" Then he remembered the names and another night, back in June. He added, "I'll never complain that you're waking up the neighborhood again."

For a moment, Jack seemed puzzled. He took a few steps toward the window and looked up. In the glow of the candle that Jack was holding, Whiting could see recognition spreading across his face. Whiting wished that he'd kept his mouth shut.

Then Jack smiled. He laughed. His hand shot up and he waved. "Merry Christmas!"

"And the same to you," shouted Whiting.

One of the carolers started singing "Joy to the World." The others joined in, and they continued up the street. Whiting listened until they had reached the top of the hill. Then he closed the window and turned back into the room. He did not notice the cold. He was thinking about something else. He had buried it again and again in the last six months, but he could deny it no longer.

"Jim, you know that donor's names are never revealed." Dr. Joseph Stanton sat behind his desk and toyed with a paper clip. It was two days after the new year.

James Whiting held up the clipping of Roger Darrow's obituary. He had been carrying it in his wallet since June. "I don't leave here until I know if this is the donor."

"Why? Why should you care?" Stanton began to bend the paper clip.

"Because I need something to care about."

Stanton snapped the paper clip in half and said no.

Whiting folded his arms and said that it was going to be a long afternoon.

And Joseph Stanton decided to tell him. It took several phone calls, a great deal of cajolery, and a few threats, but eventually, Stanton found the name and address of the donor.

As Whiting headed for the door, Stanton offered a warning. "You're going to meet people who may be shocked at the sight of you," Jim. You're going to try to touch the textures of someone else's life, and you may not be too successful. You may find that the donor was a fascinating human being. You may find the remnants of an insufferable asshole. You'll probably find someone who has the same mixture of strengths and weaknesses that the rest of us have. That's not going to help you keep the kidney, and I don't know what it's going to do for your impotence. But now that you've caused me to breach my ethics, I hope that it helps you to find what you want."

"I just want to say thanks."

THREE

L. A. FANTASIES

15

A nd we will be arriving at about three P.M. Pacific time. The weather in Los Angeles at nine A.M., sunny and clear, with a temperature of fifty-eight degrees."

James Whiting turned his watch back three hours to 9:18, and looked out the window. Through breaks in the clouds, he could see the snowy hills of central Massachusetts, and he could make out a six-lane highway that looked like the Massachusetts Turnpike.

Drinks were served over upstate New York. Luncehon—a decent steak, vegetable, rolls, a Sebastiani red wine—arrived as Lake Erie rolled into view. Then, dessert, coffee, and the Mississippi River, frozen silver in the cold.

Whiting didn't watch the movie. He preferred to listen to the classical band on the headset and watch the wheatfields and the mountains and the deserts turning on their axis below. When he flew over the Grand Canyon, with five glasses of wine and Beethoven's Eighth Symphony dancing in his head, he thought that *this* was the way Beethoven was meant to be heard. Then, the Grand Canyon disappeared. The land turned flat and brown, and Whiting wondered what sort of television jingles Beethoven would be writing to survive today.

Bong! The captain has turned on the No Smoking sign. "Please return to your seats, extinguish all smoking materials, fasten your seat belts, and prepare for the descent into Los Angeles."

Whiting checked to make sure that none of his materials were smoking, then fastened his seat belt and looked out. Although they were still over the mountains, they were dropping altitude quickly. He noticed streams of yellow-tinted mist trickling up through the mountain passes and clinging to the hillsides. It was not the viscous brown soup that boiled in the basin during the summer, but it was smog. The jet sank through it, the mountains fell away, and Los Angeles covered the land.

From the air, the city looked like a great, flat grid of streets and suburban blocks, stretching in perfect symmetry toward the sea. There were hills here and there, and cutting across the grid, like rills and rivers crossing cultivated farmland, the freeways flowed from the mountains to the water's edge and joined every corner of the expanse.

The plane was low enough now that Whiting could see cars traveling on the freeways, eight, ten, twelve lanes of steady motion, like blood cells moving through capillaries. The plane seemed to shake and growl, and the landing gear opened.

Now they were close enough that Whiting could see the Hollywood Park racetrack and the Los Angeles Forum, both surrounded by a desert of concrete on which were painted thousands of white rectangles. He remembered a statistic: Two thirds of the land in the city of Los Angeles was devoted to the movement and storage of automobiles.

When he stepped into the warm air outside the terminal, Whiting felt ten pounds lighter. The smog he had seen from the air was not visible at ground level, and palm trees were growing out of the airport sidewalk. The sun was bright, the buildings were mostly white, the streets were clean. Whiting put on his sunglasses, took a deep breath, and inhaled jet exhaust.

He climbed into a cab and said, "Bonaventure Hotel."

The cab pulled out and headed down Century Boulevard. Airport Ramada and Holiday Inn. The Tishman Skyscraper. Hughes Airwest. Live Nude Dancing, Twenty-Four Hours a Day and Hot Swedish Massage at the Airport Motel. The San Diego Freeway Overpass, the L. A. Forum, and this year, the cabby said, the Lakers were going to win another title. Hollywood Park. Motels for the horsemen. A drive-in theater. Gas stations and small shopping plazas with large parking lots in front of them. A supermarket called Ralph's. Up side streets, neat rows of California bungalows and tall, spindly palms. And billboards everywhere. The city looked like an adman's vision of Nirvana. Jordache has the look that's right. Look out for the Bull. Taste the difference. Visit Magic Mountain. And Use Afro-Sheen.

"Inglewood's a black district," said the cabby.

Compared to Boston's ghetto, thought Whiting, it looked like Westchester County. "Why is there a piece of aluminum wrapped around the trunk of every palm tree?" he asked.

"To keep the rats out of the trees," answered the cabby. "The rats like to eat the dates, and not just in Inglewood. There's even rats climbin' trees in Beverly Hills." The cabby laughed.

Jack-in-the-Box. Taco Bell. McDonald's. Aren't you hungry for Burger King now? The giant donut on top of the tiny donut shop. And then they were riding thirty feet above the ground, on the Harbor Freeway. Ahead, 180 degrees of mountains leaped into the air, forming the wall that trapped the smog and dwarfed the downtown skyscrapers. The cabby named the mountains, from the left, the Santa Monica Mountains, the Hollywood Hills, the Verdugo Hills, the San Gabriels, the San Bernardinos. And Mount Baldy, ten thousand feet, white and massive, looming out of the distant smog like Moby Dick rearing from the mists and plunging toward the *Pequod*.

He checked into the Bonaventure Hotel, a complex of five glass cylinders rising beside the Harbor Freeway. His room, in the northeast clyinder, had a view of the other downtown skyscrapers, the railroad yards, a neon sign atop a ten-story building—huge red letters proclaiming "Jesus Saves" to the freeway—and Mount Baldy. Whiting wondered why, in a town as creative as Hollywood, no one could think of a better name for a snow-covered mountain.

After he showered, Whiting dressed in gray slacks, and blue shirt. Then he sat on the edge of the bed and dialed information. A recorded voice told him that he should be using the telephone book, but since he was on the line, he could get the number if he promised to write it down. He had never been chastised by a recording before.

"What city please?" asked the human operator.

"In Pacific Palisades, Roger Darrow." Whiting spelled the name and hoped that the number wasn't unlisted. He had gotten the address from Stanton.

Whiting wrote down the number, and before hanging up, started to dial. He felt like a college freshman calling a sophomore for a date. His hands were sweating and his speech was rehearsed. The phone rang once and Whiting hung up. He had traveled three thousand miles, and he was losing his nerve.

He threw on his sweater and went out for a walk. At six o'clock, all the traffic on the wide, straight boulevards seemed to be flowing out of town, and the tall buildings turned stony faces to the few pedestrians left on the sidewalks. Eventually, however, Whiting found his way to Olvera Street, two neat rows of stucco buildings with red tile roofs and second-floor balconies, above a street just wide enough for a donkey cart. Olvera Street was the birthplace of Los Angeles, the site of the first Spanish settlement in the eighteenth century.

Whiting sat in a little Mexican restaurant overlooking a tiled fountain. He ordered a Dos Equis and two cheese enchiladas, and he watched the tourists who sat around the fountain, with faintly disappointed expressions on their faces, as though they had expected to find a Mexican Disneyland in the middle of downtown Los Angeles.

After he finished eating, Whiting rented a car and bought a map of Los Angeles. Instead of heading to Pacific Palisades and the Darrow home, as he intended, Whiting drove up the freeway to Hollywood. He parked on Vermont Avenue and looked up at the "Hollywood" sign, nine giant letters, arrayed across the Hills so that they floated in the darkness above the city, a perfect symbol for the mixture of magic and false-front artifice that was Hollywood.

Whiting spent the next several hours strolling Hollywood Boulevard, with its famous restaurants, clothing stores, car lots, porno shops, family ice-cream stores, video-game arcades, male prostitutes, tourists, and old movie palaces. It reminded Whiting of a cross between small-town America, midtown Manhattan, and Sodom or Gomorrah.

He ended at the forecourt of the Chinese Theater. He put his feet in Clark Gable's footprints. He saw the smudges in the concrete were Bette Grable had tried to leave her leg prints. And like the tourists at Olvera Street, he felt faintly disappointed. Because this shrine to the movies seemed tired, past its prime, in spite of the fresh paint and careful grooming. His imagination had led him to expect something grander. He hoped that he would not be disappointed when he finally raised the courage to visit Roger Darrow's home.

The next morning, following the directions of one of the desk clerks, Whiting drove out to Pacific Palisades, almost an hour from the hotel. It was a January Saturday morning in Los Angeles, seventy-three degrees, clear sky, and camellias starting to bloom.

James Whiting parked in the circular driveway, rang the door- bell of the Darrow mansion, ran a hand through his hair, and stood up straight. He was wearing a green LaCoste shirt, poplin trousers, and Topsiders. He stuffed his hands into his pockets so that he appeared more casual than he felt.

The door opened slowly, and Jeanne Darrow looked out. Her hair was covered by a sun viser and she was wearing a tennis dress. She looked less exotic and less beautiful than Whiting had imagined. Disappointment number one.

He smiled. "Mrs. Darrow?"

"Yes."

"My name is James Whiting. I've traveled a long way to see you. May I speak with you for a few minutes?"

"If you've traveled a long way from Salt Lake City and you want to convert me to Mormonism, I'm not interested." She started to close the door.

Whiting hadn't expected sarcasm. "I'm not a Mormon," he laughed. "I'm generally an Episcopalian and usually an agnostic. We don't have pamphlets and we don't ask for money. We just lay awake nights wondering."

She smiled. "So what are you selling?"

"Nothing. I've come to thank you for something."

She opened the door a bit wider. She seemed curious. "For what?"

He decided not to wait any longer. "Almost seven months ago, I received one of your husband's kidneys."

Jeanne Darrow said nothing. She stared at Whiting as though she did not believe him. Two sparrows were chattering in the camellia bush beside the door. Soft music was playing inside the house. And James Whiting felt the heat gathering around his collar and boiling up to his forehead.

"Is this some kind of joke?"

Maybe a simple letter would have been more effective. "It's no joke," he answered. He felt the perspiration beading on his upper lip. He quickly told his story, from the day of the transplant to his most recent doctor's visit.

When he finished, Jeanne tried to hide her shock behind a shrug and a nervous laugh. "So what do you want me to say?"

He smiled. "I want you to say 'You're welcome' when I say 'Thank you.'"

She seemed to soften a bit. "OK, you're welcome."

"Not so fast. I haven't thanked you yet." He hoped she would invite him in, at the very least, for a cup of coffee.

She did not.

He extended his hand and she took it. Her grip was strong. He wrapped the hand in both of his.

"Your husband made an act of charity, Mrs. Darrow," he said, "and I benefitted. Even if he doesn't know it, you should. It may be of some comfort to you to know that he was able to help someone else when he could no longer help himself. And it's a comfort to me to be able to express my thanks."

Jeanne Darrow felt an irrational flash of resentment. Her husband had given his final gift to this absolute stranger. "Are you comforted now?" she snapped.

"Frankly, no," he said. "I had hoped we could talk a bit more."

"About what?"

"Your husband. I'd like to know a bit about him," he hesitated, "for my own piece of mind." He should have saved that for later, but he wasn't sure there would *be* a later.

"Mr. Whiting." she said. "For six months I've been trying to learn how to live without my husband, and I haven't found any peace of mind at all. I don't think I can help you to live with what's left of him."

Whiting decided to back away as gracefully as possible and try again. "I'm sorry I bothered you, Mrs. Darrow. Perhaps we can talk later."

"I doubt it."

"I'll be at the Bonaventure for the week."

"Hey, Jeannie, what's going on?" Harriet Sears appeared from inside the house.

"This is Mr. Whiting," said Jeanne. "He's just leaving."

"Does he play doubles?" asked Harriet, sizing him up with a smile.

"Maybe another time," said Whiting. "Good morning."

Jeanne closed the door, but for a moment, she did not turn around.

"One of these days," said Harriet, "you're going to stop chasing off all the good-looking men. Who was that?"

Jeanne shook her head, as though she still didn't believe it. "Roger's kidney."

James Whiting drove west on Sunset to the ocean. He parked at Will Rogers State Beach and got out. The beach was wide and clean. He saw the waves thundering in. He felt the cold Pacific spray. He strolled along the water's edge. He watched the surfers, like seals in their wet suits, bobbing out beyond the breakers. He ogled the young bodies stretched in the sun. He sat in the hot sand and let it bake the confusion and disappointment out of him.

When he returned to the hotel two hours later, he found on his dresser a bouquet of birds-of-paradise, long-stemmed flowers that thrived in California. The card with the flowers read:

> Dear Mr. Whiting,
> I've never sent flowers to a man before, but I've seldom felt compelled to apologize to a man for my behavior. Let us talk. Please meet me in front of the L.A. County Museum at three this afternoon.
>
> Jeanne D.

The museum was on Wilshire Boulevard, a fifteen-minute drive from the hotel. Three modern buildings of precast stone and glass, two exhibit halls, and a motion-picture theater stood beside a park that was the largest green space Whiting had seen in Los Angeles. He had a few minutes, so he wandered into the park.

There were thick clumps of evergreens, the requisite number of palms, open grassy areas, paths winding through the trees, and several small ponds, the largest of which, close by Wilshire, was a rank and stagnant-looking puddle about a hundred feet long. The pond was surrounded by a chain link fence, and at either end, life-sized plaster mastodons trumpeted at each other like props from *The Lost World*.

Then, he smelled oil and realized that this was no ordinary park, but the La Brea Tar Pits, the largest fossil site in North America. The mastodons were reenacting a scene played out thousands of years ago, when animals came to the ponds to drink and were caught in the tar oozing just below the surface of the shallow pools. Thousands of skeletons—mastodons, saber-toothed tigers, prehistoric mammals of every variety, birds, and at least one human—had been preserved in the muck. And the high fence, Whiting realized, kept dogs, cats, and small children from becoming the fossils of another century.

He mounted a small platform that extended over the pond and looked down. He noticed slicks of oil floating on the surface. He smelled the odor of cold-packed road tar. He saw fat lazy bubbles expanding as the gases below oozed to the surface.

"After you've seen all the freeways, this place gives you a nice sense of perspective about L.A." Jeanne Darrow was standing on the platform beside him.

She was wearing jeans, boots, and a camel's hair sportcoat over a brown turtleneck. Her hair was short and layer cut. With a touch of blue eye shadow and simple gold hoop earrings she looked like the woman Whiting had expected to meet that morning, someone beautiful and sophisticated.

"I got here early," she said. "So I took a walk through the park and noticed you admiring the ooze."

"It's very nice ooze."

She laughed nervously. "At least it knows its place. Not like the ooze we have in the air."

"Do you come here often?" asked Whiting, dusting off a line he hadn't used in years.

"Whenever I want to be reminded that our troubles may not be as important as they seem." She paused for a moment. "And when I want to compose an apology."

"The flowers were apology enough," answered Whiting. "And I can understand your reaction. It must have been a bit of a shock to have me come knocking on your door."

"It was. It is."

"You acted at first as though you didn't believe me."

She extended her hand. "I believe you, Mr. Whiting. You look like a nice guy, and you have an honest face."

"I guess I should feel complimented."

"You should. And you should be honored that you received as fine a kidney." She meant that as a joke, but it sounded appropriate.

"I'm just glad to be alive," said Whiting. "And I'd love to have dinner with you tonight."

"Why?"

In the ooze beneath the platform, a gas gurgled and popped. On Wilshire Boulevard, the Saturday-afternoon traffic produced a steady rumble, like the sound of a single engine.

Whiting shrugged. "Because you're the only person I know in a city of three million, you seem very nice, and you're the first woman who ever sent me flours."

"Three good reasons. And the fourth? . . ."

"Fourth?"

"You want to know more about my husband," she answered sharply.

Whiting nodded.

"Why?"

This was a strange and unpredictable woman, thought Whiting. One moment she was joking with him, the next, she was asking questions for which he had no eloquent answers.

He did not know that in the last week, she had been viewing the tapes of her husband's last journey. She had traveled with Roger Darrow across a majestic landscape and into the cities of the East. She had watched him interview people who where interesting, attractive, and threatening. She had listened to narration that was by turns hopeful, cynical, and filled with despair. And she had watched him slowly deteriorating until, in the final moments of the final tape, he had lost touch with reality . . . and with her.

Whiting jammed his hands into his pockets and looked down into the oily water. "It's hard to explain," he said. "Maybe an adopted child feels this way when he tries to find out about his real parents."

Jeanne Darrow leaned against the railing. "I can't have dinner with you, Mr. Whiting," she said, "But I'm going to brunch at the home of my husband's partner tomorrow. Perhaps you'd like to come along."

"I'd love to," he said.

"You can satisfy your curiosity about my husband's world and decide if he deserves any more of your attention." She also knew that her appearance with a man on her arm might distract from speculations about the video tapes. "Now, let me give you a tour of the ooze."

"You can satisfy your curiosity about my husband's world and decide if he deserves any more of your attention." She also knew that her appearance with a man on her arm might distract from speculations about the video tapes. "Now, let me give you a tour of the ooze."

16

This, thought Whiting, was why they called it Lotus Land. One day of clear skies and bright sun followed another. The Pacific blue seemed bluer each day. The woman behind the wheel of the Mercedes convertible wore a stylish yellow hat, and the sun reflected across the down at the back of her neck. Her flowered skirt billowed slightly in the breeze. Linda Ronstadt sang on the tape deck. The car hugged the turns on the Pacific Coast Highway. The ocean rolled to the left, the Santa Monica Mountains to the right. James Whiting stretched out and enjoyed the ride.

"You're going to meet some good people today, and you're also going to meet some real stiffs," said Jeanne.

"Do I get a scorecard?"

"No. I'd rather see what you think."

"Why do I get the feeling this is some kind of test?"

"Because it is." Jeanne smiled. "If you like the right people, I'll know that kidney wasn't wasted."

After they crossed the Malibu Creek, Jeanne turned left off the Coast Road and drove down to a gatehouse. She gave her name to the guard, and the gate opened.

"Welcome to the Malibu Colony," said Jeanne.

"Not one of the original thirteen," said Whiting. "If they ever revolt out here, it won't be over the tax on tea."

Jeanne laughed. "The high price of cocaine would be more likely."

The houses perched along the water were larger than anything else he had seen on the coast. Except for an occasional tennis court or row of trees, however, they were packed as tightly as triple-deckers in Dorchester. Jeanne parked behind a Jaguar, which was parked behind a Rolls-Royce, which was parked behind a Mercedes and a Trans Am.

Howard Rudermann's house was a modern structure of red-

wood and glass, but from the road, it looked like a box with a
garage door across the front.

Sliding glass panels on the side of the house opened into a
foyer. There was a room to the right and a dining room straight
ahead, but visitors always turned first to the left, into the living
room where a two-story wall of glass looked out onto the beach
and a spiral staircase led to a balcony on the second floor. The
living room and the patio beyond were packed with people. From
the sound of things, they were having a good time, but Whiting
couldn't tell yet because his eyes were trying to adjust to the glare
from the beach and the darkness of the foyer at the same time. On
the stereo, he recognized the joyous sounds of George Benson's
guitar.

"Jeanne Darrow arrives with a man. Let me get my notebook
and write down his name." Vicki Rogers, Margarita in hand, appeared from the shadows. She was wearing a black turtleneck,
black jeans, and black boots.

"I almost didn't see you, it's so dark in here," said Jeanne.
"Now that I *have,* I guess I'll just have to ignore you."

Vicki looked at Whiting. "Perhaps you two should go out and
we'll start again."

"Either that or you could change your wardrobe," said Whiting. Already he sensed the ground rules: no open displays of hostility allowed, sarcasm and wit, if possible, to score points.

"I awoke feeling very sinister today. I think it has something to
do with my horoscope." Vicki extended her hand to Whiting. "If
Jeanne won't introduce me, I'll introduce myself. Vicki Rogers."

"As in 'On the Coast'?" Whiting was impressed.

"As in, 'Who are you, and are you worth gossiping about in my
next column,' " said Jeanne.

Vicki looked at Jeanne, "But dear, if he walked in with you, I
know he's worth gossiping about."

"Jeannie!" Howard Rudermann came up from the living room
and threw his arms around Jeanne Darrow. He was wearing a
dashiki and white ducks. "I'm so glad you could make it."

She returned the embrace. She seemed happy to see him.

He looked at Whiting. "And who's this?"

"James Whiting," said Vicki. "The name doesn't ring any
bells."

"And don't bother asking me if he makes the earth move," said

Jeanne. "He's just a friend from Boston."

Rudermann pumped Whiting's hand, took him by the shoulder, and started to lead him into the living room.

"Where are you going?" asked Jeanne.

"You know the way it works," said Rudermann. "Couples can arrive together and leave together, but at a Rudermann party, they mix."

"We're not a couple," said Jeanne.

"You came together," answered Rudermann over his shoulder. "That constitutes a couple."

Jeanne watched them step down into the living room.

"He'll introduce your friend to a few young ladies with large breasts," said Vicki, "then he'll be back to introduce you to the guest of honor."

"Who's that?" Jeanne's eyes were following Whiting through the room. She was curious to see where Rudermann would stop.

"Congressman Reuben Merrill."

Jeanne's head snapped around. A few nights earlier, Jeanne had watched Merrill dodge questions in an interview with her husband.

"I've heard that he appears on the mysterious Darrow tapes that we're all so hot to see."

"You hear a lot of things," answered Jeanne.

"Is that a denial?" Vicki's smile remained fixed. She expected unfriendliness from Jeanne Darrow, because Jeanne Darrow needed nothing from Vicki Rogers.

"I'd like a drink," said Jeanne, and she started through the doorway that led into the dining area.

"Just answer me one question," said Vicki. "Word is out that you've finally looked at the tapes. Have you?"

"Yes."

"And Howard says you're not sure what you're going to do with them."

"That's two questions," said Jeanne.

"You never stop working, do you, Vicki, dear?" Harriet Sears had pushed her way through the crowd in the living room. She was wearing a white caftan, her favorite beach outfit, and large red earrings. She was carrying two Margaritas.

Jeanne took one of them. "Thanks." She turned toward the living room. "I have to check on a friend."

"You never stop protecting that girl, do you, dear Harriet?" said
Vicki after Jeanne had gone off.

Let's drive the
put home

Rudermann introduced Whiting to half a dozen people—two actresses whose names he had never heard but whose figures he would always remember, a writer, two neighbors, and Peter Cross, the star of "Flint."

Cross was thirty-three years old, rich, famous, and egotistical enough to appear now at partys in his favorite off-time uniform— five-o'clock shadow, mussed hair, torn jeans, and a green T-shirt with the word COMMEMORATIVO stenciled across the chest. Commemorativo, he explained, had been John Wayne's favorite brand of tequila. He pulled a half pint out of his back pocket, drank, wiped off the bottle, and offered it to Whiting.

"No thanks, Pete," said Rudermann. "Mr. Whiting's hungry. And next time, try a glass." Rudermann ushered Whiting through the sliding doors onto the patio. He made no apology for Peter Cross as he led Whiting to the buffet table.

"The lox is wonderful," he said, "and inside, you'll find fruit crepes with fresh cream and eggs Benedict."

"Ah, a new face." Dr. Ben Volker strolled over to Whiting. "A nice straight nose, no puffiness under the eye, a firm jaw. Too young and too pretty to be of any interest to me."

Rudermann laughed and introduced them. "Ben's one of the top plastic surgeons in Beverly Hills."

Nancy Wright, a young actress, joined the group. She was wearing a Danskin top and a peasant skirt, and for the third time since he'd arrived, Whiting believed that he'd met the cure for his impotence.

Whiting also noticed that Ben Volker had gray hair and his stomach bulged slightly over the top of his bathing suit, but in all other respects, he looked like the product of his own workmanship. He could not tell Volker's age, or Rudermann's, or that of half the people he saw around him. It seemed that in this world, people who were middle aged might be forty-eight or sixty-two, but with the help of hairdressers, masseurs, and plastic surgeons, they had been able to halt the advance from youth to old age in a place whose only coordinates were a few wrinkles, the most artfully displayed gray hairs, and ten or fifteen years on either side of fifty. Hollywood magic, he decided.

"I'm disappointed, Jeannie," said Vaughn Lawrence, who was wearing white denim jeans, a white sweater, a gold neck chain, and sunglasses pushed up on his head. He looked casual, relaxed, almost asleep.

Jeanne looked him up and down. "About what?"

"About that." Lawerence glanced through the patio doors at Whiting.

"What are you talking about?"

"I always thought that when you showed some interest in a man again, it would be me."

"You thought what?"

"You know what I'm talking about, Jeannie."

She laughed. "I think the Quaaludes are rotting your brain, Vaughn."

"That's not 'ludes. That's laid back, honey."

Jeanne looked around to see if anyone was listening. In any other living room, Vaughn Lawrence would have been the center of attention. Here he was a face in the crowd.

"If you were interested," whispered Jeanne angrily, "why didn't you call me before this?"

"You know how it is. I didn't want to bother you . . . I'm tied up with Kelly." He shrugged. "You know how it is."

Jeanne felt her face flush. "Vaughn, from now on, don't leave the house without a member of the Writers Guild along to feed you lines."

"That's not what you used to say." He smirked.

Jeanne lowered her voice and clenched her teeth. "I don't know what prompted this after a year and a half, but forget it. I used you for a couple of months because I was mad at Roger. You used me because you use everyone. It's as simple and final as that."

Jeanne opened the door and stepped out onto the patio. She was furious. She had felt nothing for Vaughn Lawrence except distaste, which became stronger whenever she saw him. He had simply been convenient, and she had always regretted the affair.

Howard Rudermann intercepted Jeanne before she reached Whiting. "Now, just leave your friend alone for a while. Let him get to know the gang."

"If I do that, he might not be my friend anymore."

Rudermann put his arm around her. "C'mon into the library. I want you to meet the guest of honor. Your friend can look at Nancy Wright's tits."

Jeanne gave Nancy Wright a second glance. "She didn't have those the last time I saw her."

"She'd only just met Ben Volker," answered Rudermann.

When Whiting tired of talking with Ben Volker, which didn't take long, he drained the last of his Margarita and went to the bar for a refill. He sipped the liquor, sifting it through the salt around the edge of the glass, and strolled across the patio. He didn't think the couple sharing a joint in the whirlpool would appreciate his company. He decided to sit at a table and watch the party go by. On the other side of the table, with his nose buried in *Variety,* sat a young man wearing a bathing suit and a string of white shells around his neck.

"Did you see this article in here about Laura Keebler?" he asked as soon as Whiting sat down. "Luckiest broad in the world. They cancel 'Love He, Love She,' and right away, she's got another show cooking on cable. She brings the idea to Vaughn Lawrence, who loves the show, and it happens, just like that. Some people have to hustle, some don't."

"I guess that's the way it is in every business."

"Yeah, but not every business is as full of snakes." The young man spoke calmly, as though stating a common truth.

A young woman strolled past. She was short, fifteen pounds overweight, and dressed in an expensive pair of Gucci leather pants that did nothing to flatter her behind but announce to the world that she could afford a pair of Gucci leather pants. "David, guess what I just heard."

"What, Laura?"

"Peter Cross just signed a deal at Twentieth to direct a feature," said Laura Keebler.

"Direct!" David Ross almost fell off the chair. "He couldn't direct a case of the shits if he gave an actor a pound of Ex-Lax."

Nice town, thought Whiting. These people make admen look charitable.

"Mrs. Darrow, it's a pleasure to meet you." said Reuben Merrill, "and it was an honor to meet your husband back in June."

The congressman was dressed in a blue sportcoat, gray slacks, and the only necktie in the house. He was about fifty, with a long, thin face and bushy black eyebrows that bounced about when he spoke. Every other gesture and expression, including the timbre of his voice, seemed carefully controlled and polished.

"Rumor has it that after almost seven months, you've finally felt strong enough to look at your husband's video tapes," said Merrill.

"It's amazing how rumors travel." Jeanne's eyes shifted to Rudermann, who looked down at the carpet.

They were in the library, which was small, dark, and lined with books that Rudermann had never read.

Jeanne turned back to Merrill. "What brings you all the way from Washington?"

"I'm on my way to Yosemite, for a little vacation. My friend Vaughn Lawrence invited me to Mr. Rudermann's."

"A pleasure," chirped Rudermann.

Merrill's eyebrows furrowed down, then rose to the hairline. They looked to Jeanne like two caterpillars in a mating dance. "What plans do you have for the tapes, now that you've finally seen them.?"

"The tapes were a rough draft, Congressman. They're not entirely coherent. Beyond which, they have some very private moments, things that don't have much significance to anyone but Roger and me."

Merrill took her hand in both of his and smiled warmly. "Your husband was an influential and respected man. That's why I consented to speak with him in June, and that's also why the members of my subcommittee would appreciate hearing his opinions on the state of video communications in America, even posthumously."

Jeanne wanted her husband to be remembered as an influential man. She had taken great care with the tapes because she wanted to protect herself, but also because she wanted to protect his reputation and his work. Sincerely or not, Merrill had said the right thing.

Jeanne found that she liked Merrill more in person than she had on the video tape, which did not augur well for the future of his political career. "Congressman, if anyone beyond a few close friends sees the tapes, you'll be among the first."

The eyebrows rose. "I'll take your word on that."

There was a knock, and Rudermann opened the door. The sounds of the party filled the library, as though someone had turned up the volume.

Vicki Rogers poked her head into the room. "Excuse me, folks, but I thought Jeanne might be interested to know that her friend is about to get 'the treatment.' "

"They haven't pulled that in years," laughed Rudermann.

"Well, Mr. Whiting is in the cabana putting on a swimsuit. He has a big audience, and Kelly Hammerstein and David Ross have offered to go with him."

"Excuse me, Congressman," said Jeanne. She hurried out.

"This is a good cheap laugh when it works, Congressman, You really ought to watch it," offered Vicki Rogers.

Jeanne stopped at the bar in the kitchen and poured herself another Margarita.

"It looks like your friend is about to get a case of California blue balls," said Harriet. "Aren't you going to help him?"

"He's a big boy." She swallowed half the Margarita.

"What did Merrill want?"

Jeanne shook her head. "Merrill wants the tapes. And ten minutes ago, Vaughn Lawrence put the move on me. And that guy out on the patio, God only knows what he wants." She swallowed the rest of the Margarita. "For seven months, everyone leaves me alone. The minute I look at the tapes, they're all hitting on me."

"Can you handle it?"

She had the bartender pour her another. "If I have any trouble, I'll let you know."

Vaughn Lawrence slipped into the library. Rudermann was telling Reuben Merrill that he thought the tapes would make a wonderful network special and perhaps the congressman would be interested in narrating them. Merrill was listening with brows knitted and a thin smile on his face.

When Rudermann stopped for a breath, Lawrence eased him out, suggesting that he supervise the "the treatment" so that the congressman would get a good chuckle.

After Rudermann left, Merrill said, "What a windbag. He'd make a good politician."

"He's also a good producer," Lawrence said. " 'Redgates' " is top quality, and now he's producing ten hours about the Revolution, called 'A New Flag' for our American Heritage network. His work makes money for us, and you can fill a vehicle like 'Redgates' with a lot of hidden messages."

Merrill laughed. "You're going to use the American Heritage channel for propaganda?"

"We prefer to call it issue-oriented programming." Lawrence lit a cigarette.

Merrill stood. "Buzz words."

"Maybe, but Darrow fed the public about a lot of liberal crap between the car chases in 'Flint.' "

"And what issues have you explored with 'Redgates'?"

"Not too many. We *are* trying to make a profit and pick up new stations. But the Redgates don't hold slaves. They fight the Union because they believe in the importance of states' rights."

Merrill's eyebrows rose.

Lawrence took a long drag on his cigarette. He had been smoking more often as the merger date approached. "A congressman trying to decentralize the federal government could not find a more heroic family."

The eyebrows found a comfortable spot in the middle of the forehead. Reuben Merrill approved. "Maybe MacGregor's judgment about business partners wasn't so bad after all."

Lawrence sat down at Rudermann's desk and flipped on the lamp. "If you believe that, maybe you'll trust me when I ask you not to go pulling the scabs off Jeanne Darrow."

Merrill shoved the lamp out of the way and brought his face close to Lawrence's. "Just because you're behind the desk, don't try to act like you're running this show. Without me, there *is* no show."

Lawrence picked up Rudermann's gold pencil and began to draw doodles on the blotter.

"For seven months, I've been waiting for some news about those tapes," continued Merrill, "I'm on one of them, playing footsie with Darrow's questions, then acting like an indignant asshole when he tries to fuck me on camera. You take some lunatic-fringe columnist who needs to fill up space, show him that tape, and the next thing you know, I'm getting blamed for Darrow's death."

Lawrence did not take his eyes from the blotter. "You're over-reacting, Congressman. Darrow died in a boating accident."

"Yeah," said Merrill, as though he didn't believe it. "That's what they tell me."

Vaughn Lawrence began to draw hard, sharp-edged squares on the blotter. He wondered how Reuben Merrill had climbed so high in the circles of Washington power. By being careful, he decided, by playing hardball when he had to and by always remembering favors. That was why Andrew MacGregor had been drawn to him.

"We've been watching Jeanne Darrow for seven months, Congressman. We've waited for her to make her decision, but we've done nothing to raise her suspicions." Lawrence stood, came around the desk, and put an arm over Merrill's shoulder, "I guarantee you that we'll see the tapes before any lunatic-fringe columnists."

Merrill folded his arms and stared at Lawrence. He was still not satisfied. "I'm sure that'll make my staff feel much better—a guarantee from a game-show host."

Lawrence took his arm away and injected his voice with conciliation that he did not feel. "You have to trust us, Congressman. We've been working our tails off on both coasts. We're producing the right programming. We got Senator Sylbert out of the picture in Wyoming. Our stations are in place in Iowa. MacGregor's making moves in New Hampshire. And when the time is right, we'll unleash Billy Singer. But it all takes time, and the congressman's confidence."

After a moment, the eyebrows smiled, then the rest of the face. He offered his hand to Lawrence. "I'm sorry about that remark. I guess I have to trust anyone that MacGregor trusts enough to join up with."

Lawrence flashed his game show smile and shook hands. "No more worry about the tapes."

James Whiting was standing in the middle of the patio.

Ben Volker was clapping his hands and shouting, "Now, c'mon, everybody. We must have more people going in today."

"Yeah," shouted David Ross. "You don't know what you're

missing."

Kelly Hammerstein, who looked magnificent in a red Speedo racing suit, threw her arm around Whiting's bare shoulder. "We'll just have to enjoy it ourselves."

Whiting sensed that he was being set up, but he was playing along. He had mentioned to David Ross that the water looked inviting. David had suggested that they take a dip. Whiting had been ushered to that cabana, where he had selected a white bathing suit that would not contrast with the fish belly color of his legs and torso, and now he was the center of attention. He was glad he had been working out since his doctor gave him permission. What muscle he had looked hard and stringy, and his stomach was flat, despite six months of eating his way through the best restaurants in the East.

"What did you say the water temperature was again?" he asked.

"Warm," answered Ben Volker. "Real warm. That big storm off Mexico that's givin' us the good surf pushed up a lot of warm water."

"Let's quit talking and get wet," shouted David as he started toward the water.

"Yeah, c'mon." Kelly Hammerstein grabbed Whiting's hand and ran after David.

Jeanne Darrow stepped onto the patio and saw Whiting heading for the surf, with Ross and Hammerstein on either side of him. She watched for a moment, then noticed Laura Keebler beside her. Laura was standing on a chair to get a better view.

"Whose idea was this?" asked Jeanne.

"David's. Ben Volker pulled it on him the first time David ever came here. David's been dying to pull it on someone ever since."

"Anybody stupid enough to fall for it deserves it," said Vaughn Lawrence as he came out of the house.

Reuben Merrill was inside talking to a young woman in a tight-fitting T-shirt.

"I didn't know that Kelly went in for practical jokes," said Harriet to Jeanne.

"She has to get her fun somehow," said Jeanne.

Rudermann was standing beside Ben Volker, who was smiling expectantly as he waited for the plunge. "You never could resist, could you?"

Volker laughed. "I think he knows it's a joke already. He'll stop*n/* before he hits the water."

"Yeah," said Laura, "and stupid David'll probably go in."

Vicki Rogers was sitting at the patio table. "Did you see that scar on his belly, Ben?"

"I'll look when he comes back," said Volker.

"Now remember," shouted David to Whiting as they ran. "You've got to dive right in. Otherwise, those big waves'll break right on top of you and knock you out."

It was the right advice. The eight-footers were common along the California coast in winter, but Whiting had never encountered them in the East. From the moment he had seen them crashing on the beach he had wanted to try them, and he didn't care how cold the water was.

"Don't chicken out," shouted Kelly Hammerstein.

"Geronimo," hollered David Ross.

They rushed into the water. Ankle-deep: Kelly stopped. Knee-deep: David stopped. Thigh-deep: Whiting dove into the wave as it broke on top of him.

"He fell for it!" shouted Rudermann.

Volker elbowed Rudermann in the ribs. "Watch him jump up and run like hell."

"If his feet aren't frozen," said Vaughn Lawrence.

"She got him right to the edge." Rudermann looked at Frank Wheeler. The agent, who was lounging in the whirlpool with a prospective client. "That Kelly might make it as an actress yet."

"She'll make it as an actress before David makes it as a writer," answered Wheeler.

"She's been acting since she started going with Vaugh," said Jeanne. She glanced over and saw Lawrence smile.

Whiting popped out of the water. "C'mon," he shouted to David and Kelly. Then he turned and plunged before the next wave broke over him. The water was ice cold, and Whiting felt a pain at the bridge of his nose, but he wasn't coming out for anything. Besides, from his days at Bar Harbor, he remembered that after the initial shock, the pain would subside and the cold would feel pleasant.

Whiting dove through the waves, whirling his way out to where they were cresting. A roller lifted him high enough that he could see the patio and the people watching him. He raised his hand and waved, then plunged again.

"The guy has to be numb, and he's still showing off," said Rudermann.

"Which means that he's picked up the life-style already," cracked Harriet.

Jeanne Darrow was smiling. She liked Whiting's spirit. He had gone along with the joke, and now he was making it his own. He seemed completely indifferent to the cold or the danger of the powerful winter surf.

Whiting could feel the undertow, but the sense of danger had excited him and the cold had invigorated him. A wave lifted him, spun him down into its wash, and slammed him onto the hard-packed bottom. He cupped a hand over his testicles and wrapped an arm around his head and surrendered to the power of the wave. It bounced him along the bottom like a pebble. He was aware of nothing but sensation, movement, and flashes of silver light each time he turned toward the surface. For an instant, a thought was in front of him, as clear as the flashes of light: He had overcome his illness; he had never been sick.

He stayed in the water for ten minutes, tumbling, diving, and body-surfing. He caught a wave just before it crested, extended his arms and legs so that his body was rigid, and rode in triumph to the beach. Kelly and David were still waiting for him.

"I bet it's a lousy joke, even when it works," said Whiting, Then he sprinted across the beach to the patio.

Howard Rudermann and Ben Volker began to applaud.

"Hey, David," shouted Laura Keebler. "Didn't you know that trick only works on creeping weenies?"

"And Kelly Hammerstein wastes her best performance in a joke that flops," added Rudermann.

Jeanne flipped Whiting a towel and smiled. Whiting bowed to her and to the rest of the crowd. He was beginning to feel the rush that came after a cold swim. In the icy water, the blood retreated from the outer layers of skin and the vessels shrank. Now the blood was forcing its way back to the surface. His whole body tingled.

"What'll you have to drink, Whiting?" asked Jeanne.

"Margarita," he said.

The pitcher on the bar was empty. Jeanne swept it up and went into the house for a refill.

"I gotta tell you, we were stringin' you along," said Ben Volker. *143*

"I bet you only pull that on easterners in the middle of winter." Whiting threw the towel around his neck.

"And not too often," said Rudermann.

"And what's most impressive," said Volker, raising his voice, "is that you handled that surf just a few months after major surgery."

"Tell us what kind of operation it was, Ben," said Nancy Wright.

Whiting brought the towel across his abdomen to cover the top half of the scar, which showed above the swimsuit. "An appendectomy," he said.

"It's no appendectomy," said Volker. "Judging from the curve of it, I'd say it's a kidney transplant or something."

"Kidney transplant!" cried Vicki Rogers. "How exotic." Then she pulled off her glasses and looked around. "Do any of you remember when Roger tried to get us to sign organ donor cards?"

"Yeah," said Kelly as she toweled off. "Really gross."

"Well, he had one of his own signed already. And"—she took one of her dramatic-pause deep breaths—"when he died, they took his organs."

Howard Rudermann grinned at Whiting. "You don't have Roger's kidneys do you?"

Whiting shook his head nervously. "No way."

Volker snickered. "He may have one of them."

"Donors are never revealed to recipients, Ben," said Harriet. "You know that."

"But what a story," laughed Vicki Rogers. "Roger Darrow's kidney transplanted into Jeanne Darrow's latest boyfriend."

"Someone," said Vaughn Lawrence, "should tell the poor girl that they might be able to transplant Roger's kidneys, but they could never transplant his cock."

The laughter skittered across the patio, then stopped abruptly as a pitcher of Margaritas smashed on the concrete. Jeanne Darrow was standing just outside the door. "You son of a bitch."

Lawrence looked at her, then smiled at Whiting.

The animal energy was still pounding through Whiting's body. His response was a reflex. He launched his right fist at Lawrence's jaw. It glanced off Lawrence's forearm and bounced off Lawrence's mouth. It was not a good punch—James Whiting had not

144struck anyone since the sixth grade—but it was enough. Vaughn Lawrence stumbled backward, tripped over a chaise lounge, and fell into the whirlpool.

17

I've been waiting for somebody to punch that guy in the face since the first time I saw him wink at a camera," said Harriet.

The Mercedes was speeding south along the Coast Road. Jeanne Darrow was driving. Harriet was in the passenger seat, sitting on Whiting's lap.

"I thought that Wheeler guy would die," said Whiting.

"You would, too, if you were getting a hand job in a whirlpool and a game-show host fell on top of you," laughed Harriet.

"I just hope I didn't spoil the party," said Whiting.

"You did fine. We're both proud of you." Harriet patted his head.

They dropped Harriet at her apartment in Santa Monica, then went back to Pacific Palisades. It was four-thirty and getting dark when they arrived.

Jeanne suggested some tennis. She said she needed exercise. Whiting responded that he was a little rusty.

"Volley for half an hour, and I'll take you to dinner at one of Roger's favorite restaurants."

Whiting needed no further coaxing. She was inviting him to take another step into her world. Perhaps she was doing it because he had traveled so far, or she had been touched by his moment of chivalry, or perhaps she liked him. He wasn't sure. But he had been seduced by the beauty and richness of her world, by the ephemeral image of the man who had been at its center, and by the woman herself. Like any man surrendering to seduction, he was drawn on by the promise of pleasure, the hope of possession, and he ignored the warnings: that this world could be an unfriendly place, boiling with envy and deceit, that the image of Roger Darrow might hypnotize him if he gazed at it for too long, and that Jeanne Darrow was a troubled and uncertain woman.

They played tennis for an hour and a half, with Whiting wearing one of Roger Darrow's sweat suits. He played surprisingly well and won the second set. But Jeanne took the third with a barrage of powerful serves and paralyzing lobs. They finished the match under the court lights, with the temperature slipping down through the fifties. Then they went into the house to shower.

In the guest bath, Jeanne set out fresh towels, a new razor blade, and a small ice bucket containing a bottle of Olympia beer.

"Pamper yourself," she said, "and I'll do the same." She told him where he could find more beers, and she said she'd meet him downstairs in twenty minutes.

In her bedroom Jeanne Darrow dropped her clothes on the floor. As she turned toward the bathroom, she glimpsed herself in the mirror on the closet door. She was beautiful, smart, and, at the moment, more vulnerable than she had ever been in her life. But she sensed that she could trust the stranger down the hall. Because he was indebted to her husband for his life, he was, if anything, more vulnerable than she was.

After his shower, Whiting shaved and gave himself a splash of the Old Spice he found in the medicine chest. Then he put on the poplin trousers and Lacoste shirt he had worn to the party, finished his beer, and pulled on his yellow crew-neck sweater. In the kitchen, he took another Olympia out of the refrigerator, sipped, and glanced at his watch. Jeanne was still upstairs. He sipped again and looked around.

A designer kitchen," he thought. *A unique living experience in the heart of your home. A unique reflection of your personality. Kitchens by M'Sieur.* He had written copy like that himself. He didn't see anything of Roger Darrow's personality in the blue refrigerator or the aluminum colander hanging on the rack above his head. And yet, he sensed that Roger Darrow still lingered in the house.

He sipped his beer and looked at his watch. Jeanne would be another ten minutes getting ready. He looked down the darkened hallway that led from the kitchen to the rooms along the rear of the house. If she had wanted him to explore, he thought, she would have left the lights on. He sipped his beer. He looked at his watch. He stepped into the darkness.

His eyes adjusted. He passed the bathroom on the right, and then the game room. The living room door was on his left, and the baby grand piano was silhouetted in the front windows. But he was drawn, almost magnetically, to the room at the end of the hallway. The door was closed. He pushed it open.,

He did not believe in ghosts, telepathy, or psychic phenomena. He found it difficult enough to believe in an afterlife. But some rooms retained a presence, and a past. This, he knew, had been Roger Darrow's room. He stood in the darkness of the threshold and tried to feel Roger Darrow around him, see Darrow's shadow moving among the shadows of the furniture.

He flipped on the light. He saw an ornate mahogany desk, a leather chesterfield, dark paneling, bookcases, a wall covered with photographs. A television and video cassette player, a fireplace, and, above the mantel, a painting that James Whiting knew very well.

The scene is on the Grand Banks. The little dory rises against the swell. The cargo, two giant halibut, flat and white, fill the stern, weighing it down so that the gunwales almost touch the water. The fisherman, in oilskin and sou'wester, holds to his oars and studies the horizon. The schooner, his refuge, has raised sail, and the fogbank is racing to engulf her. There is a trace of fear in the fisherman's face, for he knows that if the fog moves too fast, he will be lost. But there is determination in the square of the shoulders and the tilt of the head. He will pull at the oars, and he will survive.

An excellent print of Winslow Homer's *Fog Warning* hung on the wall of Roger Darrow's study. Three thousand miles away, another print hung on the wall of James Whiting's office. Whiting was almost willing to believe that it was more than coincidence.

He looked at the photographs on the wall behind the desk: Roger Darrow shaking hands with Alfred Hitchcock; Roger and Jeanne embracing beneath a rose arbor on their wedding day. An autographed photo of Magic Johnson driving to the basket; a black-and-white shot of a little boy who looked like Darrow, standing with his parents in front of a farmhouse; Darrow and Howard Rudermann in tuxedoes, holding their Emmy Awards; a polaroid of Darrow and Robert Kennedy on a beach and the inscription, "To My Friend Roger, All my thanks for your work in the California campaign. Bob Kennedy, June 4, 1968."

"Are you looking for my husband?" Jeanne Darrow appeared in the doorway. She was again wearing jeans, turtleneck, and boots to good effect.

Whiting gestured to the pictures. "He lived quite a life. Rich, successsful, a major force in American television for more than a decade . . ."

She leaned against the doorjamb and folded her arms. "He once said that the two main functions of American television were to anesthetize and sell. It was like surgery. He put the patient to sleep, and the adman performed the operation."

Another little link thought Whiting. "He still accomplished a tremendous amount in a very tough field. And in a very short time."

"It sounds like you envy him."

"I guess I'd envy any man what he had . . . what he did."

"Don't," she said sharply.

Then, Jeanne Darrow smelled Old Spice. For an instant, the man standing on the other side of the study became someone else. She suggested that she cook dinner at home. It would be more relaxing, and she realized that she wanted her husband's scent to linger in the house.

She cooked *huevos rancheros*, a Mexican egg dish, and set the table on the kitchen counter. They drank Olympia, they ate slowly, and they talked. Jeanne heard a history of James Whiting's illness. Whiting heard the story of Jeanne Darrow's failed acting career. He talked of his safe, self-centered childhood as the son of two successful real estate agents from Brookline, Boston's rich neighbor. She described her childhood in the town of Anaheim, where on summer nights she sat on her lawn and watched the fireworks at Disneyland and dreamed of becoming famous. He admitted that his adult life, had also been safe, self-centered, and unfulfilling. His greatest achievement had been the slogan "Consider the Alternative: Sullivan Brothers Funeral Services." She told him that most people in southern California became either confirmed dreamers believing in all the myths manufactured there or cold-eyed realists reacting to the fantasy dancing around the rim of their lives. Somehow, she said, she had developed into a mixture of both, and Roger had always inspired the dreamer in her. He did not tell her of his impotence. She did not tell him of all the reasons behind her husband's journey.

But she did tell him about the video tapes.

During the course of the meal, they relaxed with each other. She no longer noticed the Old Spice. He no longer felt like a supplicant begging for whatever attention she might give. They

ing dessert, she made the decision that Whiting had been hoping
for.

"Would you like to meet my husband?"

She led him into the study once more. She took a videocassette
from the wall safe, turned on the television, and inserted one of
the tapes. She did not know if she was playing the dreamer or the
realist, but she was letting the stranger come closer.

When Roger Darrow first appeared on the hill above the
Golden Gate Bridge, James Whiting felt the magnetism. He liked
Roger Darrow the moment he saw the smile. And for the first time,
he thought he appreciated the tragedy of Darrow's loss.

Darrow introduced his tape and described his objectives. Then,
the scene changed.

*The San Francisco Peninsula is seen from the Berkeley Hills.
It looks like a toy cutout silhouetted against a reddening sky.*

Darrow steps into the shot and looks at the camera.

*"I've begun in San Francisco because it commands the edge of
the continent, and no American odyssey is complete without a
beginning or an ending at the Pacific. Moreover, Andrew Mac-
Gregor owns several cable franchises in the Bay Area, and whenever he has sought to establish another, he has always had the
political support of a former assemblyman by the name of Reuben
Merrill. Now one of the most powerful congressmen in Washington, Reuben Merrill remains a close friend of Andrew MacGregor
and the recipient of MacGregor's televised editorial support on a
wide variety of issues.*

Cut.

*Late-spring runoff tumbles down a rocky creekbed. Ponderosa
pines grow along the banks and granite ridges rise in the background.*

*"This is Chilnualna Creek," says Darrow. "Eventually this
water will flow into San Francisco toilets."*

*The camera pans to a beautiful, modern house, with large
decks and walls of glass, sited in a grove of pines. It is stained
dark brown so that it blends into the shadows.*

Cut.

The camera is looking out from the deck now, toward the creekbed. Roger Darrow steps into the shot. He is wearing hiking shorts and a bush jacket. "We are now at Congressman Reuben Merrill's mountain retreat, in a place called Wawona, about twenty miles from the Yosemite Valley. Congressman Merrill, who is also a member of the House Subcommittee on Telecommunications and Cable, has graciously consented to take time off from his vacation to discuss Andrew MacGregor, the cable television industry, and the merger of MacGregor Communications with Lawrence/Sunshine Productions."

Reuben Merrill enters the shot. He is wearing tennis shorts and a yellow jersey. He shakes hands with Darrow and they both sit in deck chairs, with the camera shooting over Darrow's shoulder. After small talk about the Dodgers and Giants, who are playing a game that afternoon, Darrow leads the discussion onto the topic.

"You're pretty conservative when it comes to government interference in the various forms of pay and cable, aren't you, Congressman?"

The eyebrows furrow. "A new industry is expanding in the private sector, Mr. Darrow. They use private wires and privately financed satellites. It shouldn't be like over-the-air television, where the FCC regulates everything as the protector of the public trust. If it's private, leave it alone, as long as no laws or statutes are violated."

"That's a position quite similar to one taken by Andrew MacGregor," says Darrow.

Merrill studies Darrow for a moment and picks at one of his eyebrows. "Great minds think alike, Mr. Darrow. I want everyone to get a crack without the government riding their backs. I want fortunes to be made in cable television. I want to see men of vision outsmart their competition, buy the right franchises, produce the programming that the public wants, and make fortunes."

"It's pretty tough for individuals to make money when they're in competition with corporate giants like Times-Mirror or Westinghouse or with powerful private companies like MacGregor Communications."

Merrill laughs. "Now there's where you're wrong. Cable offers so much and needs so much that everyone has a shot."

"Is that why a big company like MacGregor Communications

tried to gobble up Lawrence/Sunshine Productions?"

Merrill looks at Darrow the way a dog looks at a hydrant. "It's business, Mr. Darrow. Big fish are always looking for tasty little fish to swallow, but the good thing about our system is that the little fish can get rich in the bargain."

"The way this merger looks, Vaughn Lawrence may get quite a lot of power as well."

Merrill nods. He gives nothing away.

"Don't you find the joining of one of the largest cable delivery corporations in the country with one of the most rapidly expanding production companies to be rather unusual?"

Merrill shrugs. "It's all legal. What do you want me to say about it?"

Darrow laughs, almost a snicker. "That's the first time I've ever met a politician at a loss for words."

"I'm on vacation." The eyebrows furrow, and then Merrill is silent.

For several moments, neither man speaks. The tension hisses in the static on the tape. Darrow shifts in his seat, but Reuben Merrill does not move or say a word. He knows the rhetorical power of silence.

After a time, Darrow says, "An alliance like that gives both companies more power, wouldn't you say?"

"Of course. That's why they're planning to merge."

"And what do you think they're planning to do with their power?"

Merrill laughs, but he is becoming annoyed. "Beat the competition."

More silence, more tension on the tape. Darrow seems to fidget for a moment, looking down at his notes, then again at Merrill. "Maybe they have higher objectives than that."

Merrill smiles, but the eyebrows remain furrowed. "Tell me about them."

"Well," Darrow takes a deep breath. He sounds nervous. "Andrew MacGregor supported your candidacy the first time you ran, and he has been supporting you ever since. Now, on several of the television stations that he owns in California, he is saying, and I quote from one of the editorials, 'It's about time that more Americans had the benefit of Merrill's strong leadership and philosophical fortitude.'"

Merrill nods. "I have supporters all over California and all across the country. Andrew MacGregor is just one of them. And I can assure you that my only objective is to serve the people of my own district."

"I'm just trying to make a few connections, Congressman, between the people with financial power and the people with political power." Darrow pauses. "And the way one group helps the other."

Merrill sits back and stares at Darrow. The anger throbs in the little vein above his left eyebrow. "I won't even dignify that." Then he looks at the person sitting outside of camera range and says, "Jimmy, I thought this guy wanted to talk about cable and satellite."

"That's what we are talking about, Congressman," says Darrow. "The whole communications revolution. And right at the heart of it is the question of political power. The people who control cable television will have a tremendous tool for influencing the way that people think. Vaughn Lawrence believes that. Andrew MacGregor believes that. I'll bet you believe that, too. And as long as your policies are the kind that MacGregor supports, he'll support you, and throw all his weight behind you."

"Thank you, Mr. Darrow. You've had your speech, and I agree: People support the politicians they believe give them the best representation. That's why Andrew MacGregor and Vaughn Lawrence support me. Now, if you don't mind . . ." He stands.

Darrow's silhouette does not move. "I'd like to ask you a couple of more questions, Congressman, about two-way television."

"I've been in Congress for twelve years, Mister, and no one has ever impugned my ethics about anything. I don't intend to permit you the opportunity to start." He looks to his assistant. "Jimmy, turn that thing off and show this guy the door."

Blank tape.

Cut.

The camera seems to be floating above the treetops of Yosemite Valley. It pans from Yosemite Falls, across the rugged rock face of El Capitan, to Nevada Falls. The sunlight creates shadows that seem to dance as the camera moves. The colors are green, blue, and the silver of rock and falling water. But the television screen can do little to convey the majesty of the half-mile-high rocks or the vantage point that Darrow has chosen.

Then the camera readjusts and is locked down. There is a large
boulder in the foreground and, beyond it, the rim of the valley.
Roger Darrow enters the shot. He sits on the boulder and gestures
over at the granite mass on the other side of the valley. "That's El
Capitan," says Darrow. "It's a lot more beautiful when you see it
from the Ansel Adams angle at the end of the valley, but I like the
view from up here on Dewey Point, because damn few people have
seen it head on, right at eye level with the top."

Darrow laughs. "I guess I made that congressman pretty mad.
I must have asked the right questions."

He scratches the back of his neck. "The fact that he's between
the sheets with Andrew MacGregor shouldn't really hurt him.
MacGregor's a good ally to have, and so is Vaughn Lawrence.

Then there is a pause. Darrow stares over at El Capitan. His
mood is changing. He pulls his knees up against his chest, wraps
his arms around his legs and asks wistfully, "Why are people
always drawn back to places that have good memories for them?
We made love on this rock, Jeannie, in case you've forgotten."

Whiting looked nervously at Jeanne. "He's talking directly to
you."

She nodded. "He does that from time to time. It's all part of the
journey."

"Are you sure you want me to see this? It's pretty personal."

"It's my husband. Isn't he what you came for?"

Whiting turned back to the screen.

"We'd only known each other for three or four months when
we found this rock. We were still in that crazy time when we
couldn't get enough of each other.

"There's a moment in every love affair when it happens. You
realize that you may really like each other, then something clicks
and you can't keep your hands to yourself. It would be nice if the
crazy time lasted, but if it did, modern man would never have
built the Golden Gate Bridge or found a cure for smallpox or
produced the last four seasons of 'Flint.'" Darrow laughs. "Be-
cause he would have been too busy making love to modern
woman."

The shadows are lengthening and the face of El Capitan is
turning a subtle shade of red.

"People who love each other are supposed to have a pretty good

jump on life, Jeanne, because together they can face things that would destroy them if they were alone. And God knows, we faced our share."

Then he swings his legs off the rock and stands. He seems suddenly angry. "So what the hell am I doing up here all alone, without you?"

A cloud blocks out the sun. El Capitan turns a dark, ominous gray. Darrow waits until the cloud passes. His anger sinks back beneath a surface that seems smooth and settled.

He stares straight into the camera, as though trying to look into his wife's eyes. "The first time I met Miranda Blake, it was a Sunday afternoon. Harriet brought her to play tennis. Before Miranda, I had never been unfaithful, Jeannie, no matter what anybody says." He jams his hands into his pockets. "And it wasn't Miranda's fault, either. It was chemistry. She was young and beautiful and she gave me the chance to prove myself again, especially after the fertility boys gave me the bad news."

Whiting glanced at Jeanne and felt the bonds tightening. He was impotent, and Roger Darrow had been sterile. Perhaps they had known fears and frustrations they both could understand. He wondered if he should tell Jeanne of his impotence.

The sun is setting quickly. El Capitan is turning deep red behind him. He gazes out over the valley. "God, it's beautiful. The first men who saw this place must have held their breath in contemplation of its wonder."

Then his attention and gaze jump back to the camera. "I stood by you when you woke up one morning and realized you couldn't act worth a damn, but I don't expect you to stand by me now. When I promised to break it off with Miranda and try to pull our lives together, you didn't give me much encouragement. Instead, you went off looking for lovers of your own. But why did you have to screw—he almost spits the name—"Vaughn Lawrence?"

Whiting looked at Jeanne. "Vaughn Lawrence?" he whispered. She nodded. "Anger makes some strange bedfellows."

For a few moments, Jeanne Darrow and James Whiting stared at the screen. Then Jeanne flipped on the desk lamp and looked at Whiting. "Miranda Blake was a young actress who played bit parts on television shows like 'Flint.' She had an affair with my husband for six months. When it was over, she packed up and moved back to New York. That's all you need to know about her." Jeanne spoke without bitterness. "You'll have to work much harder to know Roger and me."

James Whiting could think of nothing to say.

She had allowed him much more than a glimpse of her husband and his final journey. She had let him look into their most private lives. She had allowed him an intimacy he had never expected.

"Does he talk like that on every tape?" asked Whiting after a time.

"He talks about whatever comes into his head," answered Jeanne. "About politics, our life together . . . he never intended these tapes for public consumption. They were his private journal and his personal look at America. If there were passages he thought he could use later, he planned to simply lift them out of the private material."

Whiting looked back at the screen. He felt overwhelmed.

"What did you think?" she asked.

He studied her for a moment, trying to read her face. He did not know if she was asking for approval or testing his responses to see if he was worthy to view the rest of the tapes. He decided to be honest.

"He's pretty impressive on the screen."

She nodded.

"And not a bad interviewer."

She nodded again.

"Although his monologue kept jumping around"—he took a breath—"and he must have had an ego the size of El Capitan."

She laughed. "Right on all counts. He was magnetic and brilliant and befuddled, and there were times when you couldn't help but think that he was the original pompous ass."

"I liked him," said Whiting softly. "I'd like to know more about him, big ego and all."

Her smile faded. She rested her chin on her hands. "I believe you would, Mr. Whiting. And I think you'd try to appreciate him."

18

"Famous Hollywood talent gets killed in a boating accident. One of his kidneys is transplanted into bored adman, who comes to Hollywood to meet the hot shot's family." Howard Rudermann sat back and sipped his white wine.

"Don't tell Vicki Rogers," said Whiting. "She called me at my hotel this morning and started pumping me for information. I told her that the identity of the donor was nobody's business."

"My lips are sealed," promised Rudermann. He had invited Whiting to lunch at MGM, where he was renting studio space for "A New Flag", his miniseries about the Revolution.

"I'm just trying to protect Jeanne Darrow's privacy," Whiting added.

"You can trust me." Rudermann rested his elbow on the table and looked into Whiting's eyes, as though trying to take measure of him. "Now, at this point in the story conference, we'd say, 'Which way do we take this character now?' Does he go home and go back to work, satisfied that he's said thanks?"

Whiting dropped his knife and fork and listened. He did not like this synopsis of his life, but he sensed that Rudermann was a compulsive talker, the type who abhorred silence in any conversation.

"Or," continued Rudermann, "Does he become so obsessed that he tries to become the donor, take up the donor's profession and his crusades, and take up with the donor's wife."

"You Hollywood people may not have good imaginations, but they're certainly active." Whiting picked up his knife and fork and poked again at his sand dabs.

"Hell," said Rudermann. "I wouldn't blame anybody for being interested in Roger. He was quite a guy. . . . I miss him like hell." Then, for a moment, Rudermann chewed at his lower lip and looked into his glass.

Whiting glanced around at the MGM commissary and gave

Rudermann a moment to swallow his emotions. The walls were
institution green, the lighting direct and unpleasant. Some of the
tables in the executive section were covered, most were bare. The
ceiling was high and slightly vaulted, and the place looked like the
movie set for an old Hayes-Bickford cafeteria. Except for the
mural.

On the wall at the end of the room, Leo the Lion reclined in
the pose he had taken at the end of every MGM film during the
thirties. The power today, thought Whiting, might reside with the
television networks and conglomerates based in New York, but he
was sitting in one of Hollywood's shrines.

"You must've seen a lot here over the years," said Whiting.

Rudermann looked up like an old man startled from some
dream of youth. "Me? Oh, no. I wasn't at Metro in the old days. I
was at Warners from thirty-seven right up to the sixties. We had
our share of stars, but *this* place, can you imagine what it must
have been like on a good day in 1939? George Cukor studying a
script. Groucho Marx insulting producers in the corner. Clark
Gable reading the *Racing Form*. Max Steiner whistling a new tune
while he ate his soup. Scott Fitzgerald sucking on a Coke, trying
to get up the courage to go back to the Writers' Building without
a drink . . ." He shook his head and smiled, as though he were
recalling his first love. "And the movies . . . *The Wizard of Oz,
Northwest Passage, Gone with the Wind* . . ."

"I suppose you're going to tell me they don't make them like
that anymore."

"They damn well don't." Rudermann seemed to rise from his
chair, then he sat back and shrugged. "But, what are you gonna
do? The whole world's changed. Not just the movies. If you want
to survive, you gotta change with it. That's why I got into cable."

The waitress brought two coffees and the check. Rudermann
signed for the meal and looked at his watch. "They should be just
about ready over on the Delaware River. C'mon. I'll show you some
Hollywood magic."

They walked briskly through the maze of narrow roadways and
alleys, past the office buildings where writers once labored on the
MGM assembly line, along the windowless walls of sound stages
and screening rooms, past standing sets that Whiting remembered
from scores of films but barely recognized in the bleaching sun.

There were three pictures shooting on the lot, one studio production and two independents renting space. Actors, extras and stagehands were hurrying about in the maze. Directors and executives rode in golf carts; anyone else on wheels rode a bicycle. At stage doors, knots of extras clustered in the sunshine. Redcoated soldiers from "A New Flag" huddled around the lunch wagon. Two-headed aliens from an MGM science-fiction film played cards on a packing crate. And James Whiting managed to be casual about it all. When Robert Redford ambled by, Whiting didn't look twice.

"And so," said Rudermann as they walked, "Jeanne Darrow seems pretty interested in you."

"Is that why you invited me to lunch?"

"Of course not. This is my way of saying thanks. You were the hit of the show yesterday."

They went a bit farther, then Rudermann stopped and grabbed Whiting by the sleeve. "I want you to be careful with that girl, Mister. She looks tough, but she's pretty fragile."

"We're all fragile," said Whiting.

"I don't want anybody taking advantage of her," answered Rudermann. "After six months, she's probably ready for someone to put a pair of arms around her. If you're the one, I want it to happen because you like each other. Not because she thinks you're the last piece of Roger Darrow left on earth or because you laid out some Hollywood celebrity who insulted her."

Whiting wanted to get angry, but he couldn't. "I think I know why you've stayed around this business for so long."

"Why?"

Whiting smiled. "Because you say something that should get you a sock in the nose, and it comes out sounding like fatherly advice."

Rudermann clapped Whiting on the shoulder and laughed. "That's because I'm *old* enough to be your father."

They turned another corner and stopped at a stage door. "This is why we rented space at MGM," said Rudermann. "The biggest studio tank in town."

Inside, a flotilla of boats and bateaux bobbed on a body of water about the size of a football field. A cyclorama wrapped around the far end of the tank. Lighting could make it look like the sky at dawn or in the dead of night. At the shallow end of the tank, trees grew along a riverbank, which was covered in white fluff that

photographed like snow. On the other side of the tank were two
wind machines and a compressor for making fog. A few electricians were stringing cable along the catwalks above the tank. Everyone else was at lunch.

The set was cavernous and quiet. Like a church, thought Whiting, after the service had ended. And Howard Rudermann was a pilgrim to the altar.

"I've waited twenty years to see this set," he said, almost in a whisper. "That's how long I've owned the rights to the book."

He walked to the edge of the tank. "Tomorrow we shoot the river crossing. Peter Cross plays John Trumbull. We see the whole Revolution through his eyes. He's a rower on Washington's boat when they cross the Delaware. He marches on Ticonderoga. He's at Saratoga and Monmouth . . ."

"He likes horse racing?" cracked Whiting.

"The battles, smartass."

Rudermann stepped onto one of the bateaux moored at the side of the tank and began to pace back and forth on the flat deck. "Roger should be part of all this. He's the one who pulled the script for 'Redgates' together. If it wasn't as good as it is, I wouldn't be making 'A New Flag,' and we wouldn't be running a big 'Redgates' premiere for all the cable distributors next week in New York."

Rudermann shook his head and continued to pace. He seemed angry. "In times like these, people want to look to the past. It's safe and distant, and it tells us that no matter how bad things get, we always pull through. People aren't interested in documentaries about how screwed up this country is. That's a waste."

Whiting sensed that all afternoon, Rudermann had been talking in a wide arc that was leading toward Darrow's videotapes. "Do you mean 'One Man's America?' "

Rudermann nodded. "If I'd been able to steer him off, he'd still be alive, and I wouldn't be worrying about Jeannie."

"I'd still be on dialysis," added Whiting.

Rudermann stopped pacing and walked over to Whiting. "Maybe you should just thank God you don't have to worry about that anymore. Then go to El Cholo for some good Mexican, take the tour at Universal Studios, and get on a plane and go the hell home."

Whiting was surprised by the sudden hostility. "I thought you were giving out fatherly advice. That sounds like a threat."

"Harriet told me Jeanne showed you one of the tapes. What did you do to rate that?"

Whiting shrugged. "I'm a nice guy, I guess."

Rudermann jabbed a finger at Whiting. "You may be what you say you are, mister, but that doesn't mean you can't be some cheap hustler along with it, thinkin' you can come out here and get in tight with the widow and soak up some of Roger's talent and ideas along the way."

"I came here because I wanted to thank Jeanne Darrow," said Whiting politely. "And right now, I'd like to grab those gold chains you're wearing around your neck and choke you with them."

Rudermann took a step backward and studied Whiting warily. When he was sure that Whiting would not follow through on his threat, he stepped up off the bateau so that he was on eye level with Whiting. "I may sound like a wise guy, and you may have a right to get mad, but I'm just tryin' to protect Jeannie and Roger's memory. I'm also protecting you, whether you know it or not."

"Along with your rights to 'One Man's America?'"

Before Rudermann could respond there was a commotion at the entrance and the assistant director hurried onto the sound stage. "Howard!" he shouted, "We've been looking all over for you. Peter's having a tantrum. He won't come onto the set.

Rudermann nodded and waved the young man away. Then he turned again to Whiting. "I have to go. Look around for a while, at the tank and the little forest and the lights and the wind machines, and then try to imagine what it will look like on television—Washington crossing the Delaware on a frozen December night two hundred years ago."

He took Whiting's hand and shook it. "And remember, no matter what you've seen on the tapes, in this business, there's often less to things than meets the eye."

That evening, Jeanne Darrow returned from work at six o'clock, after an exhausting day that included three car accidents; two cardiac arrests, one fatal; and a cat caught in a tree. The black Ferrari in her driveway was the last thing she wanted to see. Vaughn Lawrence was leaning against it.

"Hello, Jeannie." He was wearing a black turtleneck and Levis and puffing a cigarette. He looked like a commando or a second-story man.

"The answer is no," she said as she hurried toward the front door."

"You haven't heard the question." He began to follow her.

"It's either the question you asked yesterday or you've finally decided to start bothering me about the tapes." She unlocked the door and stepped into her foyer.

"May I come in?"

She flipped on the outdoor lights. "What are you after, Vaughn?"

"They say that you're showing Roger's videotapes to strangers, like the guy who sucker-punched me yesterday."

Jeanne noticed that Vaughn Lawrence's lower lip was swollen. She smiled. "Just the first tape."

"I'm sorry for what I said yesterday." Lawrence tried to flash his grin but stopped at half-smile and brought his hand to his lip.

"Who told you about the tapes?" she asked. "Rudermann?"

Lawrence nodded. "He was a little upset that you didn't show them to him first."

"He'll get over it. Now, if you don't mind, I'm exhausted."

Lawrence leaned against the doorframe so that she couldn't close the door. "I've always been interested in those tapes because Roger talks about me on them."

"He talks about a lot of things, Vaughn, but you were a big topic because he didn't like you," she said gently. "He thought you were a no-good bastard long before you and I used each other. You were one of the main reasons he went on that jaunt. The night before he left, he said to me that Andrew MacGregor had always shown good judgment, good sense, and good taste, until he tangled with you. He said you had something that MacGregor wanted and he was going to find out what it was."

Lawrence reached out and touched Jeanne's face. She tensed but did not recoil.

"He didn't have to go traipsing all over the country, Jeannie. You could have told him all about what I've got."

She slapped the hand away.

Lawrence's eyes opened wide for a moment, then dropped again to half-mast. "You did that the first time I touched your face." He started to step into the house.

She closed the door on his foot. "What do you want, Vaughn?"

"I think you owe it to me to let me see those tapes," he said evenly. "If his wife had stayed faithful to him, Roger wouldn't have had a reason to go after Vaughn Lawrence."

"I don't owe you anything, and I was as faithful to him as he was to me."

Lawrence tried to smile again. "That's a low blow to poor Rodge. Just tell me this, now that you've seen all the tapes: What did he say about me?"

"Less and less. By the time he got to Maine, he didn't give a damn about you or MacGregor, no matter what he thought you were up to."

"Is that how you feel about the tapes."

"I don't give a damn about you either."

Lawrence stared at her blankly.

"Does that satisfy you?" she asked sharply.

"It'll have to." He turned to leave, then stopped. "One more thing. Why, after seven months, did you decide to show the tapes first to a complete stranger?"

"Two reasons. I needed someone with a fresh perspective, and he had just demonstrated the good sense to punch you in the mouth."

After a few moments, Vaughn Lawrence offered her his hand. "I've admired you these last months, Jeanne. Roger was a lucky man."

She slipped her hand into his. He brought it to his lips and kissed it delicately. Then he turned and disappeared into the black Ferrari.

The man with the snake's eyes could be a charmer, she thought, but his visit disturbed her in the way that his presence had always disturbed her husband. Vaughn Lawrence was not to be trusted. For six months, she had expected to find her house rifled, the wall safe opened, and the tapes gone. But Vaughn Lawrence had chosen to wait, then to approach her like this, as an old and admiring lover. Now that he had made his move, she knew that he would be back.

She decided that she needed advice. She called Harriet and asked her over for a drink. "I'm going to invite Whiting, too," she added.

"Can I bring anything?" asked Harriet.

"Your eyeglasses. I'm running the tapes."

That evening James Whiting, Jeanne Darrow, and Harriet
Sears sat in the study and traveled with Roger Darrow across
America.

From Yosemite, Darrow headed to Jackson Hole, Wyoming,
where he attended a debate between Senator Thomas Sylbert and
a conservative lawyer. The topic was Wyoming land policy; the
debate was carried on a MacGregor cable station and the viewers
used Responsible to register their responses. In Iowa, he returned
to the town where he had grown up, in a county now wired for
cable by MacGregor Communications. He met one of the men who
had helped mold his youth, and he found cause for despair in the
heartland. In Youngstown, Ohio, he appeared on a program owned
by MacGregor, the Billy Singer "Good-Time Gospel Hour". There
he confronted the famous Evangelist and his own loss of faith.

By the time he reached New York, Roger Darrow's journey
had become a pilgrimage into his own soul. He did not bother to
attend the National Cable Television Association Convention,
which had been his goal in New York. He cancelled his appointment with Professor Josh Wyler, Columbia University media expert and longtime MacGregor-watcher. Instead, he went hunting
for Miranda Blake as though she were the only hope left in a
darkening world.

Finally, in Maine, he said he had found some perspective, a
place to confront himself.

When Roger Darrow again said, "I need that hope. I need a
child. I need . . ." and the final tape ran out, Jeanne turned off the
television and looked at her friends.

Harriet shook her head sadly. Whiting stared at the screen.

"Now you've seen them." Jeanne refilled the wine glasses on
the coffee table and took a deep breath. "Congressman Merrill
wants to see them. Howard Rudermann is sulking because I hav-
en't let him see them. Vaughn Lawrence has crawled out from
under his rock to take a look, too. What do I do?"

"Put the tapes back in the safe and forget about them," said
Harriet. "What ever is on them, they can't hurt you now."

"It's hard to turn off my emotions, Harriet, especially when I
listen to that last monologue from Maine." Jeanne walked over to
the fireplace. Birch logs were piled neatly on the grate. "He was
rejecting me."

"No, he wasn't," said Whiting, still staring at the screen. "He was frustrated. He was unhappy. He was looking for some kind of synthesis of everything he had found out about Merrill and Lawrence and MacGregor . . . and himself, but he couldn't nail it down. So he turned all of his frustrations onto his wife."

Jeanne brought her hand to her mouth and looked at the painting above the mantel.

Harriet glanced at Whiting. "None of that matters now. He's gone, and Jeanne should be getting on with her life."

"He loved this painting," Jeanne said dreamily. "He loved to think of himself like that fisherman, the loner, with his face to the wind, pulling against the tide."

"I'm afraid that at the end"—Harriet's fingers twined nervously around her necklace—"his dory had sprung a few holes."

Whiting's head snapped around.

Jeanne pivoted angrily. "I loved him, Harriet. I still love him. And if he'd given me half a chance to fight back, I never would have lost the son of a bitch."

"I can't believe what you said back there." Whiting was driving Harriet home. The visit had ended abruptly, with Jeanne infuriated and Harriet refusing to apologize.

"I was hard on her, but it's time that someone was," answered Harriet. "And it's time that you learned not to be so surprised by what people say and do, especially in this town."

"People are the same everywhere," said Whiting.

"Not here. Jeanne and Roger knew that. It was part of their problem. Here, life's temptations are all more refined." In the half-light cast by an oncoming car, she seemed ageless, as though she were still the Harriet Sears of pinup days. "The bodies that entice you are the most beautiful in the world."

Yes, he thought grudgingly, even an aging movie queen could still entice him.

"Everybody's always tanned. Everybody's in great physical condition. People wear the best clothes and drive the best automobiles . . ."

Whiting patted the dash of his rental and she laughed.

"Big deals are going down all over the place, and the scent of money hangs in the air like some kind of aphrodisiac gas. People are always turned on, and sex is just one more way to cut a deal, one more way to make it, one more way to stay there once you have made it."

She pulled an emery board from her purse and began to file her nails. Somehow, Whiting never imagined a sex goddess, even one past her prime, filing her nails.

"Roger Darrow is at the height of his career when he sees Miranda Blake," she said. "He is forty years old and childless and thinks that life is spinning past. He says to himself, if I could just make love to that young woman, I could steal a little bit of her youth and maybe she'd draw out of me the fatherhood that my wife has never been able to inspire."

Harriet changed hands with the emery board. "Jeanne Darrow thinks, I've faced failure in my career and pulled my life together. I have a rich, famous husband, but he's screwing someone else. I should do the same thing, just to let him know what it feels like. If I'm going to screw anyone, he should be rich, powerful, desirable, and someone my husband can't stand—Vaughn Lawrence." She said the name as though she were the announcer of a game show.

"Don't people ever do it because they love each other?" Whiting asked.

She stopped filing. "All the time. For every tale of philandering or revenge-fucking in Hollywood, there are stories of passionate love affairs lasting for years. Roger and Jeanne fell in love the week they met. They were in love when Miranda Blake happened along. They were still in love seven months ago."

Whiting was driving slowly. He knew the way, but he didn't want to reach her house until she finished talking.

"He also loved Miranda Blake," she added. "I could tell, just by looking at him."

"Just by looking at him?" Whiting laughed.

"My dear boy, I could tell because there was a time when he looked at *me* that way."

Whiting nearly went off the road.

Harriet kept her eyes straight ahead. "He was a twenty-year-old neophyte trying to sell a television script. I was a forty-year old actress recently divorced for the fourth time and feeling rather down on myself. He sent me the script. I read it. We had lunch. And he made a pass. I was probably the best-looking forty-year-old woman he'd ever seen. We made love that afternoon, and I saw to it that his script landed on Howard Rudermann's desk."

Harriet put the emery board away and closed her purse. "Roger Darrow got his job, and he and I enjoyed three months of the best sex I could remember. Unfortunately, he fell in love."

"With someone his own age?" asked Whiting.

"With *me!*" she shouted. "Fortunately, I was under contract to the American Shakespeare Festival in Connecticut. I went east to play Lady Macbeth and left him to find his Ophelias. When I returned, his ardor had cooled. I had no desire for a fifth marriage, especially to a young man who most certainly would have tired of me if I hadn't tired of him."

Harriet toyed with her necklace. "We became good friends and let the gossip-mongers be damned."

She directed him through the dark, quiet streets of Santa Monica to her apartment. When the car stopped, she reached for the door handle, then turned back to Whiting. "He loved them both, you know. He loved Jeanne because she was beautiful and smart and as steady as a gyroscope. Damn few women could look themselves in the mirror, realize they had no talent, and decide to reorganize their lives. Jeanne did. And he loved Miranda because she was beautiful and wild and completely unpredictable. At the moment when her career was about to burst open, she decided she hated Hollywood, packed up, and moved back east."

Harriet put a hand on Whiting's arm. "When Roger left Los Angeles, he simply wanted to find out which of them he loved more, and what he should do about it."

"Are you trying to tell me there's no greater importance on those tapes?" asked Whiting. "No political conspiracy?"

"There may be." Harriet shrugged, as though she didn't really care. "But Roger's own little world was what mattered to him, not electronic robber barons and Bay area congressmen."

She popped open the door. The dome light threw a shadow that made her look suddenly very old. "He said he was trying to define America at the dawn of the electronic age. That way, he turned his self-centered little journey into an epic of national discovery, filled with heroes and villains and plain folks being themselves." She squeezed Whiting's arm, "But for him, the real meat is in the soliloquys, and the real meaning is in that last little speech from Maine."

"I don't believe you," said Whiting.

She climbed out and closed the door. Then she poked her head in the window. She was milking her exit. "Never be surprised by the things people do to satisfy the itch between their legs," she said, "because usually, they're trying to satisfy a whole lot more. Especially in this town. Roger was looking for some kind of perfect love, someone to liberate him from all the frustation he felt and all the shit he saw around him."

"And loves like that don't exist for more than a few weeks?" offered Whiting.

She shook her head. "He was looking for Miranda. Whether he found her is no longer important. He should have concentrated on his wife and faced his problems like a man."

She reached in and took Whiting's hand in both of hers. "If you're looking for a lesson to draw from the Darrow tapes, that's it. Live your own life, and be nice to Roger Darrow's wife, because I think she likes you."

Harriet smiled and squeezed Whiting's hand. "If you need any further advice, I'll be at the Plaza in New York. I'm rehearsing a new play, and I have to appear at the 'Redgates' press screening next Friday."

As she went into the house, Whiting saw that one of the windows in her apartment was lit. Harriet saw it, too, but did not seem concerned. Someone was peering out. Whiting couldn't see his face, but from the build, the hairdo, and the stripes on the shirt, it looked like Howard Rudermann.

Perhaps Harriet still scratches Rudermann's itch, thought Whiting, or vice versa.

At night, the lights of Los Angeles seemed to expand endlessly, like a colony of plankton on some dark southern sea. James Whiting, driving the Santa Monica Freeway back to his hotel, felt that he was skimming safely along the surface after a day in the shifting currents.

He thought about Howard Rudermann's warning: In this town, there's often less to things than meets the eye. But sometimes, there is more.

Beneath the Hollywood exterior, a facade of confidence and rough-knocks sophistication, Howard Rudermann was frightened. The fear was quiet, vague, perhaps without reason, but Whiting had sensed it. Howard Ruderman was finally producing the films he had always considered worthy of his talents, and he was doing it without Roger Darrow looking over his shoulder. He had reached the pinnacle of his career. If nothing else, he feared falling. Or being pushed.

And in spite of the little talk they'd just had, Whiting had decided that if Harriet Sears was Jeanne Darrow's closest friend, Jeanne needed another friend. Harriet had not given Jeanne the best advice. Then, he thought, what right did he have to judge Jeanne Darrow's friends? Harriet had known Roger and Jeanne for longer than they had known each other. Whiting had met Jeanne Darrow just three days before, and he had seen Roger Darrow for a few hours on video tape.

But he felt that from those seven video tapes, he had begun to know Roger Darrow and understand his aspirations. After shooting the video tapes, Roger Darrow had given James Whiting another chance at life. Now, while visiting Darrow's world, James Whiting had found new vigor in the California surf, he had sensed the excitement of Hollywood on the MGM lot, he was feeling the liberation of speed as he drove through the Los Angeles night, and he had met a woman who attracted him in every way. He owed Roger Darrow's memory more than a simple thanks for the kidney.

Jeanne Darrow lay in bed, stared at the shadows on the ceiling, and listened to the empty house creak. Her anger at Harriet had abated, but it was growing toward her husband. He'd had no right to leave her, she thought, and no right to leave her with seven video tapes that now confounded her. Should she show them to the world, when she wasn't sure if he had uncovered anything that the world would care about? Or should she keep them to herself, because she did not want the world to witness his deterioration and her rejection?

Even in death, she thought, he would not let her go.

Then she heard a car roll into her driveway. A door slammed and footsteps crossed the walk. She felt a jolt of fear. The house was completely dark, and no one came to visit after eleven o'clock. She threw on her robe and peered out and recognized the car.

The lights came on in the foyer and then on the veranda.

"Somehow, I think I was expecting you," she said as she swung the door open.

James Whiting stepped into the house. "You told us tonight

that your husband never gave you the chance to win him back."

"Yes," she said. She was puzzled by the serious tone and the abrupt demeanor.

"Would you feel better if you at least found out what happened to him between here and Maine?"

"It might."

"Do you believe he meant it when he rejected you at the end of the tape?"

"I don't know what I believe about him anymore."

She thought she knew why Whiting had come back.

"Do you think he finished what he started?" Whiting had rehearsed every word on the drive from downtown.

She shook her head.

"Then help me to ask his questions again. We'll take a video camera, photograph his locations, interview the people he met, and find out what happened on his last trip."

"Why?" She liked the idea. She realized that she had been thinking about it herself.

Whiting stepped toward her and put his hands on her shoulders. The harsh foyer light was directly above his head. His face was in shadow. "Because he was telling us something. He wasn't sure what it was, but it was there. He was stacking dynamite around Lawrence and Merrill and MacGregor, but he just got too damn distracted by everything else to light it."

"It's 'everything else' that matters to me," she said.

"If he'd lived, he would've put it all together. We have to do it for him."

"Why?"

"Because it takes balls to set out all alone like that, no matter how you end up . . . and I owe him."

She nodded, as though she agreed, and a smile crossed her face. "The doctors were right."

"About what?"

"They said I'd expect things from you that I wouldn't ask of my closest friend."

'From now until Maine," he said firmly, "I *am* your closest friend."

She shook his hand. "Deal."

He held her hand in both of his. He wanted to kiss her, but he decided to wait.

FOUR

CHASING SHADOWS

19

Vaughn Lawrence drummed his fingers on his desk and glanced at the television set in the corner. "People and Prices" was playing with the sound turned down. "Breakfast with Vaughn" presented Lawrence as a chatty, well-informed neighbor, the perfect talkmaster. "People and Prices" told the world that Vaughn Lawrence was harmless, just another game-show host who kissed the female contestants and played mischievously sadistic games that everyone, including the victims, enjoyed. It was good to seem harmless. He liked the image. Once Lawrence/Sunshine Productions was firmly joined with Mac-Gregor Communications, he would leave the gameshow.

He had set aside a half hour to spend with Len Haley, and ten minutes were already gone. He was meeting programmers from his American Heritage network. He was planning to lunch with executives from a record company he hoped to acquire. He had no time to waste with private detectives.

"You've got seventeen minutes," he said when Len Haley finally arrived.

"Then pay attention." Len Haley sat down and opened the folder he was carrying. "Here's the Sullivan Detective Agency report on this Whiting." He began to read: "A copywriter with a Boston ad agency. No criminal record, three moving violations in the last five years. Good reputation. No wife, kids, or alimony. One mother, widowed, one sister married to insurance man. No bad debts. No balance on his MasterCard. Lives in a condo on Beacon Hill: mortgage, a hundred and twenty grand. Belongs to a Boston racquetball club, spends time with a girl named Patricia Benjamin. In perfect health before glomerulonephritis destroyed his kidneys a year and a half ago. Dialysis until kidney transplant two days after Darrow's accident. Six-month recovery has been successful. Strength and vigor have returned, although he has been examined by urologist for continued impotence."

"You guys sure can find out a lot."

"Anybody can," said Haley, "if they know where to look."

"And we can conclude that this guy is harmless, except for a sneaky right hand."

"In Nam, we used to say nothing was harmless unless it was dead," answered Haley. "But he's no threat to your sister's virginity."

Lawrence folded his hands on his desk and stared at Haley. "Conclusions?"

Haley laughed to himself. He thought of a green lieutenant trying to assert his authority. Most people were impressed by Vaughn Lawrence, but not an old veteran like Len Haley.

"My conclusion is that you call Reuben Merrill and tell him to leave Yosemite in the next few hours."

Lawrence did not move. "Why?"

Haley smiled. His front teeth were even, straight, and artificial. His own had been kicked out by a Vietnamese prison guard. "Since this guy can't screw your sister, he's going to screw you. One of my men watched him and Mrs. Darrow load her Jeep Cherokee station wagon this morning with, among other things, a video camera and recorder. He trailed them halfway over the Tehachapi Mountains."

"They're on their way to Yosemite?"

Haley swung his feet onto the coffee table. "My bet is that this kidney character's got it in his head to follow Darrow's footsteps across the country. He probably thinks old Rodge was a pretty good guy."

"And they're planning to show up in New York next Friday?"

"That was one of Darrow's stops." After a moment, Haley stood. "I think we should stop them before they get there."

Lawrence shifted in his chair, but he kept his hands tightly folded on his desk. "We should be restrained, Len."

"Bullshit," snapped Haley. He leaned on Lawrence's desk. "Restraint let Roger Darrow make it all the way to Andrew MacGregor's front porch. Restraint kept you from stealing those tapes six months ago. Restraint cost me two years in a Vietnamese prison camp. Restraint is nice if you can afford it, but it's like your sister's virginity. Once it's gone, you never get it back. You lost yours when Izzy Jackson's boat blew up."

Vaughn Lawrence pivoted in his chair and looked out at the

Los Angeles basin. At that moment, he was smiling in living rooms all over the West. He was the son of a Depression-poor hardware salesman from Pennsylvania. He stuttered until he was sixteen years old. Now he ruled a television empire that was about to triple in size. He had stopped MacGregor Communications from consuming it. He had stopped Roger Darrow from destroying it. He did not know if he could bring himself to destroy Roger Darrow's wife. Because he liked her.

"Vaughn," whispered Haley, "there aren't too many men who know where this country's going. You do, and you're going to get there first. But not if they make it to New York or find out about Andrew MacGregor."

"We'll warn Merrill not to talk to them. And we'll send one of your men up there to follow them around. If they go to Merrill's place, we'll know what they're after."

"We know already, Vaughn." Haley taunted him.

"Let's know for sure. It's a long way between Yosemite and New York."

On winter mornings, the Central Valley palette was brown and yellow, with a few splashes of green in the fields where alfalfa grew. Mists obscured the Sierra foothills to the east and the coast range to the west. The valley itself was wide and flat and rolled to the north. Rows of giant eucalyptus had been planted as windbreaks along the edges of fields and pastures. Windmills spun in the breeze. Fences slashed across the expanse. And every few miles, orchards appeared, like layed on the landscape. The mist, which began most winter days as a thick fog, never dissipated completely. It hung in the distance like a watercolor wash that bled softly into the browns and yellows of the earth and obscured the boundaries between land and sky.

"The symmetry is perfect," said Whiting.

"I suppose." Jeanne did not sound enthusiastic.

"You have Reuben Merrill right where he was in June, and in New York, you have another big media show with Andrew Mac-Gregor as the star."

"And you have three thousand miles of winter along the way." Jeanne Darrow was having doubts about the journey. As they crossed the Central Valley, she realized that Whiting had been right about one thing: Setting out on a trip like this took courage. She was scared.

James Whiting was not. Roger Darrow's excitement could have been no greater than his own as he started across America. But James Whiting had taken a step to focus public attention on their journey. He had given Vicki Rogers their itinerary, and he had promised to call her with updates as they traveled.

He knew that Jeanne disliked Vicki Rogers. He did not especially like her himself. But he also suspected, after seeing the video tapes, that Roger Darrow's death might not have been accidental. He trusted Vicki Rogers enough that she would recognize a good story, and her televised face talking about the trip would provide them with an extra measure of protection, if his suspicions were correct.

They picked up Highway 41 west of Fresno. The rangeland was green from the winter rains, and after a few miles, it began to undulate, in great sinuous waves, as though the earth were preparing for something more dramatic. The waves slowly worked themselves into foothills. Then, at the crest of one wave that was higher than the rest, the drama unfolded before them. The Sierra Nevadas, the backbone of California, rose from the earth bleached white with snow.

James Whiting felt a chill.

Late that afternoon, Len Haley received a telephone call from Ken Steiner, his man in Yosemite.

"Merrill ducked out about an hour before they got here."

"Did they go to his cabin?" asked Haley.

"Headed straight for it, as soon as they pulled in the gate."

"Where are they now?"

"They checked into the Ahwahnee and then went skiing. Should I stay with them?"

"No," said Haley. "We know they're headed for Wyoming. I'll let Bert McCall pick them up there, before they make themselves into a pair of nuisances."

"And now for a follow-up. A few days ago, we introduced you to James Whiting, the newly crowned Golden Gloves Champion of the Malibu brunch circuit. We wondered if he had been the recip- ient of one of the late Roger Darrow's kidneys, and whether he might become one of the first to look at the video tape documentary that Roger Darrow was working on when he died.

"Well"—a deep breath and a dramatic pause—"we were right on both counts. Informed sources report that at this moment, Mr. Whiting and Jeanne Darrow, Roger's widow, are motoring east from Yosemite determined to retrace Mr. Darrow's steps and update his tapes for possible broadcast later this spring. No air date has been set, but it's my bet that the networks will be clamoring, especially if the cross-country travelers come back with the prize that eluded Roger Darrow, a taped interview with Andrew Mac-Gregor.

"Until tomorrow, this is Vicki Rogers, on the story, 'On the Coast.' "

On television sets all across the West, Vaughn Lawrence was smiling. The Vicki Rogers report always ended "Breakfast with Vaughn." He waves. "So long and see you tomorrow. Make it french toast, make it waffles, make it oatmeal, make it farina, but always make it for 'Breakfast with Vaughn.' "

"Why, Vaughn, dear, to what do I owe this pleasure?"

Vicki Rogers made no attempt to cover herself. It was a half hour later, and she was sitting in the private sauna that adjoined her office. She had very small breasts, very white skin, and jet black hair.

Vaughn Lawrence had changed to tennis shorts and a jersey shirt. His day was far from over, but in Hollywood, it was perfectly acceptable for the man in charge to go to meetings wearing athletic clothes.

"I want to know what you're after, Vicki," he said.

"First of all, I'd like to know how you got in here."

"Your secretary goes for coffee at ten-twenty." He reached into his pocket and pulled out a key. "I still know the way in."

"I must remind myself from now on to change locks when I change lovers. You're sweating, Vaughn."

Lawrence pulled off his jersey and kicked off his shorts, then sat down on the redwood bench. He wiped the perspiration from his forehead and snapped it onto the coals glowing in the corner.

The coals hissed.

She crossed her legs. Even in the sauna, she was very cool. "Something must be bothering you, dear."

"I'd like you to tell me before you go on the air with any more reports about Whiting."

"I don't clear my material with anyone except my lawyer."

"Where did you get the information you ran this morning?"

Vicki uncrossed her legs. Lawrence glanced down. Then she crossed them in the other direction.

"Apparently, you didn't hear my report. I quoted anonymous sources." Vicki Rogers liked to think of herself as a serious journalist. She also liked to think of herself as a tough negotiator.

Lawrence smiled and wiped a trickle of sweat from the bridge of his nose. "You're such an honorable woman, Vicki, I sometimes wonder how I ever let you go."

"You didn't, dear. I let you go."

He pretended to ignore her and looked her up and down. "I guess it was the tiny tits."

She glanced at his lap. "Tiny what?"

Lawrence felt his heart beginning to race, as it always did after a few minutes in the sauna. "I'll make a deal with you, Vick. Let's say it's in honor of what we once had."

Vicki smiled. "How quaint. You forget, however, that half the people in Hollywood have had affairs with each other. If they were all nice to each other in honor of the past, this would be a very dull tinseltown."

Lawrence managed a smile, although he would have preferred to lock her in the sauna.

Vicki stood and wrapped a towel around herself. "What's the deal, Vaughn?"

"Clear reports about Jeanne Darrow and her kidney with us before you air them, and you'll get another two minutes of time on 'Breakfast with Vaughn.' "

"Give me a half hour every night and the money to do 'On the Coast' the way it deserves to be done. Then put it on your superstation or your strongest cable network."

"Too expensive, Vicki. I can't."

Vicki stared at him for a moment, then put her hands on his knees and brought her face close to his. "What's on them, Vaughn? Strictly off the record. Strictest confidence."

"I don't know, but Roger Darrow didn't give a damn about 179
Andrew MacGregor when he left. He was trying to destroy me and
everything I've worked for in the last ten years."

"Why?"

"Because I screwed his wife."

Slowly, Vicki Rogers smiled. It was a motivation she could
understand.

"Strictest confidence," repeated Lawrence.

"I bite my tongue, but strictest confidence." Unless I need an
advantage, she thought. "Now, just to refresh my memory, dear,
what, outside of a long enemies' list, have you been building for
the last ten years?"

He laughed. "You coined the phrase yourself. A video empire."

She opened the sauna door. "I'll shower first."

He called to her and she turned back to him. He swung one of
his legs up onto the bench, revealing more of himself. He was
looking for a position of power, because the negotiations weren't
over.

"I've just decided to change the deal. If you don't tell me who
your source is and let me clear your copy, your little syndicated
gossip spot will no longer be carried on 'Breakfast with Vaughn.' "

He smiled and stretched out his leg.

That was a serious threat. Vicki knew that without "Breakfast",
her national ratings and the amount of money she could command
in syndication would drop dramatically. She looked toward his
groin and said, "You'll have to do better than that."

When Roger Darrow left Yosemite in June, he traveled east,
down the steep, winding descent of the Tioga Pass, picked up
Route 395, and reached I-80 in Reno five hours later. But in winter, the Tioga Pass was packed in snow twelve feet deep.

At eight o'clock on Tuesday morning, Jeanne Darrow and
James Whiting loaded the Cherokee and headed west.

The day before, after missing Merrill, they had rented skis and
traveled to Dewey Point, the spot a mile above the valley from
which Roger Darrow had spoken to the camera. A fresh fringe of
snow had covered El Capitan, and the sound of the waterfalls had
echoed across the valley, filling the air with softness. Jeanne and
Whiting had climbed onto Roger's rock, and for almost an hour,

they had sat in silence before the splendor.

"What am I doing here?" Jeanne had said finally her eyes fixed someplace in the middle distance between Dewey Point and El Capitan.

"You came here to see a congressman who was conveniently called away."

"No," she had said. "I mean right here on this rock."

"You're trying to hold on to something."

She had turned to Whiting. "And what are you doing here?"

"I'm not sure. Trying to find something, I guess."

An hour and a half after they left Yosemite, they reached Highway 49, which wound north through the Sierra foothills where in 1849 gold nuggets appeared in streambeds and transformed California from a backwater territory into one of the richest states in the Union.

At U.S. 80, they turned east, and the eight-lane highway rose up into the Sierras once more. Along the roadside were billboards: dancing show girls wearing flowered headdresses, Frank Sinatra holding a microphone, Don Rickles wearing a silly grin, two happy gamblers with a roulette wheel spinning behind them. *Visit Harrah's Tahoe at the MGM Grand and See You at the Sands*. Then, at the 5,800-foot level, above the snow line once more, they drove past a town called Truckee, and Whiting saw a sign for Donner Memorial State Park.

"Is this the Donner Pass?" he asked.

Jeanne nodded. In 1846, eighty-nine people tried to get their wagon train through the pass before the snow. They did not make it. They were trapped for five months. After their food was gone, they began to die from starvation. To survive, the living ate the dead.

James Whiting found it difficult to feel secure about the comforts of modern life here in the middle of the Donner Pass. In spite of the billboards, the gas stations, the motels, and the snowfighters keeping the highway clear, he felt a deep bond with the people who once wintered there, and a deeper bond with those who survived, because they would do anything, risk everything, for the chance at a new life.

Then Whiting had a strange thought. Like half the Donner party, Roger Darrow had died within reach of his goal. And Whiting, like the rest, had cannibalized the dead to continue life.

20

That night, they stayed in separate rooms in a motel in Salt Lake City. After dinner, Jeanne went to bed. Whiting bought himself a six-pack of Coors beer, a light lager that was more like a temperature than a taste, especially in the 3.2 Utah version. Then he connected Roger Darrow's video cassette player to the television and inserted the tape marked "Wyoming," which was to be their next stop. Until after midnight, he played the tape and took notes, as though he were a film editor condensing two hours of material to thirty minutes.

Emerald-green grass, blue sky, deeper blue river. The camera sits on a small rise three or four miles from the Grand Tetons, a row of jagged peaks that looks like the teeth of a saw cutting through the rangeland. The camera tilts down to a log ranch house surrounded by cottonwoods. Nearby are a barn and a windmill. Cattle graze on the range around the house.

Cut.

The camera is now shooting from the front porch of the ranch house. A young woman rides her horse toward the house, dismounts, and tethers the horse. She wears a sweat-stained cowboy hat, leather chaps and gloves, and a work shirt.

"This is Lynne Lee Baker," says Darrow, "a rancher in Jackson, Wyoming. Her family has been friendly with Andrew MacGregor for over thirty years, since MacGregor first bought land here. I've come to talk with her about him, and about the political debate—which she helped organize—that the MacGregor cable system will broadcast from here tomorrow."

Cut.

It is much later. Lynne Baker sits on a rocking chair at the corner of her front porch. The sun's rays slant in under the porch roof, glinting off the windows, reddening Lynne's tanned-brown face and the brown bark logs of the house. She is wearing clean blue jeans and a fresh white blouse. Her blond hair is pulled straight back and looks damp; she has showered. Her right leg is drawn up to her chest, so that her heel is perched on the edge of the chair. Her bare foot is long, graceful.

She takes a sip of beer from the can on the table beside her, then rests her chin on her knee. She seems more relaxed than exhausted. She pivots her head toward the camera. "I'm glad you tracked me down."

"So am I," Darrow says softly.

She smiles. She seems to like the man behind the camera.

"I found your name by looking up MacGregor's neighbors at the County Seat. That's where they told me you were one of the leaders in the fight against development in Jackson Hole."

She looks out across the range in front of her house. "I'm just tryin' to hang on to what we have here. Good land, clean air, what's left of the peace and quiet. My brother and me, we're cow people, like my folks before me, and theirs before them. There ain't much money in it. You can sell this land right now for twenty-five thousand dollars an acre, if you want to see it developed. But I want to hold on as long's I can. So do most of the ranchers."

"There's a developer around here named Jack Cutler who says you're just trying to keep Jackson Hole to yourself," offers Darrow.

She straightens up angrily. "There's four million people pass through this valley every year, mister. That's enough. Guys like Jack Cutler want to see more condos, more ski runs, more of everything." She pauses. "The way I look at it, it's a damn good thing that Andrew MacGregor likes to buy land around here whenever it goes up for sale, because all he wants to do is keep the place open, like it was forty years ago. Of course, when he goes, I don't know what'll happen to his holdings."

"Maybe he'll leave it all to the National Park, the way Rockefeller did," says Darrow. "When was the last time he was here?"

"I guess it's been four or five years." She begins to rock in her chair. "MacGregor and my dad were real good friends. They used to hunt sage grouse together, and we always waited for his phone call tellin' us he'd be arrivin' in October." She smiles. "He was full of life and he loved to laugh and he was one of the best wing shots I ever saw. Even better than Dad." She looks out toward the Tetons. "Now that Dad's gone and MacGregor's gettin' over the hill, we never see him, 'cept when he shows up on TV to give one of his

"What are they about?"

"Free enterprise, free television, the importance of strikin' a balance between all this beauty—she gestures toward the mountains—"and gettin' the oil out of the ground in northwest Wyoming."

"He favors development?"

"You get that feelin' when you listen to him, and when you see him buyin' up cable television systems all over the state. But I know him pretty good, and when you get down to it, he still believes like a lot of us around here. Northwestern Wyoming is one of the last places left where the earth still works like it's s'posed to, one of the last places where there's clean air and room left for big game. We gotta protect it from developers and oil drillers."

"How can yo be certain MacGregor agrees with you?"

"He said 'sure' when I asked him to run the big debate on his cable stations tomorrow night."

Cut

"Whenever it's come to be ass-kickin' time, Andy MacGregor's always sided with me." Jack Cutler folds his hands on his huge belly. He wears a heavy blue shirt with double-breasted front. His belt buckle is a silver steer's head. He weighs close to 250 pounds. His beard is salt and pepper and all but covers his face. His nose is red from sunburn and alcohol, and while his laugh is as jovial as his appearance, his eyes are small and black and hard. He is sitting behind a large desk in a room lined with mooseheads, elk antlers, and antique guns.

Cutler leans forward. *"And I'll tell you this. Senator Tom Sylbert's gonna get his ass kicked tomorrow night."*

"You mean the debate?"

"Damn right, boy." And Cutler adds, with a pride most men reserve for their children, *"It was me set the whole thing up, not Lynne Baker. Sylbert's on the right side in most fights, and folks think he might make a run at the White House one of these years, but last month, to soothe the e-cologists and the Lynne Bakers and all the folks who think development is next door to nuclear war, he introduced a bill puttin' all the lands in northwest Wyoming off limits to oil exploration. That's public lands and private."*

"I bet folks out here don't take kindly to that."

Cutler cracks his knuckles. "Stupidest damn thing you ever heard. Especially if you got any money invested in these parts. The man's a damn Communist."

"And Lynne? What's your opinion of her?"

Cutler smiles, as though he genuinely likes her. "A nice gal with some wrongheaded notions. If her daddy was around, God rest him, he'd of agreed with me when I said we had to give this Tom Sylbert a chance to cook in his own juices. I called up Andy MacGregor and asked him if he'd organize that debate. You know, MacGregor owns four or five cable TV franchises in Wyoming. . . ."

"All bought within the last three years."

Cutler nods, as though he's impressed by Darrow's knowledge. "And he's got that public affairs show called 'Open Forum.' And folks with his service got the little gizmo that lets 'em answer questions while they watch the show. No waitin' for some guy to interpret it all. Question, answer, bang. Just like that."

"Just like that," echoes Darrow.

"Tomorrow night," continues Cutler expansively, "we'll have the senator tradin' shots with Eve Merriweather, a bright lady from the Western Mountain Legal Consortium. And all over Wyoming, folks'll sit with their fingers on the buttons waitin' to say what they think. It'll be like an e-lectronic town meetin' for the whole state."

Jack Cutler smiles and cracks his knuckles again. They sound like walnuts breaking in his hands.

Cut.

Roger Darrow stands in front of the camera. He is wearing jeans, a white western-style shirt with snap buttons and red piping trim, and cowboy boots. It is early evening. Behind him, people are streaming into the ranchers' hall.

"This," he says, "is another classic Old West confrontation, like the cowboys and the Indians or the ranchers and the sodbusters. It's the ranchers and the ecologists against the oil companies and the developers. Instead of six-guns, they're using two-way interactive television, and Andrew MacGregor is right in the middle."

Cut.

Inside the hall, perhaps two hundred people fill the seats and line the aisles. A blue backdrop has been erected behind three

leather swivel chairs. There is an American flag stage left, a Wy-
oming flag stage right, and a podium for each debater. Sylbert, in
his forties, with the sharp features and crisp tailoring that make
him look like a news anchorman, is studying a map at the side of
the stage. Eve Merriweather, a handsome blond in a tweed skirt
and camel's hair jacket is feverishly studying a set of notecards.

The red light flashes. The debaters turn toward the camera.

"Good evening, ladies and gentlemen. *The MacGregor Cable*
Broadcasting network welcomes you to 'Open Forum,' a series
devoted to exploring state and local issues that affect everyone
along the MacGregor network. And as always, Respondsible lets
you at home join us at the studio." The delivery is crisp, cheery,
filled with emphasis. "My name is Frank Barry, and I'll be your
host." *He looks like a Vaughn Lawrence retread.*

Cut.

The debate is under way. Eve Merriweather stands in front of
a map of North America. A thick black line runs from Prudhoe
Bay in Alaska to the Gulf of Mexico. "Northwest Wyoming sits on
the edge of the Western Overthrust Belt, the richest oil-bearing
formation left on the continent, a resource that we cannot lock
away forever."

Cut.

Senator Thomas Sylbert is at the podium. He is casual, re-
laxed, and speaks softly, as though he knows that he is not ad-
dressing the people in the hall but those watching television. "It
would be immoral for us to allow drillers and developers to disrupt
the last intact ecosystem in the lower forty-eight, and that's what
we're talking about here."

Cut.

Eve Merriweather is making her final summation. "We who
live in the West know best how to use the resources of the West,
including the oil. in the Overthrust Belt. Development will certainly accompany growth and exploration, but it is immoral for
us not to use the resources that God has given us, and we demean
ourselves if we believe we cannot manage them wisely."

Cut.

Senator Sylbert concludes, "I believe I speak for all the people
of Wyoming when I say that Jackson Hole, the Bridger-Teton
National Forest, northwest Wyoming itself are a national trea-
sure far more valuable than a few months' supply of oil. That is

why I urge all of you to support my bill to protect northwest Wyoming."

Cut.

"And now, let's find out what you at home have decided." Frank Berry glances at his clipboard, then looks into the camera. "After hearing all of the arguments, do you support the position of Eve Merriweather and the Western Mountain Legal Consortium, or Senator Thomas Sylbert? Press Button A for Merriweather, Button B for Sylbert."

The words Answer Now flash on the screen.

Cut.

Numbers now show on the screen: 49,368 households responding; Merriweather—25,330; Sylbert—24,038.

Cut.

"Soooo," says Barry, "the people of Wyoming, listening along our network, have decided to back Eve Merriweather's position over Senator Thomas Sylbert." Barry turns to the senator. "Reactions?"

"My congratulations to Mrs. Merriweather," says Sylbert, "but I've taken two private polls on this issue, and three Wyoming newspapers have also taken polls, and every one has shown a sixty-forty split in favor of my position. I find these results surprising and somewhat misleading."

"I don't think you're being fair, Senator," says the host.

"Yes," says Eve Merriweather coolly, "the numbers don't lie."

"I never said they did." Sylbert smiles. "I simply registered surprise at them, since it was apparent to me and the people in this auditorium that the strength of my position was once again demonstrated."

Sylbert looks out across the audience for applause, and he gets it. Most of the ranchers are behind him.

"Heh, heh." Barry laughs nervously. "Maybe we should have respond boxes out there in the studio audience tonight."

"That's a good idea," says Sylbert. "It might help me to cut into Ms. Merriweather's margin. But then, the MacGregor polling computer might surprise us again. You never can tell."

"The Wyoming voters surprised you," says Eve Merriweather. "Not a computer."

"No, I suppose not," responds Sylbert, although he doesn't sound convinced. "Nor was I surprised by any eloquence from my opponent."

Cut.

It is early morning. The foreground is darkened by long shadows, but the sky is light blue and the sun is already hitting the upper peaks and glaciers on the Tetons, which form the backdrop for the scene.

Roger Darrow is sitting at a picnic table. Beside him is a tent. His Jeep Cherokee is parked nearby. The Colter Bay Village Campground—tents and tent cabins, cars and vans—stretches out behind him. A heavy film of dew covers the picnic table and the windshield of the Cherokee. Darrow's hands are wrapped around a cup of coffee that steams in the cold air. He is wearing a Dodger-blue baseball jacket with knit cuffs over a darker blue turtleneck. He has slipped back into a Hollywood wardrobe.

He shivers and hunches up his shoulders. "It may be June, but it's damn cold up here in the morning." *He takes the coffeepot from the Coleman stove and pours more into the cup. He tries to sip, but the coffee is too hot. He looks at the camera.*

"Jack Cutler's a windbag," *he says,* "and he worships the dollar like a network president, but I think he may be someone you can trust.

"Lynne Baker is a independent woman. She fights for what she believes, she does what she feels, and society be damned. She cooks a good meal for a stranger, and I've gotten to know her pretty well in the last few days." *He smiles.*

"As for Andrew MacGregor, I'm not really sure of what he's trying to do in Wyoming. He buys up the land, ostensibly to protect it; he builds or buys out cable television franchises wherever he can. And when Jack Cutler wants to cook a senator, MacGregor heats the oven.

"After the debate last night, Senator Sylbert made some pretty angry remarks to the press about instant plebiscites and the dangers of electronic polling. I don't know if somebody at the MacGregor computer was actually trying to screw him on those Respondsible votes, but after seeing it in action, I'm inclined to agree that in the wrong hands, two-way polling can be a dangerous tool. The question is, how do we know whose hands are the wrong ones?"

The sound of an automobile interrupts Roger Darrow. He looks over his shoulder as the front of a car pulls into the shot.

Darrow stands and steps back. He doesn't like what he's seeing. A car door slams, then a big man wearing a fringed suede jacket and a cowboy hat enters the shot.

"My name's Bert McCall. I work for Jack Cutler." The two men face each other from opposite sides of the picture frame. McCall towers over Darrow like a hulking grizzly. "My boss wants his video tape. He decided he don't trust you."

"Your boss did all the talking," responds Darrow. "I just asked a few questions."

McCall extends his hand. "I'm doin' my job, mister. Hand over the tape."

Darrow studies Bert McCall for a moment, and the stubbornness seems to harden at the base of his spine. He straightens and says, "Not a chance."

McCall takes a step. Roger Darrow sweeps the coffeepot off the Coleman stove and holds it as though he is about to throw it.

McCall stops. "If you were plannin' to throw that thing, you should have down it right then, mister. Now that I know it's comin', you might just as well put it down, or you'll get yourself hurt."

Darrow keeps his eyes on McCall and knocks the lid off the coffeepot. "This was boilin' when you pulled up, mister. And besides, I can't give you back the tape because I already sent it to Los Angeles."

"Maybe I'll just have a look around, then."

Darrow swirls the coffee once more. "It's not worth gettin' your nose burned off, mister. The tapes aren't here."

McCall studies the coffeepot, then Darrow's face, as though trying to decide if Darrow will do it. Then he backs away. "You're courtin' trouble, mister," he warns. "If you show Jack Cutler on TV, he'll sue you into the ground, 'cause he didn't sign a release."

"I'll see that he gets one."

McCall points a finger at Darrow. "And you see that you stay out of my way the next time you're in Jackson."

Darrow watches McCall return to his car and drive off. Then he lets out his breath and looks toward the camera. "I wonder what that was all about. I guess he didn't know he was performing for posterity."

Darrow laughs nervously as the tension drains away. He seems pleased with the way he handled himself. "Maybe Cutler's something of a snake after all. And maybe that remark about cooking Sylbert in his own juices was more than colorful cowboy talk."

Roger Darrow had not lived long enough to see the results of that debate in Wyoming. If he had, he might have been more suspicious about the Respondsible system. In Los Angeles, Whiting had gone through Jeanne Darrow's magazine rack to the *Newsweek* November election issue. He carried the article with his notes, and reread it before going to sleep.

In Wyoming, Senator Thomas Sylbert lost his seat to Samuel Bragg, a relative unknown thrown against him. In June, Sylbert held a three-to-one margin in the polls, but that was before his disastrous debate over Wyoming oil and gas policy on "Open Forum," a cable television program.

Sylbert lost the debate, according to an on-air poll, and then he lost his cool, sniping at the host Frank Barry and opponent Eve Merriweather. One of Sylbert's pet bills was thrown out of committee the following week, and he began a slow but steady slide in the polls, especially in those taken on "Open Forum," which monitored the race closely.

"Open Forum" polls indicated an erosion of Sylbert support that was showing up nowhere else. Eventually, Sylbert believes, the television polls became a self-fulfilling prophecy: His support began to slip because he was slipping in the polls, and not the other way around.

Sylbert also hinted, rather darkly, that it is very difficult to monitor systems like MacGregor's Respondsible, to check for accuracy and honesty, or to guarantee that the mountains of personal information that Respondsible provides, in areas of program preference, viewing habits, political attitudes, financial information, and security data will remain private.

John Meade, MacGregor Communications spokesman and nephew of the reclusive chairman of the board, said he would be happy to allow Senator Sylbert access to the company records or polling computers. He added, however, that Sylbert's best course would be simply to accept the will of the Wyoming voters and start looking toward the next election.

Sylbert had been viewed as a possible contender for the presidential nomination in two years, but now he'll be going back to

Cody, and he claims he has no plans beyond seeing his cattle through the winter.

Apparently, by January, Thomas Sylbert had decided that his cattle could survive the winter on their own. When Whiting had called Sylbert earlier in the day to arrange an interview, he had been told that the senator was in the Caribbean on vacation. Whiting would have to content himself with interviewing Lynne Baker and Jack Cutler and hope that he could discover the reason why Cutler sent Bert McCall to threaten Darrow on the morning he left Jackson.

21

Never a lift line, never a wait. Eight great slopes of the freshest packed powder in the West. And for you, flatlanders, hundreds of miles of cross-country trails. So ski by day and relax by night at the Cutler condos, Jackson, Wyoming. And while you're in town, pardner, drop by the Cutler Eating Emporium and Trading Post for a tasty steak and a good dose of western hospitality.

It was around two o'clock in the afternoon when Jeanne Darrow and James Whiting drove up the main street of Jackson. The journey from Salt Lake City had taken seven hours.

Winter in the high plains and mountains of the West was not the gentle season that Whiting had found at Yosemite. The temperature was in the teens. The snow was deep and endless. The sun hung low to the horizon all day. And the road into Jackson, in some places, was no more than a long stretch of two-lane blacktop. But the snow-fighters kept the road clear, and the skiers found their way.

They clogged the streets in their sports cars and four-wheel drives. They jammed the sidewalks in their cowboy hats and heavy plastic boots. Ski racks were as common as windshield wipers. And skiwear, it seemed to Whiting, came only in the brightest colors—lime green, Day-Glow orange, red, yellow. The town looked like a dude ranch invaded by a school of very large tropical fish.

Whiting preferred cross-country skiing. Usually he wore wool sweaters with jeans or knickers. His skis were twenty years old and made of wood. People had told him that once he tried the excitement of downhill skiing, cross-country would never interest him again. He said that no one who had ever listened to the rhythmic kick of his own skis across a frozen meadow could ever be bored by cross-country.

They found three motels loaded with skiers before renting ar oom at the Grafton Motor Inn.

"It's the only room we got," said the woman behind the desk, who looked to be about sixty and had a face as craggy as the mountains around her. "From what I hear, it's the only room in town."

"We'll take it," said Whiting.

"There's two beds and you've got your own shower. I don't suppose you'll want both beds made up, will you?"

Whiting glanced at Jeanne.

"We will," she responded. "And we won't be sharing bath towels either."

The old woman looked at Whiting. "You better get this gal aired out on the ski slopes, mister, or you two won't have any vacation at all."

"We're here on business." said Whiting.

The room was on the second story, right at the top of the outdoor staircase. The bathroom window looked onto the roof of another motel. The front windows looked across the parking lot to a very crowded Shell station.

Jeanne snapped open the front shades. "Welcome to the Wild West."

Whiting dropped himself onto the bed and it nearly sank to the floor. "Where the old bunkhouse bed feels like a hammock and the lady at the desk has a dirty mind."

Jeanne glanced over her shoulder. "I hope she's the *only* one."

Whiting jumped up. "Listen, lady, if you don't trust me, just say so. We've been traveling for three days, and I haven't touched you, and I don't intend to." Whiting was not telling the truth.

"That was the deal," snapped Jeanne, "two celibates crossing America together. Anything else is a complication."

She popped open her suitcase and she began to rummage through it, as though she weren't quite sure of what she was looking for.

Whiting sat on his bed and watched her until her hands stopped moving through the pile of clothes and she looked up.

"What's wrong, Jeanne?" he asked.

"I'm not going to enjoy meeting this Lynne Baker woman," she said. "I may reveal my jealousy."

"Jealousy."

"He was drawn to her," she said angrily. "You could hear it in the way he talked to her. You could see it in her face when she looked at him. She's blunt, earthy, in great shape, and with that blond hair, she even *looks* like Miranda Blake."

Whiting had sensed the attraction as well. "I don't think you're being fair to either of them."

"I didn't come this far to be fair. I came to find out what happened here."

"Even if he made love to Lynne Baker, that's not all that happened to him here."

Jeanne put her hands on her hips. "I just want to look her in the eye. If I can do that, I know I'll be able to look Miranda Blake in the eye when we meet her."

A short time later, the Cherokee made its way down the snowy roads that led to Lynne Baker's house. Out here, in the middle of the valley, there were no cheerful crowds. Out here, in the heart of winter, the Tetons rose in majesty. The eleven jagged peaks breached from an ocean of snow, bleak white against the blue, cold purity itself.

Out here, there was work to do—firewood to split, hay to spread, water holes to free of ice, paper work to finish before calving time arrived and the season turned, if it ever was to turn. The brightly colored snowmobiles speeding along the roadsides looked frivolous, faintly ridiculous against the backdrop. And the little groups of cross-country skiers were like pieces of woolen lint blowing across the expanse.

Lynne Baker's pickup was parked in front of her ranch house, and a stream of smoke was curling out of the chimney. It was nearly three o'clock on a Friday afternoon, and an icy wind cut across the rangeland, blowing up little williwaws of powdery snow.

"Roger Darrow's wife?" said Lynne Baker. She seemed surprised, almost shocked. Her eyes shifted to Whiting. "And who's that?"

"His name is James Whiting," said Jeanne. "We're retracing my husband's last journey, meeting the people he met, photographing the places he stopped."

Lynne Baker eyed the two of them, then opened the door.

She was taller than Whiting had expected, nearly six feet. Her hair, worn in two braids, was not quite as blond as it had looked on the tape, and her skin was red and windburned. She was wearing boots, blue jeans, and a heavy cable-knit sweater over a blue turtleneck.

A while later, a fire in the wood stove warmed the living room, and a pot of tea steeped on the coffee table. Lynne Baker was sunk deep in an old leather chair. Whiting and Jeanne sat on a sofa with hard, saddle-leather arms and upholstery—horizontal stripes of red, orange, yellow, brown, and white—that looked like a saddle blanket.

The walls were paneled in rich pine and decorated with family photographs, along with several oil paintings of Jackson Hole scenes. Above the fireplace was a moosehead and an antique Sharps buffalo gun, and on the table beside her a stuffed owl. It was a masculine room, but Lynne Baker seemed comfortable there. "I'll be glad to tell you what I can about your husband," she was saying to Jeanne, "but I'm afraid you won't be able to meet Jack Cutler." She paused. "He's dead.

Jeanne and Whiting looked at each other. Whiting was not surprised. He had almost expected to encounter something like this between Los Angeles and Maine.

"He went off the road comin' home from his club one night back in November," Lynne leaned forward and poured a splash of tea into a mug, then filled all three, handed one to each of her guests, and sat back with her own. "Jack was a drunk, and I guess he went the way you would've expected."

"You don't sound convinced," said Whiting.

"Jack Cutler was a dyed-in-the-wool son of a bitch, and I didn't agree with him on much of anything, but he and my family went back a long way, and I was pretty broken up when he died." She sipped her tea and glanced at Jeanne. "And I'll tell you, Mrs. Darrow, I was pretty broken up when your husband died, too."

Jeanne managed a smile. "Thanks."

Whiting saw the lines of tension around Jeanne's eyes. He turned to Lynne. "If you know Roger at all, maybe you'll be able to understand why we're doing this. And why we're interested in Jack Cutler."

Lynne sipped her tea and studied her two visitors. She seemed to be sizing them up, deciding if she could trust them. "What're you plannin' to do, once you been all the way to Maine?"

"Intergrate Darrow's original tapes with our own and see if we have enough material to get 'One Man's America' onto one of the networks," answered Whiting.

"Are you some kind of producer or something?" she asked.

"No," said Jeanne firmly. "He's a family friend, and he's helping me. There's no guarantee we'll do anything with this stuff until we see what we have. If it's too personal, nobody's damn business, I may just bury it."

Lynne looked at Whiting—"You're after a good story"—then at Jeanne—"and you're just looking for the truth."

"You're simplifying things, but yes," said Whiting.

Almost unconsciously, Lynne reached out and began to stroke the feathers on the stuffed owl. "Well, I think I got a good idea about what happened to Jack Cutler, and it ties right in with all the stuff that Roger Darrow came up here to find out. I ain't told this story to too many people, 'cause it might leak like a buckshot cistern if some lawyer started pourin' water into it."

"We're not lawyers," said Whiting.

"A point for you." Lynne leaned forward and looked at Jeanne. "I only knew your husband a few days, but I would've trusted him enough to tell him this. I guess I'll trust you, too."

Jeanne's expression did not change.

"Can we tape this?" asked Whiting.

"Not yet. Just listen for a while."

She began to stroke the owl once more. "It was about a week after the election. My brother and his wife and I were at the Jackson Saloon for a drink. Jack was sittin' there with Bert McCall, and he invited me to join them, which meant that he was drunk, 'cause he usually didn't drink with me, 'less we were alone.

"I sat down, and he joshed me a bit, 'bout my side losin' a big voice in the Senate. Then he leaned close and nudged me in the ribs and said, 'Old Tom Sylbert didn't know what he was gettin' himself in for when he came up here in June.'

"Out of the corner of my eye, I could see Bert McCall start to bristle, like somebody'd dropped a lizard on his neck. I said to Jack, 'You don't mean he was up against a stacked deck when folks started pushin' buttons all over Wyoming, do you?'

"And McCall shook all over, like he was tryin' to get that damn lizard off. Jack sort of smiled and rolled his eyes. Then McCall chimed in, real angry, sayin' Sylbert lost 'cause he was just plain stupid."

Lynne finished her tea and swirled the leaves around in the bottom of the cup. "A week later Jack was dead."

Jeanne sensed Lynne's discomfort. She picked up the teapot and offered it toward Lynne's cup.

"Thanks." Lynne held out the cup, and Jeanne filled it. After a few sips, Lynne continued. "When the accident happened, I thought about that night, and the way Bert McCall kept lookin', but I figured that maybe I'd been puttin' words in Jack's mouth."

"Are you saying that Bert McCall killed his own boss because his boss was saying the wrong things about Tom Sylbert's defeat?"

"I been thinkin' on it," said Lynne. "Though it's not an idea I'd feel comfortable takin' to the sheriff."

Whiting remembered the last scene on Darrow's tape. He thought Lynne might be right about Bert McCall. "Do you think we could talk to this guy? Ask him a few questions about himself?"

Lynne laughed. "He's nothin' but a leg-breaker, mister. He came up here from L.A. to work for Jack Cutler."

"Why would Jack Cutler need a leg-breaker?"

"The Cutler Brothers, Inc., have money in a lot of things. Oil drilling, condos, fast-food, motels. Whenever MacGregor Communications buys a cable franchise in Wyoming, they subcontract the wiring to Cutler Construction. It's a big company, and most big companies have security people, especially when the competition's tough. At least, that's what Jack told me."

"And Bert McCall won't talk to outsiders?"

Lynne shook her head. "But if you want to talk about that debate, maybe I can set you up with one of the participants."

"Sylbert's in the Caribbean," said Whiting.

"Eve Merriweather's right here in Wyoming."

"Do you know her?" asked Jeanne.

"We been on opposite sides of the fence for so long, we're like neighbors," said Lynne. "She has a place up here, and this bein' a Friday afternoon, we'll prob'ly find her at the Cutler Ski and Gun Club, if she's not on the slopes."

James Whiting and Jeanne Darrow rode with Lynne Baker in her pickup. Bert McCall followed them, as he had followed Darrow and Whiting to the Baker ranch. Len Haley had called the day before with a description of the Jeep Cherokee and a few suggestions on slowing down the occupants. McCall had been waiting for them.

The pickup went through the village of Kelly, then traveled along the northern edge of the National Elk Refuge.

By the road, Whiting saw the carcass of an old male elk, now mostly antlers and rib cage and a red stain on the snow. A pair of wolves, with thick white winter fur and bloody muzzles, were tearing at the remains. Lynne slowed down for a moment. The wolves looked up like sullen children caught in mischief, then they returned to their meal. One grabbed the remains of a haunch, the other buried his face in the guts.

"They must be awful hungry to be this close to the road," said Lynne. "But better some elk on his last legs than a prize calf in my pen."

Whiting watched the scene recede through the rearview window. Both wolves began to pull at the same piece of haunch, dragging the carcass back and forth in the bloody snow. The elk's head flopped about, as though looking to see where its belly and flanks had gone. But the wolves paid it no mind. Once felled, the elk did not exist except as food. There were no personalities in nature, and the only metaphors, thought Whiting, were man's.

The Cutler Ski and Gun Club, less than a year old, was built in several levels, so that it seemed to climb up the side of the hill, like a redwood and glass flight of stairs. The lounge was arranged in five tiers, to take full advantage of the glass wall that looked out at the Tetons. On the top tier was the bar, sleek and modern. On the tiers beneath it, tables, chairs, and sofas were arranged around freestanding fireplaces, and the smoke rose through shiny flue pipes that were the only obstruction to the view.

After signing at the door, Lynne led Jeanne and Whiting to the bar. It was four o'clock, and the après-ski crowd had not yet arrived. There was seating for about 150, and the room looked no more than a third full. A soft tape was playing on the sound system, and nothing louder than the tinkling of an ice cube or a young woman's laughter broke the mood.

Lynne stepped to the bar and ordered three Coors on tap.

"You surprised me," whispered Whiting to Jeanne. "I thought you were going to get mad at her."

"I may yet," said Jeanne. "But the thing is, I like her."

They found Eve Merriweather sitting at her usual booth on the middle tier.

"Your husband still out on the slopes?" asked Lynne as she approached.

Eve Merriweather glanced up and said hello. Her blond hair was tied back with a blue ribbon. Her features, thought Whiting, were New England Yankee, especially the strong, prominent jaw, which barely moved when she spoke. "It's always 'one final run before we lose the daylight.' You know how it is."

Lynne introduced Whiting and Jeanne Darrow. Eve greeted them without much enthusiasm.

Lynne squeezed into the booth. "I hope you don't mind if we join you, Eve. These two folks are from Hollywood, and they said they wanted to meet you."

Bert McCall had waited a few minutes before flashing his membership card and strolling into the Mountain View Lounge.

He was at the bar now, a mug of beer in his hand and the heel of a cowboy boot hooked into the stainless-steel rail. His eyes were focused on Eve Merriweather's booth where Darrow's wife and The Kidney were. Already they were sticking their noses into trouble.

McCall strolled along the upper tier until he was standing almost directly above them and could hear most of their conversation.

"We were impressed by the tape of your debate with Senator Sylbert," said Whiting.

"The high point of my career," Merriweather answered, and she glanced at Lynne Baker, as though she sensed what was happening.

"Most analysts agree," said Whiting, "that the debate was the beginning of the end for Tom Sylbert."

Eve nodded. "I have no problems with that."

"The surprising results of the television poll . . ."

"They were not surprising at all," she said evenly, "to those of us on top of the issue."

For a moment, Whiting could not think of a response. He glanced at Jeanne.

She said, "They were surprising to a lot of people around the country, not the least of them Senator Sylbert himself."

"Good leaders know the strength of the opposition," responded Merriweather curtly. "Sylbert didn't. We were doing the state and the nation a favor by exposing his weakness."

She looked at her watch. "Well, I guess Hal decided to stay for some night runs. I'm in no mood to wait for him." She pulled one of her business cards out of her pocket and handed it to Whiting. "Contact me at my winter address and maybe we can talk more." She flashed a perfunctory smile and prepared to leave.

Then Lynne Baker spoke. She did not raise her eyes from her beer mug, and the brim of her cowboy hat obscured most of her face. "There's one more thing."

Eve Merriweather looked at the top of Lynne's hat. "What?"

"These folks know what Jack Cutler said about Sylbert bein' up against a stacked deck in those TV polls."

Eve Merriweather straighted up. "Sylbert was a sore loser, Lynne, and so are you." She was ready to leave, but was trapped in the circular booth. Lynne Baker and Jeanne Darrow sat on one side, Whiting on the other.

"And what about Jack?" Lynne Baker looked up at last.

Eve Merriweather's expression remained set. "Jack Cutler was a drunk." She pushed the table back and started to climb over Whiting.

"Are these people bothering you?" The voice was high-pitched, almost shrill, just as Whiting had remembered it on the tapes.

Lynne Baker turned her head so that she was looking at McCall's boots. He was standing at her shoulder. "I didn't know this club was droppin' its standards."

McCall pretended to ignore her. "I asked if these people were botherin' you, Miz Merriweather."

"No," she responded. She seemed unsettled at the sight of him. "I was just leaving."

"It sounds to me like these people were askin' you questions you didn't want to answer." McCall looked at Whiting. His features were squashed together and his head a size too small for the rest of his body. "That ain't very polite."

"When did you ever worry about polite?" grumbled Lynne Baker. "And what business is it of yours *what* we're talkin' about?"

"Miz Merriweather's a friend of mine, and it looks like she's outnumbered. Now, who the hell are you, mister?" McCall demanded of Whiting.

"You don't have to tell him a damn thing," said Lynne.

The few people sitting around them had stopped chattering. On the sound system, the Bee Gees were singing "Stayin Alive." Appropriate, thought Whiting.

"You stay out of this, Lynne," said McCall. He turned again toward Whiting. "I asked you a question. Who are you?"

Whiting was swirling the beer around in his mug. He was frightened.

"Don't tell him anything," Jeanne said softly.

McCall turned his face to her. "Shut up."

Whiting was still watching the beer. Little pieces of ice from the frosted mug were floating on the head. Without looking up, he said, "This isn't something you want a frostbitten nose about." He gulped as he said it and he almost swallowed his tongue.

Oh, you can tell by the way I use my walk, I'm a lovin' man, no time to talk . . .

Bert McCall leaned forward, with his hands on his knees, as though he were talking to a child. "What?"

Eve Merriweather tried to squeeze past Whiting. "I don't think I enjoy being the excuse for an argument."

Whiting took a deep breath. Boiling water was more of a threat than cold beer. He should have known. He wished he could take back that last remark. He put the beer mug down and wondered if he could dissolve into it.

"Did you threaten me?" said McCall.

Whiting looked into the beer mug.

"Nobody threatens me." A pair of huge hands grabbed Whiting and lifted him completely out of the booth. He flew about five feet and landed on his back.

Eve Merriweather jumped out and called for help.

Lynne Baker leaped to her feet. "Stay on the floor, Whiting."

Jeanne Darrow stood with her mug in her hand. She remembered Bert McCall threatening her husband.

Bert McCall wiped the beer from his face.

The bartender shouted for the bouncer.

Whiting rolled over and climbed to his knees. He hadn't been hurt.

Stayin' alive, stayin' alive. . . .

Bert McCall stood over Whiting. He did not have the sadistic smiles some men wear when they pick their fight. His expression was calm, contained. He was a professional doing his job.

"C'mon," muttered McCall.

Whiting did not want to run. He had already lost his chance to reason.

"C'mon," taunted McCall.

Jeanne Darrow fired the beer mug. It hit Bert McCall on the cheekbone, just hard enough to make him mad.

He turned on Jeanne, pushed the palm of his hand into her face, and slammed her against the back wall of the booth.

Eve Merriweather shouted for help.

The bartender called for the bouncer again, but he did not budge from behind the bar.

Whiting cursed himself for watching Darrow face down McCall with a coffeepot the night before. Then he stood slowly and tried to remember the moves his sister had shown him when she first started studying karate.

Stayin' alive, stayin' alive. . . .

"Back off, Whiting," said Lynne Baker.

Bert McCall cracked a backhander into Lynne's face. She fell backward.

A young skier, all muscle, blond hair, and white teeth, grabbed McCall by the arm. "Hey, bub . . ."

McCall swung his arm and sent the skier crashing into a table on the other side of the tier.

Everybody's thinkin' it, everybody's thinkin' it,/Stayin' alive, stayin' alive . . .

"C'mon," he muttered to Whiting again.

The bouncer appeared at the door of the lounge. He saw MacCall and said, "Shit."

Whiting looked at Lynne Baker. She was on her hands and knees, with blood trickling from the corner of her mouth. He looked at Jeanne Darrow. She was slumped in the booth. He looked at McCall's legs and wondered which one to grab for.

The bouncer told the bartender to call the sheriff.

McCall stepped toward Whiting.

The legs are too big.

But the head's about the size of a grapefruit. Whiting took a shot. His fist clipped McCall on the chin. McCall didn't blink. From the pain across the back of his hand, he thought he'd dislocated one of his knuckles.

Then McCall's fist crashed into Whiting's chin, opening an ugly gash.

Whiting's legs turned to jelly and he fell into a sitting position. He was dazed. He looked down and saw the front of his yellow sweater turn red with blood. He tried to get up, and McCall's boot took him hard in the chest. The sickening thud echoed through the lounge, where no one was talking, but the Bee Gees were still singing.

Stayin' ali————ve . . .

Lynne Baker was on her feet again.

The bouncer was still on the top tier.

Whiting was trying to stand, like a wounded animal who knows that if he stays down, he's dead.

McCall came at him with the boot again, but the young skier jumped in front of it. McCall turned his foot into the skier's groin and lifted him off the floor.

Whiting was up but groggy. He wobbled backward a few steps, then wobbled toward McCall.

Eve Merriweather screamed for them to stop. Jeanne Darrow screamed for help. But after the skier, no one would come near McCall. He was not drunk, and he did not seem angry. He was in total control.

Then Lynne Baker jumped on his back and began to gouge at his eyes. He spun about, and as he did, Jeanne Darrow jumped from behind the table and kicked him in the shins. He swatted at her and knocked her aside.

The bouncer decided to make his move. McCall spun around so that Lynne Baker's body hit the bouncer and knocked him off-balance. Then he spun toward the fireplace while prying at the hands around his neck.

Lynne felt the heat on her behind and decided to jump. She caught her heel on the edge of the fireplace and burned her hand as she fell.

The bouncer came again, and Bert McCall shattered his nose

with a right hand. The bouncer stumbled back, blocking McCall's view. James Whiting slipped in as the bouncer went by and sent a Timberland hiking boot into Bert McCall's groin.

McCall started to collapse. Whiting watched for a moment, then closed his eyes and kicked again. Bert McCall bellowed and sank to his knees.

Something was telling James Whiting to kick again and keep kicking until Bert McCall was senseless. But Whiting knew nothing of the killer instinct. He thought the fight was over when McCall fell forward.

Then McCall looked up and made eye contact. The cool, controlled mask was gone. There was something irrational in the gaze. Whiting took a step back and looked around. Where the hell was the sheriff? Why wouldn't anybody help him? It was the loneliest moment of his life. But in a way, one of the most triumphant. He was doing what Darrow had been ready to do.

McCall's hand shot forward and closed around Whitings ankles. Whiting's feet flew out from under him. He smashed onto his back. McCall leaped on top of him. A fist crashed into the wound on Whiting's chin. The blood splattered, and Whiting could feel himself passing out.

McCall raised his fist again, and a wine bottle shattered against the side of his head, opening a bloody hole just below his temple. He shuddered, looked up at Jeanne Darrow, who held the neck of the bottle in her hand, and keeled over.

Ah, ah, ah, ah, stayin' alive . . .

James Whiting, Jeanne Darrow, Bert McCall, Lynne Baker, and the young skier were arrested and taken to the Jackson jail. They were charged with disturbing the peace, disorderly conduct, damaging personal property, assault, battery, (charge, countercharge), and each was released on five hundred dollars' bail. McCall left with a bandage on his head. Lynne Baker had the burns on her hand wrapped. And Whiting's face was stitched.

That night, on Lynne Baker's advice, they returned to her ranch. She said it would be safer there, because there was no predicting a man like Bert McCall after he had been bloodied and beaten.

Whiting, who had been given a strong codeine compound, fell

asleep as soon as they returned to the ranch. Jeanne lay awake most of the night, listening for the sound of a car or snowmobile that might bring trouble, and wondering what she would say to Lynne Baker in the morning. Lynne managed to sleep peacefully, despite her burned hand, because her brother Tom was perched in the hayloft with a Thermos of hot coffee and a Winchester repeating rifle.

At six o'clock, Jeanne threw three logs into the wood stove in the kitchen and put on a pot of coffee. She looked out the window. They sky to the east showed streaks of red and pink.

"It'll be a nice day for travelin' . . ."

Jeanne was startled. She turned to Lynne. "Traveling?" We're not supposed to leave, are we?"

"You'll be jumpin' bail, I guess. But if I was you, I'd be about my business, and let the Wyoming courts catch up when they can." Lynne sat at the table. She was wearing a woolen bathrobe and a flannel nightgown. Her hair, released for the night from its braids, was draped over her shoulders. Her left hand was wrapped in bandages, and the last remnants of sleep still scratched in her throat.

Jeanne placed a cup in front of her and filled it, then poured one for herself.

"This is nice," said Lynne. "I like houseguests, but I think you've learned what you can around here. Now, about all you can do is get hurt."

"We haven't learned much of anything," said Jeanne. "We haven't even gotten Eve Merriweather on tape."

"After that scene yesterday, you probably lost your chance." Lynne sipped her coffee. "If the people who boss Bert McCall got somethin' on her she's been given word to wait you out. I'd also bet it's pretty hard for them to control Bert McCall when he's way up here."

"Who's they?"

Lynne shrugged. "You'll prob'ly find out, whether you want to or not."

Lynne went to the refrigerator and took out a pound of bacon and a dozen eggs. Then she peered out at the barn. "My brother gets damn hungry when he stands watch the whole night. Best cook the pound."

"It's nice of him to give you a night's sleep."

Lynne shrugged, "He don't like that McCall guy much, either."

The bacon began to sizzle.

Lynne cracked the eggs into a bowl. "Bert McCall's a hired gun, but when it comes to bein' a mean, vengeful son of a bitch, he's his own man." She looked at Jeanne. "Whatever came across your friend, that he threatened Bert McCall with a mug of beer?"

"I guess he's a little crazy." She thought she knew the reason. "Probably from watching too many video tapes."

"Well, unless one of you is carrying a sidearm, you'd best be headin' out after breakfast." Lynne poked at the bacon, breaking it into individual strips.

Jeanne took down another frying pan, put some butter into it, and set it on the stove next to the bacon. She turned up the gas and the butter began to melt, Lynne dumped the eggs into the pan, then took a loaf of bread out of the cupboard and began cutting it into slices. Jeanne shook the skillet. Lynne brought out a tray of English marmalades.

Jeanne took a deep breath and asked the question. "Did you sleep with him, Lynne?"

Lynne took the orange juice out of the refrigerator and filled four glasses. "What do you want to know that for?"

"Did you?"

Lynne handed Jeanne a glass of juice. "That's been a stone in your hoof since you first walked in here, hasn't it?"

Jeanne put the glass down. She would not let Lynne put her off. "I'm trying to understand what was happening to him on that last trip, so that I can accept the way he ended up. Two weeks after he left here, he rejected me. A day later, he was dead."

Lynne dropped two slices of bread into the toaster. "And you figure, if you can find some gal who shook her tail at him, you'll have someone to blame?"

Jeanne resolved to remain calm. "This isn't easy for me, Lynne."

"I hate to disappoint you, but I don't drop my drawers for every man who knocks on my door, even when he's a good-lookin' Hollywood producer with a fine line of small talk." Lynne went over to the stove and turned off the flames. Then she lifted the strips onto a paper towel.

"I'm sorry," said Jeanne, almost happily.

"No need." Lynne looked at Jeanne and unconsciously began to braid the strands of hair that reached almost to her breasts.

"You're the lucky one. Even if he's gone, you had five or six years with a good man. In my life, I've had maybe four or five months. Then I always scare 'em off. I'm too demandin', they say, too much in love with my ranch and my cows to love any one man too long."

She finished the braid. One side of her face now looked hard, almost craggy. The other was still softened by a tangle of blond hair. "Your husband was a real temptation, and the night he had dinner here, he was sending out all the right signals. But I figured, he'd be gone the next day, and a quick roll with a stranger never satisfied me yet. I'd rather have nothin' at all."

"Why are you telling me this?" Jeanne picked up the skillet and poured the bacon fat into an empty soup can at the back of the stove.

"Because I'm still here, lady, still gettin' along, man or no man." She began to make the second braid. "I didn't think your husband was worth gettin' worked up over for a few days of fun, and I don't think he's worth whatever you're goin' through seven months after he's gone."

Jeanne dropped the skillet back onto the stove. "What do you mean?" she asked angrily.

"It won't bring him back." Lynne finished braiding. Two ropes of hair now lay across her shoulders, giving her once again the rugged, invulnerable look that she presented to the world. "If I was you, I'd give up chasin' the ghost."

"But you're not me," Jeanne managed a smile.

Lynne looked at Jeanne for a long time. "It's nice to be in love," she said. "But it's nice to be your own woman. And if there's a choice between lovin' a ghost and bein' independent, I'd favor the second."

"I can't," said Jeanne. "At least not yet."

Feeling like fugitives, Jeanne Darrow and James Whiting left an hour later heading for Hunter, Iowa.

In June, Roger Darrow had driven from Jackson Hole on 287 to Yellowstone, where he had photographed Old Faithful. Then he had driven east on 20, over the Continental Divide and the Big

Horn Mountains, to Buffalo, at the edge of the grassland.

In the heart of winter, 287 north and 20 east out of Yellowstone were buried deep in snow. The fastest route to Iowa would have been south, through Casper to I-80, and then across Nebraska. But Whiting wanted to follow Darrow's route as closely as possible, which meant spending the night in Buffalo, Wyoming, and travelling an extra six hours to get there.

They had been gone an hour when Lynne Baker heard a knock at her door. Her brother had headed home. She went to the door, moved her shotgun to within easy reach, and peered out. Bert McCall was standing on the porch. She opened the door and looked over the chain lock. "What do you want?"

"I want to talk to your friends," he sounded very calm. "Where are they?"

"I wouldn't know."

McCall's eyes were bloodshot. Lynne could smell liquor.

"I expected to see you about six this mornin', Bert. You must be hung over."

He glowered at her for a moment. There was a red stain on the bandage over his temple. "Open up."

"You ain't bein' very professional about this, Bert," she taunted. "I figured you'd be more subtle. Maybe get them drunk and run their car off the road. Somethin' like that."

"Open up," he said again.

"They ain't here, and I don't know when they'll be back."

Bert McCall smashed his right forearm against the door and tore the chain lock out of the frame. The door hit Lynne Baker and spun her backward. The frigid air rushed into the house. McCall grabbed Lynne by the collar of her turtleneck and almost lifted her off the floor.

"I asked you nice, now I'll ask you again. Where are they?" He squeezed his hand tight so that the collar closed around her throat.

"I don't know."

"I think you do." He dragged her across the room. He swept the stuffed owl off the table and held it in front of her face. "Tell your friend."

"I don't know," she rasped. "And if I did, I wouldn't tell the damn owl."

He closed his fist around the bird's head and crushed it. The glass eyes dropped onto the floor and bounced. Sawdust and paper pushed out through the sockets. The beak snapped. The skull of feathers collapsed.

"Nice work, asshole," grumbled Lynne. "You want to try that with my moose on the wall?"

"Unless you tell me where they went, I'm gonna try it with you."

"No, you ain't." The muzzle of Tommy Baker's Winchester pressed against the back of Bert McCall's neck. "Now let my sister go."

McCall did nothing.

"Blow his brains out," said Lynne.

There was the metallic in-out-out-in sound of a rifle being cocked.

"That's a good idea, sis," answered Tommy. "A lot of people'd be damn glad to see it. But if I do it right here, what brains he's got'll make a mess of your nice hairdo."

"You got a point, there, Tommy. But I can always duck if you give me a signal."

McCall's eyes shifted, then he released Lynne.

"Don't turn around too fast." Tommy stepped back and lowered the gun until it was pointing at McCall's midsection.

"Someday, you won't have that thing with you."

"Don't bet on it," answered Tommy. He looked at his sister. "You want to have the sheriff come out and arrest this bastard."

Lynne shook her head. "He'd be bailed out two hours later."

Without another word, Bert McCall stalked out.

"It's a good thing I forgot my Thermos," said Tommy.

"Yeah." Lynne walked to the front door and watched McCall's car pulling away.

"You should have called the sheriff," said Tommy. "If McCall figures out the road your friends took, they'll be glad for a few hours' head start."

"You may be right." Lynne picked up the telephone.

22

And now, for another installment in the trek of Roger Darrow's kidney," said Vicki Rogers.

It was a Saturday, but Vicki Rogers was on the air. In Hollywood, she said, important things were happening seven days of the week. On Friday nights, she taped two extra reports that were fed to local news stations across the country on the weekend. Occasionally, she brought in a crew to tape if a big story broke. She called the program "Over the Weekend On the Coast." Vicki Rogers was nothing if not ambitious.

In Los Angeles, on the patio of his Laurel Canyon home, Vaughn Lawrence studied the television set and lit a cigarette. At his office on Alvorado, Len Haley did isometric exercises at his desk and stared at the screen.

In other time zones, Vicki Rogers had appeared earlier. The Reverend Billy Singer had listened at his media center in Youngstown. Congressman Reuben Merrill had skipped a tennis date with an influential lobbyist to see to the program. And at his Manhattan penthouse, John Meade had watched and begun to wonder if one loose thread, one moment of compassion, was going to unravel the fabric he had woven and stitched with Vaughn Lawrence.

"Yes," said Vicki. "The producer's widow and James Whiting are winding their way across America, retracing Roger Darrow's steps, and expanding the documentary that Darrow was dreaming when he died in a mysterious boating accident."

Not mysterious at all, thought Len Haley. A professional job that looked totally accidental.

"Well," she said in her most conspiratorial tone, "they've had a rough row of it. In Yosemite, they tried to talk with Reuben Merrill, and he wasn't there."

Merrill had choked on his croissant when he heard his name.

"Then they headed to Jackson Hole, Wyoming, to investigate

the background of the famous Sylbert-Merriweather debate."

It *is* coming apart, John Meade had thought.

"My sources tell me that they didn't get much dope on the debate, but Mr. Whiting and Mrs. Darrow got themselves into a fine old western brawl in a rather chichi après-ski cowboy saloon. It seems that one of the locals objected to their questions. Could it be that they're touching raw nerves among the rawhides of the Old West?"

No, thought Len Haley. They've simply made the wrong man mad, and not even Len Haley could control him.

"Stay tuned," continued Vicki. "Their next stop is a small city called Hunter, Iowa, where a MacGregor cable TV franchise recently began operating."

"After that, they're hoping for an audience with the greatest TV preacher of them all, Billy Singer."

It shall be given, Billy Singer had decided.

"Then it's on to New York, and we'll be with them every step of the way."

James Whiting was stiff and sore, and he had a painful bruise on his ribs from McCall's kick. Better there than the abdomen, he thought. He feared that he might be pushing his body too hard, expecting too much from a fragile system, but he had to keep going. He owed it to Roger Darrow, and to himself.

And in spite of the pain, he felt satisfied, proud of himself. He had faced the threat, just like Darrow, and with some help, he had won the fight.

They went over the Continental Divide at Togwotee Pass. On the west side of the divide, every hill, river, and stream flowed to the Pacific, or evaporated in an alkali sink. To the east, water flowed into the Atlantic or the Gulf. In a geological sense, they had left the West.

Togwotee Pass cut through the Rockies at nine thousand feet, above the treeline. As they rode, Whiting recalled Darrow's thoughts on Sylvan Pass, where he crossed the mountains seven months earlier.

"The narrow road winds upward, the transmission begins to strain, the engine may sputter because the oxygen is getting thin, and you really don't notice that along both sides of the road, the vegetation is changing: The big trees are becoming thinner,

*smaller, the shrubs are growing skimpy. Then, but for stubborn*ll
mosses clinging to the rocks, the green is gone. You are above the
tree line. You are at the top of the world. And a bleak place it is.
The wind booms through the passes and blows so hard that no soil
can hold. The sun is high and intense, but without warmth. The
sky is a deep blue, unblemished by smog, haze, or the dust of
the farming valleys. There are no other colors but white and gray,
the white of the snow that never melts and the gray of the rock
that surrounds you: great, desolate piles of rock, giant boulders,
sheer walls, heaps of slag that have eroded and slid onto the road-
side.

"When you're through the pass and realize that you're heading
down again, you are filled with a sense of relief. You have seen the
worst, most inimical place on the continent, and you are descend-
ing with new appreciation to the valleys, the grassland, the

green."

In winter, thought Whiting, the desolation was heightened
because the snow covered everything.

By noon, they were crossing the Wind River Indian Reservation, which sat on the plains in the middle of the state. Whiting
was asleep. Jeanne was wondering if Lynne Baker had yet been
visited by Bert McCall or the sheriff.

Bert McCall was two hours behind them on 287. The Teton
County sheriff had issued a bulletin for McCall, who was now
wanted for one count of breaking and entering and another of
assault and battery.

The sheriff had not asked about, nor had Lynne mentioned,
James Whiting and Jeanne Darrow. As far as he was concerned,
they were someplace in Teton County awaiting their hearing.

At noon in the mountain zone, it was 2:00 P.M. in Washington,
D.C.

Reuben Merrill, back in his office after a lunchtime spent with
the congressional masseur, placed a call to Vaughn Lawrence in
Hollywood, where it was 11:00 A.M.

"I thought you had an agreement from Vicki Rogers," said
Merrill angrily.

"She's her own woman, Congressman. She refuses to reveal

her source, and she's stopped doing favors for me."

"I don't want to become a regular character on the gossip spots, Lawrence. If she starts mentioning my name every time she talks about Darrow, especially in Wyoming, somebody may try to make a connection between us and the defeat of Tom Sylbert. Then, the shit starts to rise."

Lawrence laughed. "As any congressman knows, shit has a lot of buoyancy, so you'll float right on top of it."

"Don't humor me, Lawrence. I'm not a contestant on one of your damn game shows."

Vaughn Lawrence lit his tenth cigarette of the day. "I'll lean on Vicki Rogers a little bit, and maybe we can get her to bury the story."

"That's what I want to hear, Vaughn," said Merrill. "And what about Darrow's wife?"

There was a long silence on Lawrence's end of the line. He did not know what to do about Jeanne Darrow. He had not been able to slow her down, frighten her off, or make the decision to stop her permanently. "Don't worry about her, Congressman. If we can silence Vicki Rogers, Mrs. Darrow will just evaporate."

"I'll take your word for that," answered Merrill. "And the next time I'm talking with him, I'll put in a good word for you with MacGregor."

You do that, thought Lawrence.

James Whiting was driving. He had negotiated the last hairpin turn, and now the Cherokee was gliding down the gentle eastern slope of the Big Horn Mountains. A Mozart piano concerto was playing on the tape deck, and the town of Buffalo was a half hour away.

Jeanne gazed down onto the white plains, which rolled ahead of them to the Appalachians, and she thought about Lynne Baker's advice. But she could not give up the chase, because the Roger Darrow she had seen on the last tape was not the man she had known for seven years. Once, Jeanne Darrow had been the center of her husband's existence. She had refused, even after seeing the tapes, to believe that he would have been able to move out of her orbit forever. She had faced failure in her career. She had accepted it and moved on. She could not accept it in her marriage to a man she had never stopped loving. She was going to prove to herself that she could have won him back from Miranda, even though he had been gone for seven months.

At five o'clock, Whiting turned on the weather report. A snowstorm had begun to blow on the other side of the Big Horns. It was expected to drop over a foot in the higher elevations, and six to eight inches when it reached Buffalo.

"Will the snow hold us up?" asked Jeanne. She had grown up in Orange County, and she had never traveled in a snowstorm.

Whiting smiled at her. A bandage covered the four stitches in his chin. "If Bert McCall couldn't stop us, a little blizzard has no chance at all."

She heard the edge of boyish excitement cutting into his voice. She thought it was a tone that all men possessed, because she had heard it in Roger's voice whenever he decided to do something stupid or dangerous, like body-surfing during a coastal storm.

"You should never have threatened that guy with the beer yesterday," she said.

"I threatened him and you threw the beer. I thought we made a good team." He shrugged. "Of course, I think we just scratched the surface of what went on back there."

"I found out what I was after."

Whiting ignored her and kept talking. "Lynne Baker had some good theories. Eve Merriweather seemed pretty hostile, which told us something. And Bert McCall said plenty just the way he acted."

"Can you tie McCall or Merriweather to MacGregor or Lawrence?" she asked impatiently.

"Well, no, but that doesn't mean the connections aren't there."

When they reached the flatland, Whiting said, "We'll have more luck with that Lyle Guise in Iowa. His connection to MacGregor is as clear as the Wyoming air."

"Lyle Guise is to be treated with respect," said Jeanne firmly. "He helped to raise my husband."

"The bitch won't budge," said Vaughn Lawrence.

"Did you threaten to drop her show?" asked Haley.

Lawrence nodded. "She told me she'd be glad if I did. She claims she's getting nibbles from CBS."

"She's lying. Call her bluff. Drop her segment on Monday. When she goes crazy, tell her to call your lawyer."

Vaughn Lawrence and Len Haley were drinking wine on the

redwood deck behind Lawrence's home. It was seven o'clock and the temperature was in the low sixties. Lawrence got up and dipped his toes into the hot tub. Then he stripped off his terrycloth bathrobe, shivered in the cool night air, and slid into the water.

"Sure you won't join me?"

Haley remained in the deck chair beside the tub. "The last time I took a bath with friends was in the Mekong River. I was captured in my u-trou. Worst day of my life. I'm a shower man now."

Lawrence lay back, tipping his head into the water.

"You relaxed?" asked Haley.

Lawrence groaned.

"Now what about Vicki?"

Lawrence looked up. "Let's give her until tomorrow. If she makes another report from the middle of America, we'll deep-six her on Monday."

"That's good," said Haley, "because by Monday, I think our two friends may be dead."

Lawrence half-rose from the tub. "What?"

"There's nothing I can do," said Haley. "Bert McCall took off after them this morning."

"I didn't authorize this," said Lawrence.

"Neither did I," answered Haley. "McCall's a good man, but he's out of control."

Lawrence slipped back into the water.

"It's a good scenario," said Haley after a few moments. "They beat the shit out of him in the bar, he goes bananas, tracks them down, and kills them both. Vicki Rogers can scream all she wants, but Bert McCall has the perfect motive, especially for someone you might say is a little hotheaded."

Vaughn Lawrence inhaled the steam rising off the water. "Can he be traced back to the Haley Detective Agency?"

Haley shook his head. "I recommended him when Cutler came down here peddling shares in Cutler Oil Drilling and Exploration, but there's nothing in writing. If somebody wanted to tie us together, they'd have to go back to our unit in Nam. Bert McCall was a good man in a fight."

"Will he talk if he's arrested?"

"Name, rank, and serial number." Haley sipped his beer and stared into the palm fronds and broad-leafed tropical plants on the

hillside below the house. In the darkness, it looked liked something from his past, a nightmare, a place in Vietnam. He felt a
little trickle of perspiration gathering just below his hairline. He
wiped it away.

"What gives this McCall guy such a short fuse?" asked Lawrence. He didn't care. He was simply talking to fill up the silence.

Haley looked down into the hot tub. "He always had a short
fuse. You wouldn't understand about the things that lit it."

"He shocked the shit out of me when he took care of Jack
Cutler without bothering to consult anyone down here."

"When Bert sees a threat, he reacts," said Haley. "He thought
Jack Cutler was talking too much, and he was right."

Lawrence extended his arms and studied his hands as they
floated on top of the water. "Why do you think he'd kill Jack
Cutler, after working for him for a year?"

"Loyalty," said Haley crisply.

Lawrence laughed. "He wasn't very loyal to Jack Cutler."

"He was loyal to me," said Haley. "To what we were. To what
you're doing. But mostly to me." He paused. "Once, for us, loyalty
was all that mattered. For guys like me and McCall and Cal Bannister." He laughed softly. "That's why you got lucky when you
met me, Vaughn. Most people don't know about loyalty. But I'm
teaching you as we go along."

Lawrence looked up at Haley. He knew that he was tied to
Haley for as long as Haley wanted to hold on. He was glad that
Haley was one of the few men he had ever respected. "I hate to
see this happen to Jeanne Darrow," Lawrence said softly. She's a
beautiful woman."

"There's nothing we can do." Haley picked up the bottle of
Vouvray on the deck and filled Vaughn Lawrence's glass. "I'd go
up there myself, but Buffalo's not an easy place to get to, and the
snowstorm's closed half the airfields in the state."

Lawrence sipped the wine. The alcohol and warm water were
having their effect. He was starting to slur his words. "None of
this should have happened," he said.

"You can't control everything." Haley reached into his sportcoat pocket and took out a bottle of white tablets. He placed one
beside Lawrence's wineglass. "Worry about the important things,
like Reuben Merrill and John Meade."

Lawrence studied the capsule for a moment, then looked at

Haley. "Care to join me? I hat to get stoned by myself."

"Who's getting stoned without me?" Kelly Hammerstein appeared on the deck, wrapped in a terrycloth robe.

Haley gave her a Quaalude; Lawrence poured her a glass of wine. She took them, then dropped her bathrobe onto the deck, and walked to the edge of the hot tub. Lawrence watched her breasts sway; Haley studied the contours of her behind. She dipped a toe into the water, then eased her whole body down. As the heat rose around her, a long low growl rose from her throat. She took a deep breath, then let it out slowly. "I love California."

Bert McCall was six thousand feet above see level. The snow was so thick that the glare from his headlights bounced back into his eyes. The voice on the radio was issuing the weather-service travel advisory every five minutes; heavy snow in northeastern Wyoming, sixteen to twenty inches in the mountains, eight to sixteen on the plains, and ending by morning. It was eight o'clock. He had been fighting his way across the Big Horns for two hours, and he had three more ahead of him. In good weather, he could cross in less than two. His Oldsmobile Cutlass, with front-wheel drive and chains on the rear, was skidding on every turn and straining through the snow that was now above the hubcaps. He knew he would not make it to Buffalo that night.

A half hour later, he pulled into the parking lot of the old Big Horn Motel. In the snow, he nearly drove past it, because it was completely deserted. He left his car near the road and approached the row of cabins. The snow was swirling. A screen door had blown loose and was banging in the wind. He shielded his eyes and looked at the roof of each cabin, until he saw one with a brick chimney, which meant a fireplace. He smashed the door open and ran his flashlight around the room: a bed, three woolen blankets folded neatly on top of it, a maple dresser, a fireplace. A short time later, the maple wood roared in the fireplace, the blizzard screamed around the little cabin, and Bert McCall cleaned his .357 Magnum.

In never ends, he thought. Here is always one more battle, one more debt to pay the past. It never ends, even if you move to the mountains and leave L.A. behind. There's always a snowstorm brewing. And you never know when the past will come to call in

its mark. When it does, there is nothing for you to do but pay up.
It isn't so bad, though, when someone like Len Haley collects the
bill. He was there. He knows. He owes as much to the past as you
do.

Buffalo was small enough that he could check all the motels in
half an hour. If he didn't find them there, he would get them
someplace along I-90. They were as dead as the two ARVN lieutenants who pulled rank on him one night in a Saigon whorehouse.

Bert McCall was a sergeant. He had selected a woman with
delicate Eurasian features and a reputation for doing things that
would wear a man out for a week. He was leading her to a room
when the madam intercepted them and explained that two Vietnamese lieutenants had requested the young woman. The American could have anyone else in the house for the night. McCall told
her he had the woman he wanted and slammed the door in her
face.

He was about to take the prostitute from behind when the door
swung open and the two ARVNs burst into the room. McCall
turned, and one of them kicked him in the groin. The other opened
McCall's face with a brass knuckle, then spun him around and
delivered a shot to his kidneys. They worked him over with boots
and brass knuckles until he was a bloody, senseless pulp and
threw him naked onto the street.

A week later, Bert McCall waited outside for the two lieutenants to leave the whorehouse. As they passed the doorway where
he hid, he stepped into the light. He aimed his .45, blew off one
man's testicles, and shot the other in the head. One died instantly;
the other bled to death in agony.

No one since, until Whiting, had dared to kick him. The pain
he felt in the fight at the Cutler club had tripped all the circuits of
hatred and rage inside him. James Whiting would not escape.

Jeanne Darrow and James Whiting checked into the first motel
they found in Buffalo, which was a small town on the edge of the
grasslands and a popular stopping point for families on their way
to the Wyoming National Parks.

The motel's main office looked as though it had once been a
short-order restaurant. There was a registration desk beside a

small luncheon counter and four tables by the window. One of the tables had been given over to the motel's own historical exhibit. Two life-size manikins sat at the table. They had copper skin, high cheekbones, and silly grins outlined in red lipstick. One wore a leather vest and a reservation top hat with a wampum headband. The other was resplendent in war bonnet and buckskin suit. They had their arms around each other and their heads together, as though they were singing "Sweet Adeline." Each held an empty shot glass, and on the table in front of them was a whiskey bottle.

Someone had hung sings around their necks. "Ugh, that heap good firewater," read one. "And how, How," the other responded.

Whiting looked twice when he saw them. Two young men at the next table were sharing the bottled contents of a paper bag. They snickered.

"Do these guys come in here often?" asked Whiting.

"We can't get rid of 'em." The young men snickered again.

Whiting decided to say nothing more.

The man behind the desk seemed slightly surprised when Whiting asked for two rooms; then he shrugged and handed Whiting the register. After settling in, Whiting returned to the lobby, where he placed his nightly call to Vicki Rogers. He wondered what Jeanne would say when she found that one of her least-favorite people had been helping to protect them on the road.

23

Bert McCall woke when the wind stopped howling. He glanced at his watch: 5:45 A.M..

James Whiting was awakened around six o'clock by the sound of a plow scraping down the street. He looked out the window. The snow had stopped, and small chinks of blue had appeared in the sky. He and Jeanne had coffee and donuts with the Indians at the motel lunch counter and were back on the road by twenty to seven.

East of Buffalo lay the great Wyoming grasslands. In long low waves, the land rolled gently toward the Dakotas. The clouds were racing south before a booming Canadian cold front. The sun, just risen, sent its beams almost parallel to the earth. And a fresh coating of snow covered everything to the horizon in every direction. It was, thought Whiting, as though nature had flash-frozen all of America.

"His name is Whiting, and hers is Jeanne Darrow. They're driving a green Dodge Cherokee with California plates. Have you seen them?" asked Bert McCall.

The solemn man behind the desk folded his arms. "Who's askin'?"

McCall noticed the Indian figures sitting at the table. "My name's Dunbar. I'm a federal agent. Whiting and Darrow are members of some pro-Indian group. They tried to stir up trouble with the Navajo down in Arizona, then they drove up here to Wind River and got the Cheyenne all pissed off. I been trackin' them since. We think they're on their way to Wounded Knee."

The man behind his desk stroked his chin. "That feller didn't seem to like How and Ugh over there, not at all."

"When did they leave?"

"Say, you got any ID?"

McCall flashed his Los Angeles private detective license, then he repeated his question.

"About six-thirty."

"Did they say where they were headed?"

"No, but they asked if I-90 would be clear."

Bert McCall was back on the highway five minutes later.

Around quarter to nine, the Jeep Cherokee crossed the frozen Belle Fourche River. Soon, they would be out of the grassland and rising into the Black Hills of south Dakota, the land the Plains Indians had once held sacred.

They passed a billboard, and it reminded Whiting of one of Roger Darrow's video tapes.

"Just ninety miles to Wall Drug. Don't forget to stop" is the slogan on the billboard.

"Wall Drugg is famous to any traveler who uses I-90 in South Dakota or Wyoming," says Darrow. Their billboards stretch for a hundred miles on either side of Wall, South Dakota. By the time you get there, you want to stop just out of curiosity, to see who on earth would go to such lengths to promote a drugstore. Well, the drugstore is about the size of a football field, and it's always crowded. The promoters should be in Hollywood."

The camera pans from the billboard onto the landscape beyond it. The green stretches to the horizon. Here and there, a house or a hillock floats on the prairie. And waves of grass seem to rise and fall as the breeze dances across the expanse.

"The Plains Indians called this the Land of the Greasy Grass." Roger Darrow steps into the shot. "When the wind blows and the grass swirls, the rough silvery side of the leaf flashes and seems to shine, as though it has been coated with bear grease.

"Once, the buffalo wandered here in the millions, and the hunting was always good. There were no towns, no farmhouses, no drugstores, no six-lanes stitching the landscape together. It was a single, seamless fabric, from the Black Hills to the Yellowstone, from Canada to the Platte River. Sioux, Cheyenne, Arapaho, Crow, and Blackfoot hunted here and lived as their ancestors had since the beginning of time, in close partnership with nature.

"The Indians are gone now, to reservations and cities. But their land remains as a tribute. And when the wind blows across

Bert McCall had made up nearly an hour's distance between himself and his quarry. If he did not overtake them soon, he would begin to make stops at restaurants and diners along the way and hope that he could surprise them in the middle of a side of fries.

From the grasslands, three thousand feet up into the Black Hills, then along the northern edge of the Badlands in a few hours. Against the snow, the pines of the Black Hills seemed even blacker. The bleak desert beauty of the Badlands, of the buttes and cliffs and eroded ridges, was given a touch of irony by the dusting of snow.

At eleven o'clock, James Whiting and Jeanne Darrow had reached South Dakota's farm belt and passed into the central time zone. The land in January had no feature save whiteness. But in a few months, the hard red spring wheat would begin to grow toward the sun.

"It's amazing that in this land of plenty, there's not one set of golden arches." Whiting had been watching for a place to eat.

"Not even a town," added Jeanne. "Let's stop at the next gas station and empty the candy machine."

They saw a sign for food, lodging, and gas, and they turned off I-90. A gas station, a post office, a general store, a motel, three run-down shacks, no trees: It was less a town than an outpost in the middle of the blowing snow. The street, which looked like a bypassed artery, ran parallel to I-90. At the end of the little strip, just before the highway on-ramp, a single story of cinderblocks squatted beneath a neon sign that said Eat. One car was parked in the snow-crusted lot.

Jeanne pulled up beside it. "Are you sure you want to go in?"

"I've heard some good things about this place," said Whiting. "It was written up in *The New Yorker*. They said, if you're ever in Nowhere, South Dakota, visit the Eat Restaurant and order the house special."

The little building had a metal chimney, a tin roof, and one window, a double-size casement facing the parking lot. It looked to Whiting as though the vibration of the heavy trucks on I-90 would eventually shake the place down. Inside, the place seemed very clean, almost unused. It did not smell of grease or coffee, but there was a faint, medicinal odor of Lestoil. The linoleum was yellow, with purple and green cross-hatchings and several holes worn through to the concrete slab. Four chrome stools were arranged neatly in front of the lunch counter. At the side of the counter was a glass case containing penny candy, water pistols, pinwheels, and trading cards. Behind the counter was a refrigerator, a stove, a microwave oven, a nineteen-inch color television set, and a young man wearing a wide grin.

"Good morning," he said, "er . . . I mean afternoon. It's a lovely day today. A bit chilly but still pl—pleasant. What can I do for you folks?" It sounded as though he had rehearsed the speech all morning.

"We'd like lunch," said Whiting, and he and Jeanne sat at the counter.

The yound man wore a wool shirt and a stainless white butcher's apron. He was very thin, with slender hands and an elongated face, as though the birth canal had been too narrow, and he had been squeezed out, like toothpaste from a tube. He wore thick glasses and a hearing aid. He stood and stared at Jeanne, and he made no attempt to hide his awe of her beauty.

She tried to ignore him, first by glancing at the local newscast on the television, then by reading the hand-lettered menu.

Hot Campbell Soup 75
Hamburger 1.00
Cheeseburger 1.25
Hot Dog 75
Cheese Sandwich 50
(stir up the Campbell, soup is good food)

Finally, she smiled at him.

He grinned, then thrust his hand forward. "My name is Eddie. What's yours?"

She took his hand and said her name.

He shook vigorously, then offered his hand to Whiting. "My name is Eddie. What's yours?"

"Jim."

"That's a good name." Eddie then turned and ducked into the men's room. They heard running water. He was washing his hands.

Jeanne and Whiting each ordered the soup, thinking that Eddie could do the least harm with something canned. They also ordered soft drings.

"I'd offer you beer," said Eddie, "but my dad couldn't get a liquor license."

"How's business?" asked Whiting.

Eddie was nervously sponging off the counter top, which was perfectly clean. "People don't like the looks of the place from the road, but once they see how clean it is and have one of Eddie's burgers, they always come back. Are you sure you don't want one of my burgers?"

"Have one, Whiting," said Jeanne.

Whiting shrugged and said he'd love one.

Eddie went to work with a quarter pound of beef, bacon, sliced tomato, cheese, lettuce, and halfway through the process, Jeanne ordered one for herself.

As he worked, Eddie kept up a constant patter of conversation, and when his hands weren't busy, he was wiping up the little drops of grease that splattered onto the stove.

"My dad built this place because he says a man needs to have a place to work and feel like he's in charge. He'd let me work the farm, but he don't think I should be near heavy machinery and such."

Whiting wondered if Eddie's limp had come from an encounter with a combine.

"And he says I'm too—too nigh-eeve to work for other people. I think that means stupid."

"No," said Jeanne gently. "It means you're too friendly. Too nice."

"A person can't be too friendly, can they?" he asked.

She shook her head.

He placed the hamburgers on the counter. They were as tempting as anything ever seen in New York or Los Angeles. He watched closely until they had both taken bites and offered compliments. Then he continued. "My daddy built this place, and I decorated it."

He gestured to the pictures behind the bar and along the walls.

Pennants from the Minnesota Twins and the Vikings, photographs of Fran Tarkenton, Wayne Gretzky, Telly Savalas, Robert Blake, Hugh O'Brian, Peter Cross, and an old poster from the movie *Rio Bravo*.

"I wrote to the athletes, then I wrote to Kojak and Baretta and Wyatt Earp and Flint. And I got a poster of my favorite movie. *Rio Bravo*'s on TV almost every month.

"I like Walter Brennan in it, 'cause he limps and everyone thinks he's an old fool, but he's got a shotgun, and he kills a lot of bad guys at the end."

Jeanne complimented him again on the hamburger.

"I limp and everyone thinks I'm a fool. . . ."

"I don't," said Jeanne.

"But," his voice became stern and he tried to frown, "if any bad guys come in here, I'm ready for them." He reached behind the counter and produced a sawed-off shotgun.

Jeanne almost gagged.

"I'm sorry," he said nervously. "I don't show that around."

"We won't tell any bad guys," said Whiting.

Eddie sensed the condescension in Whiting's voice. "Don't make fun of me, mister. I just made you a good hamburger." He turned angrily and raised the volume on the television set.

After a few moments, he was their friend again, and he was suggesting that they watch the Vicki Rogers report, which came on at the end of the news. "She tells me all about my friends and all about my favorite shows. Do you like Vicki Rogers?"

Jeanne simply smiled.

Whiting chewed on his hamburger and watched Jeanne out of the corner of his eye.

Vicki ran through the Hollywood news and gossip. Eddie cheered when she announced that one of his favorite shows was being renewed for the following season. He laughed insanely at all of Vicki's jokes. He did not react, however, when pictures of James Whiting and Jeanne Darrow were flashed on the screen behind Vicki. Nor did Whiting.

Jeanne, however, stopped chewing and for a moment, stopped breathing.

"And now, for an update," said Vicki. "Today, according to my sources, Jeanne Darrow and James Whiting are someplace in South Dakota. . . ."

"South Dakota! She said 'South Dakota!' " shouted Eddie.

". . . and they should reach Iowa by tonight."

Eddie turned to his two customers. "Did you hear that? She mentioned South—" Eddie stopped talking. He looked at the photographs on the television screen, then back at Jeanne and Whiting. "You're—you're them. . . ."

Whiting put a finger to his lips, then pointed to the screen.

"Yes, sir," said Eddie, with new respect.

"Their trip has been uneventful since the brawl in Wyoming," continued Vicki. "My sources tell me that by the time they reach New York next Wednesday night, they will have some absolutely stellar footage to incorporate into 'One Man's America.' Word from one of the networks is that Peter Cross will narrate if the show airs. And if I may be so bold, I've been getting some vibrations around town recently from some rather important people who would be just as happy if 'One Man's America' never saw the light of day. A most interesting story. Stay tuned. Until tomorrow . . ."

Jeanne and Eddie both turned slowly to Whiting.

"Do you really know Peter Cross?" asked Eddie.

Whiting gestured to Jeanne. "She does."

"You do?"

Jeanne smiled. "He's a very nice man, Eddie. Now, if you don't mind, we'd like a few moments of privacy."

"Yes. Yes, ma'am." Eddie took an earphone from under the counter, put it on, and plugged it into the television set. "It's time for 'Gunsmoke.' After that the NFL play-off is on." Eddie fiddled with the UHF dial and tuned in an old rerun.

Jeanne turned on Whiting. "Who's her source? As if I didn't know."

"I had to do it, Jeanne."

"And what's all the bullshit about Peter Cross and the networks?"

"That's Vicki's invention."

"Why did you have to do it?"

Eddie sponged the handle on the refrigerator. With one ear, he listened to Matt Dillon. With the other, he listened to the two celebrities at his lunch counter.

"So you could get on her good side?" Jeanne answered her own question.

"To protect us," said Whiting, "from guys like Bert McCall."

"How can she do that?"

"By focusing a little attention on us, so that people are less willing to take shots at us."

She thought about it for a moment. "You should have told me. It's not a bad idea."

Whiting threw up his hands.

Jeanne called to Eddie. "Is the coffee as good as the hamburgers?"

"Yes, ma'am."

She gave him the Thermos she had brought in, and he filled it proudly. As he did, he asked them everything he could about television. Was the food good at Archie Bunker's Place? Was James Garner married to the lady in the Polaroid commercial? Did Tom Brokaw like Roger Mudd? Did Flint ever get turned down when he asked a girl on a date? Was it true that Vicki Rogers could read people's minds? Was Big Bird a boy or a girl? Did Billy Singer really sleep on an old army cot and read the Bible every night? Did Vaughn Lawrence have to pay for all the presents he gave away on "People and Prices"? What state were the Smurfs born in? And would there ever be a time when there would be cameras in every house, so that everyone could be TV stars?

"You really like television, don't you, Eddie?" said Whiting.

Eddie laughed bitterly. "What else is there, besides hamburgers and keepin' my stove clean. I never been anywhere. I never done anything. I nev—never had a girl friend. My dad spends all his time workin' the farm and my ma, she never liked me 'cause I wasn't pretty, and she was always ashamed 'cause I ain't real smart."

He wiped off the counter top again. "TV's my best friend. I'd give anything if they'd bring back Pinky Lee."

"Would you like to say all that for a camera?" asked Whiting. "Any maybe someday appear on the show that Vicki Rogers was talking about?"

Eddie took off his glasses, pulled out his hearing aid, and ripped off his apron. "Should I wear a blue shirt, too?"

And Eddie Van der Hoof had a screen test. Whiting set up the video camera in the restaurant. Eddie sat at the table by the window, with the afternoon sun flooding the scene, and he talked about television. He said nothing that was consciously profound.

He simply described his best memories and the companionship that television had always provided him. He talked for twenty minutes, totally calm, totally at ease with the camera.

Had he had experience? they asked. He responded that he had been living with television since birth. How could he feel nervous in front of a camera?

After they loaded the Cherokee, Whiting and Jeanne went back into the restaurant to say good-bye. Eddie was dressed in his parka and stocking cap.

"Where are you going?" asked Whiting.

"With you," answered Eddie. "You said I was a television star now."

They explained to him they couldn't make him a star until the program had been broadcast. They weren't even sure if the show would make it onto the air.

"But I'm ready. I want to go to New York with you and be famous."

"You won't like it, Eddie," said Whiting gently.

"I want to go to New York. I never been there. I never been anywhere." Eddie stamped his foot on the floor. "I want to go to New York."

"You said your TV takes you everywhere," responded Jeanne gently.

"Well, yeah, but—but I want to go with you. I want to be special."

"You're special right where you are, Eddie. You make the best hamburgers in South Dakota," answered Jeanne.

Eddie looked at Whiting. His eyes showed hurt, confusion.

"A person's always special out here," added Whiting. "You step out your door, and you can see for miles. And outside of the telephone poles, you may be the tallest thing in sight. In New York, you'd just be another lonely ant."

"Yeah, but—yeah, but I want to go with you."

Whiting looked at Jeanne, then put his hand on Eddie's shoulder. "OK, Eddie. You can come."

Jeanne stepped very hard on his foot, but he kept talking.

"We like you, and we want you to be happy."

Eddie smiled.

"But you've got to remember, it'll mean leaving your mother and dad. And your hamburgers. And your nice, clean store. And

New York is the dirtiest city in America."

A trace of concern shot across Eddie's face.

"And one other thing," said Whiting. "No TVs."

Eddie scowled, as though he had been slapped. "Why not?"

"We have no room for yours."

Eddie looked out at the Cherokee, to see it if was filled.

"You'll be without television for four days," continued Whiting. "No 'Gunsmoke,' no news, no Big Bird. And when you get to New York, you won't have the money to buy one because in New York everything is too expensive. So, Eddie, you'd better think it over."

Eddie thought by scowling and frowning and making other expressions that he hoped they would interpret as thought. Then he pulled off his stocking cap and threw it on the table.

"Never mind," he said. "I know what New York looks like. I've seen 'Naked City.' And I always watch 'Archie Bunker's Place.' "

He took off his coat and hung it in the corner. He went back behind the counter, flipped on the television, took out a sponge, and began to clean the counter top.

He looked up after a time and said good-bye, but they were already gone.

For many miles, Jeanne and Whiting traveled in silence. The road was empty, except for two double-semis playing leapfrog with a farmer's pickup about a mile ahead. The land was wide and flat and white. The sky was clear. And back in Nowhere, South Dakota, the television was playing in the Eat Restaurant. They both wondered what Eddie was watching.

Eddie's eyes were fixed on "The NFL Today," but his mind was drifting to parts unknown. The dishes used by his last customers were already washed and stacked. The pots had been cleaned. And he was wearing a fresh apron.

He heard a car pull up in his driveway. He smoothed the apron. Business was good for a Sunday.

A big man, unfamiliar, opened the door. He stood for a moment to survey the restaurant, then he approached the counter and sat. He was huge, thought Eddie, and his blue Windbreaker made his head seem too small for his body. He had a crew cut, a broken nose, and a bandage over the left temple.

"Hi. My name's Eddie." He offered his hand. "What's yours?"

The man shook hands with him. "Bert."

Eddie's mouth dropped open. Bert McCall straightened. He sensed danger. Carefully, Eddie withdrew his hand. He remembered the name from the conversation he had overheard earlier.

"Is is—Bert Mc—McCall?"

"Yeah." Bert McCall stood slowly.

"Are you a—a—bad guy?"

"Hunh?"

"A bad guy?" asked Eddie again.

McCall tried to smile through his teeth. "I'm a good guy."

"Then how come you're chasing my friends from Hollywood?" Eddie demanded angrily.

"They were here?"

"They were here and you want to hurt them and Vicki Rogers said so on her show. You're a bad guy."

Bert McCall stepped toward the door. He saw Eddie's hands drop behind the counter. He grabbed for the Magnum in his belt, but he knew before it cleared that he was too late. As he tried to aim, his mind was facing the irony. The Mekong Delta, Saigon brothels, Hanoi prison camps. The sleaziest side of southern California. Enforcement and assassination in Wyoming. He had survived it all, to die like this.

The shotgun exploded three feet away from him. Down feathers flew. When the Magnum went off, it was simply a reflex. The bullet crashed into the counter. Bert McCall died within thirty seconds.

When the State Police arrived, Eddie Van der Hoof was carefully mopping up the blood still seeping from the corpse. He said that the man had tried to rob him. The police lietenant said that they would have to check Eddie's story, but Eddie knew that he was in the clear, because the policeman wore a uniform. Policemen in uniforms never figured anything out. To be smart, a cop had to wear a dirty raincoat or suck on a lollipop and say, "Who loves ya, baby."

24

It was near seven o'clock. Jeanne Darrow and James Whiting had just eaten hamburgers in Sioux Falls, South Dakota. They had seen little more of the city than the fast-food restaurant, the railroad tracks, and a line of old warehouses along the river. They hoped to stay that night in Missouri Valley, three hours away. The drive from Missouri Valley to Hunter, in the southwest corner of the state, would take another seven hours.

As Whiting drove south on 29 toward the Omaha bypass, Jeanne plugged a cassette into the tape player, wrapped an afghan around her legs, and slipped a small pillow between her head and the window. The cab was filled with the crystalline sound of a single violin climbing the scale with delicacy and grace.

Whiting listened, then looked at Jeanne. "I can name that tune in eight bars."

"Give it a try."

" 'The Lark Ascending,' by Vaughn Williams."

"Bravo." She applauded delicately.

"The embodiment of serenity," he said.

She smiled at him, and in the half-light, he thought he saw something in her expression that had not been there before, a new warmth or generosity.

"I'm glad we have the same taste in music," he said. "It wouldn't do if one of us liked Bach and the other wanted 'Whip It.' "

"Haven't you ever heard 'Fugue in Devo Minor?' " She laughed, then said, "Whiting, any man who can identify 'The Lark Ascending' has just gotten to first base."

"And it's only taken me fifteen hundred miles."

She squirmed around under the afghan, looking for a comfortable position. She put her head back, and within a few minutes, the music and the movement had begun to make her drowsy. "Don't try to steal any bases," she whispered.

He realized that he did not want her to go to sleep. "I wonder what Eddie Van der Hoof is watching right about now."

"Probably 'Sixty Minutes,'" she said, with her eyes closed and the sleep slowing her speech. Then she sat up, wide awake, and looked at Whiting. "I liked the way you treated him today. You were very kind."

Whiting kept his eyes on the road. "I wonder how many people there are like that, sitting by their televisions, believing everything they see?"

"Quite a few, I suppose, but not too many like Eddie."

The headlights in the oncoming lane glared into the cab. Jeanne closed her eyes and put her head back. After a few miles, she said, "I think I like you better with the Eddie Van der Hoofs than with the Bert McCalls."

Whiting liked himself that way, as well. "But you can't back away from the Bert McCalls. Your husband didn't."

"And now he's dead," she said softly. Soon, her breathing was slow and steady.

and James Whiting's mind travelled ahead to Iowa. For Roger Darrow, Hunter, Iowa, had been a personal turning point, and in a way that James Whiting was beginning to recognize, the state of Iowa was the centerpiece of Andrew MacGregor's grand design.

The camera is focused on a field of corn. The land is not flat. It undulates gently, like a blanket blowing in the breeze. The sun is high and hot and burns so brightly that the leaves on the corn stalks glare like glass. The plants have not grown to their full height, and the ears are still developing, for it is early in the Iowa growing season, but the subject is corn, from the foreground to the horizon.

Roger Darrow steps in front of the camera. He is wearing jeans, a yellow GMC cap, and a dark green work shirt—his farm country wardrobe.

"This is where I'm from," he announces. "The corn belt, the heart of America, our greatest strength." He has a clump of soil in his hand. "We are blessed here with the richest soil on earth. God has been good to us." He crushes the clod and lets it fall through his hands.

"Because this is where I grew up—on farms owned by grand-parents, aunts, uncles, and friends—I was always planning to

stop in Hunter. But Andrew MacGregor gave me another reason."
Cut.

A long shot of the Hunter farmland, taken from a silo: a great canvas of corn and soybean fields, each crop brushed with a stroke that distinguishes it from the other. The camera tilts up until, in the distance, a modern high school, a white church steeple, a main street, and a cluster of old brick buildings can be seen. We are looking across half the county.

"The tentacles of MacGregor Communications have reached into this sparsely populated, small-town county, where the distance between houses should make cable wiring expensive and unprofitable. But MacGregor has been buying up or bidding on franchises all over Iowa. I'd like to know why."

Cut.

"Unfortunately, I think that the man who lives here has the answer." Roger Darrow stands outside a farmhouse—white, two stories, L-shaped, solidly built seventy or eighty years earlier, and wrapped in a handsome veranda. A woman sits in a rocking chair on the veranda. Behind the house are a silo, a barn, and other outbuildings.

"Some of my happiest times were spent on this farm," he says. "After my parents got killed and I'd bounced from one inhospitable relative to another, Lyle and Betty Guise took me in. I lived here for two years during high school and for three summers after that, and these people gave me the kind of love I'd been missing for years.

"Lyle Guise is one of the finest men I've every met and one of the most respected and influential farmers in Hunter County. So, when MacGregor decided to compete with Hunter Broadcasting— a small, locally-owned company—for the county cable rights, they sent Lyle, and a few others around here, one of these"—Darrow holds up a letter for the camera—"a dirty but perfectly legal piece of influence-buying."

Darrow reads the introduction, then looks at the camera. "The MacGregor people explain that they're going to be competing for the Hunter cable franchise because they can offer the best service to the county. But since they're new to the area, they're going to need some local clout."

He begins to read again. " 'That, sir, is where you can help. Your presence at county meetings where licensing will be dis-

cussed, the weight of your influence within the Hunter political community, and your specific recommendations on our behalf to the county supervisors, will all be of vital importance to our effort.' "

Darrow looks up at the camera again. "Here comes the part that they call 'the American Way.' " He reads, " 'In exchange for your assistance, we hope that you will take advantage of our offer to become a preferred stockholder in MacGregor Communications of Hunter. A two hundred dollar investment will entitle you to share in a twenty percent interest, as set aside for local supporters. And after five years, you will have the option to sell your interest back to the company at a fair share of cash value.'

"In plain English, MacGregor was inviting a handful of locals to put up their influence and two hundred dollars for an investment worth a hundred times as much."

Darrow takes a step toward the camera. "Well, MacGregor won the franchise, and the folks down at Hunter Broadcasting told me that"—Darrow looks down at the ground, as though he is embarrassed by what he is saying—"my old friend Lyle was one of the locals who went into the tank for MacGregor."

Cut.

The camera is now on the veranda. The chair squeaks rhythmically as Betty Guise rocks back and forth. She wears a bibbed apron over an old, print dress. Her hair is mostly gray and has been recently permanented. Her glasses have blue frames with little rhinestones studding the corners. Knitting needles move ceaselessly in her hands.

"Bless your heart for comin' here, Roger," she says.

"I'd never drive through Iowa without seeing you two," Darrow answers softly.

"It'll make Lyle about as happy as a man can be that you thought to stop and visit."

I hope that while I'm here I—I don't make him mad."

She stops rocking. "How could you do that, honey?"

"I have to ask him a few questions . . . about the way MacGregor Communications bought itself into Hunter County."

The knitting needles stop moving and Betty fixes her eyes on Darrow. "Lyle did nothin' wrong, Roger. I'm surprised you'd even think that."

"I'm just asking," says Darrow feebly, as though he doesn't

want to ask at all.

"Well, don't do it tonight. I got a nice dinner planned. If you hit Lyle with a touchy topic straight off, it'll spoil everything." Betty is pleading. "I'd like this to be a pleasant evenin'."

Darrow smiles, as though he is happy to put off the confrontation.

Cut.

The scene dissolves to dawn on the farm. The sun appears above a cornfield. Roosters crow. Lyle Guise, a wiry man in overalls, workshirt, and John Deere cap, strides out his back door. In a carefully cut montage, we follow him through his day. Lyle Guise discusses work with his son and two hired hands. He inspects his soybean field. He drives a front loader to the edge of his huge hog pen and drops a load of corn. The hogs swarm. They are packed so tightly that their backs look like waves on a lake. He stops for a drink in the blazing sun. He makes repairs to one of his tractors. He drives across one of his fields in an old pick-up. He stands on the crest of a small hill and looks out across the land.

Cut.

Lyle Guise and Roger Darrow sit facing each other at a redwood picnic table behind the house. A trellis of roses forms a backdrop. Two cans of Coors beer are on the table in front of them.

Lyle turns to the camera. His face is lined and leathery, his eyes sharp and blue. His white hair is trimmed in a crew cut, and he has the look and bearing of a career military man.

"Is that thing on?" he asks of the camera.

"All I do is push the button," says Darrow. "It'll go automatically until the tape runs out."

Lyle regards the camera curiously, as though he had never seen one before. "Is it Japanese?"

Darrow laughs. "I don't know. It says Zenith on the label."

"Good." Lyle nods.

The two men look at each other and smile, a pair of old friends pleased to be in each other's company again.

"So," Lyle begins, "what do you want to talk about?"

"The farm, you and Betty, how things are going."

"Well, you know how it is with farmin'," says Lyle. "It's hard, back-breakin' work most of the year, and all your money ends up goin' back into it, but if you was raised on a farm, it's in your blood." He glances again at the camera. It seems to make him *uncomfortable.* "We have our good years and our bad years, but we keep goin'. What it takes is what we give."

Darrow stiffens for a moment, starts to speak, then reaches for his beer. He has seen the chance to ask his question, but he has not taken it.

" 'Course," *Lyle continues,* "you never was much for farmin' that I remember. You lit out as soon as you had the chance."

Darrow bows his head, pretending to be embarrassed that he did not stay in Iowa. "I'm sorry, Lyle. You did a lot for me. I ought to appreciate it more."

Lyle laughs and leans back. "You're damn right, sonny boy. I want you comin' through here every year, just about harvest time. Bring the wife along when you're patched up with her. You can both work, and we'll forget that for the last five years, we never heard from you, 'cept at Christmas."

Darrow offers his hand, playing the prodigal son. "Deal."

He and Lyle shake hands and laugh together. Darrow's tension is more apparent to the camera than it is to Lyle.

After Lyle takes another sip of beer, he says, "You know, Rodge, it ain't been all that easy the last few years. We've had good harvests, but we've also had inflation, high interest, then a recession, tough times . . . if you want to know the truth."

Darrow sips his beer, takes a deep breath, and looks Lyle in the eye. "It's been said that you've done a few things to hold off the creditors."

Lyle straightens in his chair. "What?"

"Is it true that you've gotten"—*Darrow hunts for a neutral word* "—tight with the people at MacGregor Communications?"

"You figure that's the truth?"

"I don't know, Lyle. That's why I'm asking you about it." *Darrow reaches into his pocket and produces the letter. His hand is shaking, and the sheet of paper with it.* "The folks at Hunter Broadcasting said you'd recognize this . . ."

Lyle Guise reads the letter, throws it on the table, and stares at Roger Darrow, who folds his hands in front of him and looks down, as though he can't bear Lyle's gaze.

Lyle drains the last of his beer, crushes the can, and slams it on the table. He watches the can rock back and forth on its twisted base, and when it stops moving, he says: "You slept here last night. You ate at my table. You told me about your wife and your *life out there in Hollywood. And you didn't say a word about this, or about your real reason for comin' to Hunter."*

"Settle down, Lyle," says Darrow. "I would've asked you about this last night, but Betty wanted me to wait."

"Even so, you could've sprung this on me before you started your camera." He looks at the lens. "This way here, it's like you're tryin' to catch me gettin' flustered or somethin'. What the hell's happened to you out there in Hollywood?"

"This isn't easy for my, Lyle," says Darrow. "I'm just trying to find out what MacGregor's after. He's wormin' his way in all over the state. like he's trying to get himself a monopoly. Iowa's pretty important politically, and he's giving out all kinds of legal bribes to get a piece of it."

"Well, by Jesus, that's great." Lyle laughs bitterly. "My own unofficial stepson thinks I took bribes."

"Maybe that's the wrong word."

"You're damn right. It was business is what it was."

Darrow looks at Lyle for a moment, as though he doesn't want to continue. "I was just surprised when I heard that you threw in with an outsider. I thought you'd stand by the local people."

"Goddamn you," says Lyle softly. "You ain't even given me a chance to explain, and right on TV you're tellin' me I sold out."

"I'm givin' you the chance now, Lyle. That's why I'm here."

"Well, son, I don't want it." He looks at the camera. "I don't rightly give a damn about the people lookin' at me through that little hole. Let 'em think what they want. None of 'em knows what it is to keep a place like this runnin'. None of 'em stops to think that without the feller who puts the seeds in the ground or drops the fishin' lines in the water, without me and them like me, this whole damn country'd go to hell in a handbasket, and all the television sets and computers and e-lectronics wouldn't be worth a shit."

Lyle Guise stands and walks off. Darrow calls after him. Lyle pokes his face back into the shot.

"You do what you have to do to get by, Rodge. And you hope that those near to you stand close." He leans forward, bringing his face to Darrow's. "Now I got nothing more to say to you. Sleep out in the guesthouse, and be on the road in the mornin'."

Lyle walks away. Darrow calls after him several times, but Lyle does not return. Darrow brings his hand to his forehead. He draws his lower teeth across his upper lip. He contemplates the table top for a moment. Then he reaches over and turns off the video camera.

25

At dusk, the winter fields were desolate and lonely. The few farmhouses seemed to huddle close to their barns because the trees were bare and offered no protection from the wind. The roads were narrow but well plowed. The snow turned gray in the fading light and disappeared into darkness before it reached the horizon.

The utility poles—carrying telephone, electric, and now, television wires—flipped past in steady, monotonous rhythm, like strokes from a metronome. Jets streaked overhead and joined the coasts. Cities grew more complex and crowded. Computers created new rhythms of life. Geneticists created new forms. But Lyle Guise was right, thought Whiting. Without these Iowa farmers, sitting by their stoves, sipping their beers, waiting for the earth to warm, nothing else mattered.

Jeanne Darrow had never met Lyle Guise, but her husband had always spoken of him with awe and respect. Lyle Guise, Roger had said, taught him that he was responsible for his own future and gave him the confidence to seek it. Jeanne hoped that now, like an Iowan Tiresias, Guise would relate the details of her husband's unhappy passage through Hunter and give her the impetus to continue.

James Whiting had other expectations. "You could see on the tapes that Roger wanted to pin Guise down a few times, and he just didn't have the stomach to do it."

"As I told you before," responded Jeanne sharply, "Lyle was like a father to him, and it devastated Roger when Lyle threw him out."

"I won't have to be quite as constrained." Whiting's voice sounded hard and aggressive. "I'll ask the tough questions that Roger avoided."

"I'd rather that you be friendly, the way you were with Eddie."

Whiting did not respond.

When they reached the fencepost marked 325 South Fork Road, Whiting turned down a long, snowy driveway, at the end of which was the Guise farmhouse.

"Stop!" cried Jeanne.

Whiting slammed on the brake and looked at her. She was smiling, and her eyes were filling with tears.

"What's wrong?"

"It's just the way he described it when he told me about his youth," she said, gazing through the windshield. "I'd like to sit and look at it for a minute."

The big old house perched on the edge of dusk and seemed to hold off the night. The sky was black and gray above and pink near the western horizon. The wind was skittering across the empty fields, blowing up puffs of powdery snow, but warm, golden light poured from the house and beckoned the travelers in from the cold.

"It's like I know this place," she said. "It's like coming home for the first time."

"I hope we get a better welcome than Roger got."

The Guises greeted them as though they were a niece and nephew who hadn't visited in far too long. Betty Guise threw four more potatoes and another half-dozen carrots onto the pot roast. She added more flour and water to the gravy, took out a bottle of Mateus rosé that someone had given them as a gift, and set the table for four in the dining room, using her best china. Lyle dumped more coal into the living room stove, served straight bourbon to take away the chill, and set out Kraft Blue Cheese Spread and Ritz crackers as an appetizer. Then he went around the house and pulled all the drapes to keep in the heat.

During dinner, Whiting and Jeanne told of their journey. Lyle and Betty talked about Roger Darrow's early years in Iowa. After the pot roast, they had strong coffee and apple pie with cheddar cheese. Betty cleared the table. Lyle poured more bourbon and leaned back in his chair.

"He was always sort of wild," said Lyle, "and he just got wilder after his parents died."

"But he was a good boy, just the same," added Betty. "And he idolized you."

Lyle nodded and sipped his bourbon and seemed lost for a time in his memories. "I just wish I hadn't sent him off mad that last time."

Whiting saw his opportunity to turn the discussion to the tapes. "Wasn't it something about the Hunter cable franchise that started the argument?"

Jeanne kicked Whiting under the table. "Jim . . ."

Lyle looked at Jeanne. "It's all right, honey. I know you seen that video tape, and that's prob'ly why you're here."

Jeanne nodded and glanced at Betty. "That's part of it."

"Well, that's just fine," said Betty nervously. "Now, why don't we all move into the livin' room?"

Lyle winked at Whiting as they stood up from the table. "She's afraid you're gonna make me mad, so she's changin' the subject. But I don't know you as well as I knew Rodge, so you can ask me just about anything and I'll be as polite as a parson." He spoke with a hard-edged mid-America accent that defined every consonant as sharply as Iowa's open spaces defined the horizon line.

In the living room, Jeanne curled up on the oversize sofa. Betty sat in the rocker between the coal stove and the television set. Whiting left the new vinyl recliner for Lyle and slumped into the stuffed chair beside it. With the drapes drawn and the coal stove steaming, Jeanne felt warmer than she had since leaving California. And she felt safety and love, as Roger must have many years before. She liked these people. She did not want Whiting to alienate them with his questions. But she knew that he had to ask them, just as she had to ask hers.

The wind growled outside. The big house creaked. A shutter rattled.

"Gettin' cold," said Betty.

"*Gettin'* cold? What was that out there today?" asked Jeanne.

"We call that raw." Lyle put two fresh glasses on the coffee table, half-filled them with bourbon, picked up one, and looked hard at Whiting. "I got no apologies for sidin' with the MacGregor company. I just regret that I got so damn mad at Roger. It was a sorry way to end up, right there on TV and all."

"As I recall the tape"—Whiting was beginning to feel like Darrow, hunting for the least offensive way to ask a question—"you became upset when he mentioned bribe-taking."

Betty drew a sharp breath. Jeanne tightened her grip on the

Lyle kept his eyes on Whiting. "That's a pretty nasty expression, 'bribe-taking.' "

"And not exactly what happened here?" offered Whiting.

"Not on your life, sonny." Lyle sipped his bourbon again and stared at the coals behind the little window in the stove. "It might not have been the best thing I ever did, but it was legal."

"And smart," added Betty. "We got nothin' to be ashamed of. We worked hard all our life, and if it's any good, that stock'll give us some security."

"It's good all right," said Lyle. "I wouldn't have wasted any self-respect if it wasn't."

"Self-respect?" asked Whiting.

Lyle frowned at him. "Why the hell do you think I'm so damn touchy about this? I knew MacGregor'd win the franchise without any trouble at all. Before I even got that letter, two of the supervisors told me they were goin' with him. Still and all, I signed on with MacGregor, after a lawyer in Des Moines told me it was OK."

"Did you lobby for MacGregor?"

"A bit, but I didn't go out of my way none." Then, suddenly, Lyle stood, like a middleweight answering the bell. "I did what I thought was best for me and my family. I didn't hurt anybody in Hunter. I didn't break any laws. Cable companies do this kind of thing all over the country. And I made out like a bandit with a big company that's got plenty to begin with."

Whiting saw the anger that Lyle had promised to restrain. He swirled his bourbon in his glass and tried to think of one of the tough questions. "What would you have done if you thought MacGregor Communications was trying to gain a monopoly on Iowa cable systems so that they could influence the presidential caucuses with their two-way polling?"

Lyle frowned. "Rodge said somethin' like that seven months ago, but he didn't have no proof. You got any?"

"Well, since then, Senator Tom Sylbert has been beaten in Wyoming. The race for the party nomination's wide open. And the man who wins Iowa gets the first leg up."

"That ain't good enough, sonny." Lyle sat, thought for a moment, then pointed a finger at Whiting. "But I promise you this: If you can prove it, or I see MacGregor comin' down hard on the side of some politician here in Iowa—"

"Reuben Merrill," interrupted Whiting.

"I promise that I'll get my two hundred bucks back, and I'll scream bloody murder against MacGregor Communications."

After a moment, Whiting raised his bourbon glass to Lyle Guise. "I'll take you at your word."

Lyle touched his glass to Whitings's. "My word is good, son. It always has been."

Betty looked at Jeanne. "My Lyle's a good, generous man, with his own kids, and poor boys like Roger. That's why it hurt Lyle so bad when Roger didn't start right off givin' him the benefit of the doubt, instead of callin' Lyle a 'bribe-taker.' "

"He didn't mean to hurt either of you," answered Jeanne. He always said you were like parents to him."

"We were proud as parents whenever he wrote and told us how good he was doin'," said Betty. "And we was never happier than when he told us he'd taken a bride. I still have your weddin' picture on my bedroom wall."

Jeanne smiled. "I'm glad you didn't take it down after his last visit, because I'm sure he talked about me while he was here."

Lyle finished his bourbon. Betty turned her attention to the bag of knitting for a moment.

"What did he say?" asked Jeanne.

Lyle looked straight at her. "He said you two couldn't talk things out, so he'd left to think things over on his own. He said you two hadn't been able to have children, and he wanted kids more than anything." Lyle filled his glass again. "He also said that you weren't totally to blame for any of it."

"Nice of him," she grumbled.

"Because you'd both made a few mistakes along the way, and the doctors weren't really sure which of you it was that couldn't have the kids."

Jeanne launched herself from the sofa. "Did he really say that?"

"Is it true?" asked Lyle.

"We couldn't have children because he was sterile. He'd known for six months."

"The poor boy," said Betty, and she brought a hand to her mouth.

Lyle ran his knuckles over his crew cut and swallowed more bourbon.

Jeanne dropped back onto the sofa. "I can't believe that he said that to you." Then, after a moment, she changed her mind. "Maybe I can."

Lyle looked at Jeanne. "He wasn't too happy, Jeanne. He wasn't happy about his work, or himself, or what he thought he was seein' in this country. And I'd guess he wasn't too happy to think that his old friend Lyle had sold out to MacGregor." Lyle drained his glass. "And all his unhappiness was comin' down on your head."

Betty began to knit. "Honey, nobody knows what goes on between two people when they're fallin' in love or when their love is startin' to turn sour. Nothin' they say to anybody else matters. It's what they say when they look at each other."

Jeanne pulled her knees against her chest. "I'll never have the chance to do that, Betty. That's why I've come this far." And for the first time, she was beginning to think that she had come far enough. Her husband had told lies about their relationship to his "step parents." Did she really want to know what he said to Miranda Blake a week later in New York? Jeanne heard Lynne Baker's advice rattle through her head.

Whiting left his chair and sat beside her on the sofa. He moved his hand onto the cushion between them, so that she could touch it if she wanted. She did not.

"We've told you what we could," said Lyle. "We only really got to talk one night, then in front of the TV camera. Then . . . well, we never got the chance to tie up our loose ends."

"Neither did we," said Jeanne.

Lyle filled his bourbon glass again, then Whiting's. He took a long swallow and shut his eyes tight. Whiting didn't know if the bourbon was burning him or the memory.

Betty looked at Jeanne. "Don't take nothin' to heart about Roger until you met Billy Singer and he tells you what they talked about after the TV show. I think Roger hoped that Billy could set him straight about a few things."

Lyle burped. "He told me he was goin' to see Billy Singer because he wanted to see an asshole in the flesh."

Betty jumped up angrily. "Lyle, I'll not have talk like that in my house, especially on a man of God. You sit there and drink every night, then you start your blasphemin' . . . Thank God that Reverend Billy gives me the strength to cope with the likes of you."

"Good Lord, save us from holy women and Jesus Jumpers." Lyle rolled his eyes toward the sky, then drank more bourbon and offered the bottle to Whiting, who declined.

Betty glanced at her watch. "Since you two kids are headin' east to see the reverend, I think you ought to get acquainted with him, and eight-fifteen on a Monday night's as good a time as any. We missed the sermon, but the show runs an hour. You can get a good idea of what he's like." Betty turned on the television set.

Lyle threw down the rest of the bourbon and picked up the bottle again. "I think I need another drink."

Billy Singer appeared on the television screen. He was sitting behind a desk, like any talk-show host. He wore an expensive suit and a silk tie. Every hair and every expression were in place. They listened to Singer chatter mindlessly with Jed Lee, his sidekick, for an eight-minute segment. After a message from the Singer Watchguards, Singer reappeared.

"It's time now," he smiled into the camera, "for the nightly Singer survey. Today in Washington, a God-fearing congressman you've seen many times on this show, Reuben Merrill, introduced a bill to control the showing of uncut X- and R-rated entertainment on cable television."

Whiting looked at Lyle, whose bourbon glass was at his lips and whose eyes were riveted to the screen.

"I'm not going to ask you if you support the bill," said Singer, "just the principle behind it. Push Button *A* if you think Reuben Merrill is on the right track, Button *B* if you don't."

The words *Answer Now* flashed on the screen.

Betty Guise picked up the little box that was connected to the television.

"It's nobody's goddamn business what I watch," said Lyle, "especially if that Reuben Merrill is involved. Hit *B*."

"We're good Christians, Lyle, in spite of our faults. And if Billy Singer trusts Reuben Merrill, I do, too." She held up the box and pushed Button *A*.

James Whiting saw what was happening. Andrew MacGregor and his men were reaching through the television camera, along the cables strung across the Iowa night, and into the homes of people like the Guises. The possibilities were frightening.

Lyle glared at his wife until he was sure she sensed his displeasure. Then he turned to Whiting. "Remember, son, you got my word. If I been duped by this MacGregor, so that he could elect 245 Reuben Merrill, I'll be the first to say so."

Whiting smiled, because a man like Lyle Guise could allay his fears. Roger Darrow had come to Iowa expecting to meet the yeoman farmer he had remembered from his youth. Whiting had expected something less, or someone more sinister. Instead, he had found a man who tried to hold to his values but sometimes faltered, and who drank too much bourbon. Lyle Guise was pragmatic and tough and a bit flawed, but that was all right, because Whiting believed that when the MacGregor machine finally began to grind, Lyle would do the right thing.

26

Jeanne Darrow and James Whiting stayed the night at Lyle Guise's farm.

Whiting slept well and awoke refreshed. He knew that he was beginning to make sense of all that Roger Darrow had seen, and he was going to be able to finish Darrow's work. At breakfast, he ate three eggs, four sausages, and a stack of Betty Guise buttermilk pancakes.

Jeanne lay awake the whole night, listening to the wind, wondering what she would learn at their next stop, and wondering now if the knowledge would do anything to improve her life. At breakfast, she sipped at a cup of coffee and said little.

The clouds were thick and heavy when they left. Lyle told them there would be snow by afternoon, and they should be careful. Betty made them promise to return in the summer, when the corn was high.

At eleven o'clock, they reached the Mississippi. The winter sun was bright, and the river, frozen beneath several inches of ice, looked like a stream of silver through the snow. They crossed near the Quad Cities on the I-80 bridge, a long, flat span that was serviceable, but with none of the majesty that the river demanded. It was not until they reached the middle of the mile-wide bridge that Whiting had the perspective to be properly impressed by the Mississippi. To the north, the river meandered down from the Canadian border and the Minnesota lakes, cutting a broad path through hills and farmland. To the south, it transcribed a great, lazy arc around one of the haunches of Illinois, and rolled on, unperturbed, toward the Gulf. Downstream, it absorbed the Missouri, the Illinois, and the Ohio. It nourished the great cities, the plantations, the farmlands of the delta. It carried with it the commerce, the water and the waste of half the continent.

"We have to stop," said Whiting.

"In the middle of the bridge?"

"Of course not. On the other side, at the turnoff where your husband stopped."

Near the base of the bridge, on the southeast side, was a little parking lot, four picnic tables covered in snow, and a stand of winter-windburned maples. Beyond the trees was the frozen river. Whiting climbed out of the Cherokee and walked to the edge of the picnic area. A bitter wind was blowing from the west, gathering force as it swept across the Mississippi ice, slamming into the eastern bank with a chill factor of five below. And a bank of clouds, fat with snow, was advancing from Iowa.

The picnic tables are empty, except for one, where Roger Darrow sits. The sunlight dapples down through thick layers of maple leaves. The wind rustles gently through the trees. And the traffic is heavy on the river. An old stern-wheeler, speedboats, and barges loaded with ore and grain churn through the earth-brown water.

"We're in the East now," says Darrow, a note of trepidation in his voice. "There are two ways to tell. First, we've just crossed the

Mississippi. Second, the minute I came off the bridge into Illinois, the road turned into washboard."

Darrow is wearing a green sweater and looks tired. The trip is beginning to wear on him.

"I wanted to stay longer in Iowa, but there's nothing there for me anymore. Whatever roots I had in that soil were plowed under long ago. Despite its fertility, it has become an alien place. And damned depressing when an honest man like Lyle Guise knuckles under for a few extra bucks."

Darrow looks down at his hands, which are folded on the table in front of him. He works them against each other and the muscles in his arms flex. "It is sometimes hardest for us to be understanding with the people who need it most from us. Lyle Guise didn't have the strength to say no to MacGregor's money and his take-over of half the cable franchises in Iowa. And I couldn't find it in me to say, 'It's OK, Lyle, I probably would've taken the money myself.' "

He shakes his head. "You want to believe that your parents are incorruptible, especially if you pick them, like I did with Lyle. You want to believe it, no matter how old and jaded you get. Just like you want to believe that in the heartland, the old values still means something."

He squeezes his hands against each other again. His biceps bulge and his neck muscles tighten. "But damn," he says through clenched teeth, "why did he have to do it?"

He looks away again and stares at the river. The old stern-wheeler is paddling along, raising a little waterfall in its wake, filling the air with smoke and the squealing of its whistle. He watches until it disappears around the bend, then he turns back to the camera.

"After you see that thing go by, you almost expect to see Huck and Jim floatin' after it on their raft." He pauses and thinks about the analogy. "I guess you could say that my Mississippi has been the Interstate. I'm only halfway downstream, and as Huck would say, I've already seen enough of 'sivilization.' Unfortunately, I still have the big cities ahead of me. But then, I've never thought of Manhattan as too 'sivilized.' "

He stands to leave, then looks back into the lens. "Huck was lucky. He had someone to talk to. All I have is this camera. If you were along, Jeanne, you could be my Jim. Or maybe, I'm Jim, and I'm runnin' away, and someplace up ahead are the free states where a man can get good and lost."

They had an early lunch in Rosalie's Family Restaurant, overlooking the river, about a half mile north of the bridge. Rosalie's was clean and spacious, with a big lunch counter, booths along the window, and an open area of tables to the left of the lunch counter. There was a feeling of the 1950s about Rosalie's. It was the sort of place that hadn't been built since the advent of fast-food restaurants. At midday, Rosalie's was crowded with retired couples and young mothers taking their toddlers to lunch.

Jeanne ordered a grilled cheese and coffee, Whiting a cheeseburger, french fries, and a milk shake. He was starving. She took a few bites, sipped her coffee, and pushed her plate away.

"I've decided that Billy Singer is not worth meeting," she announced.

Whiting looked up.

"And Roger hated Manhattan with a passion. He called it his own little vision of hell."

Whiting stopped chewing. "You mean you want to head straight for Maine?"

"No," she answered. "Roger had seen enough by the time he

reached the Mississippi, and so have I."

Whiting dropped his hamburger.

"It's time to turn back," said Jeanne. "And close your mouth."

"I don't understand."

"Lynne Baker was right. He's not worth it."

Whiting just looked at her.

The waitress refilled Jeanne's coffee cup, but Jeanne did not take her eyes from Whiting. "I've decided that I want to go home. I'm just chasing a ghost, and I can never catch him."

"You really don't know what we're doing out here," he said angrily, "do you?"

His tone caused heads to bob and turn around them.

"You don't know what *I've* been doing." Jeanne raised her voice, then dropped it an octave when she saw people look in her direction. "I realized last night that this trip should be my way to gain independence, to become my own woman, like Lynne Baker said. And all I've been doing is playing Roger's slave, just like you."

Whiting sat back, as though she had swung at him. He looked around, and he noticed, at the end of the lunch counter, a black man in a leather bombardier's jacket. The man was listening to them and smiling faintly. Whiting glared at him for a moment, and the man looked away.

Whiting turned back to Jeanne. "We're going to be in Youngstown tonight and New York by Thursday afternoon. We haven't traveled almost two thousand miles just to stop on a whim."

"We began on a whim," she said. "I'm stopping after thinking it all through. I was awake all night."

"What you needed," snapped Whiting, "was a good night's sleep."

"I'm sorry, Jim."

Whiting shook his head. "Am I seeing the actress or the paramedic? The dreamer or the realist? And what have I been seeing for the last thousand miles?"

"You've seen someone trying to prove to herself that her husband still loved her at the end, when the fact is that he didn't. Lyle was right. So were you. Roger saw the world falling apart around him. He got more depressed at every stop. And he turned all his anger and frustration onto me because he couldn't leave a child in the middle of the mess he'd seen."

Whiting placed a hand on her forearm. "He thought things were a mess because he didn't live long enough to see how that old man on the coast of Maine was pulling them all together."

Jeanne shook her head. "We're talking about two different things, Jim."

"You're just looking for a reason to run away."

"No," she said firmly. "Roger was running away. I'm going home. I felt warm and safe in that house last night. I want to go back to where I've always felt that way. I'm going home."

"Jeanne, that house on the Iowa prairie is no safer than any-place else? . . . Now, we're almost to New York."

She put her hands over her ears and looked down at her plate. By now, half the people in Rosalie's were glancing at the table after every swallow.

"Billy Singer is expecting us . . ."

Jeanne kept her hands over her ears and began to shake her head.

Whiting gave up. "You think you know what you're doing, but you're being about as rational as a three-year-old." Then he muttered something that he regretted immediately. "No wonder he left you."

In a flash, Jeanne grabbed the water glass and flung it at him. He ducked, and the glass shattered against the back of the booth. Now, everyone was staring, and the black man was smiling.

"Here! Here!" shouted the waitress with the name *Rosalie* embroidered on her uniform. "What's goin' on here?"

"A little private dispute that's just gone public," explained Whiting. "We're very sorry."

"Well, this is a family place. We don't like trouble."

"I'm very sorry," said Jeanne. She was trembling. "We'll pay for the glass."

After a moment, Rosalie patted her on the shoulder. "It's all right, honey. Take your time and finish up, and you two patch up before you leave."

Whiting felt his face begin to burn. Part of it was embarrassment, part of it was medication. After Rosalie left them, he excused himself and slid out of the booth. He went into the men's room, turned on the cold water, and rinsed his face. He dried himself with a rough paper towel. He looked in the mirror and straightened his hair. He took a few minutes to compose an apology, then he pushed through the swinging door, went back into the dining area, and stopped. Jeanne was gone. He approached the booth. His parka was folded on the seat and six dollars with change had been placed neatly on top of the check. Whiting looked out the window, at the space where the Cherokee had been parked. Empty. He started for the door, fumbling to put on his parka as he went.

"She gone."

Whiting stopped at the end of the lunch counter.

"She gone, and that fancy four-wheel drive gone with her." The black man stared into his coffee cup. He looked like he weighed over 250 pounds. A piece of apple pie smothered in ice cream sat on the table in front of him. "She gone," he repeated, looking up at Whiting. "And so's that dude who came in right after you."

"Who?"

"He came in right after you and sat down th' other end of the counter. The minute your lady head for the door, the dude pay his check and beat feet right up her tail. When she pull out, he follow her in his red Buick."

"Did you get his license?" Whiting couldn't think of anything else to say.

"What I look like? Superman, with X-ray eyes or somethin'?"

Whiting turned and went out into the cold. He buttoned his parka and looked down the road. He felt stranded, helpless. He hoped that she was just driving around to cool off. He walked to the edge of the parking lot. From there, he could see the bridge. Traffic was not too heavy, and he was able to pick out the green roof of the Cherokee gliding along above the parapet. And a few hundred yards behind her, he saw the red roof of a car that could have been a Buick.

"Yeah," said the voice behind him. "It look like she headin' west, and haulin' ass, too."

Whiting turned to the black man. "What the hell do I do? She left me with no car, five bucks, and a credit card that expired a week ago."

"First you want Superman. Now you want Dear Abby. But they white. I can't help you, man." The black man stood near six five and would have been mostly muscle, except for the roll of truck-stop fat around his middle.

Whiting turned and stared at the bridge.

"Say, man, is she your number-one lady?"

Whiting shrugged but did not take his eyes from the bridge.

"You know what I mean. Your main squeeze. The chick who keeps your head on straight."

Whiting laughed. "She's not doing much for my head right now. And I guess she hasn't squeezed me too often, either."

The black man whistled through his teeth. "She don't squeeze, she mess up your head, and still you standin' here like a deballed he-dog at the bitch-pound gate. Man, you pussy-whipped. You better go after her, 'fore that other dude catch up to her and screw her all the way to San Looie O-bis-po."

"How?"

"Now *there*, I can help you." The black had a big, leonine head, a broad, flat nose, a carefully trimmed goatee, and a smile that said he had been everywhere and done everything."

He pointed to the tractor-trailer rig parked at the far end of the lot. The trailer was unmarked. The cab was a red Mac, with chrome smokestacks and mudguards and the Mac bulldog polished to perfection on the hood.

On the side of the cab, a carefully lettered sign in gold leaf read, "Henry Baxter, Independent, Newark, New Jersey."

"I got a load to drop in Des Moines, and one to pick up in Iowa City, and every time I cross the Mississippi, the black population in Iowa goes up by two percent. So let's get a move on."

The inside of the cab was luxurious. Henry proudly said that he had designed it himself. It included two leather seats, a padded leather dash, an instrument panel worthy of a jumbo jet, and a state-of-the-art stereo cassette player. A partition with a locking door separated the front of the cab from a small compartment that contained a three-quarter-size bed, a footlocker, a small refrigerator, and a Sony six-inch television set. The walls of the compartment were padded in a thick, brown shag rug, and a picture of an older woman, Henry's mother, hung on the wall.

"You like it?" asked Henry as he maneuvered out of the parking lot.

"All the comforts of home," said Whiting.

"Yeah, except for the hopper, but I like it just fine. Gives me the kind of freedom most cats'd kill for, and there ain't no place in this country I ain't been."

He shifted into second. Whiting felt the engine hesitate an instant, then a surge of power shook the cab.

"On the road, you your own boss. Nobody but stiff-brims and the smartasses on the loadin' dock to give you shit. And if things get real irritatin' just flip 'em all the big digit and head for the Coast."

The truck approached the I-80 ramp. A sign read, "Davenport, Iowa City, Hunter, Des Moines." Up the ramp in first gear, and then they were on the bridge, sliding smoothly into the traffic. Snow had begun to fall as the storm raced east. Whiting squinted through the flakes that swirled in the wind currents above the river. Somewhere up ahead, Roger Darrow's wife was careening back in to the West, and somebody was following her.

The truck rolled off the bridge and Henry Baxter settled smoothly into third. He pulled a cassette from beneath the seat and snapped it into the machine. A familiar sound filled the cab. Whiting smiled.

Henry glanced at Whiting and chuckled. "I bet you was expectin' James Brown or some other screamer."

Whiting laughed. "I didn't know what to expect."

"Well, you get him later, if you stick around. But after lunch, I like to soothe the soul with a little *Vie*-valdi."

Whiting recognized the music now. It was from '*The Four Seasons.*' He did not, however, correct Henry Baxter's rendition of the composer's name.

"It's called 'Inverno.'" Henry said the title with the perfect Italian inflection and a little smile, enough to tell Whiting that he really did know how to pronounce it.

"Since we headin' into the know, I thought 'The Winter' would be apropos."

For a short time, they listened to the music, and Whiting peered ahead. Although it was midday, headlights were appearing in the eastbound lane, and Henry Baxter had turned on his windshield wipers.

"All right, then," said Henry with a new note of authority in his voice, "who's the dude on your lady's tail?"

"I don't know."

"You ain't shittin' me, are you?" It was more of a threat than a question.

"I don't know who he is," repeated Whiting. "Her husband got killed eight months ago on a cross-country journey. We're retracing his steps. For all I know, the guy in the red car may have tailed her husband when *he* crossed the Mississippi."

"Did you say 'killed' as in 'dead'?"

Whiting nodded.

Henry whistled through his teeth. "Are you a dealer or somethin', man? You carryin' coke that you ain't offerin' any toots on?"

"She's the widow of the television producer who made 'Flint.' I'm her cameraman."

Henry perked up. "You mean the Peter Cross 'Flint'?"

Whiting nodded.

"You gonna take my picture if we catch up to your lady? Put me on TV?"

"We'll do a whole story on Henry Baxter and his rig."

"Good," Henry nodded once, then again assumed his tone of authority. "Does she know how to drive in snow?"

"She's from L.A."

"Well, this stuff gonna get pretty slippery pretty damn quick. At least she got four-wheel drive." He reached over and flipped the switch on his C.B. radio. "Does she drive with her radio on?"

Whiting shook his head.

"Well, we see if we can talk to her anyway." He picked up the microphone. "Breaker, breaker, this is Big Mama's Baby callin' Miz Cherokee Flint."

"Who?"

"Big Mama's Baby. That's my handle."

"The other name."

"Miz Cherokee Flint? I made it up."

"She'll never get it."

"Why not." He seemed offended. "She's drivin' a Cherokee, and her old man made 'Flint.' "

"Well . . . let's say she's got no imagination."

Henry pressed the button on the microphone again. "Breaker one-four, breaker one-four. This is Big Mama's Baby callin' . . . " He glanced at Whiting.

"Jeanne Darrow."

Henry tried calling her on several frequencies, but there was no response. He hung up the microphone but left the receiver turned on.

"Is this woman crazy or somethin', drivin' off into a snowstorm when she never drove in snow before?"

Whiting shook his head. At the moment, he didn't know who was crazy.

"Hey, Big Mama's Baby." A woman's voice scratched over the C.B. speaker.

Henry picked up the microphone and turned down the volume on the tape deck.

"We hear you're lookin' for a woman. Over."

Henry seemed to preen in front of the microphone. "To whom do I have the pleasure of speaking to? Over."

"Laverne and Shirley. Over."

Whiting looked at Henry. "Laverne and Shirley?"

"Yeah," said Henry. "Two lady truckers. Always travels together. One wears leather T-shirts and combs her hair like John Travolta. The other one likes pink sweaters with her initials on the tit. But nice chicks. Real nice chicks." He said it as though he meant it, then he pressed the talk button. "Good afternoon, ladies. Long time, no squawk. I'd ask what you doin' out on such a bad-assed day as this, but I know we all just tryin' to make a buck. I hope you feelin' fine. Over."

"Never better, Big Mama." It was another, softer voice. "What's your location? Over."

"Westbound on I-eighty, about ten minutes into Iowa. Light snow gettin' heavier, and maybe fifteen minutes before we need sleigh bells. Over."

"We're about fifteen minutes ahead of you," came the voice. "And it's gettin' a bit hairy. Wouldn't be so bad if we didn't have a lot of Little Red Riding Hoods goin' off to Grandma's house. Over."

"Speakin' of the color red, I got a feller here, he got a thing goin' on with a Mrs. Jones in a green Cherokee. And this Mrs. Jones, she got a thing goin' on with a dude in a red Buick. You seen either of them? Over."

"Mm-hmm." It was the deeper voice again. "Sounds kinky, Big Mama. But as a matter of fact, we been playin' leapfrog with that rat's ass of a Buick for the last five miles, and the Cherokee passed about ten minutes ago, doin' damn near seventy."

Seventy! Whiting felt one of his internal organs rise to his throat. He hoped it wasn't the kidney. He swallowed it back.

The voice continued to scratch on the speaker. "We been expectin' to see her off in the corn stubble ever since. Over."

"Well, ladies," said Henry. "Don't do nothin' foolish, but if you can catch up to that chick, I'd appreciate it if you'd tell her to turn on her C.B. Over."

"For anyone but you, Big Mama, we'd say up yours," answered the stronger voice. "But we remember that truck stop in Boston. So we'll do our best. Over and Out."

"Right on." Henry hung up the microphone and turned to Whiting, who had lost all the color in his face. "Don't worry man, they'll catch up to her. They owe me one."

"Why?"

"Well, one night in a diner in Boston, some trucker tried to pick up Shirley. Laverne got pissed and took a poke at him. If I'd a hadn't jumped in, that truck stop woulda been servin' Boston baked les-beens for breakfast."

Whiting laughed nervously.

"And don't worry, man. Nobody can keep up seventy in weather like this."

Heavy, wet snowflakes were splattering against the windshield and piling up on the sides of the road. The traffic was still steady enough that the snow had not accumulated in the travel lanes, but the surfaces were wet and slick and the visibility was deteriorating. Henry turned up the volume on the Vivaldi, pulled on his headlights, and squinted into the snow.

Fifteen minutes ahead of them, the highway was down to two lanes, with an average speed of forty miles an hour and the slick wetness freezing as the snow began to stick.

"Breaker one-four. This is Laverne and Shirley callin' Big Mama's Baby. Over."

Henry kept both hands on the wheel and told Whiting to take the microphone. "Press the button and give 'em your handle. Say, what *is* your name, anyway?"

Whiting told him, then pressed the button. "This is Big Mama's Buddy. Over."

Henry laughed and nodded. He approved.

"We're comin' up on your Mrs. Jones," the softer voice said. "And doin' it at extreme peril. She's in the right lane, doin' about forty-five, and drivin' too damn close to the van in front of her. Over."

"Did you see the red car?" asked Whiting.

No response. Henry reminded him to say "Over."

"Over."

"Yeah, he's back there somewhere. But he's not crazy enough to be drivin' as fast as Mrs. Jones. Over."

Whiting didn't know what else to say. He looked at Henry, who grabbed the microphone.

"We be waitin' on you, ladies. Over and Out." He hung up the microphone.

Laverne and Shirley, whose real names were Valerie and Rebecca, drove a big, yellow Kenworth, and they were hauling a load of cable spools to Des Moines.

As they pulled alongside the green Cherokee, Shirley opened her window and looked down at Jeanne. "Hey!" she shouted over the roar.

Jeanne Darrow did not look up. Her hands were frozen to the steering wheel and her eyes were fixed on the lights of the van in front of her.

Laverne fired three loud blasts on her horn. Jeanne swerved momentarily, but held on. Perspiration was beading on her upper lip. She wanted to slow down, put her foot on the brake, but she was afraid to stop quickly. Whiting had told her that stopping quickly would send her into a skid. Now, this damn truck was blowing its horn, frightening her half to death.

When she felt that she had control again, she shot an angry glance up at the truck. Then she looked again.

A young woman in a pink monogram sweater, with blond, bouffant hair, and bright, red lipstick was leaning out the window, into the driving snow, and waving frantically to Jeanne.

Because it was a woman who was waving to her, an probably because the sight was so bizarre, Jeanne carefully took a hand from the wheel and rolled down the window. Cold air and wet snow whacked her in the face. "What?" she shouted, but the words didn't carry.

The blond pulled her head back into the cab, then reappeared with a C.B. microphone in her hand. She gestured to the microphone, then motioned for Jeanne to turn on her receiver. Jeanne reached over and flipped the switch.

"Breaker one-four. This is Laverne and Shirley calling Big Mama's Baby. Over."Henry answered.

"My hair's an absolute goddamn mess," said Shirley, "but we got her. Give Mrs. Jones a call. Over."

"Many thanks, ladies," said Henry. "We owe you a permanent and a big, wet kiss. Over."

"Yech," said Shirley. "Over and Out."

"Breaker. Breaker. I'm calling Mrs. Jeanne Darrow. Mrs. Jeanne Darrow. Over," said Whiting.

No response.

"I thought she was your old lady," said Henry. "Don't be callin' her missus. Call her sweety-pie or honey-babe or some shit like that. And tell her your goddamn name so she don't think you're some horny motherfuckin' trucker."

Whiting pressed the button again. "Breaker. Breaker. This is Whiting calling Jeannie. Whiting calling Jeannie. Come in please. Over."

Henry shook his head. " 'Come in please.' We ain't heard that one on the road since Marconi."

The voice crackled over the speaker in the Jeep Cherokee, startling Jeanne again.

"This is Whiting calling Jeannie. If you hear me, pick up your microphone and push the button and say so. Over."

She reached for the microphone, then drew her hand back. She wouldn't talk to him. She wouldn't let him convince her to turn around again. She was confused enough. She was sorry to leave him in an Illinois restaurant in the middle of a snowstorm, but telling him so wouldn't change it.

Brake lights flashed and the van in front of her began to fish-tail. She was going forty miles an hour, and she knew she couldn't stop, in spite of the four-wheel drive. She grabbed for the stick and moved her foot to the clutch. She remembered Whiting's instructions: In snow, don't slam on the brakes; downshift.

The brake lights in front of her went off. The fishtailing stopped. She dropped back into second and glided over the slippery patch. For the first time in nine years, she wanted a cigarette. She gripped the wheel and kept her eyes on the taillights in front of her. A hundred yards down the road, the lights of Laverne and Shirley's Kenworth were disappearing into the snow.

The average speed was down to thirty miles an hour now, with treacherous conditions made worse by the long, gentle grades and the rolling curves of the Iowa landscape.

"Breaker, breaker. Jeannie, this is Jim. Will you please answer? Over."

She was driving. She was concentrating. She was trying to keep herself alive. She could not distract herself. She was also frightened. She told herself again that Lynne Baker had been right. Roger wasn't worth all this. And neither was the man now calling her on the radio. She reached over to turn it off.

"If you won't answer me, just listen," said Whiting through the speaker. "There's somebody trailing you."

She glanced into her rearview mirror. She could not see beyond the swirling snow or the headlights.

"We don't know who he is. But he followed us into the restaurant earlier today. You've got to be careful, Jeannie." The voice faltered, then added. "You've got to answer me, Jeannie. Please. Over."

The static hissed on the C.B. speaker in Henry Baxter's truck.

"Why won't she answer?" said Whiting.

"Don't ask me. She's your woman. I just drivin' the truck."

Whiting looked at the radio, as though it would help him to see the person on the other end of it. "C'mon, Jeannie," he whispered. "Talk to me."

"Hello—Whiting—" The voice was weak, tentative.

Whiting snatched the microphone and pressed the button. "Jeannie. Hello."

"Hey, man," said Henry. "She didn't say 'Over.' She can't hear you till she take her finger off the button. Wait till she say 'Over,' then lay into her."

After several moments of static and confusion, Jeanne's voice crackled again. "Whiting? If you can hear me, let me know."

Whiting pressed the button. "Jeannie, we're about ten miles behind you. These are two-way radios. When you want me to answer you, say 'Over.' Got it? Over."

"Over?" came the reply.

Whiting pressed the button. "Yeah. 'Over.' Over."

". . . a red Buick behind me. Over." The voice on the speaker finished a sentence that Whiting had missed.

Henry Baxter began to laugh. "No wonder you two havin' such a bad time of it. You don't know how to communicate."

Whiting pressed the button. "Can you say that again? Over."

"Who's *we*? And how do you know about a red Buick behind me? Over."

"*We* is my friend Henry Baxter and me. And I know about the goddamn red Buick because I saw it."

"Good boy." Henry liked Whiting's tone. "Show her who's boss."

Whiting continued. "I have to talk to you, Jeannie. You have to stop. If the guy in the red Buick doesn't get you, the weather will. Over."

"You bastard!" she shouted, and she fought a skid. "I'm scared enough as it is without you makin' it worse. I'm going home. Over and out."

She hung up the microphone and reached for the switch.

"Jeannie," pleaded Whiting's voice, and again she let him speak. "Just pull over for a few minutes so that we can talk. Over."

She grabbed the microphone. "And let the guy in the red Buick pull over with me? We don't even know who the hell he is. Over."

"And that's the problem," answered Whiting.

Her knuckles were white on the steering wheel. She had to concentrate on the road. But he was right. They had to talk. She could not leave him stranded in the middle of Iowa. She was going home, however impulsive he thought she was, but at the very least, she could give him back his luggage.

She pressed the button. "I'm—I'm—" She hated to admit it. "Dammit, I don't think I know how to stop on this ice. Over."

"Jeannie, four-wheel drive is the safest . . ." static . . .

Jeanne reached over and fiddled with the dial.

". . . Over."

Whiting looked at the speaker and waited for a response. Static. He looked at Henry.

"Maybe she didn't hear you. Sometime, the reception go in bad weather. It'll come back. Talk again, and this time, tell her she got one of the best damn truckers in the U.S.A. to coach her. That'll make her feel good."

Jeanne picked up the microphone and pressed the button. "Whiting, Whiting. I've lost you. Can you hear me? Over."

Static.

She called again and peered into the swirling snow.

Whiting could barely hear her. He pressed the button, looked down at the cars crawling through the storm ahead of him, and answered.

Faintly, she could hear his voice. She had to talk to him now. She had been crazy to run away from him.

The Cherokee reached the crest of a gentle hill and was start- ing down into the trough. Jeanne held one hand on the wheel while she fiddled with the radio dial.

Then brake lights flashed, and the van in front of her began to slide.

Jeanne grabbed the shift and dropped back into first. She thought she was under control. Then the van started to fishtail, and just ahead of it, she saw the flash of a headlight. What was happening?

She slammed on the brakes instinctively. In front of her, she sqw more headlights. The van had gone into a spin and she was heading straight for it. This was all happening in an instant.

The sedan in front of the van was smashing into the guardrail and swinging broadside into the road. The van was hitting the sedan. Jeanne was pumping the brakes and trying to remember if she had fastened her seatbelt.

She saw the rear of the van stop, and the sedan in front of it seemed to bounce. She swung the wheel hard and tried to swing around the van. She heard the sickening bang as she hit the van sideways. The sedan bounced again. She looked to her left and saw the headlights of the car behind her. They were heading straight for her door. She closed her eyes and felt the metal crunching.

Henry Baxter saw the flashing lights first. He reached over and turned the radio to the police band.

"We'll need all your available units," the policeman on the scene was saying. "With fire and medical. We've got casualties, and it looks like we may have a fatality. Over."

"Ah, how many vehicles did you say? Over."

"Eight."

Henry had managed to slip in behind a snowplow conga line just after Jeanne's last transmission. Each plow pushed the snow into the lane beside it until the last plow pushed it off the road while automatic spreaders hurled sand from the back of each truck. In spite of the clear roads, the traffic had slowed once more. Now, Henry realized the reason.

"That looks like a mighty big accident."

Whiting saw the red and blue lights oscillating through the

storm. Neither of them noticed the red Buick, now covered in snow, at the side of the road.

"Yeah," the policeman on the radio was saying. "Eight vehicles. Seven with Iowa plates, and a Jeep Cherokee with California . . ."

"Oh, Jesus," said Whiting.

Henry put a hand on Whiting's knee. "Just relax, man. Don't go crazy till you got a reason."

For fifteen miles, Whiting had been helpless, out of touch, angry at Jeanne and angry at himself for driving her off. Now, his heart was pounding in his ears.

Henry Baxter pulled into the breakdown lane. He crawled close to the accident site, and a state trooper flagged him down.

"We need to get emergency vehicles in here," shouted the trooper. "Get your rig on the road."

Henry said that Whiting was married to one of the people in the accident. Then, Whiting leaped from the cab and started to run.

"Remember, man, don't go crazy," shouted Henry.

Eight cars piled into one another. Shattered windshields. Front ends disintegrated. Broken glass crunching underfoot. A headlight still shining off the snow. Whiting ran.

The smell of gasoline. The smell of hot antifreeze. Someone screaming. A paramedic shouting instructions. Two women, wrapped in blankets, standing by the guardrail. A policeman taking a report from a driver. Three fireman and a paramedic prying open a compact car. Whiting ran.

A siren screamed as an ambulance rushed off down the highway, its flasher fading into the layers of snow.

A gurney rolled across Whiting's path. He almost fell over it. A blanket covered the body.

"Watch it!" shouted the paramedic.

Whiting looked down at the body.

"Whiting! Over here!"

Jeanne was kneeling beside another gurney. She was holding a bottle of Ringer's lactate that was being fed intravenously to an injured man. She was trembling.

"Are you all right?" Whiting's voice cracked.

She nodded. Then she nodded again, several times.

A paramedic took the IV bottle. Jeanne stood and stepped back from the gurney.

She looked up at Whiting. She blinked back the snowflakes collecting on her eyelashes. The wind whipped against the both of them, and Jeanne shivered. She wore no hat and a light down vest. Whiting threw his arms around her. She unzipped his parka, *how* slipped her arms into it, and wrapped them around his waist. He let his warmth warm her.

27

By midnight, eight inches of fresh snow blanketed the Iowa corn stubble, and a new cold front was pushing across the Midwest. The black sky above Des Moines was studded with icy stars. I-80 had been plowed and sanded and was open from Nebraska to the Mississippi and beyond.

Henry Baxter had delivered his load of I.L.G.W.U. clothes to a wholesaler in the Des Moines suburbs. Now, he was headed east. He would pick up a refrigerator unit at a small meat-packing plant in Iowa City and deliver a load of frozen pork trimmings to a processor in Youngstown. At the moment, his only cargo were two very tired travelers, their luggage, and their video recording equipment.

"We'll be hittin' Iowa City in a couple of hours," said Henry. "We'll snooze at the dock till six, get the load, and be on our way. We should make Youngstown in time for tea with Billy."

The Jeep Cherokee had been totaled in the accident, but because of its size, Jeanne had escaped with just a few scratches and a stiff neck. The Cherokee had been towed to a gas station, where an insurance agent would pronounce the last rites. Jeanne had been taken to a hospital, treated, and released.

Henry Baxter had stayed with them because, he explained, he liked company, they were all heading for the same town, and he had always wanted to meet Billy Singer. In exchange for getting them to Manhattan by Friday, he made them promise to introduce him to the evangelist. When Whiting agreed, Henry smiled and said, "Praise God."

"Now, you two ain't been alone yet today," said Henry. "Climb into the back there, help yourself to the bar, snuggle up, and just do what comes natural."

Jeanne looked down at her shoes. "Right now, that means sleep."

"Well, you go to sleep and let Whitey, here . . . " He chuckled.
A few hours earlier, in a moment of inspiration, he had found the perfect handle for a man named Whiting. " . . . let Whitey do what come natural to him. I don't thing he is too sleepy, just yet."

Jeanne looked at Whiting, who seemed to be blushing, even in the darkened cab. She laughed. She was glad that Henry was there to help smooth things between them. He knew exactly what to say, when to be serious, when to be lecherous, and when to be quiet. And she was thankful that he had been in the restaurant that morning. Otherwise, she and James Whiting might be separated by more than the miles she could have covered in a day.

"Go on," said Henry. He gestured back into the little compartment. "Just draw the curtain and don't worry about me. I got my coffee to keep me awake and my Walkman to keep me mindin' my own business."

"You know they're illegal," said Jeanne.

Henry looked at Whiting. "This gal be a real killjoy. First she sleepy. Now she tellin' me"—he turned to her—"say what's illegal?"

"The headphones," she answered.

"Yeah, and so's climbin' back into my little bed if you two ain't married." He pulled the headphones over his ears. "I won't tell if you won't."

Whiting and Jeanne said good-night and went in to the compartment. For a long time, they lay together in the narrow bed and listened to the steady rumble of the road. their shoes and sweaters lay on the floor. A blanket covered them. They were both exhausted.

"I'm sorry," Jeanne whispered after many miles of silence. "I'm sorry I ran off today."

Whiting stroked her hair. "It's all right."

"We'll have to go all the way to Maine," she said.

"I'll stop whenever you want," Whiting responded.

She looked into his eyes. "It wasn't just Roger I was running away from."

He slipped his arms around her. He felt the softness of her breasts pressing against him. "I'm glad you ran," he said. "It made me chase you."

"That's not why I ran, but someplace back there I realized I need someone who cares, not someone who's dead and may have stopped caring long before he left."

Passing headlights sent splashes of luminescence into the little compartment. For an instant, they could see each other's faces. Then they were in darkness again.

She brought a hand to his cheek. "I thought of you, just before that car hit me."

He kissed her. The kiss lasted a mile or more.

Whiting let his hands slide down to the pockets of her jeans. Lights flashed again and streaked across the ceiling of the compartment. Their lovemaking did not go further that night. Whiting was still not certain that he *could* go further. And neither of them wanted to put too much weight on a fragile structure, especially when time and privacy would strengthen it. Instead, they lay in each other's arms and felt the rhythm of the road and eventually slept.

They awoke briefly when they felt the truck slowing, then backing up. Whiting looked out and saw that they were at a loading dock. A few dismal light bulbs illuminated the platform. Two other tractor rigs were parked, but there was no activity. Whiting glanced at his watch: 3:30.

The engines stopped rumbling. Whiting heard Henry shift from the driver's seat to the passenger's side, make himself comfortable, and fall asleep.

Whiting turned back to Jeanne and closed his arms around her waist.

"Where are we?" she whispered groggily.

"The slaughterhouse."

She nodded, as though she approved, then drifted back to sleep.

"I love you," he whispered. He did not know if she heard him.

The noise began at five-thirty. Whiting heard Henry rouse himself, climb out of the truck, and shout an obscene greeting to someone on the dock. The engines had been off for two hours and Whiting could see his breath in the compartment. He shivered and got out of bed.

Then he looked out the window. The first shift was arriving—

a long line of cold, sleepy meat-cutters, with a few bright ones chattering to the rest.

Iowa corn fed Iowa pork and beef. Iowa meat-cutters butchered the stock that fed America. Like meat-cutters everywhere, they faced the occupational hazards: fingers lost to their own sharp knives slicing too quickly on the assembly line; hands mangled in meat grinders and food processors; and a taste for alcohol antifreeze that developed when a man worked all day in a refrigerator.

A few feet away, a truck backed up to the dock. The trailer had wooden-slat sides, and through one of the slats, Whiting could see hooves and hay. Through another, halfway up the side of the rig, he saw big, bovine eyes peering out at him. Disembodied, the eyes seemed intelligent, perceptive, aware of what awaited. Whiting smelled the stink of cattle and shit and fear. It almost gagged him.

They were back on I-80 by six o'clock, dragging pork noses and pigs' feet to a sausage maker in Youngstown. As they crossed the Mississippi, the sun rose out of a bank of purple clouds that were the last remnants of the previous day's storm.

They came off the bridge, Henry glanced into the rearview mirror, and laughed. "He's a persistent mother, whoever he is."

Whiting looked into the other mirror. The red Buick was back on the road, about a quarter mile behind. "I thought we lost him."

Henry chuckled. "Maybe he's one of Billy Singer's angels, and he watchin' over us."

"These people are not operating in the best interests of MacGregor Communications, Lawrence/Sunshine Productions, or the Gospel Church of Evangelical Sainthood," said Len Haley. "I urge you, Reverend, not to receive them."

Billy Singer sat behind his marble-topped desk, his hands folded on the blotter. It was a clean space, uncluttered by paper work or pens. To his left was a simple telephone. To his right a framed photograph of his family and a pewter crucifix. Behind him, a picture window overlooked the valley where Youngstown smelters produced steel and pig iron. At the side of the window, a Bible was open on a reading podium.

"I don't turn pilgrims from my door, sir," he said.

"It would be better if you avoided them, Reverend. I had a man pick them up at the Mississippi, and he puts them in central Illinois. They'll be here tonight." Haley spoke respectfully, although he had no respect for churchmen, whether they were television evangelists of Episcopal archbishops.

Singer leaned across his desk. "I've been watching that Vicki Rogers on television. She makes it sound like these people are uncovering some sort of conspiracy, and we're all part of it."

"She gets carried away."

"You're damn right she does. We're just usin' the tools that God gave us to spread the message, and I'll tell that to anyone including Roger Darrow's widow and his kidney."

"Then I can't convince you?"

Singer shook his head.

"They may destroy everything that Andrew MacGregor, Vaughn Lawrence, and you have been working toward for the last two years."

"Andrew MacGregor is a disciple of my church," said Singer evenly. "Through him, my ministry has grown. I have no truck with Vaughn Lawrence."

"Well, as of Friday, you'll be working for him," said Haley with a little smile.

Singer did not move.

"According to the contract on file at the MacGregor offices in New York, you have agreed that the MacGregor Communications Corporation, its subsidiaries, and its assignees, for a period of five years, have approval rights over all programming decisions made by the Gospel-Evangelical Cable Network. In exchange for that, you have the studio MacGregor built and turned over to you, the computer system to organize your church, and two-way Respondsible to reach your people."

Billy Singer got up and went over to his Bible stand. "Tell me one thing, Mr. Haley. What does your boss have on Andrew MacGregor? How can a game-show host fight off a corporate takeover and a year and a half later become the chief executive officer of the company that tried to conquer him? By what miracle can this happen?"

"First of all," answered Haley, "Vaughn Lawrence is my client, not my boss. He and MacGregor see eye to eye on many things. They believe that like-minded men should join together to take advantage of the systems they have developed."

"But Vaughn Lawrence and Billy Singer don't see eye to eye on matters of the spirit, do they? A man of God and a man of Mammon?"

Haley smiled. "Billy Singer and Vaughn Lawrence agree on the potential of Reuben Merrill as a candidate for national office."

Billy Singer sat slowly, as though this were something of special interest.

"You're both influential men, Reverend. You both know how to reach people through the picture tube. You recognize, as my client does, that with MacGregor behind you, you can begin to change the way this country thinks."

Singer studied Haley as though he were inspecting a young man seeking a ministry in the Gospel church. "We can indeed, Mr. Haley. We can change this country spiritually. We can make it what the Lord intended it to be. But that still doesn't explain why I should not see Roger Darrow's wife."

"She and her friend are trying to shake down the structure that MacGregor has erected, an electronic mansion where the chapel has been reserved for you." Haley smiled, pleased with his eloquence.

Singer played with the ruby ring on his little finger. "A nice phrase, Mr. Haley, but until I hear it from MacGregor himself, a big load of cowflap."

Billy Singer stood once more and his arms began to move about as though he were on a pulpit. "I will see whomever I want. I will tell them whatever truth I know. And I will make no apologies. As for you, I wouldn't try to interfere. I placed you under surveillance the moment you called for an appointment. Three men will be watching you until you leave Ohio, which I suggest you do soon."

Len Haley stood. He did not like to be thrown out of anyone's office, but Billy Singer was one of the most influential men in the Bible Belt, and that was where their strength would first rise. "We work toward the same goals, Reverend."

Len Haley left the office and returned to his motel. He was followed by three men. He knew he could not try to stop Jeanne Darrow and James Whiting in Ohio.

Henry Baxter's truck passed Joliet, Illinois, around eleven o'clock. The red Buick was still a few hundred yards behind. The sun was shining hard off the snow. The Interstate was clear and the traffic was light.

Henry looked into the rearview mirror. "I guess that guy's plannin' to follow us all the way to Billy Singer's altar."

"I sure would like to know who he is," said Whiting.

"Whoever he is, I'd like to get him off my tail." Henry wiggled around in his seat. "He startin' to make me nervous."

"Do you think he could be telling someone where we are?" asked Jeanne.

"Beats the hell out of me," said Whiting.

"No antenna, so he got no C.B.," said Henry. "But I seen him stoppin' at rest areas where they got phone booths. Maybe Miss Killjoy's right. If what you all say about Bert McCall is true, the dude in this Buick may be tryin' to set your asses up for some kind of surprise. A truck accident or somethin'."

"I've had my share of accidents this week, thanks," said Jeanne.

"Yeah, well, I don't like puttin' my truck in danger either. And that's what I'm doin' haulin' you two across the country."

Whiting looked nervously at Henry.

"Now," continued Henry, "I could put you two out, which means my truck'd be safe, but I'll never get to meet His Eminence Billy Singer."

"Whiting smiled. "Damn right."

"Or I can take action. And as Shakespeare tell us, better a live Fortinbras than a dead Hamlet, any day of the week."

Jeanne's head snapped around. "What?"

"I am a man of great erudition, honey." Henry wagged a finger at her. "Never be surprised where your next pearl of wisdom is comin' from."

Henry turned on the C.B. and picked up the microphone. "Breaker. Breaker. This is Big Mama's Baby lookin' for a chat. Hello? He repeated the greeting several times and waited.

"Big Mama's Baby?" A male voice with a southern accent scratched over the speaker. "This here's the Redneck. What you doin' to keep the flies off the watermelon? Over."

"I eatin' it, baby. I eatin' it." A pause, a wink at Whiting and Jeanne, then, "Say, since when they start lettin' po' white trash drive trucks through Illinois? Over." Henry laughed. He knew the Redneck. They had talked like this before.

"I'm just exercisin' my civil rights. Now what kind of welfare you after today, Big Mama? Over."

"Fact is, I need some real help, and you may be just the man to do it. Over."

"I'm haulin' a load to Manhattan, but I'll do what I can. Any man with a rep as good as yours gets help on automatic. Over."

Henry asked the Redneck's location. The Redneck was about a mile behind.

"OK, then. This may be a little fun for both of us." He described the situation and the setup. He called it "road hospitality."

"Hot damn." The Redneck knew exactly what he meant. "I'll be comin' up behind that Buick in about two minutes."

Henry hung up the microphone and looked at the others. "If he'd heard about any stiff-brims, he woulda suggested we back off. The constabulary don't like us playin' tricks on the Interstate."

"Is this going to be dangerous?" asked Jeanne.

Henry looked out of the corner of his eye and snorted. "What ain't?"

Whiting buckled on his seat belt.

Henry chuckled, wrapped his hand around the stick, and began to down shift.

Whiting watched the speedometer drop from sixty-five toward fifty. The pitch and beat of the engine changed with the gears. In the rearview mirror, Whiting watched two cars pull out and pass the truck. Then he saw the red Buick growing larger as Henry slowed. He hated driving on heavy truck routes, because the trucks were always tailgating and bullying their way along. But right now, he was glad to be sitting in Henry's cab.

Henry glanced into his mirror. "There's my man!"

Whiting saw a big black cab and van bearing down on the Buick from behind. Henry's speedometer had dropped now to forty.

The left directional began to flash on the Buick. The car pulled out to pass. Henry shifted, snapped the wheel, and accelerated into the passing lane. The Buick swung back into the middle lane, accelerated quickly, and started to pass agian.

"He's on your right," shouting Whiting.

"So he is," laughed Henry. "And damned if there ain't a big black Mac right on his tail."

The Buick was doing fifty-five. Henry shifted and accelerated again.

The Buick hit sixty and pulled parallel to the cab of Henry's truck. Henry shifted into fourth to stay with him. Whiting glanced at the speedometer: 65 mph. The cab was vibrating, and the Redneck was roaring along beside them.

"Hey, Big Mama!" came the Redneck's voice. "Are we havin' a sandwich today? Over."

"No. You just keep that enema comin' up his ass and we'll tell you when to turn off the water." He flipped on his directional and started to ease his way into the right lane."

The Redneck dropped back. The Buick tried to accelerate, but Henry stayed with him. They were shooting along near seventy now. Other cars were scrambling out of the way, and Whiting was sure that the Illinois State Police would soon be joining the chase.

The Buick couldn't pass. The truck was too big and too powerful.

"Them cars got guts, but not enough to outrun old Henry," he shouted.

The Buick swung to the far right lane, with the Redneck on his tail and Henry traveling close beside. The main surface of the road was wet from the midday melt. The breakdown lane was piled high with snow and that was where Henry was planning to send the Buick.

He flipped on his directional signal and started into the right lane once more. The driver again tried to outrace the truck. Henry accelerated. From third gear to fourth. Sixty. Sixty-five. Henry flashed his lights and blasted his horn.

A station wagon in front of him squirted off into the left lane. The cab was shaking. The Redneck was now a truck-length behind. A trickle of sweat ran down the side of Henry Baxter's face.

At seventy-five, Henry swung the wheel. The huge truck leaned over. There was no place for the Buick to go, except into the breakdown lane. He couldn't accelerate. He couldn't slow down. But he held his ground.

"That's one courageous motherfucker. But he's dumb."

Henry fired another blast on his horn. It startled the driver just enough. He swerved into the breakdown lane, hit the snow, and skidded.

The Redneck backed off quickly. Henry accelerated.

The Buick spun once in the breakdown lane then buried itself up to its windshield in a snowbank.

"Yahoo! Wow!" The Redneck gave a rebel yell on his C.B.

"That was a very bad dude," said Henry into his microphone, "but he won't tell Smokey nothin', 'cause he work for some dudes badder than he is. They be sittin' on him, and I be waitin' on them."

"You do that, Big Mama."

"I owe you one, Red, baby. Over and out."

Henry looked at Jeanne. "What did you think of that?"

"I thought it was the stupidest thing I've ever seen—since yesterday."

"Well," said Henry, "I ain't lettin' nobody try to stop me from meetin' America's favorite Jesus Jumper in the flesh. My mama been watching Billy Singer since 1960, and I just want to tell him so." He paused and laughed cynically. "Hallelujah, sister."

28

The video tape of Billy Singer's "Good-Time Gospel Hour"
for June 4:

The program opens with the Billy Singers, eight young
people straight out of conservative colleges where the
dress code is as important as the grade-point average. They sing
in a kind of treacly harmony learned from long years of studying
at the easy-listening band.

"He takes our hands and travels at our side./He walks with
us across the river wide.

The camera pans from face to beatific face.

"And all he asks is love. All he asks is l-o-o-o-v-e.

The camera sweep across the audience as the applause builds.
"And now," says the announcer. "Here is the man who makes
it happen in the Gospel Church of Evangelical Sainthood, your
friend and mine, the Reverend Billy Singer!"
The applause rises. The orchestra begins to play an upbeat
version of "Amazing Grace."
Billy Singer raises his hands and the audience grows quiet. He
is an imposing figure behind his television podium. His suit is
conservative gray, well-cut, and offset by a carefully chosen ma-
roon tie. His hair is gray, well-cut, and carefully blown into place.
He has no wrinkles on his face or his suit. His only jewelry is the
small ruby pinkie ring he plays with when he is nervous. But Billy
Singer is rarely nervous. He looks like a long-lost uncle, returned
rich and successful from distant shores. He seems familiar to the
viewers, but he maintains a ministerial distance, because he has
found the truth and brought it home to his nieces and nephews.
He fixes his eyes on the camera in front of him, and his mag-
netism reaches through the lens, into the diodes and cathodes and
transistors of every set tuned to his face.

"My friends," he begins," "I have a reading for tonight, and a message for the times."

He reads from the Bible, then, in measured tone and gesture, he expatiates on the reading and relates it to the lives of every person in the audience. The message, in the opening sermon or monologue, is always the same and always very traditional: Get Satan behind you and turn your eyes toward the light. Pray for guidance and your prayers will be answered. Embrace Jesus, and he will embrace you.

The corollaries to the message, which relate to politics, First Amendment issues, abortion, resource policy, busing, welfare, and the need for everyone to support the various projects of Billy Singer's church, are neatly woven into the rest of the program.

After the opening sermon, there is a message. Or, in less spiritual terms, a commercial. Billy's announcer and sidekick, Jed Lee, offers the viewing audience a chance to purchase the Singer Bible, an American vernacular version with Leatherette binding, the owner's name embossed in gold on the cover, and Billy Singer's autograph, all for seventy-five dollars.

When the program resumes, Billy Singer is sitting behind a desk and Jed Lee sits on a chair beside him. They chat for a while, discuss the latest news from the Singer missions, punctuating their conversation with ejaculations like "Praise the Lord" and "Goodness Gracious." Jed Lee tells a cute little joke about "the Catholic, the Jew, and the Gospel Evangelical walking down the street." Billy draws a little parable from the joke, something about people learning from one another. Then Billy runs down the guest list.

"And as a special surprise," he says, "sitting in our audience tonight, come all the way from Hollywood to interview us here in Youngstown, is a man whose television programs you all know well. . . ."

"And," adds Jed, "a man who comes originally from the heartland—Hunter, Iowa."

"Praise the Lord for that," says Billy. "He's out in the audience and he doesn't know we're planning to call him up here. . . ."

The cameras begin to sweep across the audience.

"We'd like to give a big, Evangelical Sainthood welcome to the man who created Jess Flint, one of our favorite TV detectives . . ."

"Most of the time, that is," chortles Jed.

"*Mr. Roger Darrow!*"

The camera finds Darrow. He is seated in the third row wearing a sportcoat over an open-collar shirt. He is laughing and shaking his head. No, he doesn't want to come up.

"C'mon. It's not often that we get a real Hollywood celebrity to visit," says Billy.

Darrow relents, mounts the stage, and shakes hands with Billy and Jed. He sits in the guest's chair. Jed, following the usual protocol, moves to the sofa.

Singer and Darrow exchange pleasantries, Singer seems relaxed, mildly amused at Darrow's on-camera discomfort and annoyance.

"So," says Billy, "what brings you here to Youngstown and the Gospel Church of Evangelical Sainthood?"

"Well, Reverend," Darrow fidgets with the arm of the chair. "I've heard about your program and the beautiful studio that Andrew MacGregor has built for you here."

"MacGregor and all the good people who listen," comments Singer. Many people have helped build this studio on a hill. Now, then, let's talk about Jess Flint and Hollywood. To the good young people out there in the middle of America, you're a traveler from a distant place. Yet your thoughts and ideas enter their homes every night, a fact that I have always found to be one of the great ironies of our society."

Darrow shifts in the chair. His smile does not waver.

"But Andrew MacGregor and modern cable technology gives you a share of power that very few people ever have, even in Hollywood."

"You mean Respondsible?" Billy smiles. "Perhaps we can let you see it in action and at the same time we can give our viewers the opportunity to tell us what they think about Jess Flint."

Darrow leans back. "I'd like to see how you use the system here in the East. Out west, I saw Respondsible blow Senator Tom Sylbert clean out of the water."

"Well, you know"—Singer smiles—"Respondsible is a new innovation for us, but our viewers have always had the Singer WatchGuards to do their bidding and protect the airwaves."

Darrow laughs, although he is not amused. "I know."

"And usually, they gave high marks to 'Flint,'" says Billy. "The show always tried to emphasize human dignity and decency, *and usually you tried to do it without sex or volence."*

Darrow smiles, but his face seems tense, as though he knows what's coming.

"But sometimes," continues Billy, "he started lookin' for human decency in some mighty strange places."

Darrow's expression doesn't change. "I'd like to think you can find human decency wherever you find human beings."

"In one show I remember," *says Singer, oblivious to Darrow's remark,* "Flint championed the cause of someone who taught school in the suburbs by day and played in San Francisco's homosexual dens of iniquity by night."

Darrow pulls himself up straight in the chair. "Flint's conscience always bothered him when he saw someone victimized by arbitrary authority or self-appointed moralists."

Billy Singer pats Darrow on the arm. Even when he is being challenged, he keeps the conversation friendly. "I do believe that you're taking a little shot at the Singer Watchguards."

"Why not? You people have taken shots at some good television programming, including 'Flint.' You even tried to stop that homosexual episode from going on the air."

"The watchguards took a stand, Mr. Darrow. They had every right to do it."

"Amen," *adds Jed. Then he begins to applaud and the audience joins in.*

"No one has a right to deny other people the programming they want to watch," *says Darrow.*

Singer's calm is unruffled. "It's a free country, Mr. Darrow. The free expression of opinion is a cornerstone for all of us."

"That's why we have the First Amendment," *says Darrow.*

"That's why people write angry letters to network executives and boycott sponsors," *chortles Billy, keeping the atmosphere light.* "We may not have the penetration level of a producer who can reach millions, but we have all of his rights."

"Or damn close," *cracks Darrow.*

Jed leans into the conversation. "Maybe we should include our listeners in this discussion, Reverend."

"Right you are, Jed. A Singer Survey." *Billy Singer looks at Darrow.* "Any objections?"

"Who's asking the questions?"

"We'll each ask one."

Darrow nods.

Billy Singer looks directly at the camera and fixes his gaze on every viewer. "Do you believe that a religious group has the right and responsibility to protest when it sees a television program that violates its beliefs or standards of morality."

Singer turns to Darrow. "Speak to my congregation. They'll give you a fair hearing."

Darrow looks into the camera. "Do you believe a religious group should deny a man the right to express his opinions, even if they run counter to the beliefs of the group?"

"A fair question," says Billy.

They break for a message, and when they come back, the results are in.

"So," says Billy expansively. "My listeners show their support of the Singer Watchguards, and at the same time, they display their open-minded sense of fair play.

The results flash on the screen.

Question 1:   *Yes 91%*   *No 9%*
Question 2:   *Yes 17%*   *No 83%*

"Over ninety percent believe that we have the right to protest when something runs counter to our beliefs," Billy explains, "but over eighty percent also believe that we don't have the right to deny a man his freedom of expression."

Singer looks at Darrow. "It's that kind of consensus that shows me the real strength behind our cause and our faith. . . ."

"Dammit, Reverend!" Darrow slams his hand on the desk. Jed jumps halfway off the sofa. "What the hell's happened in this country when religion is something that we determine by consensus? Religion is a matter of a man's conscience and his personal relationship with God."

"T'was ever thus, Mr. Darrow." Singer's tone doesn't change.

The orchestra begins to play softly, offering Billy Singer a little avenue of escape.

Darrow ignores the music. "It has nothing to do with the way a hundred thousand people answer two simplistic questions that are just opposite sides of the same damn coin."

The music plays a bit more loudly. Billy glances offstage, toward the producer.

"Unh, Billy," says Jed nervously. "I think it's time for a message."

"No, it isn't," snaps Billy Singer. "Let the man say his piece."

"You can't learn anything from these stupid surveys. They're just a tool for whoever runs them. Who cares what the consensus is?"

Billy keeps drumming his pencil on his desk, but he maintains his outward calm. "Now, Roger, that's quite a mouthful. First of all, this country's built on the consensus . . ."

"Save your civics lesson, Billy."

"That ain't very polite," says Jed.

"Shut up, Jed," says Singer, without changing his tone.

In the rest of the studio, there is complete, shocked silence, even in the control booth, where they know they can cut this out.

"I came here to Youngstown hoping to meet the Billy Singer I admired when I was a boy," says Darrow. I listened to him on radio, and he preached love and honesty. He talked about the truth of the Bible and the importance of a man's own conscience." Darrow is standing now, looking down at Billy Singer, who sits motionless while Jed Lee fidgets with the buttons on his sportcoat.

"And I remember a time in 1960, when a group of Protestant ministers said it was their consensus that a Catholic should never be president, and Billy Singer told them all to go to hell, because every man deserved the same chance, whether you agreed with him or not. That's the Billy Singer I hoped to meet here tonight, the one I admired. For that Billy Singer, faith came first, and it was all that mattered."

"And what about you, Mr. Darrow?" asks Singer. "Since you know so much about faith, what kind of faith motivates you?"

Darrow stares at Singer for a moment, as though searching for an answer. He can find none. He walks off the set, leaving the audience stunned and Jed Lee quipless.

Singer looks straight into the camera. "That, ladies and gentlemen, was an angry man. He was also an honest man, and honest men are hard to find. Especially in his neck of the woods."

"Praise God," mutters Jed Lee.

The orchestra begins to play.

"We'll be right back after this," says Billy Singer.

29

"N o," said Billy Singer. "I didn't talk to your husband again, except for a brief exchange backstage. I think he figured that I was so darn offended by his outburst that I wanted nothing more to do with him."

"Were you?" asked Whiting.

"Oh, heck, no. It was good television, and I looked good because I let him say his piece, as I would with any man."

A dreary winter rain splattered against the windows in Billy Singer's office suite. The view of Youngstown was obscured by thick gray clouds and smoke that rose from the city's smelters and mills. In Billy Singer's office, a fire crackled on the grate, a pot of hot coffee, and a dish of cakes sat on a table between two leather sofas.

Billy Singer wearing a cardigan sweater, perched on the edge of one sofa and rubbed his hands by the fire. Jeanne Darrow and James Whiting sat opposite him and sipped coffee. The camera was set up behind the sofa, ready to roll.

So far, Whiting and Jeanne had gotten Eddie Van der Hoof on video tape, along with wintertime shots of Darrow's summer locations, and a tape of Henry Baxter describing his truck. Lynne Baker had declined to discuss the death of Jack Cutler, and Lyle Guise had refused to say anything to the camera. Whiting had little photographic experience, but everything had been well-exposed and in focus.

Whiting turned on the camera and the light. The room was filled with a harsh, blinding glare, but Billy Singer did not seem to mind. He sat back casually, threw an arm around the sofa, and crossed his legs.

"How does this look?" he asked.

Whiting approved. He started the camera on automatic, then came around and sat again on the sofa.

"Now, before we proceed," Singer, "let me just say a bit more about Mr. Darrow."

"You said plenty at his funeral," said Jeanne without any trace of warmth.

"But I was just looking for the good things. I always try to find good things to say. That's been my philosophy since day one."

"And the good things with 'Flint' start after the episode on homosexual teachers?

Billy smiled. "Mrs. Darrow, the last time I saw your husband, he wasn't a very stable man. He'd fielded questions like mine a hundred times before without flying off the handle. That's why I thought I could bring up the issue on the air. Nothing like good, rational discussion to help folks understand things."

"Are you saying my husband wasn't rational?" asked Jeanne through clenched teeth.

"No. I'm just not sure why he came here, and he never made it clear."

"He came to ask you about your relationship to Andrew MacGregor," offered Whiting.

"And I told him the simple truth: Andrew MacGregor believes in the word as I preach it. He believes the nation should hear that word, so he built me this studio and helped me organize my religious network."

"Plenty of other evangelists have been able to survive without someone like MacGregor. Why did you need him?"

"Mr. Whiting, the building you're sitting in is the envy of my industry. We have four sound stages, a chapel, an eight-story office building, and our very own computer. Into that computer, we log all the information we receive on everyone who follows our ministry."

Whiting's mouth dropped open.

Jeanne looked from Whiting to Billy Singer. "Isn't that an invasion of their privacy?"

"My dear, a person's private life, his deepest thoughts, and how he puts them into action are the things a minister must be most concerned with. Nobody complains when a Catholic goes into a little box and reveals his innermost thoughts and feelings to a priest."

"Yeah," said Whiting, "but the priest doesn't put it all on a computer card."

Billy laughed. "And neither do we. But we log in names, addresses, the amount contributed, and if they write to us about a problem, we have a little code for that, too."

Jeanne Darrow shook her head. "I can't believe you're telling us all this in front of a camera. How will your viewers react?"

Billy stood and began to walk back and forth. "With trust, as they always do. Because they know that I would never do anything to hurt my followers."

"What about MacGregor and his organization?" asked Jeanne. "Don't they have access to this information?"

Billy stopped pacing. "When a follower of mine offers to build me a television studio, I say Praise God and let him do it. And when he offers my followers the electronic tool through which they can express their opinions on all the major topics of the day, I don't turn him down simply because some Hollywood liberal thinks the system might invade somebody's privacy." Billy sank back onto the sofa and stared at the fireplace. For a moment, the room was silent.

Then, Whiting's voice rose from behind the camera. "Are you telling me that the results from the Respondsible surveys are tablutated on your computer as well? And all the answers go onto those little cards of yours?"

Billy Singer did not answer. He folded his arms and looked at Whiting with one eye brow raised in righteous indignation.

"That way," continued Whiting, "you have not only your moral profile, but also a political profile of all the people who listen to your show?"

"I don't really think you understand the exigencies of the electronic church and our role in the modern world," said Billy softly. "Now, I'll be happy to discuss these things with you and give you a tour of the facilities, but not until you've satisfied me that you're not out to gore my ox."

"We're just trying to make a few connections, Reverend," said Whiting.

"Between what?"

"These men with the financial power, those with the political power, and those who wield the emotional power."

Billy Singer's face reddened. "My power is religious. It is not merely emotional."

"We're trying to learn how one group of power-brokers helps another," added Whiting.

"By Christ!" Billy Singer jumped to his feet.

"We're simply trying to finish my husband's work," said Jeanne, trying to soothe the reverend.

"Then your husband's work was the work of the devil." Billy Singer crouched down, bringing his face close to Jeanne's. "Do you know what your husband said to me backstage after his sorry performance? He said he had forgotten one thing on the air. He had forgotten to call me decadent." He spat the word in her face, then shouted it at the camera. "Decadent! If that is the work you have come here to finish, call me decadent *and* degenerate, then leave." He looked at the camera in all his wrath. "And let your viewers decide who is decadent and who is degenerate."

"My husband came here," answered Jeanne softly, "because he wanted to know how you fit into Andrew MacGregor's plans."

Billy Singer pulled himself up straight and looked down at Jeanne. "The question, young woman, is how does Andrew MacGregor fit into my plans? And how do the two of us fulfill God's plan?"

Billy turned and strode to his desk, pulling off his cardigan as he went. He picked up the telephone and barked, "Have Jed and Johnny in the control room in two minutes. He slammed down the receiver and turned to Whiting. "I assume your camera is portable?"

Then Singer threw on his sportcoat and headed for the door. Whiting strapped the VCR to his waist and slung the camera over his shoulder.

Billy Singer marched into the reception area of his office with Whiting and Jeanne behind him. "I am a tool of no one but the Lord."

"Then shout hallelujah, brother!" Henry Baxter jumped up from the sofa where he had been waiting.

"Who's this?" growled Singer.

"He's our—our driver," said Whiting. "He always wanted to meet you."

Singer's expression brightened at the promise of adulation. He shook hands with Henry. "Pleased to meet you, son. You can come along if you like."

"Thanks, boss." Henry fell into step behind Whiting and muttered, " 'Son.' I guess. That's better than 'boy.' "

They marched through the outer offices to the elevator. Singer was silent as the elevator dropped three flights. He was regaining his composure.

When the doors pulled open, he turned to Whiting. "Start rolling."

Whiting pressed the button and the little battery-operated light on the top of the camera threw an ugly glow into the marble foyer.

"I am a man of God," Billy announced as he pushed through the crowd of people waiting for the elevator.

"Amen to that!" shouted one of his employees.

"Praise God!" yelled another.

"A single man doing his best to spread the Word as he understands it." He careened around a corner, then another, and down a long, narrow corridor. "From everywhere in the United States and Canada, my people call unto me. For thousands upon thousands, I am the only conduit to the Lord Jesus."

He rounded another corner, with his little entourage hurrying along behind him, and he led them onto the sound stage. Cables slithered across the floor. The ceiling was covered in lights and microphones. Three cameras on rolling tripods sat in front of the set. The orchestra stand was stage left, Billy's desk and sofa, stage right. The seats for the audience rose behind the cameras. The glassed-in control booth and the giant clock stared down from above the audience. Jed Lee and another man were sitting in the booth looking puzzled.

"My church is flung to the four winds, but the Lord, working through Andrew MacGregor, has allowed me to touch my every parishioner every day, more surely than any country preacher screaming hellfire and damnation once a week in some West Virginia mountain meetinghouse.

Billy strode across the stage to his pulpit. Whiting followed with the camera. Billy straighted his tie, looked Whiting in the lens, then looked up at the booth. He raised his hand, as though commanding the waters to part, and said, "Lights."

All shadow disappeared. Billy Singer took on new life.

"And this"—he flung his arms out—"was what the good Lord gave us to preach his word and spread his truth. The electronic ministry, the modern miracle that can join the faithful, from Maine to California."

Whiting could not take his eye from the viewfinder. Jeanne Darrow was transfixed. Billy Singer was magic, no matter what he was saying.

"We have answered the call of Jesus. We have gone into the highways and the byways. We have reached into the homes and hospitals. We have used this wonderful tool to spread the good news."

Jeanne and Henry Baxter had drawn closer now, just out of range of Whiting's camera.

"It is my firm belief, stated many times, that if Jesus Christ had had this tool"—Billy shot his finger toward the lens—"eleven apostles would have been enough." He paused and smiled and looked around.

"But that would've nixed out old Judas."

Billy Singer turned his gaze onto Henry Baxter.

"Yeah," continued Henry. "And if there wasn't no Judas. There wouldn'ta been anybody to betray Christ. So He wouldn'ta got crucified or woken up with a hangover three days later." Henry smiled at the preacher.

But Billy was not flustered. This was the Chatauqua tent Billy Singer, the man who faced down hecklers with a quip and a prayer and turned them into God-fearing Christians. "I see a blasphemer among us today. A man who believes not when the truth shines so clear in his eyes."

Billy lifted the Bible from his podium and held it toward Henry Baxter. "Don't be blinded by the light, son. It may burn, but it cleanses. Accept Christ and all your pain will be lifted, all your sorrow forgotten. If not today, then tomorrow. And if not tomorrow, there'll come a day when death stares you in the face, and you'll cry, 'Oh God, please help me.' On that day, you will remember what I have told you here today. You will accept Jesus Christ, and you will be saved."

Jed Lee shouted "Amen!" through the director's microphone, and his voice reverberated in the empty studio.

Henry Baxter said, "Bull-sheeyut." Then he stepped up onto the stage, into the cirvle of light surrounding Billy Singer.

Billy's sanctuary had been violated. He turned to face the intruder, who was three inches taller.

"I already looked death in the face, man. Night watch. Quang Tri Province, 1968. And you know what death look like? A Viet Cong. And you know what I do to death? I kill the motherfucker, 'fore he kill me."

"I offer my hand to any man who has fought for our country," said Billy with sudden solemnity.

"I shake your hand after I had my say," answered Henry. "I wouldn'ta had to go off, 'cept for dudes like you sayin' what a good thing it was for us to be fightin' that ol' Godless ol' communism. But this was just another way for you to make more money."

Billy turned to the control booth, raised his hand, and commanded, "Lights."

"The lights went off, leaving the stage in the glare of Whiting's camera key light.

"Singer turned back to Henry. "I don't know what you're talkin' about."

Whiting's eye was glued to the lens. Jeanne could not move.

"On every show," said Henry, "you promised folks you'd pray special if they wrote and told you their boy'd been shipped out. My mama, she watched you all the damn time when you was on syndication. The day I leave, she start sendin' you ten bucks a week to pray for me. She get nice notes from your computer, tellin' her how hard you prayin' and how glad you are to get that contribution, so she keep sendin' it and sendin' it, even after I get back.

"I say, 'Mama, why you doin' that?' And she say, ' cause you came back alive from Nam. That was Reverend Billy's doin'."

Billy's hands were at his sides now. The trance had been broken. Henry Baxter, it seemed, was reaching something inside the television preacher.

"A black lady from Harlem with six kids, a lousy job, and a husband dead of a heart attack at forty-two, sendin' you money she can't afford 'cause she think you saved her boy."

"It was Jesus saved you," said Billy Singer softly. "I would tell her that today."

"The only reason her life is any better now is that I send her a check." Henry poked a finger into Billy's chest. "And I don't let her give none of it to you. I say, 'Give it to a black preacher right here in New York, somebody who'll do somethin' for the c'mmunity . . . build a youth center or somethin'. Don't throw it away on some transistorized white guy who just wants your money and don't give a damn about anything 'cept how he looks on TV.' "

Unconsciously, Billy ran a hand through his hair. But he made no response.

"That's all I got to say."

"I'm—I'm truly sorry if I've ever caused your mother any pain," said Billy. "It may not mean much, but I'll pray for her."

"Pray for yourself first, man." Henry walked off the stage.

Billy looked at the others. "I have always tried to be a decent man. I have always striven to be humble."

Henry stopped. "Like hell. You so full of yourself, I bet you ain't even listened to what these people been tryin' to tell you this morning."

Singer looked at Whiting and his camera. "Most of what I've heard has been polemics, along with a few more rumors for Vicki Rogers's show."

Whiting lowered the camera and turned off the light. "Will you let us fill you in and ask a few questions?"

"What is there that you can tell me?"

"Plenty," said Henry Baxter. " 'Less you know all about it and you're in on the plot."

"I know where my church is going and what I must do to help it there."

"Does that mean shakin' hands with Satan?" asked Henry.

Singer stepped off the podium. "Satan has no part in my church," he said softly, almost apprehensively. "My church is the work of God."

"Touched by the tainted hand of man," said Jeanne.

Singer shifted his eyes to her, but the fire had gone out of them.

"It's the truth, Reverend," added Henry. "Like you say, the truth may burn, but it cleanses."

A smile flickered across Billy Singer's face. His own words were coming back to him. He walked across the set and sat on the edge of his desk. "Tell me your story."

"Tell your assistant in the booth to turn off the microphones," said Whiting.

Singer gave the command, then he looked at Henry and offered his hand.

Henry took it. "You listen good to my friends' story."

30

The voice seems distant, driven, almost spectral in its intensity.

"I am not, in the formal sense, a religious man. I grew up Protestant, an Iowa Bible reader responding to the drama of the King James, if not to its truth. I have felt the sense of serenity and calm, the real optimism, that descends on a congregation at a Catholic funeral. I have known the magic of sitting with a Jewish family at the Seder. I have been struck by the spare, simple churches and the spare, simple doctrines of the Unitarians.

The camera is sitting on a hillside, looking down across a stand of trees toward Youngstown. The city looks gray and brick-red, even in the summer light. Smokestacks dominate this view, and the sky is smudged with their effluence.

Off camera, Roger Darrow continues to talk, as though he no longer cares to put his image on the screen. "If I have a religion, it is, I suppose, a sort of California pantheism. I see God in the order of nature, in the L.A. mountains that rise unperturbed above the smog, in the surf that crashes endlessly along Zuma Beach, in the flowers that bloom all year at Descanso Gardens, in the perfect roundness of a young girl's bottom, and the sublime fullness of a young woman's belly at eight months.

"But here, technology has subjugated religion and taken away its magic and mystery." The camera spins crazily, a 180-degree pan, so that it now focuses on the huge Gospel Evangelical complex. The exterior is white, precast stone and glass, an eight-story tower surrounded by several sound stages. Above the entrance is a huge crucifix. Darrow zooms toward it. "We bring God with our technology . . ." He pans and zooms to the television disc antenna at the rear of the complex. "But we have made technology a god."

Cut.

The camera is now looking down a street in a small city. "We have forsaken the past, our national heritage, our architectural *treasures . . .*

He pans to a six-story office building, probably erected around the turn of the century. A crane swings a wrecking ball into the side of the building. Bricks fly. Dust billows. The building shudders.

". . . And moved our commerce into ugly boxes."

Cut.

A shopping mall spreads itself across the landscape. Precast glass, surrounded by the roofs of automobiles reflected the sun like a single, multicolored mirror.

Cut.

The scene is now a quiet, sylvan place. Trees, a broad field, a church steeple in the distance, statues and walkways. Cannons pointed at the sky.

"Sometimes I feel that our future is all used up," continues Darrow, in his strange, crazed voice. "Television cables and telephone lines aren't the nervous system. They're the tendons that hold the corpse together.

"Once, we fought for ideas in places like this. . . . Little Round Top, where the Yankees repelled Pickett's Charge . . .

"Now, we struggle to gain control of cable television stations so we can keep the people under our influence. We fight over who will have the last drops of oil and who will see the last sweeping vistas before the derricks and smoke obscure them. Men of the earth, giants of the earth, are brought low by bribes and dishonesty. Men of God are brought low by technology and their own pretensions. . . ."

"And if the future is Manhattan . . ."

Cut.

A long shot of New York City on a hot, hazy day. The skyscrapers rise from the smog.

". . . it will not be bright. ʌ

Cut.

"It is the richest place in America. . . ." The camera is traveling along Central Park East, with its co-ops and condos and Gilded Age architecture.

Cut.

". . . and the poorest." The camera moves through Harlem, past boarded buildings, burned-out hulks, playgrounds so covered in broken glass that they sparkle like stretches of steamrolled quartz.

Cut.

"It is a place where people do not care . . ." On Fifth Avenue, uptown ladies step around a well-dressed man who has passed out on the sidewalk. ". . . for anything but insulation from the disorder that threatens their lives each day." Near the bandstand in Central Park, a mounted policeman gallops after a black teenager who runs in panic.

Cut.

"It is the seat of our culture . . ." The Metropolitan Museum of Art.

Cut.

". . . and the symbol of our decay." From the base of one of the bridges, an image rises in carefully composed tiers: mold-green water oozing in the river, derelict automobile on the bank, an elevated structure in the middle distance with a graffiti-stained train rattling along the tracks, and the skyline of Manhattan barely visible through the late-afternoon pollution.

Cut.

Roger Darrow is now standing in Washington Square, near the archway. "I have lost my interest in all this. I will not go to the cable television convention. I will not meet the famous Professor Wyler from Colubmia. All that matters to me in New York now lives in Greenwich Village." He brings his face close to the lens. "But you will not meet her here."

31

Vicki Rogers sat in the back of a Central Park carriage with a microphone in one hand and a clipboard in the other. The snow in the park was white and fresh, the Midtown skyline a mass of angles and shadows backlit by the rising sun.

Vicki was wearing a white, fox-fur coat, matching hat, and leather gloves. Her red lipstick was the only note of color in the outfit.

It was 6:54 A.M. Her broadcast was about to be fed live to East Coast eye-opener news programs and put on tape for syndication in the West. The cameraman rode beside the carriage driver. The remote truck was parked about a hundred feet down the road, at the spot where the carriage would stop, and a cable connected the cameraman to the truck's transmitter.

A mounted New York police officer rode beside the carriage.

"You'll keep the curiosity-seekers away?" Vicki asked him.

"It'll be mostly joggers this time of morning," said the officer. "And besides, you could take off all your clothes and dance with your pet dachshund in front of Saint Patrick's, and ninety percent of the people in New York'd walk past and pretend they didn't even see you. The other ten percent'd ask if they could cut in, and most of *them*'d want to dance with the dog."

Vicki laughed. She felt terrific. She had five minutes of meaty copy. She had negotiated everything that she wanted. She looked gorgeous. And this was going to be the best remote she had ever done.

In hotels all over new York, guests left 6:45 wake-up calls so that they could watch "On the Coast."

In her suite at the Plaza, Harriet Sears threw on her old flannel bathrobe, curled her legs under her, and sipped coffee.

In the Saint Regis, Howard Rudermann cursed the jet lag after five hours of sleep, phoned room service for coffee, urinated, turned on the television, and climbed back into bed.

At the Essex House, Vaughn Lawrence and Kelly Hammerstein shared a VIP suite. She slept. He sat up, smoked his first cigarette of the day, and hoped that there would be no surprises from Vicki Rogers. He was up to a pack a day.

On another floor at the Essex, Len Haley did fifty push-ups with one arm, then fifty with the other. Ken Steiner, one of his associates at the Haley Detective Agency, was asleep.

At the Roosevelt, Billy Singer read the Gideon Bible as he did every morning before he dressed. He had never met Vicki Rogers, but silently he thanked her for watching over the people who had come to him the day before. They had asked questions that he could not answer. They had made him wonder if Andrew MacGregor and Vaughn Lawrence were using Billy Singer and, through him, Jesus Christ for the furthering of illicit goals.

In his brownstone on upper Riverside Drive, Columbia professor Josh Wyler ate Cheerios and watched the report. He had received a phone call from James Whiting, and he had consented to an interview that day. Whiting had suggested that he watch "On the Coast."

When John Meade was not in Palm Beach or Easter's Haven, he lived in the penthouse of the Park Avenue headquarters of MacGregor Industries, parent corporation of MacGregor Communications. Meade had risen, as usual, around six. He had jogged the four-mile run in Central Park and returned in time for the broadcast. He had sat at the kitchen table, beside the expanse of glass that formed the south wall of his suite, looked out across Manhattan, and ate his morning concoction of wheat germ, honey, yogurt, and raisins.

James Whiting and Jeanne Darrow shared a suite at the Algonquin. They did not share a bed. After comforting each other in the back of Henry Baxter's truck, they had slept in separate rooms the following night in Ohio. They had arrived in New York late the night before, and Henry had dropped them at the hotel. Jeanne had showered first and climbed into bed. When Whiting had come out of the shower, she had been sound asleep.

Henry Baxter had returned to his mother's apartment in Morningside Heights. He had carried with him a framed photograph of the television preacher. The inscription read, "To Sarah Baxter, A woman who lives in the Lord. My Highest Regards, Billy Singer."

"In just a moment," said the New York anchorman, "we'll have

Vicki Rogers, 'On the Coast.' "

"What did you tell her this time?" asked Jeanne.

"I just brought her up to date. She think's it's quite a story."

"I still don't trust her," said Jeanne.

"She's been laying her career on the line for us," responded Whiting. "Lawrence threatened to drop her show if she kept talking about us, but she wouldn't stop. Without her, that guy in the red Buick might have gotten a lot closer a lot sooner." Whiting sipped his coffee. "When I see that woman, I'm going to give her a nice big kiss."

"Good morning everyone, from a gorgeous, snow-covered Central Park."

"Here's our gal." Whiting turned up the volume.

"They say that the January thaw is coming today, with temperatures in the mid-forties." Vicki pretended to shiver. "Certainly not beach weather to California girls like me, but the New Yorkers will gladly take it, at least until the snowstorm they're predicting for late in the day."

The sound of horse's hooves clopped on the sound track as Vicki's carriage moved through the park. First, she delivered her daily report on the ups and downs and the gossip of the industry, mixing business news and gossip together, so that they sounded like part of the same story. So-and-So had been photographed with Such-and-Such leaving Chasen's. Francis Coppola had bought the rights to a new best-seller. Young Oscar winner Cheryl Deems was, yes, at it again. She had been picked up by the L.A.P.D. on drug charges and was now undergoing therapy. The latest episode of the *Star Wars* saga had gone before the cameras in England.

"And now," said Vicki, "you're probably wondering what I'm doing here in the Big Apple. Well, Lawrence/Sunshine Productions and MacGregor Communications have collaborated on the most expensive epic ever produced directly for cable television. And believe me, it's a big deal. Stars Peter Cross and Harriet Sears are here, along with producer Howard Rudermann and Vaughn Lawrence, and they'll all be attending today's big screening for stockholders and selected members of the press, including yours truly.

After the screening, so the speculation goes, the great man himself, Andrew MacGregor, will appear on video tape to announce the final SEC approval of the merger between Lawrence/

Sunshine Productions and MacGregor Communications.

"Sources close to the negotiations tell me that all parties are pleased, especially Vaughn Lawrence, who just eighteen months ago fought off a full-fledged take-over bid by Mr. MacGregor. Now, the future looks rosy for the MacGregor/Lawrence Cable Broadcasting System."

Vicki took a deep breath. "All of which brings us to James Whiting and Jeanne Darrow, who thought they were tracking down the real story.

Vaugh Lawrence lit another cigarette. Len Haley stopped his workout. Billy Singer looked up from his Bible.

"Apparently," Vicki smiled. "Their journey across America is over. After traipsing from Los Angeles to Ohio and, we think, on to New York, they have decided to give up their quest for Andrew MacGregor."

Whiting lowered his coffee cup.

Jeanne looked at him. She was not surprised. "A nice, big kiss?"

"They have decided that Roger Darrow was chasing shadows when he set out to do his exposé of MacGregor Communications. And after a carefuly analysis, so have I."

"That bitch!" Whiting snapped off the television set. She's just left us to the wolves."

"We still exist," said Jeanne, "whether she acknowledges us or not."

"She's been using me since the first time she called me in Los Angeles." He walked into the bathroom and looked at himself in the mirror. "Idiot," he said, then he went back into the living room. "Why did she do it?"

"Business," said Jeanne. "Vicki probably wanted something from Vaughn, and she used you to get it. Now you're expendable."

"That bitch," said Whiting once more. "I should have known."

"Relax," said Jeanne. "In Hollywood, it's very easy to misjudge people. At least you never had an affair with Vaughn Lawrence." She smiled. After a moment, she laughed. She realized that she had never been able to joke about the affair before.

Whiting sat on the edge of his bed and folded his hands in front of him.

"If you think we're in danger, Jim, all we have to do is go to the police."

"With what? Speculation? Video tapes that prove nothing? The confession that we jumped bail in Wyoming?"

"Wyoming is a long way from here."

"Maybe we ought to go straight to Maine. Skip the big screening and the interview with Professor Wyler, and leave Billy Singer to blow the lid off things in New York."

"No," said Jeanne firmly. "I came to New York for a reason. There's someone here I have to see."

After Vicki signed off, Billy Singer slammed his Bible on the table beside him. "Damn that woman."

"What's wrong, Reverend?" said Jed Lee.

"She's betrayed the young folks." Billy Singer picked up a pad of paper and scrawled a note to himself. "I must mention that when I ask my other questions today."

"At the screening?"

"I intend to present them to the press," said Singer, "if they cannot be answered satisfactorily in private."

The butler brought the telephone to John Meade's breakfast table. "Reverend Singer, sir."

On the television screen, the national newscaster was discussing the economy, and the knot in John Meade's stomach was loosening. Vicki Rogers had gotten what she wanted and backed away from the story. Now, it would be easier to stop James Whiting and Jeanne Darrow.

Meade knew that once a televised face like Vicki Rogers stated an opinion, it gathered validity. If stated often enough, it became fact. With Vicki's continued assistance, the disappearance of James Whiting and Jeanne Darrow would become a footnote to her tale.

John Meade had resolved that, unlike the last time, he would not interfere with Vaughn Lawrence and his men. He picked up the receiver and said hello to Billy Singer.

Len Haley knocked on Vaughn Lawrence's door. He was dressed in gray slacks and white broadcloth shirt. He was not wearing his gun.

Lawrence opened the door. He was puffing another cigarette. The metallic smell of the smoke hung about his head like a wreath. He was still in his bathrobe. His morning stubble looked thick and mostly gray. The skin beneath his eyes looked dark and sunken, as though someone had punched him.

Haley closed the door behind him. "Where's Kelly?"

"The shower."

"Vicki's opened up our options for us. I don't think we should mess around with Whiting any longer." Haley jammed his hands into his pockets and flexed his biceps.

The shower stopped running.

"Turn that back on," shouted Lawrence.

"I'm done," answered Kelly.

Lawrence walked over to the door. His robe fell open, revealing his sagging pectorals. "Turn the shower on, I said!"

"I'll be a goddamn prune!"

"They're delicious."

The shower started again. Lawrence turned back to Haley and knotted his bathrobe.

"There are too many questions," said Haley. "There's too much Whiting may know or put together. And if he gets out of New York, he's sure to go to Maine."

Lawrence folded his arms across his chest and listened.

"I'd rather kill Whiting than be faced with the possibility of having to put the old man out of his misery."

"I'd rather not kill anyone else." Lawrence turned and looked out the window. The sun had risen, casting long shadows onto the street below.

"It's too late to be developing scruples, Vaughn."

It wasn't scruple. Vaughn Lawrence still thought that Jeanne Darrow was one of the most attractive women he had ever known.

"You have to learn what we learned in Nam," said Haley. "Play to win."

Lawrence picked at his stubble. "Winning doesn't always mean killing the other guy . . . or the other woman."

"In this case, you lose if they live. You lose the chance to control one of the most powerful cable television organizations in this country. More real power than any of the networks, because you have a wire in every home."

Haley dropped his voice an octave. "You'll lose that, and I'll lose my chance to influence you."

Lawrence turned to Haley.

"I won't let that happen," said Haley.

Lawrence looked out the window again, at the masses of people, in cars, buses, taxis, and on foot, hurrying through the New York streets. Individually, they did not matter. But banded together behind a product or an opinion or a politician, they meant power and riches.

"I'm not in this for my health, Vaughn, or for yours." Haley stood very close to Vaughn Lawrence and spoke very softly. "I know the power of television. I know it better than you. I know what it means to sit in a Vietnamese prison for four years, living like an animal, eating rice and fish every day and never knowing when you go to sleep at night if you'll wake up the next morning, losing thirty pounds, losing your wife to some draft-dodging screenwriter, losing everything but your anger. And you lay there every night, and you say, why the hell don't we win it? Why the hell don't we come in here and blow these gooks away? We can do it. We have the gas. And it doesn't happen. And every week, some gook lieutenant comes in and tells you that you're forgotten back home, that the American people have turned against you, that they're rioting in the streets to stop the war that's taken everything you can give. And you spit in his eye because you don't believe it. And you get the shit beaten out of you and they throw you in the hole with the rats."

Haley's voice had descended to a hoarse, angry whisper. "When you finally come home, you find out that the gook was right. There was no support, because television turned against you, and every night, the news was bad. Television cost us that war because it drained our will to fight. It showed every mother in America what her little boy had gone through that day in the jungles or was headed for after he got drafted. Television left guys like me and McCall and Ken Steiner and Cal Bannister—it left us to rot."

Haley put his hands on Lawrence's shoulders and gently turned him around. Television is power, Vaughn, and I'm going to get a piece of it. That's why I'm holding onto my piece of you. And I'm not letting anybody screw up your plans."

After a few moments, the shower stopped running. "I think

I'm drowning," shouted Kelly from the bathroom.

Lawrence glanced at the door. "All right." Then he looked back at Haley. "Even if Vicki pulled the plug on him, people still know that Whiting is sniffing around the story."

Haley nodded. "So who would be crazy enough to kill him? Certainly not anyone who would want to attract attention."

"What about Jeanne?" muttered Lawrence.

"New York's a tough town. Anything can happen here."

Lawrence looked out the window. Too tough, he thought, to be sentimental.

"Yes, this is Professor Wyler."

"This is James Whiting calling, Professor. You won't believe it, but I misplaced the address where we'll be meeting."

"I'll give it to you again." He read the address slowly. "It's a MacGregor company construction site in Brooklyn Heights."

"What's over there, again?"

"An old warehouse that's going to be turned into co-ops with up-to-the-minute video, computer, and cable equipment, as I told you last night.

"Indeed."

"And the question we all should be asking," said the Columbia media expert, "What does MacGregor intend to do with the power that he is amassing?"

"Yes. At the appointed time, then?"

"Right," answered the professor. "Nine o'clock. I'm driving so that I won't be late."

"Good-bye, then." Len Haley hung up the telephone. He had gotten Wyler's name from Vicki Rogers.

He placed a call to Newark, to a man named Johnny Mendoza, an independent hit man favored by the ruling families in the tri-state area. Mendoza was not a veteran, but Haley had worked with him before and trusted him. Mendoza was fast, efficient, and psychopathic. In the driveway beside his house was a red Buick Riviera with a smashed grille and a shattered windshield.

"Yeah?"

"This is Haley. I need you and another man today. I'm giving you a chance to get back at the folks who left you in an Illinois snowbank."

Haley gave Mendoza the address of Professor Josh Wyler. "Get someone good to follow him around this morning. When he heads for Brooklyn Heights around twenty to nine, I want him to have an accident. Total his car if you can, send him to the hospital if you must. But I want him to be at least a half hour late for his nine o'clock appointment."

"What else."

Haley gave Mendoza an address in Greenwich Village. "I have a hunch that Jeanne Darrow and possibly her boyfriend will show up there. If they do, they're all yours. And make it look like a real crazy go to them."

took a at ?

32

I've been waiting to hear from you," said Harriet when Jeanne called her around eight o'clock.

"You knew that I'd be in touch."

"We have to talk, honey, before you go any further."

Jeanne was winding the telephone cord around her finger, then letting it unwind itself. She glanced nervously at Whiting and said, "I want to talk to Miranda Blake first."

"Do you really want to see her? Are you sure?" asked Harriet.

"By the time Roger got here, she was his only hope," answered Jeanne.

Whiting put his elbows on the table, wrapped his hands around the sides of his face, and listened. He could not help her to conquer her obsession with Miranda.

"Her number's unlisted and I don't have her address," said Jeanne to Harriet. "With or without your approval, I'll find her. Where does she live?"

Harriet decided to give her the address. Then she added, "What time do you want to see her?"

"Why?" Jeanne was suspicious.

"I know her schedule."

"Nine o'clock."

"She should be in," answered Harriet.

"Good," said Jeanne. "Whiting and I will see you for lunch, Grand Central Oyster Bar, twelve-thirty.

Harriet agreed, and Jeanne hung up.

She looked at Whiting. "I have to see her."

"Jeannie, Roger's dead. Whatever happened between him and another woman doesn't matter anymore. Not as much as what happened between him and Vaughn Lawrence, and certainly not as much as what's happened between us."

Jeanne sat down beside Whiting. She placed her hand on his arm. "That New York tape keeps playing in my head—the world going to hell, Miranda's the only one that matters, and he won't even let us see her."

She moved her hand under his sweater cuff, up his arm toward the crook of his elbow. Whiting found it difficult to resist her touch.

"I have to see Miranda," she said. *"Alone."*

"No," answered Whiting.

"This is between Miranda and me," said Jeanne. "I have to make this part of the journey alone."

"No," he said firmly.

"You won't do me any good. You'll just complicate things."

"It's too dangerous."

"I'll ask Henry Baxter to come with me. He can wait outside."

After a time, Whiting grudgingly agreed.

"And if Greenwich Village is too dangerous," she added, "maybe you should think twice about going to Brooklyn Heights. Roger never even bothered to interview that Professor Wyler."

"That's the reason I have to meet him," answered Whiting. "Roger was losing it when he reached New York. He didn't even go through the motions. I'm going to do the things he didn't do, even if I have to do them alone."

She brought a hand to his face. She would not try to dissuade him. In a way, she was happy, because he was trying to cut himself loose. She hoped that she could do as well.

Howard Rudermann sat in the Carnegie Deli and sipped coffee. In front of him were two fresh bagels, lox, and cream cheese. Whenever he came to New York, he visited the Carnegie. He soaked up the pungent aroma of cucumber dill pickles, vinegar, and rye bread. He eavesdropped on the conversations of the young actors and actresses who haunted the Carnegie. And he ate. But this morning, he wasn't hungry.

In his pocket, he had the telephone number of the Algonquin. Harriet had given it to him. He had not dialed the number, however, because he did not know what he would say. Today was going to be one of the most important days of his life. With the screening of the first episode of "Redgates of Virginia," people would begin to realize that Howard Rudermann had always been as talented as his young partner. He wanted nothing to detract from his triumph.

He reached into his pocket and played with the change he had gotten for the pay phone. He wondered what he would say to Jeanne or Whiting. He knew that they were in danger, now that Vicki Rogers no longer watched over them, but he did not want them coming to the press conference or spoiling his premiere. He decided to finish his breakfast and think things over.

Billy Singer stepped off the elevator in the small, dark foyer of John Meade's penthouse. He had come alone to confront Mac-Gregor's nephew.

Meade's butler greeted the reverend, took his coat and hat, then turned and opened the inner doors. Billy Singer felt as though he were stepping into a secular cathedral. The entire south side of the penthouse was plate glass from floor to ceiling. The rays of the morning sun were slanting in, clean and golden. The New York beyond the windows looked like a field of concrete and glass flowers stretching themselves toward the morning light.

There were two levels to the living room. The walls of the upper level were lined with books and paintings that, to Billy Singer's untrained eye, looked like originals. The lower level was a rectangular space, three sides of which were reserved for leather sectional pieces, the fourth for wall-size television, stereo equipment, video recorders, and speakers.

"Reverend Billy!" John Meade appeared, wearing a perfectly cut light gray suit and a gray silk tie that looked almost silver. His hair, damp from the shower, was blond and shiny. His face was shaved smooth and glistened with a splash of Pierre Cardin after shave. He greeted Singer warmly, ordered two coffees, and led Singer down to the lower level of the living room.

John Meade was not happy to see Billy Singer, but John Meade did not demonstrate displeasure unless he had a purpose. "We're glad you could make it for the screening, Reverend. Your presence will add a great deal to the ceremony of the day."

"That's not really why I'm in New York." Billy Singer sat on the edge of the sofa and played wiht his pinkie ring. He was wearing a dark blue suit with white shirt and polka-dot tie. He looked like a stockbroker, which gave him, in New York, a degree of anonymity that he preferred. "I'm here for some answers from the man himself."

"My uncle is in Maine," answered Meade evenly. "He has made a video tape to be presented to the press this afternoon. I can show it to you if you like."

"No thanks, John. A video tape can't answer questions."

Meade leaned back and locked his hands around his knee. "All right, then," he said pleasantly, "fire away."

Billy Singer took a deep breath. "There's people out there, John, who think I'm a windbag, people who think that what I say on television about truth and honesty doesn't hold in my own life."

"I've never heard that, Reverend—"

Singer raised his hand. "And sometimes, they're right, John. But I had a visit yesterday from Roger Darrow's young widow and that fellow who got the kidney transplant."

Meade nodded. "We've been following their journey on television."

"I gave these folks my word that I'd ask a few questions that they ain't been able to get answers on, and I keep my word." Billy paused. "Now, John, what's your opinion of Vaughn Lawrence?"

John Meade said nothing.

"Or Reuben Merrill?"

"You've been a Merrill supporter since he first went to Congress, Reverend. You know him better than I."

Billy stared at Meade and played with his ring, as though he weren't satisfied with the answer.

Meade rose and folded his arms. "Let's get to the point, Reverend. I have a long day ahead."

Billy stood. He was a head taller than Meade, and his thick waist and dark suit made Meade seem lithe and youthful in contrast. Billy wiped the perspiration from his sideburn. "These are the questions I want you to answer in good faith: To what end has MacGregor Communications joined forces with Lawrence/Sunshine Productions? And what do you see as the role of the Gospel Church of Evangelical Sainthood in this new corporate entity?"

"Is that all?"

"No," answered Billy Singers. "Was Roger Darrow's death really an accident? And are those two young people in danger?"

John Meade did not answer immediately. He turned away from Billy Singer, walked up to the second level, and strolled to the windows. He stared out for a few moments, then he spoke.

"We are wiring the society to hold it together, Reverend." He began to pace beside the window, and his shadow danced on the beige carpet. "Our system brings entertainment, ideas, home security, the means to bank and do business without ever leaving the house, the enlightenment of your teaching"—Meade pivoted back to Singer—"and a new phenomenon. Teledemocracy."

Bill tried to speak, but John Meade was moving again, his shadow chasing him like a sprite as he advanced on Billy Singer.

"With Respondsible, we can protect our freedoms and project our independence from our own living rooms. Think of it, simply by pushing buttons and letting the world know how we think. Your followers have already done it through your own church."

"In the right hands, it's a powerful tool for good, in the hands of a man like Andrew MacGregor. But after listening to Darrow's widow and the Whiting man, I believe that your uncle has aligned himself with someone who's no damn good." Billy Singer stepped into the sunlight surrounding John Meade. "Why?"

John Meade turned his face to the window.

In the entryway of a three-story brownstone in Greenwich Village, Jeanne Darrow pressed the button beneath the name *Blake*. A familiar voice answered on the intercom. Then the door buzzer squawked and Jeanne jumped back. The buzzing continued until she grabbed the door handle and pushed.

The foyer was dark and smelled of disinfectant. There was a door on her left, and the stairs rose to her right. She went up. At the second landing, the foyer brightened. She turned, climbed to the third floor, and knocked on the door.

"Jeanne?" the voice was muffled, familiar, but not Miranda's.

Someone looked through the peephole, then the bolt was released and the door opened.

"Harriet!"

"Hi, honey."

Jeanne stood on the threshold. "Did you tell her I was coming?"

"She's not here," said Harriet.

"When will she be back?"

"I don't know." Harriet hesitated. "Actually, she's not around too often."

The buzzer rang. Harriet looked at the intercom. It rang again
and she decided to answer it.

"Jackie?" asked the man at the other end of the intercom.

"There's no Jackie here."

"Oh, sorry. I pressed the wrong buzzer."

Downstairs, Johnny Mendoza had completed his survey. He
had pushed all the buzzers. No one was home on the first floor or
the second. Jeanne Darrow and some vaguely familiar old woman
were on the third floor.

Jeanne was standing in the living room. It was neat, clean,
sparsely finished with oak, maple, and flowered-print fabrics. The
walls were white and hung with old theatrical posters. To the right
was a small hallway that led to the bedroom. To the left was a
dining table. The kitchen was tucked into what had once been a
closet in the hundred-year-old building.

"OK," Jeanne said to Harriet. "Why are you here instead of
Miranda?"

Harriet smiled. "I'm her understudy."

"No jokes, Harriet. I've traveled three thousand miles to see
her."

"I've followed you, along with Vicki Rogers. I didn't believe
what she said this morning, but I agreed with her."

"About what?"

Harriet turned away and stood by the living room window,
which looked across an alley to another window. "I agreed that
you've just been chasing shadows."

"Like Miranda's?"

"Yes." Harriet brought her hand to her throat. "And Roger's."

"I'll never be able to catch Roger's." Jeanne put her hands on
her hips. "But I may wait right here for Miranda."

"She doesn't want to talk to you, Jeannie."

"Why are you protecting her," Harriet?"

"I'm protecting you."

Jeanne turned and walked over to the dining table. She ran
her hand along its surface and felt the grain of the oak. Roger had
probably eaten here before going on to Maine. She wondered what

he talked about with Miranda.

Then, her eyes shifted to the kitchen. It was just large enough for one person, or maybe two. Oak cabinets, butcher's block counter tops, Design Research canister set with brown plastic covers that matched the color of the stove and refrigerator, a bulletin board with bright pushpins holding postcards, notes, and the pages of a script in place: It was perfect Miranda. Just organized enough, just sloppy enough, natural and plastic and . . .

Jeanne stepped closer to the bulletin board and felt her stomach turn over. Attached to the upper-right corner with two red pushpins was a bright green card. Across the top it read, "Easter's Haven Ferry Schedule, October 31 thru April 1."

"Come here, Harriet."

In the Carnegie Deli, Howard Rudermann had finished his bagel and was sipping his coffee. He had decided to talk to Whiting and Jeanne. He was going to warn them. He went to the telephone at the back of the restaurant, dropped a dime in the slot, and dialed the Algonquin number. He asked for Whiting's room and then counted ten rings. On the twelfth, he hung up.

James Whiting was in a taxi heading for the Brooklyn Bridge. On the seat beside him was the lightweight camera, video power pack, and tripod. He wore jeans, Timberland hiking boots, and a wool sweater over a turtleneck. This was the first time in ten days that he had gone anywhere without Jeanne Darrow. He was worried about her and nervous about the trip to Brooklyn.

But Whiting had decided that he would meet Professor Wyler wherever Wyler suggested. He would not be frightened off because the queen of the gossips had deserted him, and in a way, he was glad that he was traveling alone, because now, he was doing this for himself, not for Jeanne Darrow or her husband. When Darrow reached New York, he had been filled with despair and running blindly. James Whiting had decided he would not run.

The sun was swinging southward and glaring through the windows of John Meade's penthouse. Meade was looking at the city. Billy Singer was looking at Meade.

"The alliance with Vaughn Lawrence makes my uncle more powerful, Reverend. It gives him control over programming networks as well as delivery systems. And when my uncle's power is augmented, so is yours. You help my uncle to fulfill his goals, and my uncle helps you to attain yours."

"But he has always stood in the light," answered Singer, "with you beside him. Now, you've permitted this man of Mammon to join you."

Meade looked at Singer, "Save me the biblical phraseology, Reverend."

"You've convinced me of nothing, John. I have to go to the press."

"That's a mistake, Reverend."

Singer swallowed the tension in his voice. "If thine eye offends thee, pluck it out, John. I'm sorry." Billy Singer started for the door.

"Reverend," said Meade.

Billy stopped and turned. He hoped that Meade would give his conscience a reprieve.

"Would a meeting with my uncle help to convince you that our intentions are honorable, that Vaughn Lawrence is to be trusted?"

Billy smiled. "Yes, John, it would make me feel a lot better. I haven't spoken privately with him in many years."

"He speaks with few people," said Meade. "But if he believes you're about to desert the fold, I know he'll come personally from Maine. Will you wait until tomorrow to see the press?"

Billy walked back into the sunlight. "I'll wait until next week if I can speak with your uncle."

Just until tomorrow, thought Meade. He smiled, and the sun sparkled around him. Andrew MacGregor had worked his magic once more.

In Miranda Blake's apartment, Jeanne Darrow and Harriet Sears were seated on the sofa. Jeanne had jammed herself into the corner, against an armrest. Harriet was perched on the middle cushion.

Down in the street, Johnny Mendoza was becoming impatient.

"I'm going to Maine," Jeanne was saying again.

Harriet was trying to convince her to go home. "Miranda never wanted people to know that MacGregor was her uncle or John Meade was her brother. She felt it would give her some kind of unfair advantage. She wanted to make it on her own."

"If she's on Easter's Haven now, I'm going to see her." Jeanne stood.

Harriet grabbed her by the hand. "Don't go, honey, please. I don't even know if she's there."

Jeanne knelt and took both of Harriet's hands in hers. "I know you too well, Harriet. What's going on?"

"I don't know, and I don't think Roger did either. If he did, he didn't really care by the time he got here." Harriet threw her arms around Jeanne's neck and the two women held each other close.

Jeanne knew she could not suspect Harriet of anything but the best intentions. "I still have to go to Maine," she said softly. "Today."

Harriet grabbed her by the shoulders and pushed her back. The two women looked into each other's eyes. "When you get there, I don't know what you'll find. But just remember what I told you, never be surprised by the things people do to scratch the itch, whether it's between their legs or at the bottom of their soul. And most people think that satisfying the first goes a long way toward taking care of the second."

A few minutes later, they were ready to leave. Harriet opened the door. The old building was silent. The sunshine was pouring through the skylight directly above them and filtering down to the foyer three floors below. It illuminated the green paint peeling from the hallway walls and the dust particles dancing about in the drafts.

A shadow passed above the skylight. A bird, thought Jeanne, or perhaps an airplane.

Suddenly, the glass was shattering. Shards were flying. Slices were smashing on the staircase. Small, lethal granules were exploding like buckshot.

Jeanne screamed. Then something was flying through the skylight. She saw heavy boots coming straight at her and an orange ski mask with brown trim around the eyes and mouth. The eyes were round and empty; the mouth was knit into a permanent, silent wail.

The boots hit her in the chest and sent her reeling.

Harriet tried to close the door, but the body slammed into her and spun her away.

Then the creature was inside, kicking the door shut with his boot. A switchblade materialized in his hand. He pushed a button, and six inches of steel sprang to life.

"An old bitch and a new one," he growled. "My lucky day." He pulled a coil of rope from inside his suede jacket and flung it at Harriet. "Do like you're told, and I'll give you both something nice to remember me by."

Jeanne was sitting on the floor, gasping for breath.

Harriet was catching the rope and grabbing for the telephone at the same time. The creature kicked the phone from her hands, smashed her across the face, and with one surgical stroke, cut the telephone line.

Jeanne caught her wind. She sprang for the door. A powerful hand grabbed her by the collar and threw her back across the room. She screamed at the top of her lungs.

"Forget it, honey," said the creature behind the mask. "There's no one home but the three of us. And we're gonna play house. I'll be the daddy"—to Harriet—"you'll be the mommy"—and to Jeanne—"you'll be the little bitch who's broken up our marriage."

He looked at Harriet again. "Tie your friends hands behind her back."

Harriet didn't move."

"Do it," he growled.

"Jesus Christ," muttered Harriet.

"Henry!" screamed Jeanne.

The mask turned to her. "Henry?"

Jeanne jumped to her feet, ran to the front window, and screamed for Henry.

"Shut up," rasped the mask.

The creature's back was to the door. He turned to lock it. Bang! It burst open, smashed into his face, and nearly flew off its hinges. Then Henry Baxter was hurtling into the room.

Harriet rolled out of the way.

The creature crouched.

"He's got a knife," screamed Jeanne.

The knife flashed upward, under the leather bombardier's jacket, but missed the roll of truck-stop fat.

Henry's forearm came crashing and hit the mask in the nose.

Jeanne heard a crunching sound, a dog biting a bone in half.

The creature fell back against the sofa. Blood was already pooling at the mouth of the mask.

Henry was breathing hard. The creature was snorting and grunting, trying to get air through the remnants of nose that Henry had just shattered.

Henry picked up an oak captain's chair. "You ain't knifing me, motherfucker."

The orange face was turning a deep, clotting crimson.

Henry glanced at the women. "Get out."

The creature was on his feet again. The knife was clenched in his right hand. The blood was running down from under his mask, dripping off his chin, and onto his jacket.

The women were crouched by the kitchen door. The distance between them and the front door was about fifteen feet.

Henry moved himself to a point where he was halfway between the two doors. The creature in the mask pivoted his body and his knife as Henry moved, but he did not leave his spot. Henry expected him to lunge for the exit or for one of the women.

"Go on," said Henry to Jeanne and Harriet. "I'll cover you."

They scurried along the wall behind him, and he moved his body with them.

Harriet slipped out the door. Then Henry glanced over his shoulder as Jeanne ducked out.

The creature lunged.

"Look out!" screamed Jeanne.

Henry swung—a hard, vicious stroke. He caught the creature full force with the back of the chair. The spindles shattered against the side of the head. The seat and legs flew into the *Chorus Line* poster on the wall. The glass shattered. The creature staggered, fell back, but did not fall.

Henry couldn't believe that the man was still standing. He looked at the two pieces of oak, like belaying pins, that he now held in his hands.

The creature's legs stopped wobbling. Suddenly, he leaped forward. His knife slashed through Henry's leather jacket and through his shirt. Henry twisted and the knife skittered along his rib cage.

Then the knife flashed back. The blade was covered in blood. The creature lunged again. Henry swung his body out of the way and smashed with a piece of oak. It caught the creature behind the ear.

Jeanne and Harriet were standing in the hallway beneath the skylight. They saw the creature fly out the door, crash through the railing, and hit the flight of steps below.

Henry lurched out of the apartment after him.

The creature wobbled to his feet. He looked up. He started to climb the stairs, then he turned back and staggered down the next flight.

They listened to the footfalls receding; then they heard the front door slam.

"Motherfucker," growled Henry.

33

When the Continenal army drew up at New York in 1776, George Washington decided to fortify Brooklyn Heights. It afforded a view of lower Manhattan, yet it was protected by the deep, fast-flowing currents where the East River met New York Harbor. Command Brooklyn Heights, he believed, and command New York.

A hundred and seven years later, the Brooklyn Bridge, the architectural and engineering wonder of the age, linked Brooklyn to Manhattan. Two granite towers, the tallest structures of their time, formed the Victorian archways to America's greatest city and supported an Aeolian harp of spun-steel cable that in turn supported the roadway to New York.

A hundred years later, the bridge served many of the 3 million commuters who injected themselves into Manhattan each day. And the Brooklyn Heights meadow of Washington's time had become one of New York's best neighborhoods.

James Whiting had friends in Brooklyn Heights and visited often. He loved to explore the shops and restaurants along Henry Street, or stroll down the fruit streets, as they were called—Pineapple, Cranberry, Orange—and admire the brownstones and bowfronts that dated from the nineteenth century.

And eventually, he would find his way out to the Promenade and one of the most famous views in America. The Promenade ran for about a half a mile along the edge of Brooklyn Heights. Below it, like terraced steps, were the Brooklyn-Queens Expressway, Front Street and the Brooklyn docks. And across New York Harbor rose the skyline of lower Manhattan. When he had walked the Promenade at night, when it seemed that every window in every building was illuminated, when Manhattan gazed at Brooklyn Heights like a benevolent god about to bestow its gifts of knowledge and light, James Whiting had found it easy to understand all that New York had once symbolized.

Whiting was waiting for Professor Josh Wyler in front of an old warehouse on Water Street. The area's proximity to the Brooklyn docks had once made it a convenient spot for factories and warehouses. Now its proximity to Wall Street and its views of the bridge and Manhattan made it an attractive location for young executives.

In a square near the base of the bridge, there were restaurants, a museum, and several condominium conversions. Exterior brickwork had been repointed. Old broken windows had been replaced. Gardens and trees had been planted. For the interiors, Whiting imagined all the elements of refurbished chic—exposed brick walls and ceiling timbers, refinished floors of oak or hard pine, stark white paint, track lighting. And in each unit developed by the construction subsidiary of MacGregor Industries, there was an entertainment center like a Hollywood screening room: windowless walls padded in an acoustically perfect combination of rubber and fabric, a four-foot screen, eight stereo speakers, and a control console containing computer head, television cable, video cassette recorder, tape deck, laser disc player, *all the electronics to make life worth living . . .*

Good copy, thought Whiting. Maybe MacGregor would hire him to promote the new concept.

Renovations had begun on a building at the edge of the square, a few hundred yards from where Whiting was standing. Construction trucks were parked outside, workers were milling about, and the sound of jackhammers rattled down the street. The row of buildings where Whiting was to meet Josh Wyler, however, was vacant and deteriorating. The windows on the first and second floor were covered with plywood. Newspapers and trash had molded themselves into the corners around the entrance. Beer bottles had been broken on steps and walls and shattered against the sign fixed to the front of the building: "Phase III, MacGregor Bridgeview Condominiums, Computerized Luxury Homesites for the New York Professional, Opening Soon."

Someone with a can of spray paint had scrawled "Fuck all you rich assholes" across the front of the sign.

Whiting knew why Professor Wyler had asked him to meet here. Wyler was an academic. He would be looking for comparisons. To understand where we were going, it was necessary to see where we had been. So, Wyler wanted Whiting to see the guts of a deserted old warehouse. Then they would go back to the square and see the transformation of another old building into computerized luxury homesites.

Whiting had already photographed the exterior of the building, the docks behind it, and the Brooklyn-Queens Expressway across the street. Now he stood on the sidewalk, kicked at the pile of soot-crusted snow, and felt the sun on the side of his face. The temperature was above forty degrees. In New York, the January thaw had begun. It might last a day and end with a snowstorm as predicted; it might continue for a week.

Whiting glanced at his watch: 9:10. He wondered where Wyler was.

Professor Josh Wyler was in his 1972 Volkswagen, halfway across the Brooklyn Bridge, and hurrying because he was late for his appointment.

He did not notice the beat-up station wagon that had followed him down from the West Side and that was now coming up on his left. He did not notice when it pulled up beside him, doing forty miles an hour on the bridge. He did not notice it until it was half a car-length ahead of him with its right signal flashing.

There was almost room for the station wagon to slip between Wyler and the car in front of him, but Wyler accelerated. The mild-mannered professor became a New Yorker behind the wheel. He closed the gap, but the station wagon kept drifting, as though Wyler weren't there.

Wyler leaned on his horn. He slammed on his brakes. And the station wagon hit him broadside.

Tires squealed and screamed. Glass shattered. Metal crunched. Wyler swerved to his right and bounced off the guardrail. Mirrors, door handles, and fenders flew. Wyler's VW scraped to a stop with his bumper hooked into the left-front wheel well of the station wagon and the other driver screaming obscenities.

"Mr. Whiting! Up here!"

Whiting looked up. A young man wearing a hard hat was leaning out a broken window on the fourth floor.

"Come up the stairs at the rear!" he called.

Whiting waved back, picked up his VCR and camera, and walked down the driveway at the side of the building. The driveway had once led to the loading docks, but now the loading doors were all bolted shut. Whiting walked past the empty platform to the edge of the driveway, where the land fell away. He went down a flight of steps and around the corner of the building, which was a block deep.

The rear door was made of iron, a fire exit. It had been chained shut, but the padlock had been released so that Whiting could enter. He opened the door and stepped into a concrete and metal stairwell that stank of urine, even in January. The door slammed behind him.

"Fourth floor!" shouted the young man.

"Professor Wyler?" Whiting's voice echoed up the stairwell.

"Nice to meet you, Mr. Whiting! C'mon up!"

A rat scuttled out of one of the corners and across the first step.

Whiting started up. His footsteps rang hollowly through the metal staircase, which had once rumbled every day under the weight of hundreds of workers.

The walls in the stairwell had originally been tan-colored, with a crimson stripe running, at shoulder level, like a directional line, all the way to the roof. At each landing, the floor number had been painted in crimson above the stripe, and a hand with a pointing finger had been stenciled below it. The finger pointed to the door, and below the finger, a sign described what went on behind the door.

The crimson paint had faded to a dried-blood brown, the tan paint had dissolved into the plaster, and mold grew in the corners where drunks had urinated, but the little signs still conveyed authority.

"1st Floor: Shipping, Receiving, Reception. Worker's Entrance." Old newspapers on the stairs. A muscatel bottle on the landing. An empty mayonnaise jar.

"2nd Floor: Main Administrative Offices." An empty six-pack. Rat droppings. More newspapers. An old leather shoe with the sole worn through. On the landing, a pallet of newspapers six inches thick. An old hypodermic needle. Broken pieces of plaster. Shattered glass.

"3rd Floor: Storage." A stink, like human feces. More newspapers. A Haffenreffer beer bottle. Two filthy overcoats. A large old blood stain. What happened there? What the hell am I doing here?"

"4th Floor: Storage."

A man with blond hair and an ugly scar on his chin greeting Whiting. "Good morning, Mr. Whiting. I'm Wyler."

Whiting extended his free hand. "I thought we were meeting downstairs."

"Sorry about the mix-up." A Viet Cong mortar round had nearly torn away Ken Steiner's jaw. Plastic surgery and dental work had repaired his face but left him with a slight speech impediment. "Sorry" became "shorry."

Whiting had not recalled the impediment from his phone conversation with Wyler the night before. He wished that he had seen a photograph of the professor before coming to meet him here.

The man handed Whiting a yellow hard hat like the one he was wearing. "Regulations of the MacGregor Corporation."

"You have permission, then?"

"Oh, yes." said Steiner. "Professors can get permission for almost anything."

He opened the door, and Whiting stepped onto the main floor, where thousands of tons of goods had once been stored. Now, the floor was empty of crates, partitions, workers. From the back entrance to the front of the building, almost three hundred feet, nothing stirred, except for the pigeons nesting on the windowsills. The sun poured through the windows on the right side and slanted halfway across the width of the building. Concrete pillars, arranged in diamond patterns across the floor, supported the ceiling and weight of the building. Behind one of them, Len Haley waited.

A gust of wind blew through the broken windows. Old newspapers and pigeon feathers swirled across the floor, catching themselves on pillars or old studs that were the remnants of partitions.

"I'd like to set up right here," said Whiting. "The light's perfect and we have great . . ." He fumbled for the word. He wanted to sound as though he knew what he was talking about. ". . . perspective . . . depth, right from this spot."

"Fine, fine," said Steiner, "but first let me walk you around the floor and show you the points of interest, architecturally."

Len Haley pulled at the leather gloves already molded to his hands. He had given his camel's hair overcoat to Steiner. He was perspiring in his tweed jacket, and the sweat felt cold as it rolled down his flanks.

Whiting picked up his camera and followed Steiner.

"These are going to be real luxury places."

"With a spectacular view thrown in," said Whiting. Outside the north windows, the Brooklyn Bridge split the sun's rays like a prism.

Keep walking. Keep talking. Len Haley listened to the conversation drawing closer. He would not punch. He would not thrust. He wanted no unusual bruises. He had no special relationship with the New York medical examiner.

"What do you think these developers are after, Professor?"

Steiner laughed. "What everyone else is after. Money."

"But you implied that there was something more ominous going on."

The young man laughed again, but he did not turn around. In fact, thought Whiting, he had barely made eye contact since they shook hands.

At the elevator shaft, Steiner stopped and turned to Whiting."Why don't you set up your camera here?"

"Is there something specific to shoot?" asked Whiting.

"Well, the special video rooms are going to be installed, for structural reasons, in the old service elevator shafts. It might be good to show an empty shaft, then photograph one of the rooms in the new building."

Whiting agreed. He set up the tripod. Then he noticed that the elevator shaft was open. The two-by-four gate that should have been nailed across its mouth was lying on the floor beside the shaft. The sign nailed to the gate read Danger.

Haley looked around the pillar.

Whiting was nearly in position. He was holding the camera in his left hand. The tripod and video unit were just to his right. When Whiting moved a few feet closer, Haley would spring.

"Before you put the camera on the tripod," said Steiner, "perhaps you should get a shot looking straight down the shaft."

"You've got to be kidding," said Whiting.

Haley heard the change in Whiting's voice. He peered around the pillar. His gaze met Steiner's. Whiting saw Steiner's eyes shift. He spun as Len Haley leaped at him.

"No!" The scream escaped from Whiting's throat, and reflexively, he pulled back to throw the camera. The cable between the recorder and the camera snapped taut and caught Len Haley around the ankle. Haley stumbled and lost his momentum.

Steiner grabbed at Whiting's sweater. Whiting slammed the camera into Steiner's chest and hit him just below the throat, in the only spot that wasn't padded with camel's hair.

The camera drove the necktie into Steiner's Adam's apple. He gasped and stumbled backward. Whiting pulled the camera back again, and the cable knocked Haley's left foot out from under him. Haley fell. Then, Whiting threw the camera as hard as he could. Steiner caught it in the stomach. It knocked him back another step, and he slipped over the edge.

Whiting shouted.

Steiner screamed. He dropped a foot below the floor level and hung. He was still clutching the camera, and the cable was strong enough to hold him for a few seconds.

Len Haley grabbed at the cable wrapped around his ankle and began to pull gently, gingerly, hand over hand.

A sound of panic escaped from Ken Steiner.

"Just hold on, babe," whispered Haley through clenched teeth.

Whiting should have been running, but he stood and watched.

Haley pulled on the cable once more and cursed. At the spot where it turned over the edge, it was starting to stretch. The rubber was giving way and turning white.

Haley managed to get up onto one knee. The cable was stretching fast. Another second and Steiner would be lost."

"Help, Lieutenant!" shouted Steiner.

"Your hand," screamed Haley.

Steiner swung his left arm up. Palm slapped against palm and Len Haley held tight.

Whiting was still standing there. He knew he should have been running. He looked over the edge and saw the frightened eyes. Four flights below, pieces of broken glass reflected the light.

"Drop the camera," rasped Haley.

The camera fell another five feet and hung.

"Grab the ledge."

Ken Steiner swung with his right arm and caught the metal floor plate at the edge of the elevator shaft.

"You're halfway there," growled Haley. "Now hang on."

Haley tried to lift. Whiting saw the cords in his neck standing out like the piping on a piece of fabric.

Another strange cry, this one like a sob, escaped from Ken Steiner.

"Hold on, Steiner," groaned Haley. He was standing at the end of the shaft, trying to lift straight up. He needed leverage, something to hold on to.

He looked around frantically. The sweat was pouring off his forehead. Every muscle was strained tight. If he leaned forward another few degrees, he and Steiner both would go down the shaft.

Haley looked at Whiting and held out his left hand. "Help me." His face had flushed a deep, beefsteak red.

Whiting did not move.

Pain and draining strength screamed up from the elevator shaft.

"Help me," rasped Haley once more.

"You just tried to kill me," said Whiting.

"You're wrong."

"I can't hold on much longer, Lieutenant Haley," said Steiner.

Whiting knew that the man in the elevator shaft was about to die. Whiting could save him.

"Please," groaned Haley. "Help us."

Whiting stepped toward Haley. He started to offer his hand, then he stepped back. They were there to kill him.

"Bastard," growled Len Haley.

Whiting looked around. A pile of half-inch chain lay at the base of a nearby pillar. It looked like the remnants of an old chain-fall, a pully for lifting heavy loads.

"Help me, you bastard."

Another cry escaped from the shaft.

Len Haley looked down at Steiner. He knew he could not hold on much longer. He was thinking about letting go and tossing Whiting after him. But Ken Steiner was one of his men. He would not let go of one of his men. In battle, a man did not fight for country or ideals, but for himself and the handful of men in the same foxhole. Haley screamed again at Whiting.

Whiting could not run. He was either too crazy or too human. He grabbed one end of the chain, wrapped it around a pillar, hooked it onto itself. He picked up the other end of the chain and slid it across the floor to Haley.

Then he turned and ran.

Haley wrapped one hand around the chain. Now he had leverage.

Whiting slammed through the steel door at the rear of the

building and leaped for the stairs, taking them two at a time, past the dried blood, past the old coat and newspapers and beer bottles, down to the third floor. He stumbled and fell.

Ken Steiner was halfway out of the hole.

"Lift your leg up," Haley shouted.

Steiner caught his toe on the bottom of the support beam, pushed up, then collapsed exhausted on the floor in front of the elevator. Len Haley turned and raced after Whiting.

Whiting heard the door slam above him. He was on the landing between the second floor and the first. Then, two more leaps, his hard hat flew off, and he was out of the building. As he reached the street, he slipped in the snow and fell on his face.

"Whoa, take it easy dere, buddy."

Whiting looked up.

Two construction workers were walking past the old building. It was coffee time, and they were sharing a brown paper bag, special blend.

"Yeah," said the larger one. "You'll hurt yourself runnin' around like dat."

Whiting had reopened the gash Bert McCall had given him on his chin. The blood was oozing out through the stitches. The sweat was pouring down the sides of his face and starting to drip off the tip of his nose. He tried to speak. He couldn't get his breath.

"You guys . . ." he swallowed. "You guys gotta help me. There's someone after me." He gestured over his shoulder. "In there."

"Someone in *dere* is after you?" the beefy one with the red hard hat began to laugh.

"Yeah," said the skinny one in the stocking cap. "He stole some junkie's needle to stitch up his face, now every junkie in Brooklyn's after him."

They laughed and kept walking.

Whiting wobbled to his feet and looked over his shoulder. Len Haley was appearing at the far end of the building. Whiting began to run again. He lurched down the street. A car was coming toward him. He tried to wave it down, call for help. The car swerved around him. He kept running, past the construction site, through the square, and up one of the side streets that led toward the Height's.

He glanced over his shoulder. A surge of traffic swept down

the street and Haley could not get across.

Keep running, Whiting told himself. He thought his lungs would explode. Keep running.

He turned a corner onto Hicks Street. Up ahead, he could see the town house where his friends lived, a New York brownstone converted to co-ops.

Keep running.

He reached the stoop in front of the apartment. He ran up the steps and leaned on the bell.

Alice, please be home, be late for class. Bill, be home sick with a big hangover or a case of the blue Fridays.

No answer. He leaned on the other bells. No answer. No one at home in Brooklyn Heights. No policemen walking on Hicks Street at 9:14 on a balmy winter day.

He looked down the street. Len Haley was just turning the corner. Whiting jumped off the stoop, turned onto Pineapple Street and started to run.

He approached a gap in a row of joined town houses. It looked like a little park, and beyond it, he saw open sky. The Promenade. He rushed through the little park. The trees fell away. The vista opened. Manhattan rose in front of him. He looked to his left: The parallel lines of the Promenade merged in the distance. People were strolling, sitting on benches, leaning at the railing, jogging, and enjoying the warm winter sun. He looked to his right: more people on the walkway that curved gently back toward Water Street and the bridge.

He turned to his right and started to run. He felt safer, but he could see no New York police walking in tandem, protecting the populace, and he did not think that the populace would do much to protect him. Two old ladies tottered along, led by a fast-moving Pekingese on a leash. A father was watching his nine-year-old son try out a new bicycle. A college girl sat on a bench and read Balzac. A cabby sat beside her and ate a hero sandwich.

Whiting's lungs were burning again. He had to stop. He slowed down and glanced over his shoulder. Haley was standing at the entrance to the Promenade and looking in the other direction. To Whiting's right, a young woman in a bright sweater was hurrying across the harbor. She was wearing a pair of Walkman headphones and seemed to be in another space and time. Her ten-speed bicycle leaned against the railing beside her.

"Sorry," he muttered, although he knew she did not hear him. He grabbed the bicycle and jumped on.

He had not ridden a ten-speed in years, but the bike was well-adjusted for his height, and in two quick pumps, he was under way. He glanced over his shoulder; the girl's eyes were closed and she was swaying back and forth. He wondered what she was listening to.

Len Haley saw Whiting beginning to skim away. He knew he would never catch a man on a ten-speed.

"That's all, Bobby. Let's go!"

"Haley turned. "Aw, Dad, just one more ride." The little boy on his Christmas bicycle was pleading with his father.

The father was tall and slender, with glasses, a turtleneck, and a cardigan sweater. He dressed like someone who worked at home. He cupped his hands to his mouth and shouted, "You're supposed to be home sick from school. One more turn, and that's it!"

"Sure, Dad." The boy was within a few feet of Haley.

A flash of leg, a well-placed shoulder, and Bobby was on the pavement with his bicycle on top of him.

"Bobby!" shouted the father, and he started to run.

"I'm sorry, son," said Haley. "Really sorry. I guess I didn't see you."

"You clumsy jerk," shouted the kid. "Whyn't you watch what you're doin'?"

"I'm really sorry." Haley lifted the bike off the boy. The boy started to get up. Haley swung his leg over the bike, and, with a foot on the flank, knocked Bobby to the ground again.

"You're supposed to be home sick," he grunted.

"Daaaaaady!" screamed Bobby.

"Bobby! What's wrong?" the father was rushing toward his son.

The daydreaming businessman stopped gazing at the skyline. The Pekingese spun toward the noise. The college girl lowered her Balzac. The cabby stopped chewing, as Len Haley came toward him.

"Bobby! What happened?" shouted the father.

The little boy wiped the tears from his eyes and shot a finger at Haley. "That fuckin' asshole stole my bike!"

"Hey!" shouted the father. "Bring back that bike."

Haley pumped two or three times, wobbling a bit before he

could get underway. He glanced over his left shoulder. The father was running after him, screaming for him to stop. He found a comfortable position, shifted gears, and the cabby's half-eaten hero sandwich hit him in the ear.

The cabby jumped up as the bicycle shot past. "Give the kid his bike, you son of a bitch!" Then, the taxi driver began to pound after Len Haley.

The little boy and his father shot past. The Pekingese had broken loose and was yapping at the boy's heels. The girl reading Balzac saw the Pekingese go by, pursued by two old ladies. She grabbed for the dog's leash, but she missed.

"Come back! Come back! Chairman Mao! Mao!" One of the old ladies was screaming. The dog's name was Mao.

The girl shoved her Balzac into her pocket and began to run after the dog.

Whiting was approaching the end of the Promenade now, and his thigh muscles were aching. He heard shouting and glanced over his shoulder. Haley was chasing him, and people were chasing Haley.

"My bike! My bike!" The little boy sped past the young woman wearing the Walkman. Her tape had just ended. She heard the boy go by, then she realized something was missing.,

"*Your* bike!" she screamed. "Where's *my* bike?"

She saw it speeding away from her, and she began to run.

A pair of joggers with huge necks and sweat shirts displaying the Brooklyn Heights Nautilus Club insignia were running toward Len Haley.

"Stop him!" shouted the father.

The two joggers looked at each other, then at Haley, who was about to drive between them. One of them jumped in front of the bike, the other went at Haley.

Haley swerved. One of the joggers grabbed his handlebars. Haley shot a vicious elbow into the thick neck, and the man fell, gasping. The other tried to grab Haley but missed. Haley kept pumping, and the crowd of pursuers was now joined by the two joggers.

Whiting reached the end of the Promenade. If he went down Water Street, he would be back in the square at the base of the bridge. But if he turned to his right, onto Cranberry Street, he could spring across to Cadman Park and then onto the bridge.

Haley nearly fell off the bike when he jumped the curb onto Cranberry Street. Then the tires slipped on a patch of ice. He had no more than a fifteen-yard lead on the joggers, and Whiting was two blocks ahead of him. But Haley had found the rhythm, and he was starting to close on Whiting. He expected that he would lose his pursuers in the next block if he could make it across the busy intersection at Henry.

As he approached the intersection, Whiting jumped off his bike. A double-parked delivery truck had forced the traffic into one lane. Horns were blaring, drivers were shouting, and nothing on wheels was moving. He lifted the bike above his head, and moved as fast as he could through the bumper-to-bumper traffic.

"You got the right idea, buddy," shouted a man in a pickup truck.

Whiting looked over his shoulder. Lieutenant Haley was still a block from the intersection, and the crowd a block behind him. Whiting jumped back onto the bicycle and felt the stitches in his face pulling. He had stopped bleeding. The blood was drying and cracking.

Cranberry Street ran a short distance more, past a modern, ten-story apartment building, and then opened into Cadman Park. Patches of dirty snow dotted the park, but the paths were clear, and on the other side, the great bridge rose toward Manhattan. Whiting pushed the gear shift up several notches and streaked across the expanse of brown grass and bare trees. He felt a new rush of strength.

As Haley approached Henry Street, he picked a path through the cars. If he could get across without getting off the bike, he would gain ten or fifteen seconds on Whiting. He shot into the intersection, past one car, then another, and then a third inched up, closing off his path. He tried to brake but slammed into the front fender of a new Chevrolet Camaro.

The driver leaped out of the car and began to scream.

"You jerk! You just hit my new car!"

Haley leaped onto the hood of the Camaro, picked up the bike, and swung it over the side of the car. The driver screamed. Haley jumped on and pushed for Cadman Park. The Pekingese came barking out from under the Camaro and streaked after him. The two joggers scrambled over the hood of the car. The driver screamed again. The Walkman woman scrambled after the joggers. The driver threw up his hands and sat on the curb.

The father was carrying his little boy piggyback-style, through the traffic jam.

"C'mon, Daddy. We can do it. We can get him," the boy was shouting.

The two old women scurried into the intersection, one of them holding up a white cane with a red tip, the other shouting for Chairman Mao.

"He's down the street havinv' dim sum with Brezhnev!" shouted the man in the pickup.

"Stinkin' lousy louse of a maggot!" the cabby stumbled into the intersection, leaned against a lamppost, and gulped for air. The college girl wandered after him with her nose buried again in the Balzac.

Whiting had crossed Cadman Park and had reached the entrance to the bridge. He lifted the bike, took a deep breath, and started up the staircase to the walkway above the automobile deck.

Haley was about fifty years from Whiting and pumping hard. He was beginning to feel the exertion now, but his body was well-tuned.

James Whiting was near collapse. Unlike Haley, he had no reserves of energy, strength, and coordination. All he had left was his will and his refusal to stop. He told himself to keep going. He had to survive. And someplace inside him, he made a connection between the old James Whiting and the man with Roger Darrow's kidney. The old James Whiting had never given up. He had survived in agony for over a year. He could survive in agony a short time longer.

He reached the top of the stairs just as Haley arrived at the bottom. The crowd had fallen back now. Only the joggers and the woman with the Walkman were still running. The rest were walking or stopped for breath. What was driving these people? he wondered.

Haley picked up his bike and ran up the stairs two at a time.

Whiting jumped onto the ten-speed. The walkway was nearly deserted. He put his head down and kicked for Manhattan with whatever strength he had left.

Haley got to the walkway with the two joggers a flight behind him. He leaped onto the bike, pumped about five feet, and ground to a stop. The front tire had taken a nail and gone flat. The joggers were appearing at the top of the stairs. Haley lifted the bike above his head and heaved it at them. Len Haley turned and ran after Whiting.

Whiting was moving slowly. Haley thought he might still be able to catch Whiting before he started his downward glide toward Manhattan.

Whiting could barely see. His head was pounding. The sweat was pouring off his face. His heart felt as though it would burst.

In front of him, he saw the midpoint of the bridge. He felt a little surge of strength. Pump. Pump. Pump. The pain was screaming through his body. Every last drop of glucose and gram of carbohydrate had been consumed. His muscles were feeding on themselves. And then the pain eased. He had reached the center. He looked over his shoulder and almost laughed out loud. Haley was on foot now, far behind. Whiting pumped a few more times, then sat back and let the slope do the work while he gulped oxygen and looked up at the artistry around him, at the cables hung with geometric precision, at the magnificent granite tower, at the delicate play of light on stone and steel. And he listened to the musical hum of the cars speeding below him. He skimmed through one of the archways in the Manhattan tower, and up ahead, he saw two blue jackets with parallel rows of shing buttons: N.Y.P.D. He stopped in front of them.

"Mornin'," said one of the cops.

There's somethin' funny goin' on back there," said Whiting. "There's some guy shoutin' like a crazy man and runnin' across the bridge."

The two policemen looked at each other, then started to run. Whiting gave the bike a push and glided down toward City Hall.

Len Haley saw the police coming toward him, and he knew that the joggers were someplace behind him. He leaped onto the little parapet that protected the walkway from the automobile deck below. He grabbed a girder, held tight, and swung out over the traffic eighteen feet below. Using every last ounce of strength, he grabbed one of the support cables and lowered himself, hand over hand, to the automobile deck. He waited for a lull in traffic, jumped into the nearest lane, and waved at the car speeding toward him.

The car stopped, and traffic squealed to a stop behind it. An old man was driving. Haley jumped in and flashed his badge.

"Police business. I need a ride to the Manhattan side."

James Whiting left the bicycle on the staircase at the Manhattan end of the bridge. He ran down to the square, hailed a cab, and headed uptown.

34

Twenty minutes later, Whiting was back at the Algonquin. He hoped that Jeanne would be waiting for him. He turned the key and pushed. The door swung open. For a moment, Whiting stood in the hallway.

"Good thing you back, Whitey," said a familiar voice. "Miss Killjoy gettin' awful friendly."

Whiting stepped into the room. Henry Baxter, naked from the waist up, was sitting on the edge of the bed with his arms above his head. Jeanne was beside him. Her first-aid kit was open, and she was applying the last of five butterfly stitches to a six-inch gash across Henry's rib cage.

"Hold still," she told him.

Whiting closed the door and locked it. Then his knees began to tremble. His mind finally allowed his muscles to relax.

"New York's a tough town, ain't it, Whitey?"

Whiting laughed nervously and dropped onto the bed. Jeanne finished closing the gash. Then she attended to Whiting's chin. And they exchanged their stories.

"Well, what you plannin' to do now that folks chasin' you two all over the Big Apple?" asked Henry as he pulled on his shirt.

"Get the hell out," said Whiting.

"To where?" asked Henry.

"Maine." Whiting looked at Jeanne. "There's isn't much point in going to Lawrence's press screening. We know what will be announced, and we know what Billy Singer is going to do afterward."

"What you *hope* he's going to do," said Henry.

"He'll do it," said Whiting. "And maybe we ought to get on to Maine before he sends the press scurrying up there."

Henry watched Jeanne methodically close up her first-aid kit, pack it into her suitcase, and pull out the green ferry schedule. "I ain't seen no statistics on it, but for you two, that Easter's Haven may be more dangerous than Bed-Sty."

"You put your man out of commission today," said Whiting. "And I think that lieutenant character got himself arrested. How many more guys like that can they have?"

"Guys like that are all over the place, man. Like weeds."

"Maybe, but when Billy Singer tells the world that we're going to the island, and he beseeches Andrew MacGregor to grant us an audience, I think we'll be safe."

Henry shook his head.

"Can we make it up there today?" Jeanne asked.

Whiting looked at his watch, then the ferry schedule. "It's ten-fifteen now. We can be in Boston by eleven-thirty if we catch the next shuttle. We'll get my car, drive the rest of the way, and make the four-o'clock ferry with time to spare."

"This'd be a good time to play Miss Killjoy," Henry said to Jeanne.

"This is why we came east," she responded. "To go to Maine, to meet MacGregor, to look Miranda Blake in the eye."

"You may look more 'n her in the eye if you ain't careful. I watched that dude in the ski mask this mornin', right outside that apartment. I was waitin' on him to make a move. Then he go walkin' off, and I hear my sixth sense sayin' he ain't gone for good. But I wait till I hear that glass shatterin' before I get my ass in gear. Honey, you're messin' with some dangerous, unpredictable shit."

Whiting got up, stuffed his underwear and socks into his suitcase, and snapped it shut. "Henry, you were ready to risk your rig when you thought you had a chance to look Billy Singer in the eye."

"Yeah."

"And we have to take a few more risks to get where we want to go."

"But Whitey, *I* know how to take care of myself."

Whiting smiled. "I didn't do too badly this morning."

"No, I guess not. I guess you been payin' attention to me the last coupla days."

Jeanne pulled on her down vest and picked up her suitcase.

"Will you drive us to the airport?" Whiting asked.

Henry looked from one to the other. "Damn the two of you for makin' me think I oughta go along, but I just decided that whatever's up there, you gotta face it alone, together, without Henry Baxter jumpin' through doors to save your ass whenever you get in trouble. Big Mama's Baby mothered you long enough."

"We're not asking you to go Henry." Whiting threw an arm around Henry's shoulder. "But we'll always remember what you've done for us."

"Just be careful," Henry grumbled.

"We'll be back to see you in a few days." Jeanne brought a hand to his face and tugged gently on his goatee.

"You better be." He smiled at the both of them. "But there's some things folks gotta do for themselves. Some motherfuckers you gotta look straight in the eye. And if you don't get killed, you come back stronger than ever."

"Like that motherfucker on night watch, Quang Tri Province, 1968?"

"Something like that," said Henry. "Besides, when you get to Maine, you won't want to look conspicuous. I might be a drawback on that score. And I don't like islands."

"Manhattan's an island," said Jeanne.

"Who ever said I liked Manhattan?"

The drive to La Guardia took twenty minutes, the flight to Boston a little over half an hour, and the cab ride from Logan to Beacon Hill, ten minutes.

The Boston Common covered in snow, the golden dome of the State House, the drivers, the potholes, the red brick and sandstone: Whiting was happy to be home, if only for a few hours. The familiarity of the city seemed to welcome him, and at the same time it made him feel comfortably anonymous. Nothing had changed in two and a half weeks.

Except for the cars, nothing on Mount Vernon Street had changed in almost two hundred years. Most of these buildings were here, he told Jeanne with some pride, when Los Angeles was nothing more than the pueblo around Olvera Street.

Whiting let himself into the foyer, recognized the familiar smell, and told Jeanne to wait downstairs. he walked up, past his own door, to the third floor. He knew that Dave Douglas, the all-night disc jockey, would be at home, and probably asleep.

After Whiting pounded on the door several times, Douglas appeared in his pajamas. He blinked the sleep out of his eyes and focused. "I thought you were in California."

"I just got back," said Whiting. "I'm sorry to bother you, but I need a favor."

"If you're here for a cup of sugar or something, I'm going to be real mad."

"I need to borrow your gun," blurted Whiting.

"Huh?"

"I just went to let myself in and I thought I heard someone in my apartment."

Douglas frowned, grunted, and reappeared a moment later with a nickel-plated .22 revolver held, pointing upward, at his shoulder.

"Let's go," he said sternly.

Dave Douglas positioned himself on the right side of Whiting's door, like a television cop. "Open it," he whispered to Whiting.

"Just take it easy, Dave. There's probably nothing in there." Whiting inserted a key into the dead bolt and turned. Then he unlocked the secondary lock.

Dave looked at Whiting. "Go ahead. I'll be right behind you."

"Good man." Whiting smiled.

A few moments later, he thanked Dave Douglas for his help and called Jeanne up the stairs. It was all just a precaution, he explained.

"Anytime," said Dave. "This gun for hire. If you don't mind my saying so, you could use a shower, James. And with an electric razor, you wouldn't cut up your face like that."

Whiting introduced Jeanne when she appeared in the door.

"Well," said Dave, his eyes sliding up and down her frame, "I've heard of bringing souvenirs back from California, but usually it's an ashtray from Alcatraz or a set of Mickey Mouse ears."

Jeanne pulled her lips across her teeth in the best smile she could muster.

"Say good-night, Dave," muttered Whiting.

Dave smiled. "You two enjoy yourselves, and don't worry about waking me up. I sleep like a rock."

While Whiting showered, Jeanne Darrow poked about in the kitchen and thought about Henry Baxter's sixth sense. *He ain't gone for good.*

Jeanne had a sixth sense of her own, and from time to time, it had said the same thing. *He ain't gone for good*. She had always ignored it, even when it awoke her from a deep sleep. But now, after the New York madness, just a few hours from Maine, with Miranda Blake's ferry schedule in her pocket and Harriet Sears's advice rattling around in her head, she was finally starting to listen to her own sixth sense.

Fifteen minutes of hot water eased the tension in Whiting's back and neck. He stepped out of the stall and pulled one of his bath towels from the shelf. It was thick and soft and a rich crimson color. The feel of it made him want to lay out and take a nap. Thick bath towels had always been one of his vices, and a shower was not complete until he had wrapped himself in one. The feel of the towels was the feel of home.

He went into the bedroom. Jeanne was standing in the sun by the window.

"I like having you here." he said.

"I like being here. It feels very peaceful." She folded her hands in front of her. "I'd like to spend some time here."

He stepped around the bed and went over to her. "You will." He put his arms on her shoulders and kissed her gently."

She slipped her arms around his neck. They held each other. They felt the warm sun on their shoulders. They listened to the midday silence in the apartment.

"We could give up right now," he said, looking into her eyes. "Not go any further. Just dump the tapes into somebody's lap, forget about ghosts and evil wizards spinning out their plans for polluting the minds of America. Just concentrate on you and me. Right here." He kissed her again, longer, harder.

He pressed himself against her, and she rested her face against his chest. His body was still warm from the shower. His skin was soft and smooth. She raised her eyes to his once more and let her hands slide down the muscles in his back, then along the top of the towel. She ran her hand across his flank and loosened the knot in the towel. It dropped to the floor, and James Whiting was naked. Gently, almost curiously, she touched him.

The moment, he thought, had arrived. In his own room, after three thousand miles of traveling with her and learning about her, he had found with Jeanne Darrow what his doctors had called the right emotional context. He felt firm, erect, and, for the first time in over a year, confident.

For Jeanne, this was a small moment of sanity. The confrontation with her husband's death was just a few hours away, and
James Whiting was giving her the chance to reaffirm life.

In an instant, she was naked with him, rubbing her breasts
against his chest, sliding one of her long, smooth thighs back and
forth between his legs, biting his neck, kissing his lips, helping
his hands explore every part of her, feeling his fingertips enter
her, excite her, prepare her.

He pushed her onto the bed. She wrapped her legs around his
waist and rubbed her heels on the backs of his thighs. He brought
his mouth down on hers.

James Whiting realized that he was leaving Roger Darrow behind. Then, all thoughts drained out of him and all his senses
focused on the delicate hands caressing him.

"Love me, Jim," she whispered.

"Yes," he said.

Afterward, they lay on top of the bed with the sun falling across
their bodies. Whiting traced his finger along the flecks of blond at
the base of her neck. She leaned herself against him and rubbed
like a cat.

"How do you feel?" he asked.

"More relaxed than I should feel."

Whiting put his head back. "So am I."

"We'd better get going or we'll never make the ferry."

Whiting did not respond. He simply stared at the ceiling.

She leaned an elbow on his chest and brought her face close
to his. "Henry was right, Whiting. We have to look this motherfucker in the eye."

Whiting raised his head. "Lynne Baker was right, too. Being
your own person is more important than following Roger Darrow's
trail."

"The only way I can get free is to follow it right to the place
where he died. You have do it, too."

He pulled her face to his and kissed her. "From now on, I do it
for myself, and you."

After he dressed, Whiting went upstairs and woke Dave Douglas again. He gave Douglas the original Darrow tapes and those that he and Jeanne had shot in the last two weeks. He did not give Douglas any details. He simply told him to look at the tapes if Whiting did not contact him within forty-eight hours. Whiting then borrowed Douglas's video camera and recorder, and, after some argument, his .22.

At the Charles Street Garage, Whiting threw suitcase and video equipment into the trunk of his Volvo. Then he strapped cross-country skis—his own and an ex-girlfriend's—to the roof of the car. The shower, the lovemaking, and a hamburger had revived him. Although he knew he shouldn't, he was ready to push himself the rest of the way.

"The skis make us look like a harmless pair of tourists hunting for a winter experience on the Maine rocks."

They got into the car, and Jeanne grabbed Whiting's wrist. "You know, sane people wouldn't be doing this."

"I know. But don't worry. Billy Singer's watching over us."

"And Roger's still got a hold on us."

"We've got a hold on each other. He can't break that." Whiting turned the ignition. After three weeks, the car started on the first crank.

Three hours later, Vaughn Lawrence, Vicki Rogers, and Kelly Hammerstein were traveling back to Hollywood on Lawrence's Lear jet, escaping the snowstorm that had descended on New York City. The press screening and the final announcement of the merger had gone perfectly. "The Redgates of Virginia" would be a huge success. John Meade had seemed cordial and happy. Billy Singer had watched the film quietly from the back of the theater. And the video tape appearance of the recluse from Maine had been dramatic and convincing.

Kelly Hammerstein was mixing drinks. Vaughn and Vicki were talking. Two nights earlier, Vaughn had agreed to produce a half-hour nightly version of "On the Coast" and distribute it on the new MacGregor/Lawrence system. In return, Vicki had agreed that she would stop her reports on Jeanne Darrow and James Whiting. None of it had been in writing, of course, but she had gotten what she wanted, and now she was ever so thankful.

"You're not concerned about Jeanne Darrow and Whiting are

you, Vaughn?"

Lawrence shook his head. He did not tell her that Len Haley had been dispatched to Maine. "There's nothing on Darrow's tapes that can hurt us. I'm sure there's nothing on Whiting's either."

"If they do try to pin anything on us, you'll always have me to prick their balloon. You know, his communications to me were sometimes rather bizarre. One might even call them unbalanced. I've put them all on tape."

"If they were unbalanced, why did you put them on the air?"

She laughed. "They made for a good story."

Kelly served the Scotch and sodas.

"But now," continued Vicki, "I'm on your side again. I'll attack Whiting's credibility on the air and in print." She sipped her drink. "I feel like Louella Parsons ready to fight for her boss, William Randolph Hearst."

"Fight hard," said Lawrence, "because if we win, we'll have our hands on all the power that Hearst ever dreamed about."

Vicki pulled off her glasses and looked at Vaughn. She would have put her hand on his knee, but Kelly Hammerstein was sitting on the other side of the compartment. Until Vicki had reestablished herself, Kelly was still the woman—or the girl—in Vaughn's life.

"William Randolph Hearst dreamed of being president," Vicki said.

"I know," responded Vaughn Lawrence.

About an hour after they left Boston, Jeanne Darrow and James Whiting had crossed the bridge in Portsmouth, New Hampshire, a short distance from the Maine border. The sunshine had been brilliant and bright.

Whiting had noticed a MacGregor Communications Cable Service van in the next lane. "I didn't know they had franchises in New Hampshire."

"Neither did Roger," Jeanne had answered. "Why do they want cable franchises in New Hampshire?"

"For the same reason they wanted them in Iowa."

FIVE

MAINE

35

"Well, Jake, how does it look?"

"Ain't seen it yet, Sandy, so I can't tell."

Whiting turned to Jeanne. "Why can't these radio weather guys give the forecast, instead of trying to sound like a pair of Down East smartasses?"

Jeanne shrugged. She was beginning to feel seasick, and she did not know what he meant by "Down East," anyway. She knew it had something to do with the state of Maine.

The little ferry, which held twenty cars, was plowing through rough seas in Penobscot Bay. Whiting and Jeanne were sitting in his Volvo, and Jeanne was staring at the radio dial, which, although she might not have known it, was intensifying her seasickness.

"In New York City, Sandy, the temperature dropped twenty degrees between noon and two-thirty. It's been snowin' there for the last hour. Now Logan Airport and Chatham Weather Station are reportin' flurries. This one's movin' fast."

Clouds had appeared on the horizon to the south and southeast, but the sun was still shining brightly at four-fifteen. Its long, low rays slanted over the ferry's shoulder and cut hundreds of gray-green gems of granite and pine out of the Atlantic blue. According to the map that Whiting held against the steering wheel, Easter's Haven, the largest and most distant of the gems, was seven nautical miles from the ferry slip.

"Well, then, Jake, I guess by now, you musta smelled snow in the wind," said one of the voices on the radio.

"Nope. Ain't done that, either. Been watchin' the radar, though."

"And?"

"It'll go one of two ways. If the storm hugs the coast and hits us head on, we're good for five or six inches, and them inland skiin' spots'll get a good ten. Or it might veer off Cape Cod, head toward the Maritimes, and we can forget about it. Or—"

"You said two ways."

"I never said I could count, Sandy." Jake laughed. "The storm should veer off Cape Cod, pick up some steam out over the water, and come cowtailin' back at us from the northeast. That means twenty to twenty-five inches, and most of it gettin' dumped right on the coast."

"Sounds like a big 'n.'"

"Eh-yeh. If I was plannin' to get off of one of the islands, I'd be doin' it in the next few hours."

Whiting flipped off the radio.

On the far side of Easter's Haven, the *Ellie B.* rocked on the swells and churned steadily toward the harbor. She rode low in the water, her hold heavy with Gulf of Maine shrimp, her stern rigged for dragging. In the small cabin, Cal Bannister held the wheel while Harry Miller poured two cups of coffee from his Thermos.

Harry handed Cal a cup of coffee. "You sure you don't want me to take 'er in? There's nothin' worse than a followin' sea."

"I can handle it," said Cal.

Harry sipped his coffee. "Never said you couldn't."

"I ask for help when I need it."

Harry nodded. "That's why you're learnin'."

A waved crashed over the stern and slapped against the bulkhead.

"Give 'er a bit more," said Harry. "Another shot like that'll swamp us."

Cal Bannister leaned on the throttle and the boat kicked ahead. The windows in the cabin were steamed from the coffee and the breath of two men perspiring inside winter cocoons of wool and rubber.

A woman's voice crackled over the speaker on the radio. She gave her call numbers and then the *Ellie B.*'s "Come in, please."

Harry picked up the microphone and responded with his call numbers.

"Harry, this is Lanie Bannister." Her voice sounded tense, even on the tiny speaker. She asked for Cal.

Harry handed Cal the microphone and took the wheel. "Gettin' us in is a job for two hands and a clear head. Nobody pilots my boat and talks to his wife at the same time."

"This is Cal. What do you want? Over." He was annoyed and a bit concerned. Calls to the boat were supposed to be for emergency only.

"A man called a while ago from New York. He said to tell you he was the lieutenant, and he was going to be here before the snow."

Cal's eyes shifted to Harry, who held his gaze steady on the rolling water in front of him.

Lanie's voice squawked again over the little speaker. "He said he expected you to be here when he arrived. I told him you were out and might not be back until . . ." A wave of static washed through the sentence, then receded ". . . and it was like he ignored me. He just said for you to be here, and that was that."

Harry glanced at Cal, then looked at the bow of the boat. He could see the number-three buoy at the mouth of the Easter's Haven Thoroughfare.

Lanie was saying something, but the static was crackling. Cal sucked the inside of his cheek between his teeth and chewed nervously.

"We get static sometimes when there's a storm movin' in." Harry explained. "I got the feelin' were're in for a monster."

Lanie's voice faded in once more, and with it her sense of alarm. "He said he wants you to watch the Brisbane Road and make sure no one goes up there."

Harry's head snapped around.

"Who is he, Cal? What does he want?" asked Lanie.

Cal glanced at Harry again, then pushed the transmit button on the microphone. "An old business pal, Lanie."

"He said he has work for you, Cal. What kind of work?" She spoke as though she knew. Over."

"I'll tell you when we get in." Cal hung up the microphone and turned down the volume on the speaker.

Harry worked the wheel and throttle. Cal Bannister stared straight ahead and chewed on his cheek.

"Ain't none of my business," said Harry after a time, "but if you got a problem and you need some help, just yell."

Cal looked at Harry. "Thanks, old man."

As the months had passed after the explosion of the *Fog Lady*, Cal had begun to hope that his last assignment had been given, that he would be forgotten in this distant corner of America. He had begun to live within the rhythms of the island. He had found, in the changing moods of the sea, a sympathy for his own angry soul. Now, the lieutenant himself was coming to the island, and Cal Bannister knew that his fragile peace was about to be shattered.

Lanie's voice cried faintly over the static on the radio. Cal turned it off.

Harry Miller held the little boat on coars. As he approached the number-two buoy, with Saint Bartholomew's Fields covered in snow off the starboard, he threw out the words *Brisbane Road.*

Cal Bannister stiffened.

"Stoppin' folks on Brisbane Road ain't too friendly."

"You don't want to know about it." Cal did not threaten. He spoke gently, as if to warn a friend. "I'm more than just a fisherman."

"Most folks're more than they seem," said Harry. "Or less."

Cal said nothing.

"I might just take a ride up Brisbane Road when we get back," said Harry. "Make sure old Andy has enough Scotch to get through the storm. . . . If it's all right with you."

Cal did not move or look at Harry. He simply nodded.

At Brisbane Cottage, the telephone rang.

Edgar Lean, impeccable in butler's waistcoat and jacket, answered.

"Where's the old man?" demanded the voice on the other end of the line.

"Mr. Meade?" said Lean.

"Yes, Edgar." Meade's voice sounded strained. "I'm in New York."

"And how did the corporate presentation go this afternoon?" Lean asked politely.

"Fine, fine," grumbled Meade. "Now, we've been trying to get you since this morning. Where have you been?"

"A little excursion to the mainland, sir. An antidote for cabin fever."

"I've asked you never to leave the island without reporting to this office."

"I'm sorry, sir," said Lean.

"Where's the old man?"

"Out for his afternoon ski, sir."

"Is Dodd with him?"

"No, sir."

"Where's he?"

"Reading, sir."

"Some bodyguard," muttered Meade. "Send him out to find our friend, and when they get back, I want the two of them to come to New York right away."

"But sir, there's a storm approaching. . . ."

"I want them to leave the island this afternoon."

"Yes, sir."

"And you may be getting a visit from someone who presents herself as Roger Darrow's wife. It would be best if no one at Brisbane Cottage talked with her or her companion."

"Of course not, sir," said Edgar Lean with a touch of anger in his voice. He had been in the service of the MacGregor family for more than thirty years. He did not need to be reminded that the family guarded its privacy, especially now.

"I want the old man off the island as soon as possible," repeated Meade.

"Yes, sir."

Edgar Lean hung up and looked out the kitchen window. The late-afternoon sun glinted off the glass bubble of the helicopter. He told his wife that they would be eating alone that night, then he went into the library, where Tom Dodd, who served as both bodyguard and helicopter pilot, was hidden behind the latest Spenser detective novel. Dodd lowered the book and looked up. He was mostly shoulders and chest, with a square jaw and a square head.

"Put on your cross-country ski boots," said Lean.

John Meade looked out toward the Empire State Building, just visible through the thickening snow. He did not like to bring people down from Maine so abruptly. But he wanted the old man to have no part in any unpleasantness.

It was all in a good cause, he told himself. He was fulfilling Andrew MacGregor's vision. He was the only person who understood it. He had been forced to make concessions, but he was keeping the company in a position, as his uncle had always counseled, "to be ready to take advantage of whatever came next."

In Bangor, Len Haley chartered an airplane. The pilot, a crusty old Down Easter, charged an exorbitant rate for flying into the approaching storm, and he refused to lay over.

Len Haley had brought Ken Steiner and Johnny Mendoza with him. Ken Steiner had a cracked rib from hitting the support beam in the elevator shaft. Johnny Mendoza's eyes were black and his nose was heavily bandaged. All three were dressed for winter in wool sweaters, down vests, thermal underwear, and insulated boots. And each carried a Schmeisser .22-caliber machine pistol.

Len Haley had resolved that nothing Jeanne Darrow or James Whiting had learned would leave Easter's Haven. Their death or, if it could be arranged successfully, their disappearance in the storm would be of less consequence than their continued interference.

Len Haley knew from experience that once the shooting started, you did not negotiate, you did not hold back, you did not stop until you knew you were safe. He had learned the hard way, and he had finally been able to teach Vaughn Lawrence.

Jeanne Darrow and James Whiting stood on the little superstructure above the ferry's automobile deck and gazed ahead into the Easter's Haven Thoroughfare. The four links in the Pentecost Island chain unwound to starboard. On the port side, the granite cliffs of Easter's Haven rose.

The clouds had moved farther north and were now surging from the east and northeast as well. They were absorbing the late-afternoon sunlight and quickly shrinking the swatch of blue between Easter's Haven and the mainland. As the clouds advanced, the ocean lost its color and flashed iridescent, like an oil slick. The darkening water seemed to be flowing westward ahead of the clouds, rushing through the thoroughfare, spilling into Penobscot Bay, and surrounding the base of the island while the sun played off the pines and cliffs above.

The wind in the middle of the thoroughfare was blowing hard and bitter, and the little ferry bucked against it. Jeanne Darrow and James Whiting, bundled in their parkas, with their ski caps

pulled down over their ears, were the only people outside the pas-355
senger's compartment. The few others riding the ferry that Friday
afternoon—a handful of fisherman, their wives, and several pre-
schoolers—sat in the warmth of the cabin and entertained themselves with comments about the strangers courting frostbite at the
rail.

But Roger Darrow had introduced the island from this angle.
James Whiting and Jeanne Darrow were compelled to see it first
from the deck of the ferry. Whiting stood close by Jeanne, so that
his body was touching hers.

"I'm scared," she said.

"So am I," he answered. He reached into his pocket and pulled
out Dave Douglas's .22-caliber pistol. "You can take some comfort
in this."

"How did you get that?"

"I promised Dave I'd introduce him to your sister if I could just
keep the gun overnight."

"My sister's married."

Whiting shrugged. "That's never stopped Dave before."

Except for the strip of blue along the western horizon, the
clouds, gray and gravid, covered the sky.

36

Harry Miller brought the *Ellie B.* into Easter's Landing and moored her at the ice house, where members of the island cooperative stored their catch before shipment to the mainland. Across the harbor, the ferry was backing out of is slip. Its running lights glowed through the first flurries, and five cars sat on the main deck.

Harry watched the ferry for a moment, then glanced over toward Brisbane Road. He saw a foreign car emerge from a stand of trees and cut across Town Meadow. He called to Cal, who was already on deck opening the hold.

Cal looked up and saw the headlights.

"If you were s'posed to stop them," Harry said, "you missed."

Cal watched the car cross the meadow and disappear into the trees. Then he looked at Harry. "I'll worry about Brisbane Road after I unload the boat."

"That's good." Harry nodded once. "The catch comes first."

The snow was falling in little bursts, and the wind was snapping in from the northeast, causing the flurries to swirl in front of the windshield. Whiting drove past a row of lobstermen's houses that looked out on the breakwater. Some were dark. Lights glimmered here and there, and beyond the houses, the ocean had turned black and angry.

As they moved away from the town, there were fewer houses, and sometimes as much as a quarter mile between them. They passed a cottage with the name *Bannister* on the sign hanging from the lamppost, and then the road turned away from the water, into the pine woods of Louder's Point. It was dusk everywhere else on the island, but here, the deep gloom of a stormy night had already descended.

They drove for half a mile through the woods, and when they

emerged near the Louder's Pond Inlet, the rest of the island had
grown darker and all the grays had sunk toward black. Up ahead,
lights glowed in the windows of a lobsterman's house. They drove
across the inlet, and Jeanne told Whiting to slow down.

He shifted. "Why?"

She glanced at the map, then looked out to the thoroughfare,
where the ferry was cutting through the heavy seas. "Roger's boat
blew a hundred and fifty yards from the mouth of this inlet."

Whiting stared at the menacing waters for a few moments,
then stepped on the gas. This was not the time to be contemplat-
ing that spot.

Whiting followed the road back into the darkness of the woods
and came to a fork in the road. A sign pointed left to Rumrunner's
Bulge and right to Brisbane Road. Jeanne directed him to the
right.

The land began to rise through the woods. They traveled almost a mile, along switchbacks and steep grades, until they
reached the gates of the MacGregor estate. The road had leveled
out, but they were still deep in the pines. Granite pillars rose on
either side of the road, supporting heavy, wrought-iron gates that

were, surprisingly, swung open. On one pillar, an old, gilt-lettered
sign read "Brisbane Cottage." On the other, a newer sign, in red
letters, said "Private Property. No Trespassing." Beneath it, a
smaller sign warned "Danger: Attack Dogs."

They drove another half mile before the thick cover of pines
fell away, and Brisbane Cottage rose before them.

A snow flurry swirled around the house, giving a fresh coating
of white to the red roof and the half acre of lawn already deep in
snow. In the whiteness, the house itself seemed without color,
merely a shadow, but shafts of yellow light spilled from every
window. Brisbane Cottage was not the forbidding place that Whiting had expected. But then, he remembered Howard Rudermann's warning that there is less to things than meets the eye . . .
and sometimes more.

"It's beautiful," whispered Jeanne.

Whiting pulled up in front of the house and climbed out. He
heard dogs barking and saw two angry Dobermans running back
and forth in a pen beside the house.

Through the evergreens at the top of the cliff, he could see the
ferry, looking tiny and threatened as it hurried for the mainland

ahead of the storm. He slipped his hand into his pocket and wrapped it around the handle of the gun. He turned to Jeanne. She was standing in front of the house, looking up at the fieldstone pillars that supported the porch roof. Her cheeks were rosy from the cold. Her eyelashes were sprinkled with snowflakes. Whiting took her hand, and together they went up the stairs.

Harry Miller's pickup pulled into Cal Bannister's driveway. The afternoon light was almost gone.

"A good catch," said Cal.

Harry nodded.

"Thanks for the lift."

Harry nodded again. Cal started to open the door.

"Who are you, Cal?"

Cal froze. He looked at Harry for a moment. Then Lanie Bannister pounded on the window.

Cal rolled it down. Cold air and snow blew into his face.

Lanie stuck her head into the truck. She had a wool jacket thrown over her shoulders. "He called again," she said to Cal.

"Who?"

"The guy who calls himself the lieutenant. He said he'll be at the airstrip at five-thirty. He wants you to pick him up."

Cal glanced at his watch.

"What's so damned important that he has to get over here tonight?" she asked.

"Who is he, Cal?" asked Harry at the same time.

Cal told Lanie to go in the house. "I'll tell you when I come in."

She hesitated a moment, then said good-night to Harry and went in.

Cal rolled up the window.

"Well," Harry demanded, "Who are you?"

"I'm just somebody tryin' to get along. That's all." The muscles in Cal's jaw began to flex.

"Son," said Harry angrily, "you've fished from my boat. You've ett from my table and I never once asked you a thing about where you come from or what brought you here."

"And I appreciate that, Harry."

"A man's past is his own business. If he wants to start fresh, this island's a good place to do it. But if you're bringin' trouble here, Cal . . ."

"There's trouble everywhere, Harry," Call growled. "You can't escape it." He started to open the door.

Harry grabbed his arm. The grip was strong. "What kind of trouble is comin' to my island?"

"I don't know, old man, but I don't want it any more than you. And I don't want you involved."

"Is this trouble followin' you? Did you bring it?" demanded Harry.

The snow hurled itself suddenly against the windshield, and for a few moments, Cal was silent. Then the flurry ended.

"I'm just the point man," he said. "I'm here because people from Los Angeles want me here. They don't trust the people around Andrew MacGregor. They want someone on the island, an enforcer."

Harry squinted at Cal, looked him up and down as though they were meeting for the first time. "You enforced anything yet?"

Cal shook his head. He was telling the truth. "I was hopin' I wouldn't have to enforce nothin'. I'm still hopin' that."

"Then don't go to the airstrip. Let your friend freeze up there."

"I can't." Cal popped the door. "He saved my life."

As Cal climbed out of the pickup, he heard, above the rising wind, the distant rumble of an airplane engine. He looked toward the sound and saw the red wing-lights approaching the island.

Jeanne Darrow and James Whiting heard the sound as well. They were in the car again, parked on the side of the road, just outside the granite gateway to MacGregor's property.

They had been rebuffed by Edgar Lean, who said that Mr. MacGregor did not receive guests and Miranda Blake could be located in the Manhattan telephone directory. Lean had added that Mr. MacGregor's bodyguard would answer the door if they knocked again, and the guard dogs would be released to roam the property.

The single-engine plane burst from the clouds two hundred feet above them.

"Jesus!" Jeanne jumped.

For a moment, the car shook with the noise. Then the roar abated as the plane continued on to the airstrip.

"Who the hell would be flying to this island tonight?" asked Jeanne.

"Only someone with urgent business," answered Whiting.

Whiting got out of the car. He took a thermometer from his pocket and put it on top of the snow. Then he took his skis from the roof.

Jeanne got out on the other side. "What are you doing?"

"We came to meet MacGregor." Whiting opened his trunk and took out a plastic box containing waxes, scrapers, and corks. "We can cross the top of Cutter's Point on skis and get to within twenty feet of the house."

"What about the dogs?"

"Maybe they won't see us."

"And what do we do when we get to the house? Shinny up the drainpipe to the master bedroom? We don't even know where MacGregor is."

Whiting looked at the thermometer. "Twenty-two degrees. We'll need blue wax." He took two tubes of wax and two scrapers from his box and offered a set to Jeanne. She took them and put them on the hood.

Whiting leaned his skis against the car and began to scrape them. "It's always best to get off the old wax. Especially when you've got a soft wax on the ski, like a red, and you want to put a hard blue over it."

"We took our shot at MacGregor," said Jeanne. "Let's try to find Miranda."

"She's his niece. She'll be there, too," he insisted. "Now, the blue wax we'll be using should be good all the way down to zero."

Cal and Lanie Bannister heard the plane pass overhead. Cal was leaving for the airstrip. Lanie was stirring the stew she had been simmering all afternoon.

"You said this would never happen, Cal," she muttered. "You said that when we came here, things would be different."

"That's the way they've been, haven't they?"

"No. After that TV producer got killed, you barely spoke for a month. And this is part of the same damn thing."

"Where do you think we got the money to move here and buy this house?" asked Cal angrily. "From the tooth fairy? From your life savings of forty-four bucks plus tips? It came from the man on that plane and the people he works for."

"That doesn't mean he owns you, Cal. No one owns you. You can say no to this guy."

"I'd like to." He threw his arms around her.

She squeezed his waist, working her hands under his parka and into the roll of fat that her cooking had given him. "I'll stand by you," she said.

"I know, babe. But I knew the man on that plane before I knew you. I knew him in Nam. Without him, we wouldn't be here." He kissed her on the forehead. "So you be nice to him, and feed him some of your fine fish stew."

He went out into the fading light and walked over to his Bronco. Lanie was watching him from the kitchen window. She brought her fingers to her lips and kissed them. He waved.

Whiting was about twenty feet ahead of Jeanne, following a ski trail that ran along the edge of Cutter's Point. On his left, to the east, the land dropped two hundred feet, down a succession of granite steps that were the scars left by the Cutter's Point quarry-men fifty years earlier. At the base of the cliff were the cottages and pine groves of Rumrunner's Bulge.

At the tip of Cutter's Point, Whiting stopped and waited for Jeanne, who was still struggling along the trail. The snowflurries had stopped. The wind, for the moment, had died down.

"Kick and glide. Kick and glide," he shouted. "I thought you liked cross-country skiing."

"Once a year. I'd rather play tennis."

Whiting looked to the west toward Brisbane Cottage. He saw the staircase that led from the top of the cliff down to the dock. A row of pines grew across the top of the cliff and shielded the house from the view of the ferry. Beyond the pines, he could just see the dark mass of the house, the tall chimneys, and the yellow glow of the lights.

"We'll keep to this side of the pines, and maybe the dogs won't see us," said Whiting. "When we get close, I'll run across to the little terrace at the back of the house. Maybe I can get in through the french doors."

"And when you get in, what then?" Jeanne's nose was red and

starting to run in the cold.

"I'm hoping that the back room is where the old man spends his time. It looks like it could be the library, and there was smoke coming from the chimney."

They kicked toward the house.

The single-engine plane was lifting off into the clouds as Cal Bannister arrived at the airstrip. He saw three men, Len Haley, and two others, standing in front of a ramshackle two-story house, which served as control tower and terminal. Bannister got out of the truck and walked over to the men.

Len Haley extended his hand and said Cal's name as though he had seen him earlier in the day. He introduced Cal to Steiner and Mendoza, who looked as though someone had recently closed a door on his face.

"Let's go," said Haley.

The white and blue guide lights along the airstrip flashed off, then the caretaker stuck his head out the door. "Hey, Cal, you must be havin' some kind of party if your friends'd hire a plane to get over here on a night like this."

"They like snow."

Bannister slipped in behind the wheel. Haley sat beside him. The other two sat in back.

"You've done well," said Haley. "They treat you like one of their own."

"They're good people," answered Bannister.

He pulled out of the rutted lot and back onto the Midland Road. They traveled a short distance in silence, then Haley told Cal to stop. Bannister stepped on the brake.

Haley rolled down the window and looked up at the Easter's Haven television tower. It was red and white and the upper half had disappeared into the cloud cover. Warning lights were flashing all along its length, and they suffused the clouds with a red glow, as though the tower were spreading its energy into the atmosphere, instead of drawing energy from it.

"This is where it all began," whispered Haley.

37

The snow was beginning to fall again. The flakes were big and soft and floated lazily to earth, like the snowflakes in a glass ball.

James Whiting and Jeanne Darrow took off their skis in the pine grove beside Brisbane Cottage. They had not aroused the Dobermans, who were still huddled in the doghouse, in spite of Lean's warning.

"It'll be pitch dark in a few miutes," said Whiting, mustering the courage to sneak across the lawn. "Maybe I should wait."

"Suit yourself," said Jeanne, "but a few minutes of sitting here is sure to give me cold feet." She shivered and sniffled back the fluid gathering at the tip of her nose.

"Once you stop moving, the perspiration freezes and the toes go numb."

"It's not the cold that will give me cold feet." She wiped her sleeve across her face.

Whiting looked at the house. The light was still burning in the room at the rear. Smoke was curling out of the back chimney. He could smell the aroma of a wood fire.

"All right," he said. "Go down the stairs until you're just below the top of the cliff. I'll try to get in and see MacGregor. If you don't hear from me in fifteen minutes, try to get back to town and see what they have for law enforcement around here."

"Fine," she answered. "And if you hear the sound of gagging, it's only me throwing up."

He reached into his pocket and pulled out a handkerchief. "Blow your nose." Then he slipped off into the pine grove that would give him cover until he was twenty feet from the house.

Jeanne moved down the steps a short distance, brushed the snow away, and sat. The cold wood stung her bottom. She rose to one knee and felt another shot of cold sneak in around her neck.

Then she heard a door slam. She looked down toward the little boathouse at the dock. A man had just come out and was starting up. She scrambled back to the top of the stairs and hid in the trees.

She looked toward the house, but she could no longer see Whiting. She looked back down the staircase, which rose in eight flights from the water to the top of the cliff. The man had climbed one flight and was stopping to rest. Jeanne squinted into the snow, but at this distance, she could tell nothing about him.

Whiting crouched at the edge of the pine grove and looked toward the house. He was close enough now that he could see the books lining the walls of the room at the rear of the house.

He took two or three deep breaths, got up, and ran. He crossed the lawn. He reached the terrace. He leaped up the steps. He jumped to the french doors. He stopped for a moment and looked around. The Dobermans were still in the doghouse. No one was looking out the windows above the terrace. No one stirred in the library. On the opposite wall was the fireplace, to his right, the desk, to his left, the sofa, and behind it a library table on which some sort of game board lay open. Directly in front him, back to the door, was a leather wing chair. A novel was open on the arm of the chair and a glass of whiskey sat on the table beside it. Whiting could not see the old man, but he was sure that Mac-Gregor was sitting there now, nodding off perhaps, or staring at the flames.

Whiting expected that alarm bells would start ringing as soon as he stepped inside, but he did not care if he could face Andrew MacGregor for a few seconds. He swallowed hard, reached down, and turned the handle. Unlocked. No bells. No bodyguards.

Whiting closed the door behind him. A log crackled in the fireplace. It startled him. He swallowed and whispered, "Mr. MacGregor."

No response.

He said it again. No response. Then, he stepped around the table. He moved out of the lamp's glare and looked at the chair.

Empty.

Jeanne Darrow watched the man ascend through the blowing snow. He would climb two flights of stairs, then stop for several minutes to catch his breath before starting again. There was just enough light left for her to see his features; she felt her stomach turn over. It was him.

Whiting stood very quietly in the middle of the library and listened. Somewhere on the first floor, a radio was playing. Old jazz, from the thirties.

The house creaked, and, for a moment, Whiting froze. He heard pots banging and two people talking. The maid and the butler were preparing supper. To his right, a set of pocket doors were pulled together, closing on an archway that led, he assumed, to the living room. He put his ear against it and heard nothing. Ahead of him, just to the right of the fireplace, another door was half-open. It led to a hallway. Whiting gently pushed the door until it was almost shut.

Then he returned to the desk, a massive piece of mahogany, ornately carved, carefully polished. A blotter covered the desk. A brass lamp with an Italian green glass shade illuminated it. There was a telephone with a rotary dial on one side, a gold pen and pencil set in a gold stand on the other, a six-inch length of television cable encased in Lucite, a polished granite paperweight, and a black-and-white photograph.

Whiting picked up the photograph. It had been taken someplace in New York, in front of the Dakota, perhaps. From the look of the cars in the background, it had been taken during the thirties. A beautiful young woman in a mink coat and fur hat held a newborn baby. The mother smiled broadly. The baby was wrapped in hand-knitted blankets and wore a crocheted bonnet. He looked like any baby a week or two old, and the young woman looked as proud as any mother who had ever held a newborn for a camera.

Whiting gently replaced the photograph and went over to the library table behind the sofa.

What looked from a distance like a Monopoly board was actually a large map of the United States, covered with colored pushpins, arrows, movable pieces, and printed legends.

Beneath the name of each state, four sets of figures were written: the number of cable franchises, the number held by MacGregor, the total population, and the electoral votes.

The red pins indicated MacGregor cable franchises. The black pins, which covered much of the map, especially in heavily urbanized areas, were listed on the legend as "the untouchables." Then, in parenthesis, were the names of some of the largest, most powerful cable delivery systems, "Warner/Amex, Continental Cablevision, Westinghouse," etc. White pins, the legend said, represented "municipalities about to offer franchises." Green pins were "franchises set for renewal." A yellow pin inserted beside a white or a green pin meant, according to the legend, "a target franchise."

Like a general overseeing a battle, Andrew MacGregor had made a judgment on the status of every cable television franchise in America. There were red MacGregor pushpins scattered across the map, in the Bay Area of San Francisco, in many of the rich suburbs around New York City, and a pin with a star on it in Brooklyn. He had franchises in Maine, New York, and Massachusetts. In certain states, however, he had concentrated his efforts. In the east, New Hampshire was peppered with red pins. In the west, he had covered Wyoming and Iowa. And in Los Angeles, the home of Lawrence/Sunshine Productions, there was a single, large red pin.

James Whiting was looking at more than the remains of a corporate strategy session. This map was a political battle plan, and it confirmed all of his suspicions. MacGregor had amassed enough franchises in Wyoming to defeat one of America's most powerful and respected conservative voices. He had strung his cables across New Hampshire and Iowa, two of the most sparsely populated yet politically influential states in the nation.

Moreover, he had covered Ohio, Texas, and Illinois with yellow pins. He was heading to those states next, to buy up as many cable franchises as he could, because in a close election, they were always the pivotal states, bringing huge blocks of electoral votes for the most minuscule margins of popular-vote victory.

Here, thought Whiting, was the final proof for Lyle Guise, for Billy Singer, for Lynne Baker. Andrew MacGregor was going to try to put Reuben Merrill into the White House, or close to it. He would spend whatever was necessary to win Iowa franchises. He would abuse those who believed in his good will. He would manipulate polls if he could destroy a rival. And he would kill anyone who endangered his plans, like Jack Cutler . . . or Roger Darrow.

In the kitchen, Tom Dodd was brushing the snow from his jacket. "I skied on all his trails, and there's no sign of him anywhere."

"Did you look down in the boathouse?"

Dodd shook his head. "What the hell would he be doing down there?"

"From time to time, he goes down to the boathouse and declaims speeches from Shakespeare," explained Lean. "He says it's the only place where he can rehearse out of earshot of the rest of us."

"Yes," muttered Mrs. Lean. "I think the old boy is a few eggs short of a dozen."

"Why didn't you tell me to look down there?" demanded Dodd.

"Because he left on skis. Usually, he walks."

The old man had reached the top of the stairs. He stopped and looked across the thoroughfare. A red buoy light was flashing, and the snow was not yet thick enough to obscure it. He watched it blink at him several times, then turned and started to walk up the path to the house.

His shoulders were stooped. His head was down. He carried a book under his arm.

Jeanne stepped out from behind the pines and stood in front of him. He almost walked into her before he looked up.

She saw the surprise on his face turn quickly to fright, then when he saw that she was a woman, his expression slipped back to surprise. For a time, they stood in the snow, their faces close together, the darkness closed in around them.

"Mr. MacGregor?" she said, just loudly enough to be heard above the sound of the wind.

He was squinting. His face was long and thin and lined. "Who are you?"

"Roger Darrow's wife."

His mouth dropped open. Then it closed slowly. His face, in a few moments, went through a range of emotions, from surprise to curiosity to renewed fear. Then, suddenly, he looked up at the wind and the sky and the trees, and shouted, "A horse! A horse! My kingdom for a horse!"

Whiting was still studying the map when he felt the gun against his neck.

"Don't turn around," said Tom Dodd.

Whiting obeyed. He stood up straight while Dodd rifled his pockets and pulled out the pistol.

"Lean!" shouted Dodd. "Somebody left the terrace doors unlocked!"

Edgar Lean hurried into the study and saw Whiting. "Oh, my."

"Someone also failed to activate the alarm system," accused Dodd.

"I believe that's your job," responded Lean testily. "I answer the door and run the house."

"Who's with you?" said Dodd to Whiting.

"He was here earlier," said Lean, "with a woman."

"He was here earlier, and you didn't turn on the alarm?" Dodd was infuriated.

Lean shrugged. "I'm an old man now. I must be getting forgetful."

"Where's the woman?"

Whiting shrugged.

Jeanne was still standing in the pine grove. "Please don't turn us away, Mr. MacGregor. We've come three thousand miles."

The old man was listening closely to Jeanne, but he had said nothing since calling for a horse.

"We want to talk to you about my husband's visit and about the merger between your company and Vaughn Lawrence's."

He studied her a moment longer, then hunched himself up, lowering his head until it seemed to grow out of the middle of his chest, and he answered, in harsh voice and British accent, "I cannot tell. The world is grown so bad/ that wrens make prey where eagles dare not perch."

"What?" said Jeanne.

Then he tried to step around her. She blocked his path. She would not be cowed by the stature of Andrew MacGregor or by this strange performance.

"Mr. MacGregor, please." The wind gusted suddenly, driving the snow against them. "I must talk with you. And I must see Miranda Blake. I know she's here."

Then a door was opening on the terrace. Powerful quartz lights, the sort usually found in urban crime areas, were flashing on all around the compound. The snow on the pines and spruces turned orange in the glow, and someone began to shout.

In the strange light, the old man seemed to change once more. He pulled himself out of his bizarre slouch and into a new, more confident character. He looked toward the light, then have Jeanne his jovial MacGregor smile.

"Mr. MacGregor. Mr. MacGregor!" Tom Dodd was shouting.

Lean was opening the chain link pen and loosing the dogs.

"Over here!" shouted the old man. "In the pine grove." He stepped around Jeanne and stared to walk toward the house.

Jeanne grabbed him by the arm. "Where is Miranda Blake?"

He turned and pointed out toward the flashing buoy light. "She's on Saint Matthew's Island. But take the advice of an old man, and leave her alone.

Harry Miller stood in his living room and looked out the window. He was sipping a hot toddy. Ellie was preparing a crab-meat casserole and chattering from the kitchen.

"Big storm blowin' up. Glad you made it in."

"Eh-yeh."

"S'posed to get a foot and a half."

"Yeh."

"How's the toddy?"

"Fine."

Harry was watching the buoy light flashing near Saint Matthew's Island. It warned of a dangerous shoal of rocks.

"Ell," he said.

"Eh-yeh?"

"There been any cars on Brisbane Road lately?"

"Just one." She was sprinkling bread crumbs on top of the casserole. "A foreign car with skis on the roof. Funny thing was, they slowed down right here, looked at the house, then got goin' again."

Harry did not know what was happening, but he suspected that the Easter's Haven world he had striven to protect and insulate for forty years, the world for which he had created myths and told lies, was about to meet reality.

"How long before we eat, Ell?"

"Oh, forty minutes or so."

Harry finished his drink and walked out into the kitchen. "I think I'll take a drive up to MacGregor's."

"Tonight? What for?"

Harry was already putting on his coat. "I'm beginning to think that there might be some trouble."

Ellie's face lost its expression. She wiped her hands on her apron and left a little trail of bread crumbs.

"What kind of trouble?"

"Not sure," Harry pulled on his heavy pea coat.

"Is it the people in the foreign car?"

"Can't say. Don't know." He put on a red-and-black checkered cap with a visor. He pulled the earlaps down.

"I just want to check in."

"Be careful, Harry."

"I'll be back before that casserole's done."

Len Haley looked at the dark woods on either side of the Midland Road. "It seems pretty deserted."

"Only the eastern half, the part MacGregor owns," said Bannister. "There's more people down near town."

"Any loose women?" asked Steiner from the back seat.

Haley laughed. It sounded more like a sniffle.

"None that I've seen," said Cal. "But then, I ain't been lookin'."

"You're happy here?" asked Haley.

Bannister nodded.

Haley said, "Good." He sounded as though he meant it. "It's good that somebody can escape."

Bannister looked at him.

"We'll try to be careful, so nothing goes wrong for you," Haley continued. "We just want to get in and get out and leave you in peace."

"For good, if you can arrange it," said Bannister.

Haley nodded. "We'll be as neat as we can. Just do what we tell you and give us the information we want."

Cal nodded. "All I can." Already he had lied to them. He had said he hadn't seen any cars driving up Brisbane Road that afternoon. He had decided that whoever was in the Volvo, he was going to give them some time.

James Whiting and Jeanne Darrow were standing in the library. Tom Dodd stood by the door. The old man sat in the leather sofa. Edgar Lean stood beside him, with one of the Dobermans at his feet.

Mrs. Lean appeared in the doorway, carrying a suitcase. "Here you go, Mr. MacGregor. Everything you'll need for the trip."

MacGregor's body dropped again into its bizarre slouch, and once more he spoke in his harsh voice. " 'Foul, wrinkled witch, what mak'st thou in my sight?' "

She smiled. "Ah, my lord, I see you've been reading *Richard the Third* again."

"Never mind that. What mak'st thou with my bags?" he demanded.

Jeanne and Whiting exchanged glances.

"Mr. Meade requested that you leave the island tonight," said Lean. "He wants you in New York tomorrow."

The old man stood and pulled himself out of the slouch. " 'I'll not leave this island, this other Eden, demi-paradise,/ This fortress built by Nature for herself . . .' "

"Ah, yes, John of Gaunt," said Lean. Then he glanced at Whiting and his lips formed the word *senile*.

"I am not senile," roared the old man with his own, powerful voice. "And I am not John of Gaunt."

Whiting glanced at Jeanne again, but her eyes were fixed on the old man's face. In the light, she recognized the Andrew MacGregor she remembered from the few photographs she had seen of him in the last few years, but she thought she saw something more.

"Sir, we really think you should be leaving." Dodd grabbed him by the elbow.

The old man pulled away. " 'Whither wilt thou lead me? Speak. I'll go no further.' "

"New York," grumbled the bodyguard.

"You certainly know your Shakespeare," said Jeanne.

The old man bowed. " 'Brush up your Shakespeare, and they'll all kowtow.' "

Jeanne knew him now. And more, she knew what her husband had discovered. She looked at the old man. "Have you ever heard of an old character actor by the name of Ben Little?"

A smile flickered across the old man's face.

"He used to do a one-man Shakespeare show in colleges ten years ago. Then, he dropped out of sight."

"Oh, dear," said Lean softly.

"You bear a strong resemblance to this Ben Little, Mr. Mac-Gregor."

The old man smiled broadly. "How interesting. Is he a good actor?"

"I was impressed by his show," continued Jeanne. "I remember that Richard the Third was his best character."

For a moment, no one spoke. Outside, the wind gusted, rattling the french doors. James Whiting had never heard of Ben Little, but he was convinced that if this old man was the center of everything, the center was hollow. Whether the old man was a senile Andrew MacGregor or an failed Shakespearean actor, Whiting now understood why his identity had been protected. He also realized that this discovery had probably caused Roger Darrow's death.

Edgar Lean dropped a topcoat over the old man's shoulders and looked at Dodd. "Can you still fly the helicopter?"

"If we go right now. But the wind is pickin' up."

The old man dropped the coat on the floor. "No one has given me a reason to go to New York tonight. I would prefer to stay and discuss acting with this young woman."

Lean went over to the desk and picked up the telephone. "Perhaps Mr. Meade can convince you."

"What, Ariel! My industrious servant Ariel! Perhaps indeed. Call him." The old man turned and smiled at Whiting and Jeanne. "All the world's a stage/ And all the men and women merely players."

Whiting looked at Jeanne. "Why did I expect to hear that?"

Lean spoke a few words into the receiver, then handed the telephone to the old man.

"Hello, John," he said. "I take it my performance was well-received by press and public this afternoon . . . But I see no reason to travel on a night like this . . ."

Whiting could guess at what was being said on the other end of the line.

"To meet with Billy Singer?" The old man's eyebrows rose, as though he were impressed. "Why, yes."

Whiting looked at Jeanne. Billy Singer had failed them, or the magnetism of Andrew MacGregor, which neither of them felt at this distance, had been too strong for Singer to resist. They real-

ized now that they were here alone, without the protection of
anyone on the outside.

"My lines are written and you'd like me to study them tonight?" the old man was saying into the receiver. "We're on our way. Give me reason to fly into the storm, and I am at your command."

He handed the receiver back to Lean, then looked at Jeanne and Whiting. "Once more unto the breach, dear friends, For God, Harry, and MacGregor Communications!" He picked up his coat and threw it around his shoulders.

Edgar Lean spoke for another minute or two, glancing up from time to time at Whiting and Jeanne. Whiting knew that the person on the other end of the line was talking about them. Lean said good-bye, and Whiting noticed that his hand trembled slightly as he replaced the receiver and picked up Whiting's pistol.

"Can we go now?" asked Whiting cynically.

"I'm afraid not," said Lean.

Andrew MacGregor raised his hand. " 'Do not infest your mind with beating on/ The strangeness of this business: at picked leisure,/ Which shall be shortly . . . I'll resolve you . . . till when, be cheerful/ And think of each thing well.' " He gave a wave, told Dodd to come along, then opened the french doors, and stepped out into the blowing snow.

Dodd looked at Lean. "What about these two?"

"Mr. Meade requested that we hold them here. People will be coming for them soon."

"Will you need help?"

Lean looked down at the Doberman seated by the desk. "My assistant and I will do whatever Mr. Meade has instructed."

"Are you sure?"

"Long before you were born, I was serving as Mr. MacGregor's personal valet and bodyguard."

Dodd left. Edgar Lean told his wife to make tea. Whiting and Jeanne stood in the middle of the room and kept their eyes on the dog, who growled and bared his teeth at the least suggestion of movement from either of them. Outside, the beating of the helicopter rotors became a roar that rose, then receded into the night.

The three stood in the middle of the room until they could no longer hear the helicopter. On the mantel, the ticking of the Seth Thomas clock seemed to grow louder. The wind rattled the french doors.

"Once more unto the breach, dear friends," said Lean with a touch of sarcasm. He opened the french doors. Cold air and errant snowflakes blew into the room. Lean whistled and the dog ran out.

"It's going to be a terrible night for travel," he said as he locked the doors. "I don't imagine they'll get much beyond Rocktown. But that will give them a good start toward New York in the morning."

"Lucky them," said Whiting.

"Benighted fools, all of them." Lean crossed the room and handed the pistol to Whiting.

"You're letting us go?" asked Whiting, suspecting a trick.

"I'm no longer a bodyguard, sir."

"But there is someone else on this island who is going to do your work for you?"

"No one on this island has offered to answer the door or clean the floors, if that's what you mean." He pulled a handkerchief from his pocket and dusted the desk.

"I mean someone who'll make sure we're not going to get off this island with what we know."

The butler studied both of them for a moment, then told them to sit on the sofa. Years of conditioning kept Lean standing in the middle of the room.

"I can offer you a hot meal and a bit of advice, but very little more."

He folded his hands behind his back. "Find a safe place to stay tonight, and get off the island in the morning."

"Why are you doing this?" asked Whiting suspiciously.

Edgar Lean looked down at the carpet. "I have served this family faithfully for over thirty years. I have done its bidding and I have kept its secrets, the most bizarre of which you have just met."

His body trembled, as though he were suddenly about to break down. He brought a hand to his mouth and waited for a moment to regain his composure. "I have done whatever has been requested of me. But the Andrew MacGregor I was proud to serve would never have asked me to hold a gun on two people until company security men, whom I have never met, arrive to—"

He stopped speaking. The dogs had begun to bark. Mr. Lean wife hurried in from the kitchen. "Harry Miller's truck is coming up the drive."

A few minutes later, Edgar Lean led Harry Miller into the room.

Whiting came around the sofa and shook Harry's hand. "We've already met you on the video tapes."

"You were one of the last people to spend any time with my husband," said Jeanne.

"I'm sorry for your loss," Harry answered.

His hand felt callused and cold, and Jeanne saw something in the face that the video tape had not revealed, an strength and honesty almost weathered into the creases.

"I don't get involved in people's business as a rule," he said, "but I'm wonderin' what folks like you are doin' up here in the dead of winter, and I'm thinkin' that maybe you should be gettin' off this island."

"Tonight?" asked Jeanne.

"Well," Harry scratched the back of his neck. "That might be a problem. But you're outsiders, and there's more outsiders just arrived on an airplane, and from what I can figure, they ain't very friendly."

"How do you know?" Whiting had not yet decided if he should trust this old lobsterman.

"I don't, for sure. But you might know better than me." He pulled his pipe out of his pocket and went over to the tobacco canister on MacGregor's desk. "Anybody been chasin' you lately?"

"You could say that," answered Whiting, glancing at Lean.

"Well, I'd bet they're still after you." Harry looked at Jeanne. "Your husband seemed like a decent feller. I'll try to help you two as best I can."

"Why can't we just stay here and call the police?"

Harry laughed as he packed his pipe. "There ain't no police. There's a sheriff for the islands, but he lives over on North Haven. And he won't come out in this storm, I don't think. We could call the Coast Guard, but it'd take damn close to half an hour for them to get their helicopter up here. And with this storm gettin' worse by the minute, I don't guess they'd want to fly. Tom Dodd'll be lucky to make it to the mainland himself. But suit yourself."

Harry sucked on his pipe.

"All right," said Whiting. "Let's go."

Whiting and Jeanne went out onto the terrace to get their skis. The snow was falling more heavily now, already accumulating an inches over a foot-deep base.

"What do they know?" Harry Miller asked Edgar Lean while the others were outside.

"That Andrew MacGregor is either senile or an imposter named Ben Little."

"For Ben's sake, we'll tell 'em he's senile." Harry pulled on his hat. "What do they know about Saint Matthew's Island?"

"That Miranda Blake lives there. That's all."

"Good." Harry turned to leave.

"What did we get ourselves into four years ago, Harry?" blurted Lean.

"We liked him too much to let him die, I guess." Harry sucked on the pipe again.

"We loved him, and his nephew loved his power," answered Lean. "We should have let him die and his dreams with him."

"If we let him die," said Harry, "this island would have had to face the future. We never wanted that."

38

A nd what time did the car go by?" demanded Haley.

"About an hour ago," answered Lanie Bannister.

Haley looked at Cal. "You missed your assignment."

"I was unloading at the dock," said Cal.

Few people could intimidate Cal Bannister, but Len Haley was one of them.

"Just one car?" Haley said to Lanie.

She nodded.

Haley looked at the Easter's Haven map spread out on Bannister's kitchen table. Steiner and Mendoza were in the living room watching television and eating Lanie Bannister's fish stew.

Haley pointed to Rumrunner's Bulge. "What about these places down here?"

"Ten or fifteen summer cottages," answered Cal. "Deserted in winter."

Lanie glanced at Cal. She knew he was lying.

"Good," said Haley. "That means that between MacGregor's house and yours, Harry Miller is the only lobsterman?"

"Yes, sir," said Cal. He almost saluted.

"And there's no one for another half mile back toward town?"

"No," answered Cal.

"Anyone live with Miller?"

"His wife," said Lanie. It was the first time she had spoken without being asked.

"Is she a friend of yours?" asked Haley.

Lanie nodded. "She is a very nice lady."

"Harry is MacGregor's closest friend on the island," offered Cal.

"Why are you bringing the Millers into this?" Lanie demanded.

"They're in it already, dear," said Haley. "They have been for about four years. Now, did you get the make of that car?"

"Why should I?" Lanie was becoming hostile.

Cal muttered her name, as if to warn her.

Haley patted her arm. "No reason at all. Your husband should have done it." He turned to Bannister. "Let's see if we can find it now."

Haley called to the others, and he and his men went out into the snow.

Cal put his arms around Lanie. "It'll all be over by morning."

She pulled away from him. "I don't care what happens to me. I should've known what I was gettin' into with you. But if anything happens to the Millers, anything . . ."

Haley stuck his head in the door. "The sooner we finish this, the sooner we'll leave you two alone."

"Right," said Cal. He kissed Lanie on the forehead.

"One more thing," said Lanie after Haley had left. "Harry Miller's truck went up that road ten minutes ago."

Cal kissed her again and went outside. The snow was falling heavily now. The wind was gusting. The preliminaries were over. The blizzard had arrived.

Cal threw the hood of his parka over his head and looked out toward the road. A dark figure was climbing down the utility pole in front of the house. It was Steiner.

"Hey!" shouted Cal. "What are you doing?"

Steiner jumped off the pole and toppled into a snow bank.

"That's a precaution," shouted Haley from the Jeep. "They also disconnected the radio in the living room. Your wife seems like the nervous type. We don't want any errors in judgment."

Cal stood for a moment in the blowing snow. He was wearing his heaviest Greenland parka, thermal underwear, and insulated boots. But he had never felt colder.

"Let's go," shouted Haley.

The tire chains jangled steadily as Harry Miller's old pickup crawled through the storm. The snow was now coming down so hard that the wipers could not keep the windshield clear. Whiting, Jeanne, and Edgar Lean were riding with him. At the gate, Edgar Lean climbed out. He was carrying snowshoes, and he was going to hide Whiting's car on one of the carriage paths north of the house.

Then Harry Miller started the slow, slippery descent down

Brisbane Road. "If I had seat belts, I'd tell you to put them on. I've driven this road a thousand times in snow, and I ain't enjoyed it yet."

Halfway down, he stepped on the brakes. The truck skidded and began to slide sideways. Jeanne squeezed Whiting's arm. Whiting dug his fingernails into the dash. The truck came to a stop astraddle the road, with its headlights pointing down into a dark gully. As soon as he stopped moving, Harry turned the headlights off.

"Why did you do that?" asked Whiting.

Harry was looking down the road, into the darkness. "We'll see it again in a second, when the road turns. There!"

Somewhere off in the storm, a set of headlights flashed, then disappeared.

"What is it?" asked Whiting.

"A car. The folks comin' after you, I guess."

"How do you know?" asked Whiting.

Harry leaned around Jeanne and fixed a contemptuous squint on Whiting. "You don't think an islander'd be out on a night like this, do you?"

Whiting did not respond.

"So what do we do?" asked Jeanne.

"You'll have to get out. I'll see if I can talk these fellers back to where they come from."

"They've come a long way," said Whiting.

"Eh-yeh." Harry pulled on his headlights again. The beam cut through the snow and into the gully. "Beyond that gully," said Harry, "there's about a hundred acres of pine woods, all of it goin' downhill and kinda dangerous. Once you get to the bottom, you'll be on Rumrunner's Bulge."

The headlights of Cal Bannister's Bronco truck flashed around another bend, this one much closer.

"You'll still be in thick woods," continued Harry, "but every so often, you'll find a summer cottage." Then he paused and looked into Jeanne's eyes. She did not know what she saw on his face. Affection? Pity? For a moment, he seemed confused, unsure of himself.

"What, Mr. Miller?" she asked. "What is it?"

He began to speak again. "Keep goin' toward the water until you find a cottage with the name 'Knudsen' on the door. It's right on the thoroughfare."

Bannister's headlights appeared again. The beam was pointing upward. The truck was climbing. It was very close.

Harry kept talking. "Go to that cottage, build a fire, and stay there. When the storm ends, I'll come 'round in my boat and pick you right off the rocks."

"What if we get lost?" asked Jeanne.

Harry looked her in the eye. "You'll freeze to death. But if I was you, I'd rather take my chances with the storm than them headlights."

The beam was growing larger, the light stronger.

Harry looked at Whiting. "You got no choice that I can see, but you knew there'd be trouble."

Whiting nodded. "Are there any landmarks between here and the cottage?"

"Go toward the sound of the waves and try to keep the cliffs on your right." He reached over and popped open the glove compartment. "Take my flashlight."

Whiting grabbed it and got out of the truck. For a moment, Jeanne hesitated.

"Go!" shouted Harry. "Before they kill the three of us."

She jumped out.

"Walk up the road a ways in my skid marks so you don't leave tracks," Harry had to holler over the sound of the wind. "And don't put your skis on until you reach the flat of the bulge. You can break you leg skiin' down through them woods."

"We'll never hear the ocean," shouted Whiting. "We'll never see the cliff in this storm."

"Navigate by the wind!"

The snow was swirling into the cab and covering against the windshield. Cal Bannister's headlights had disappeared again. Harry knew there was one last bend in the road before they reached him.

"How?" shouted Whiting.

Harry leaned across the seat, grabbed Whiting by his parka, and pulled him into the cab. "This is a nor'easter. You want to be headin southeast. The wind is whippin' all around and whistlin' against the cliffs. Just try to keep the brunt of it hittin' you in your left ear and the whistlin' in your right." Harry paused a moment. "And one more thing. You might see a light there. I don't know."

He pushed Whiting out of the cab. "Now go!"

Whiting slammed the door. Jeanne was already running up the road, keeping her tracks in the middle of one of Harry's skid marks. Whiting grabbed his skis, threw them over his shoulder, and followed her.

Harry threw the shift into reverse and backed up until his rear wheels dug into the snow at the side of the road. Then he stepped on the gas and let the wheels spin a six-inch hole. He was blocking the road.

He turned up the collar on his pea coat, pulled on his mittens, and jumped out. He walked back and forth several times, obliterating the other footprints around the truck. He grabbed a snow shovel from the back of the truck and began to dig at the holes beneath the tires.

The headlights swung around the last bend and stopped a few feet from Harry's truck. Harry looked up the road. He saw nothing but sheets of snow. Whiting and Jeanne had disappeared. He heard a truck door slam. He saw Cal and another man running toward him.

"Am I glad to see you," he said.

James Whiting and Jeanne Darrow had plunged off the road, down into the snowy, knee-deep blackness of the gully. They saw the beams of Harry Miller's headlights lancing off into the trees. They felt the wind on their left side. They heard it whistling and screaming all around them, tearing through the tops of the trees and driving the storm against the cliffs.

They were stumbling downhill, and now, through the snow, they could see little pinpricks of light peering from the road.

Jeanne grabbed Whiting and crouched down. "They have flashlights. They're looking for us."

Whiting puller her up. "They can't see us. C'mon."

"I'm scared, Whiting," she hollered.

"So am I. And I'll bet that old man back there is terrified."

Len Haley did not have to squint in the snow and darkness. He was wearing a pair of ski goggles and shining a flashlight in Harry Miller's face. "You say you were driving up the hill when you skidded?"

"Eh-yeh."

The rumble of Cal Bannister's engine had been added to the wailing of the wind on Brisbane Road. Johnny Mendoza was still shining his flashlight into the gully. Cal Bannister and Ken Steiner were shoveling snow away from Harry's back wheels.

"I don't believe you," said Haley.

"Don't care," answered Harry.

"I believe him," shouted Cal.

Haley glanced at Bannister. "Keep digging."

Cal stared at Haley for a moment, then jammed his shovel into the snow again. Harry had expected Cal to slam the shovel into the side of Haley's head.

"How could you end up pointing downhill when you skidded going up?"

"Spun out," shouted Harry.

"That's not what the tracks show."

"I don't give a damn, mister." Harry stepped around Haley. "I'll give 'er the gas and you guys give 'er a push."

"They're here to steal the secret, Harry." Len Haley did not turn around, but he spoke loudly enough to be heard above the wind.

Harry stepped off the running board and looked at Haley. "What secret?"

"The one you've protected for four years."

Cal looked up. He thought Harry would laugh or turn away. But Harry stood there, a pile of snow rising on the visor of his hat, and stared into Haley's goggles.

"We're here to help keep the secret, Harry. Don't bullshit us."

"Look around for tracks in the snow if you think I'm helpin' them."

"I didn't say you were helpin' them, Harry." Haley slipped a gloved hand under the lapel of Harry's pea coat. "But we're on your side, so I want you to help us."

Harry glanced at Cal, then looked back at Haley. After a moment, he nodded. "How?"

Johnny Mendoza, his orange, blood-stained ski mask pulled over his face, came trudging back down the road. "I can't see nothin'. If there was tracks, the snow filled 'em up awready." The smashed nose, the ski mask, and the pain-killers he was taking made him almost incomprehensible.

"There's no tracks," said Harry, "because they're still up at Brisbane Cottage."

Haley smiled and clapped Harry on the arm. "They better be, because you're coming with us."

Jeanne Darrow and James Whiting careened down the wooded slope, now in total darkness. The beams of the headlights had disappeared into the storm and no light shone anywhere ahead of them. The snowflakes had grown small and vengeful and felt like tiny frozen needles against the skin.

The were plowing, jumping, stumbling downward through the snow. They tripped over their skis and poles. They caught their feet on undergrowth buried beneath the snow cover. They slipped and fell forward when they moved too fast.

Jeanne's toes felt like small, heavy pieces of cold metal. She was using her skis like a pair of crutches, digging them into the snow ahead of her. Her hands were wrapped so tightly around them she didn't think she could let go. The snow had worked itself into every crevice of Whiting's clothing. He was starting to shiver. He was losing body heat. He told himself to watch for the warning signs of hypothermia. The wind was still driving the snow against his left cheek. Its whistling had grown more focused, more intense, and its backlash hit like a bullwhip.

When Edgar Lean opened the door at Brisbane Cottage, Harry Miller spoke before Haley could open his mouth.

"Are those people still here, Edgar?"

Lean studied Harry, then Haley and Bannister and the other two hulks standing on the top step. "You mean the two people who were here earlier?"

"Yeah. The ones you told me about on the telephone."

"Unh . . ." Lean was confused. He swung the door open and invited them all into the house.

Once in the foyer, Harry Miller introduced the others.

Haley pushed the goggles up onto his forehead.

Cal Bannister looked around at the heavy oak woodwork, the turned staircase in the foyer, and the massive fieldstone fireplaces in the living room and dining room.

"Are they here?" asked Haley.

"No," answered Lean. "They left a few minutes after Mr. Miller." He thought it was a good lie.

Haley looked at Harry. "You said you hadn't been here tonight."

"Never said that," answered Harry. "I said I skidded goin' uphill."

Haley smiled at his own expense. "So you did." He turned to Lean. "Where are they?"

"They left a short time after Mr. Miller." Lean glanced nervously at Harry.

"Then we'll have a look around."

"I'm afraid that won't be possible," said Lean.

Haley directed Mendoza up the stairs and Steiner into the kitchen.

"No!" screamed Edgar Lean. He grabbed Mendoza by the sleeve. No stranger had been on the second floor of Brisbane Cottage in twenty years.

Haley put a hand on Lean's shoulder. "Relax, old man. We know the truth, and we're here to protect it."

"He's going upstairs. He can't do that." Lean seemed almost dazed.

When she saw Ken Steiner's scarred face, Mrs. Lean screamed and ran through the dining room. "Edgar! Edgar! Help!" She stopped short.

"Good evening, Mrs. Lean." Haley introduced himself.

"He went upstairs, Mary," Lean said to his wife. "He really should not have done that."

Mendoza was already coming down. "Nothing up there, except a shortwave in the attic. I busted it."

"Good." Haley sent Mendoza out to look around the grounds.

"This just isn't done," said Lean. The invasion of the second floor had completely unnerved him. "When Mr. MacGregor hears about this, my job will be . . . ."

"It's all right, Edgar," said Cal gently. "He'll understand."

"But he won't," responded Lean.

Haley looked at Bannister. "That's right. He won't, because he's dead."

Bannister's head snapped around.

"You're the only one in this little group who doesn't know that," said Haley, "and yet you're the one who discovered it."

Cal looked at Harry, who nodded. It was true. Haley turned and walked into the massive living room. With its woodwork, its leather furnishing, and its stuffed-animal trophies, it looked like the Bavarian hunting lodge of a Nazi prince.

Haley pulled off his gloves by the fireplace. "You got us finger-prints on a beer bottle, then the photographs, Cal, and they were all we needed. We'd gotten his fingerprints from FBI security clearance files, and we knew from medical records that the old man had a laparotomy scar on his belly."

"Which my photos didn't show?" Call Bannister scowled, trying to hide his shock.

Haley shook his head. "Without you, Cal, John Meade would have been able to swallow up Lawrence/Sunshine Productions and spit Vaughn Lawrence into the toilet."

Steiner returned to the room. "Nothing on the first floor or in the cellar."

Haley turned to Lean. "Do you have a snowmobile?"

"Yes, sir. Two of them."

Haley ordered him to give Steiner the keys, then he sent Stei-ner outside to join Mendoza. He turned back to Bannister and folded his arms across his chest. "Knowing that Andrew Mac-Gregor was an imposter, Vaughn Lawrence was able to fight off Meade's corporate raid and force him to the bargaining table in-stead. An unorthodox way to win a battle, but you use whatever weapons you have." Haley slapped Cal on the shoulder. "Well done."

"Thank you, sir." Cal Bannister felt a little shot of pride. He had been able to affect things beyond this island after all. He was not powerless. But then, he thought, what did his power matter if the peace of this place was destroyed.

The wind drove the snow against the windows. Haley looked outside. One of the snowmobile headlights was moving back and forth beside the house.

"I don't know why you're protecting them, Harry. We're going to find them, blizzard or not. They're not going to get off this island."

Mrs. Lean looked at her husband. "What does this mean, Edgar?"

"The young people are going to die."

She brought her hands to her mouth.

"Before I kill anybody," said Cal, "I'd like to know why I'm doin' it."

Haley looked at him. "For you, it's simple. If they get off this island alive, the whole world finds out what's been covered up here, and they'll reopen the case of Darrow's death. If they disappear between here and New York, there'll be fewer questions for you, for the gentlemen who've known all along that MacGregor is dead, and for the MacGregor/Lawrence Cable Broadcasting System."

The sound of the snowmobiles was receding. They were widening their circle. One seemed to be moving southeast, toward Cutter's Point, the other north toward the carriage paths where Lean had hidden the car.

"What does any of this matter to me or the Leans?" asked Harry. "Why should we let you kill two innocent people?"

"They're not innocent," answered Haley with sudden anger. "They're here to destroy the myth."

"I'm a lobsterman," grunted Harry. "I don't believe in myths."

"That's not what Meade told us, Harry. He said that when MacGregor dropped dead out on the terrace one summer afternoon, you realized you'd be willing to do anything to help keep the old boy alive to the rest of the world."

For a time, Harry did not speak, then he looked at Cal, who still stood in the archway between foyer and living room, as though frozen there by shock.

"MacGregor was always on the right side whenever there was a fight to protect this island," said Harry. "He loved it as much as any man I ever knew, and his name still means power when we have to stop a nuclear dump or some big developer."

"His name still means power," Haley agreed. "MacGregor just snaps his fingers and keeps the modern world at bay. We need that power as much as you do, Harry."

Cal shook his head. "You blamed me for bringin' trouble here, Harry, when it was you all along."

"You may be right," answered Harry.

One of the snowmobiles was returning. The wail of the engine grew louder until it was in front of the house. Johnny Mendoza rushed into the foyer. He was covered in a thick layer of snow.

"I found their car."

"What kind?"

"A Volvo."

Haley looked at the others.

Jeanne Darrow and James Whiting had reached the flat of Rumrunner's Bulge, but they could not hear the ocean or see any of the cottages. The wind was still howling from the northeast and pounding against the quarry rocks.

High above them, on Cutter's Point, a snowmobile was skimming through the pines, looking for tracks.

Whiting and Jeanne were wearing their skis now, and the travel was not quite as exhausting. But their feet were freezing, and their uncovered faces were numb from the cold.

Whiting continued to monitor himself for signs of hypothermia. Do you feel uncontrollable chills? Are you disoriented? As long as he could ask himself the question, he thought, he was all right.

Suddenly, they burst out of the woods. The deep blackness became a shade brighter. But in the open, without the trees to obstruct it, the wind whipped the snow even more viciously.

The left side of Jeanne's face felt raw and pitted. She thought that by now most of the flesh must have been torn away.

They kicked across the little clearing, and Whiting realized they were in somebody's backyard. He saw a small cottage with its windows boarded, its shutters latched, its screen doors nailed shut.

They skied to the end of the cottage, where it offered them some protection from the wind, and they crouched down to rest.

"Whiting," said Jeanne between gulps of air. "We have to stop!"

"No!" he shouted. "It's the wrong cottage."

"I can't go much farther."

"Neither can I, but we have to try to find Knudsen's. It's the only guarantee that we'll get off this island." He turned the left side of his face to the wind. "C'mon . . ."

"Jim . . ."

"Yeah?"

"We should be someplace with our feet up in front of a fire, drinking beer."

He turned again and began to kick toward the southeast. Every few strokes, he looked over his shoulder to make sure she was close behind him. If she fell, he might not hear her call in the wind.

They kicked and glided across clearings, through backyards, past boarded cottages, across roads that seemed to lead nowhere. They moved through the blizzard for fifteen or twenty minutes before Whiting stopped abruptly.

"What's wrong?" shouted Jeanne.

Whiting put a hand over his left ear. "Listen!"

He could hear a new sound, a roar pitched just a tone lower than the wind: the ocean crashing against the island's granite lip. He turned to Jeanne and smiled, although his face was so cold it did not move.

"We're almost there."

They lunged through another stand of pines and the roar grew louder. For an instant, Whiting thought he smelled wood smoke. He told himself his mind was playing tricks. Then, up ahead, where the roar of the ocean was loudest, he saw light. It was like a flower, a golden yellow center surrounded by dancing petals of white.

They skied through the brush, past a rainhouse, a corrugated plastic A-frame roof above a concrete collecting trough, to the crest of a small rise. Below them, in a clearing, was the cottage.

"I thought this place was deserted," shouted Jeanne.

"The lobsterman said we might see a light."

The little cottage was half-covered in snowdrifts already. A snowmobile was parked beside it. Scraggly pines stretched out on either side and shook violently in the wind. Beyond them, an almost palpable blackness roared and hurled itself against the rocks. They had reached the ocean.

Whiting and Jeanne kicked off their skis. They slid down the little grade and ran across the clearing, keeping out of the beam of light that slanted through the window in the cottage door. They moved close enough to read the name *Knudsen* on the little plate beside the bell.

They peered in, looking down a narrow hallway. It was a tiny place, bathroom on the left of the entrance, bedroom on the right, the illuminated living area beyond.

A young woman appeared. She walked toward the door and turned into the bedroom. A light came on, and its glow fell out onto the snow. She bent down, then stood again with a baby in her arms. The baby was crying, but Whiting and Jeanne could not hear it for the sound of the wind and the ocean.

The woman turned and called into the living room.

James Whiting could see her face now, and he felt a chill. He knew her. He looked at Jeanne. Her face, half-covered in snow, held no expression. Her eyes were wide, fixed.

The woman inside called again. She was smiling. She seemed happy. A man appeared. He was tall, bearded, wearing a heavy lumberjack's shirt. He casually threw an arm around her. They talked for a moment about the baby, then he kissed them both.

"Oh, my God," said Jeanne.

Whiting looked at her.

"It's Roger."

39

On Cutter's Point, Ken Steiner turned off the snowmobile, let the gas fumes dissipate, and smelled wood smoke. It was rising from the land at the base of the cliff. But Rumrunner's Bulge was supposed to be deserted.

He started the snowmobile and turned back toward the house.

James Whiting pounded on the door of the little cottage, and the lights in the bedroom went off.

Jeanne Darrow was still crouched in the snow, frozen into position by the cold and, now, by the shock. But somewhere in her mind, she had expected it.

Whiting banged again. He saw the man's silhouette move out of the bedroom, down the little hall, to the living area. Then, the lights in the rest of the house went off. The outdoor light above the door flashed on and a powerful floodlight on the corner of the house illuminated the clearing.

Whiting looked at Jeanne. She was gazing up at the glare, like a primitive creature driven by the storm to a place she ordinarily avoided.

Then the door swung open. The black beard looked strange, alien, because the blue eyes were so familiar. For seven hours of video tape, they had gazed out at James Whiting, or gazed with him through the television window. Now they peered suspiciously, and the barrel of a pump-action shotgun protruded from behind the door.

In the bitter cold and harsh, glaring light, Whiting could not tell what he was feeling. He had traveled three thousand miles to find the legacy of this man, and instead, he had found the man himself. For two weeks, James Whiting's life had been wrapped in the fabric of this man's existence, and now, the man stood in front of him.

The blue eyes shifted from Whiting to the woman crouched in

the snow. They narrowed for a moment, then they opened wide.

"You!" exclaimed Roger Darrow.

Slowly, Jeanne stood. Her left side was white, coated with snow. Her gaze was steady, wide-eyed. She saw her dead husband step out of the darkness and stand beneath the light. He moved his lips, repeating what he had just said, but she could not hear him.

He moved through the little circle of incandescence. His beard began to turn white with snow. He stopped a few feet from where she stood. He stared as if he did not feel the cold or the snow or the wind lashing him.

Like a spirit, she thought, an apparition.

He shouted at her. "What are you doing here? How did you find me?"The words blowing past her were real. He was real. The wind screamed around her.

"Dammit!" Len Haley slammed his hand on Andrew Mac-Gregor's desk. "You told me Rumrunner's Bulge was deserted, Harry."

"It is," said Ellie Miller.

The little group at Brisbane Cottage had grown. Len Haley had sent Bannister and Mendoza down the road to bring back Ellie Miller and Lanie Bannister. Even in the four-wheel drive, the short trip had been nasty, and it would worsen before the night ended.

Lanie was in the kitchen, helping Mary Lean prepare a meal. Johnny Mendoza was half-asleep on the sofa, with a new dose of Percodan moving through his system. Ken Steiner, just back from Cutter's Point, was melting on the carpet. Cal Bannister studied the map on the library table. Ellie and Harry Miller sat on the sofa. Edgar Lean dusted and fussed.

"Are you sure?" demanded Haley.

"Wouldn't say so if I wasn't," answered Harry.

"Well," said Haley. "Where's the wood smoke coming from?"

"Wood, prob'ly."

Haley stared at Harry for a count of five, just long enough to signal his annoyance. Harry pulled out his pipe and began to pack it as though he didn't give a damn.

"Harry, I don't believe you."

"Suit yourself." Harry got up and walked over to the fireplace.

He struck a match. It didn't light. He tried another one.

"Wet matches, Harry?" Haley flashed across the room and pinned Harry to the mantel.

Ellie Miller gasped.

"I hate to see a man suck a dry pipe," growled Haley. His cigarette lighter appeared in his hand. The flame jumped three or four inches into the air. "And I hate to see a man suck a dry tit, which is what I get the feeling I'm doing talking to you."

He brought the flame close to Harry's chin. "Let's both stop suckin'."

Harry chewed on his pipe and watched the flame move toward the tip of his nose. "You missed the bowl."

"Where are they, Harry?"

"You got me."

"Damn right I do," said Haley. "And I'm gonna burn your nose off. Where are they?"

"Please, mister," pleaded Ellie. "Leave him alone."

"Your wife is worried, Harry."

Harry said nothing.

Cal Bannister realized that Harry would not crack. "He doesn't know, Lieutenant."

"Yes, he does." Haley's cigarette lighter was closer to Harry's nose. "Maybe a nostril instead of the tip. Burn the inside. That way, you'll have no scar."

"Got plenty already."

"If they went to the northeast, they'll freeze to death in the woods," said Cal, "or fall into one of the old quarries and die."

"That would be just fine." Haley brought the lighter close enough that one of Harry's nose hairs singed.

Ellie Miller flew at Haley, but Steiner grabbed her.

"They didn't pass us on the road," continued Cal. "They couldn't."

"Right." Haley kept his eyes on Harry. He was going to break this old man.

Harry looked away from the flame and watched Cal. His gaze made Cal feel guilty, but Cal continued to speak. "Which means that we should just head for Rumrunner's Bulge."

"Good idea," answered Haley. "You tell us it's a good idea, too, Harry."

Harry looked down at the flame. "You won't be the first off

islanders to waste your time on Rumrunner's Bulge. 'Cept you'll be stupider than most, 'cause you'll be doin' it in the dead of winter."

Haley raised the flame to Harry's nose again. "And who else is on Rumrunner's Bulge?"

"Miranda Blake," blurted Ellie, "and her—her baby. She moved over before her baby was born to be near the doctor."

"What about her husband?" asked Cal. He had lied to Haley once. He decided not to lie again.

Harry looked angrily at Cal.

"What's wrong, Harry?" asked Haley. "She must have a husband. Or do you think she got pregnant with an eighteen-pound lobster?"

Ken Steiner laughed.

Edgar Lean came into the room. He seemed to be growing more frail as the evening continued. On this one night, the house had been invaded by more strangers than he had seen here in more than thirty years. "Uh . . . my wife and Mrs. Bannister have put out the buffet supper."

"It'll have to wait," said Haley.

"Yes, sir."

Len Haley looked at Harry. "Do you have a snowmobile?"

Harry nodded. Haley demanded the key, then turned to Cal, who was standing by the map. "We'll get Harry's, then yours."

"My Bronco should make it," said Cal.

Haley shook his head. "More mobility on snowmobiles."

"Don't go, Cal," said Harry.

"Be quiet, Harry," warned Len Haley.

"He's going to ask you to kill Miranda Blake and her husband, too."

"Shut up," said Haley. "Miranda Blake is like the rest of you. She has too much to lose if the world discovers that there's no Andrew MacGregor."

"Don't do it, Cal," Harry repeated.

"It's my job, Harry."

"You don't have to do it." Harry paused. He was working on Cal, trying to save Cal and the people on Rumrunner's Bulge. "Did you rig the *Fog Lady* to explode, Cal?"

Cal looked at Len Haley, then back to Harry. "No," he said very softly. "But Roger Darrow still died on the boat."

"No, he didn't."

"What?" said Haley. "What is this?"

Cal Bannister sank slowly into a chair.

"Roger Darrow is still alive, Cal. He's the guy with the big black beard who lives with Miranda," explained Harry.

"I don't believe it," snapped Haley. He turned to Cal. "What the hell happened?"

Cal shrugged. He almost smiled. He had killed no one.

"C'mon, then," said Haley. "We'll let you finish the job."

"You don't have to go," said Harry. "You're a damn good lobsterman and guilty of nothin'."

"He's guilty of plenty," said Haley. "And besides. He's in my unit."

Then Haley instructed Steiner to pull the distributors out of the vehicles at the house. He told Mendoza to disconnect the radio in the kitchen and the C.B.s in the trucks. Haley's men went out.

Lanie Bannister was wiping her hands on a towel as she came into the library.

"Let's go, Cal," ordered Haley, and he began to button his vest.

"Go where?" said Lanie.

"Tell her, Cal," said Harry.

Len Haley turned to Lanie. "He's fulfilling the last clause of the contract that brought him here."

"Standard clause," grunted Harry. "It calls for him to kill two or three people."

"Oh, shit," Lanie slumped against the door and dropped the towel.

A gust of wind slammed into the house and the windowpanes rattled.

"He made a contract with the man who saved his life and saw him through hell on earth." Haley spoke directly to Cal. "Without me, you'd have none of what you've got now. You're part of the unit, Cal. Don't desert."

Cal looked at Haley, then at his wife. He chewed on the inside of his cheek and listened to the wind outside. Then he stood and zipped his parka. "This is my last job."

"Shit," said Lanie again.

"I'm sorry, babe," Cal started for the door.

Harry banged his pipe in his hand. "I don't make mistakes about folks too often," he said to Ellie.

Cal stopped and turned.

"There's a first time for everything," said Haley, before Cal could respond. Then he pulled on his gloves. "Now, you folks have a nice big storm raging out there, and you've got woods and ocean and granite cliffs all around you. There's no place to go, and not much to do but sit here and stay cozy and think about what Andrew MacGregor means to all of us."

"He means nothin' to me," said Lanie angrily.

"Maybe," said Haley, "but these other people have all conspired to keep alive a man they knew was dead. In the process, they have defrauded every person that MacGregor has done business with since he died."

Haley walked over to Harry. "And we should not forget what Cal Bannister means to you."

"If he's a murderer, he means nothin' to me."

Haley crouched down, so that his face was close to Harry's. "I get the feelin' you like him a lot, Harry. And if we do a real neat job, you might be willin' to look the other way. It won't be the first time you've done it."

Cal's eyes met Harry's, then Cal turned to his wife. She shook her head and started to speak, but Cal hurried out, followed by Len Haley. For a few moments, no one in the library moved. Then Lanie went into the living room and looked out the front windows. Two snowmobiles, each carrying a pair of riders, growled away and disappeared into the blizzard.

Lanie watched the snow swirling about, and then she sensed Ellie Miller standing beside her. "He won't do it, Ellie. I just know it."

Ellie placed a hand on Lanie's shoulder. "He's a good man. I can see that."

"And I'd like to count on him helpin' them people down there." Harry was putting on his pea coat as he crossed the living room, "But I don't think we can. That lieutenant's got too much of a hold."

Edgar Lean came through the foyer. He was carrying cross-country skis, boots, and poles. "Here's the old man's gear."

Ellie watched Harry sit down and put on the boots. "What on earth are you doing?"

"I'll ski around Cutter's Point to the top of the old quarry, then climb down."

"Harry! You're seventy-two years old."

"That's right, and I ain't skied since Hector was a pup."

"You ain't climbed the quarry in longer than that. You'll kill yourself on them rocks."

Harry pretended to ignore his wife. "What's the temperature out, Eddie?"

"Fifteen degrees."

"Harry," Ellie knelt down in front of him. "You can't go. You're an old man."

"I'll go," said Lanie, "I can ski. I can climb."

Ellie stood. "Nobody goes. Those people down there knew what they were getting themselves into when they came here. They have a gun. Roger Darrow has one. They'll hear the snowmobiles."

"Not until the snowmobiles are on top of them." Harry stood and pulled on his gloves.

"The snowmobiles will get there before you," said Ellie.

"It'll take them forty minutes by the time they go down to Bannister's and back," answered Harry.

"What if they go in, two to a machine?"

"Too dangerous on rough terrain," responded Harry. "They'll use four. If I'm lucky, I can get down there ahead of them."

"You can't climb a quarry in a blizzard," said Ellie.

"When we was boys, me and Andy MacGregor knew every toehold and shortcut there was. The minute I start down, I'll know just where I am." Harry put on his checkered hat. "Most of it's pretty easy goin'."

"Please, Harry." The words caught in Ellie's throat. "We don't owe these people anything."

Harry threw his arms around his wife. "If it wasn't for all of us tryin' to keep MacGregor alive, none of this would've ever happened. That Haley's right. We caused this trouble."

Lean took a flare gun and a box of flares from the front-hall closet. "We use it for signaling, Harry. It's the only weapon in the house."

Harry took the gun, shouldered the skis, and stepped out into the blizzard.

James Whiting looked at the ocean crashing on the flat table of granite six or eight feet in front of the cottage. Picture windows lined the south side of the house, and outdoor floodlights were shining into the storm in every direction. In summer, thought Whiting, the view from the windows must have been serene and peaceful: the blue thoroughfare, white sailboats, and the ferry bringing visitors to the island. Tonight, the little cottage felt warm and safe, but it perched on the edge of chaos.

It was an old place, with rough pine paneling, a low ceiling, and wide-board pine floors. The living area was about ten by twenty feet. At one end were table and chairs and a door that led onto a little patio. A bookcase ran along the south wall, beneath the windows. There were chairs scattered across the room, old hard-backed rockers, and overstuffed wing chairs with floral-print slipcovers. Three chairs were clustered around the wood stove in the corner. On the arm of one, beneath a reading light, a copy of *The History of the Decline and Fall of the Roman Empire* lay open. Good reading, thought Whiting, for a long winter's night. A tape deck in the corner played a piece by Mendelssohn that tried to compete with the wind. Whiting thought something by Musorgski would have been more appropriate.

Jeanne Darrow sat on a rocker by the wood stove, her boots and socks on the floor. She had wrapped herself tightly in a blanket and was rocking back and forth, staring at the flames. She said nothing. She looked at no one.

Miranda Blake sat next to Jeanne. Her blond hair was pulled straight back in a single braid. She wore a wool turtleneck, jeans, no makeup. She needed none, thought Whiting, because she was beautiful. Her delft-blue eyes had mesmerized Hollywood from the day she arrived, and they had lured Roger Darrow to this island. Now, she rocked silently, studied Jeanne Darrow, and glanced from time to time at the baby.

Roger Darrow appeared from the little galley kitchen off the entry hall. He was carrying a tray with four large cups of tea. He crouched beside Jeanne and offered her a cup.

She waved it away.

"It'll help warm you, Jeannie," said Roger Darrow gently.

She stared at him with wide, unblinking eyes. "Why?"

Without responding, Darrow stood. He gave Miranda a cup of tea and offered one to Whiting.

Whiting looked at the tea, then at Darrow. "That's a fair question she just asked."

"I have an even better one," he responded. "Why did you come here? Why couldn't you just let me rest in peace?"

Outside, the wind and the ocean seemed to howl at each other.

"Because of the video tapes," answered Whiting. "Because of the kidney."

"In that order?"

Whiting shook his head.

Darrow put down the tray. "You're here, living out my life, because one of my kidneys kept you alive. Is that it?"

Whiting did not respond. His reasons were now more complex than that.

"Well," Darrow turned around, raised his shirt, and showed Whiting his back. "I still have both kidneys, mister. It wasn't me."

Whiting looked at him and said, "Since you're half-undressed, why not drop your drawers and show us your ass, too?"

Darrow straightened up, frowned, then smiled, as though deciding to be amused by the irreverence. "Very good. Very good."

James Whiting had chased this man's shadow for three thousand miles. He was still numbed by the shock of meeting him, especially after the shock of meeting Andrew MacGregor, and yet he had found cause for sarcasm. He thought that was a good sign. "You still haven't answered your wife's question."

" 'Why?' is not an easy one. It's too vague. Too general."

Jeanne looked up. "I'll make it easier. Why did you let me travel three thousand miles to mourn you in that hospital when it wasn't even your body?"

Darrow knelt beside her chair. "You weren't supposed to come to Maine. It was all arranged. All you were supposed to do was sign the papers and hand over the dental records. It wasn't legal, but Andrew MacGregor could arrange anything."

"Even when he was dead?" said Whiting.

Darrow stood. "You know about that ?"

"Until now, I was speculating."

"Ben Little has been impersonating MacGregor for fifteen years. Whenever MacGregor wanted to distract the press, Little did the job. When MacGregor died, Ben Little just stepped in. He lives like a king, everybody but Harry Miller and the household staff scrape and bow to him. It's not a bad life for an old actor."

"As long as he gets to spout Shakespeare all day long?"

"He *is* a bit senile. That's a problem. But some men are so important that you can't let them die."

"That's what I've been thinking for the last few weeks," said Whiting.

Darrow smiled. Even behind the beard, it was the seductive, boyish grin that made people like him immediately. James Whiting, however, found it easy to resist.

"Thanks," said Darrow, "but there's other people you should just let die, even when they're alive. People who aren't noble and haven't made any great sacrifices. People who haven't given up their kidneys for the future of man and who haven't hesitated to give up their wives if they thought they found something better."

Jeanne raised her head and looked at Miranda. The two women stared at each other for several seconds, and then, as if by mutual consent, Jeanne looked back at the fire and Miranda at her baby.

Whiting sat down by the wood stove. He wrapped himself in a blanket and sipped the tea. He should have been exhausted. He had driven his body to the limit of its endurance. He knew that he had been endangering his fragile health for the last two weeks. But he was still running on mental energy, and his body had given him a megadose of adrenalin in the last twelve hours.

"You've wasted your time coming here to thank me," said Darrow. "If you want to thank someone, it's the surgical resident who ran routine tests on the victim of a boating accident."

Whiting sipped his tea and wondered if he wanted to hear this. Yes. He wanted the truth.

"The surgical resident," Darrow continued, "put two type-A-positive kidneys onto the computer before the chief of surgery could intervene. The accident victim was wearing my name tag. He was built like me, and he weighed about the same, but his real name was Izzy Jackson. He lived alone, out on one of the Pentecost Islands." Darrow smiled at Whiting, as though he were about to enjoy a joke at Whiting's expense. "Izzy was the local idiot."

Whiting felt a chill, but it was not the truth that brought it. This truth, he realized, no longer mattered. He pulled his chair closer to the fire. "So there was no transplant planned?"

"Oh, yes," answered Darrow. "You may have gotten his kidney, but from the moment the *Fog Lady* blew up, I was supposed to get his life-style." Darrow walked over and stood behind Miranda. "With one prominent exception."

Miranda glanced up at him. A diffident little smile danced across her face.

Jeanne looked at Miranda and the baby. She still could not believe what she was seeing.

The ocean crashed so high on the granite that the little cottage shook and a sheet of spray snapped against the windows.

Three snowmobiles had pulled up in front of Cal Bannister's house. Len Haley, Ken Steiner, and Johnny Mendoza were standing in the garage, studying the map of the island. Cal came out carrying a shotgun, a stocking cap for Haley, and three pairs of snow goggles.

"We'll go down Rumrunner's Road, then branch out and check as many of the cottages as we can," said Haley.

"And keep smellin' for the wood smoke," added Steiner.

"You won't smell much," said Haley. "We'll be goin' in upwind. Just watch for the lights." He looked at Cal. "You got any suggestions?"

"I'd say we head for the waterfront. That's where Harry would've sent them."

Haley nodded. "And remember"—he raised an index finger and pointed it at each of them—"we don't harm Miranda Blake. She's John Meade's sister. The other three are dead."

Cal pushed the snowmobile out of his garage.

"All right, Cal," shouted Haley, "you lead the way."

Cal pulled on his goggles and swung his leg over the machine. Len Haley ran his hand along the shiny metal nose of the snowmobile. "Mechanized warfare," he said. "The First Air Cav comin' in low over the treetops. You remember?"

Cal nodded.

"We were the best," shouted Haley above the roar of wind and machine. "The best."

"Then how come we lost?" answered Cal.

Len Haley's face contorted with anger. "We didn't lose. We were betrayed."

Haley turned away and climbed onto his snowmobile. Cal Bannister squeezed the throttle and roared off.

Harry Miller had reached the top of the quarry. Two hundred feet below him was Rumrunner's Bulge. But he could see only a few feet in the thick, blowing snow. His flashlight was tied to one of his wrists. He aimed it downward. The first drop was about six feet.

The quarry, as he remembered it, was like a giant flight of stairs. Some of the steps were six or eight feet high, others, where small pieces had been cut, just a few feet; some were wide and flat, others provided no more than a toehold. There were slag heaps and the remnants of rockslides, and beneath the snow, mosses and grass and a few bits of scrub clung to the granite. It was a treacherous climb on a sunny day.

The wind gusted and the snow pockmarked his face. If the climb didn't kill him, he thought, the weather would. Already he felt cold and tired, and he was only halfway there. He considered turning back. Then the smell of wood smoke rose up from below. He tied the skis and poles together and dropped them onto the next ledge. Then he lay on his stomach in the snow, grabbed the branches of a pine that overhung the cliff, and lowered himself until his arms would no longer hold him. He let go and dropped gently into a pile of snow. And he knew now that there would be no turning back. He was going all the way to the bottom, because he could never climb back to the top.

He got up and pointed the flashlight around. The next step was easy—two feet. It was followed by a three-foot drop and a succession of easy steps.

For a few minutes, as he descended from rock to rock, Harry Miller did not feel quite so old. Then the bitter, black wind rose again. Its claws grabbed him and threw him back against the granite.

"Why couldn't you just come back and say you wanted a divorce?" Jeanne was still staring at the fire, speaking in a monotone that was becoming almost hypnotic. Even the baby was silent at the sound. "Why did you have to do *this* to me? Why couldn't you have the courage to face me?"

Darrow was standing by the window. The others were still clustered by the fire.

"I was a wreck when I got here. I'd started out to show how

intertwined we all are, from one coast to the other. And when I got here, all I could see were the knots that we've tied ourselves in, the whole damn society."

"What a philosopher," said Whiting sarcastically. He looked at Jeanne and rolled his eyes. He was trying to deflate Darrow, hoping to snap Jeanne out of her shock.

She glanced at Whiting and turned her eyes back to the fire, as though she were not even listening.

Then Roger Darrow's bulk was in front of Whiting, and he was leaning forward, so that his face was in Whiting's line of vision. "You think hard on what you've seen in the last couple of weeks, mister, and you might just want to join me up here," The voice was low and harsh. "But there's no more room." He went back to the windows and began to pace.

Physically, he bore little resemblance to the Roger Darrow of the video tapes. His hair and beard had grown. His body had expanded from seven months of hard work in the outdoors. He had added several inches to his chest and shoulders. His complexion was ruddy, his hands large and callused. But the eyes, thought Whiting, were still angry, still uncertain, the eyes that had looked into the camera in Washington Square seven months earlier.

"It may be nice up here in the summer," said Whiting, "But I'm not interested in running away to any islands."

Darrow stopped pacing. "I didn't run away from anything . . . except—"

"The video tapes," interrupted Whiting. "You knew what was going on back there, even with Tom Sylbert. Didn't you?"

For a moment, Roger Darrow stared at James Whiting. His body was turned to the window, but his head was pivoted about so that he looked like some bearded bird of prey studying his next meal. Then he smiled. Then he began to laugh. He jammed his hands into his pockets. He walked across the room. He flopped onto the little couch behind Miranda's rocker. And he laughed.

Miranda watched him out of the corner of her eye.

Whiting glanced from Darrow to Jeanne, who would not look at her husband.

And Roger Darrow continued to laugh.

Then, as if shaken awake, Jeanne Darrow looked up from the flames and said, in a voice that was clear and sharp, "Stop performing, Roger."

Darrow's laughing stopped at once.

"Good girl," said Whiting.

"He used to pull this crap back in L.A. when I tried to get him to talk things through."

Whiting knew that she was going to fight back. It was all that mattered to him.

"Somehow, I guess I expected this." Jeanne looked at her husband. "A real Darrow stunt. This belongs in one of your scripts."

Darrow swung his legs off the sofa, so that his face was just over Miranda's shoulder. "If the American people are stupid enough to let television tell them who to elect to public office, then the hell with them." He got up and stalked to the windows again.

Jeanne looked at Miranda. "I'm talking about us, and he's talking about politics. I hope he listens better when you talk to him."

Miranda tried to smile. It was not the mocking expression of the mistress meeting the wife. It seemed more like an offer of friendship or understanding. The baby stirred in Miranda's arms and she murmured to it. Jeanne turned her eyes again to the fire.

"Politics," said Darrow softly, from the other side of the room, "has always been more interesting than us. Once the western wing of the party lost Tom Sylbert, thanks to some dirty polling, they would naturally turn to another westerner."

"Just as I thought," said Jeanne, feigning interest.

"That was the theory," said Darrow, turning to Whiting. "Then buy all the franchises you can to influence Iowa caucuses and New Hampshire primaries. Get yourself a Jesus Jumper like Billy Singer, screaming hellfire and damnation and taking the name of the Lord in vain in the heartland . . ."

"I think you may be wrong about Singer," said Whiting.

". . . and get men like Lyle Guise to go into the tank for you when there's no other way to win a key franchise."

"I *know* you're wrong about Lyle Guise," said Whiting.

"He let me down."

"Jesus Christ!" Whiting jumped up and went over to Darrow. "He didn't let you down. You act like the whole world revolves around you. Lyle Guise wasn't even thinking of you. He was just doing what he could to get by and get ahead, and it was all legal."

"You let *him* down, Roger," said Jeanne. "You never gave him a chance to set things straight."

"He was like a father to me," said Darrow softly. "Sometimes

394it's hard to be objective when someone you love disappoints you."

"I know," answered Jeanne.

Cal Bannister was functioning on automatic. He was a part of the machine beneath him. He had adjusted his body to its movement, his ears to its noise, his eyes to the beam of light that danced twenty feet ahead of him. He had passed Harry Miller's house and was leading the group on to Rumrunner's Bulge. He planned to head straight for the waterfront cottages, which were about a mile away.

The shotgun strapped to the seat behind him was simply another piece of machinery. He had not yet wondered if he would use it.

The wind-chill factor on the moving snowmobile was far below zero, but Len Haley did not feel the cold. He was on a mission, clearing out a final pocket of resistance. Ahead of him, the point man's taillight glowed red. Behind him, the headlights of the squadron kept pace.

Harry Miller knew that he was in trouble. From the sound of the wind and the distance he had traveled, he guessed that he was about forty feet from the ground, but somehow, he had worked himself onto a little granite platform from which there was no further descent. He aimed his light over the front of the platform but could not see bottom. To the left was a fifteen-foot drop, to the right, ten or a bit more.

He had already tried to climb back to the level above, but he had slipped and fallen twice.

He could just see the lights of the cottage now, about a hundred yards from the base of the cliff, and he could hear the ocean slamming against the granite. He cocked his head and lifted his earlap, but he did not hear the snowmobiles.

He decided to gamble. He took out the flare gun and loaded a shot. If the snowmobiles were deep in the pine cover, they might not see the flare, and it would alert the people in the cottage. He aimed the gun straight out over the water and fired.

For a moment, the granite cliffs were bathed in an unearthly white glow. The wind was blowing so powerfully that it sent the

magnesium shot streaking straight back at the cliff and smashed
it into the rocks high above Harry's head. But the few seconds of
light had shown him a way down.

He jammed the flare gun into his pocket and moved toward
the right edge of the precipice. He pulled out his flashlight and
examined the rock face again. There were several little outcroppings. He kicked the snow from the first one and stepped onto it.

"Did you see lightning?" asked Whiting.

"No. You just saw God," laughed Darrow, "or Billy Singer."

"No," said Whiting. "He's on the cable."

The conversation had quieted. They looked like two couples
seated around the fire after dinner. The shock had worn off, or
settled in, for all of them. The Mendelssohn tape had run out. The
wind and water were wailing together. The baby was sleeping.
Jeanne was staring at the fire. Miranda was rocking softly. Darrow
was talking.

"Some people, like that Professor Wyler, believe there's video
danger everywhere. According to them, you shouldn't even tune
in the box because the radiation'll give you cancer. Or the programming will rot your brain. Or if you buy one of MacGregor's
electronic condos, you'll be turning yourself body and soul over to
Big Brother, who already affects the way you think simply by the
programs he offers you. And once he has that respond box in your
house, he's got you, because we all need someone to talk to, even
if all we get to say is 'Yes,' 'No', or, 'Send me the twenty-nine
ninety-five set of bakeware.' "

The fire was beginning to die down. Darrow fed another log
through the door of the wood stove.

"Do you believe that's what's happening?" asked Whiting.

"Why do you think I'm here?"

"I'm not ready to believe that people are that gullible," responded Whiting. "Especially after the last two weeks. And I think
people should know what's been going on with MacGregor and
Vaughn Lawrence and their new cable system."

"Fine," said Darrow. "Go tell them. But leave me out of it,
because I don't really give a damn anymore."

The new log began to crackle in the stove. Whiting glanced at
it, then asked. "Do you think it's worth getting shot for?"

"Nothing's worth that, except your family and your turf."

"Well, there are people on this island tonight who'd like to kill us. They may be the same ones who wanted to kill you."

"Except," said Jeanne, "that you chose to kill yourself for them."

Darrow looked at Jeanne for a long time, then at Miranda. Then he rose and walked to the window. "Maybe I did run away from the truth, Jeanne. Maybe I should have divorced you, instead of just disappearing, but I had to run when I did. I needed something to make me believe in the beauty and order of things again, something commensurate with our capacity for wonder."

Whiting recognized a line from *The Great Gatsby*. He looked at Miranda. "Does he always go around quoting famous writers?"

"No." Miranda smiled. "Sometimes he quotes himself."

Darrow glared at her for a moment. But she smiled sweetly at him, as though she knew exactly how to soothe him.

Then Darrow turned to Whiting. The confusion left his eyes, if only momentarily. "You and I are a lot alike. You were dying one way, and I was dying another, but we both got a second chance. You have the wonders of medicine and technology to thank. And I have this. . . ."

He went over to the corner of the room and threw the switches that turned off all the lights, inside and out. The room went black, except for the orange glow from the wood stove. Miranda stopped rocking. Jeanne turned and looked at her husband. Whiting's eyes tracked Darrow as he began to pace in front of the windows. Outside, the wind blew, the snow swirled, the ocean pounded on the granite, its spray covered the glass.

Jeanne glanced at Whiting. "Remember the fisherman in the painting, the loner with his face to the wind? That's him behind me looking for a breeze."

Darrow spoke, oblivious to the sarcasm. "I have the fresh green breast of the New World. The darkest, stormiest night of the winter. Summer sunrises and the autumn flight of the Canada geese. And this year, I'll have the spring with a new little baby."

James Whiting wanted to laugh, to poke through the pretension and craziness that he saw in Roger Darrow. But he could not. Roger Darrow believed what he was saying, and he had thrown away everything to embrace his new world. Whatever he had done to his wife, his decision had taken a perverted kind of courage, and what he was saying was not really that crazy, after all.

Whiting watched Darrow stalk across the room and kneel again beside Jeanne, so that his face, half in shadow, was close to his widow's. "We had lost our capacity for wonder," he said, "in each other and in our world."

"I hadn't lost it."

He stared at her for a moment. His look turned cold, merciless, as though he were remembering some old hurt or seeking a reason to drive her away once more. "You grew up in L.A. Maybe you never had it to lose."

She looked at the fire again. She was past hurting.

Darrow turned to Whiting. "We're still the same men we always were, but now we see the world with clearer eyes. So let's get on with our lives. I'll do what I can to get you both off this island. But I don't have the courage or the fear to go back."

The baby began to stir in Miranda's arms.

Jeanne looked at her husband. "I have just two more questions," she said. "First of all, why did they let you live with what you found out?"

"Seven months ago, John Meade didn't agree with Vaughn Lawrence's tactics for dealing with a problem like me." Darrow looked down at Miranda. "Beyond that, he wanted to make his sister happy. And so did I."

Miranda opened her shirt and gave her breast to the baby.

"What's the other question?" asked Darrow.

"Who's the father?"

40

al Bannister stopped his snowmobile about a hundred yards from the waterfront, at a fork in the road. The left fork led to the water. The right fork curved back inland, past several cottages, and ended where the land began to rise. He ran a glove across the goggles and tried to wipe away the snow.

Haley pulled up beside him, and the other two snowmobiles slowed to an idle.

"Which way?" Haley demanded.

Cal Bannister did not know that he would point to the wrong fork. He had not planned it. But he did it.

"Do you have any idea which cottage they'll be in?" shouted Haley.

Bannister shook his head. "No. We just look for the light, and if we don't see any, we have to check every house."

Haley nodded once. "OK. When we get close, we stop and go in on foot."

Bannister squeezed the throttle and started off. This diversion would do no one any good, he thought. Soon enough, he would have to admit his mistake. Then they would turn back to the waterfront and kill the people they had come to kill, and Len Haley would question Cal Bannister's loyalty.

Harry Miller felt the bitter wind at the back of his neck, but he could not turn up his collar. He was standing on a little, snow-covered outcropping, about a foot square, and the fingers of both hands were dug into the crevice in front of him.

He had slipped a moment before and nearly fallen. Now, his legs were weak. His left knee was trembling, and he had nowhere to go. In the brief burn of the flare, he had seen toeholds that weren't there and others that seemed much closer than they were.

He hunched up his shoulders and tried to shield his neck. The

wind grabbed him and shook him. He was too old for this. He felt
feeble and trapped. The wind stopped gusting. He relaxed his grip.
He carefully removed his right hand from the crevice and shined
the flashlight down. He was six feet from the next level and clinging like a piece of moss to the quarry face.

Then, in the momentary lull, he heard the snowmobiles baying
through the woods like a pack of mechanized dogs. The sound
was off to his right, and it seemed to be moving toward the cliffs
instead of the water. But they had reached the bulge and were
drawing near their prey.

He looked over his left shoulder again, toward the ocean, but
he could no longer see lights around Knudsen's cottage. A power
loss in the storm? A precaution? Or had the snowmobiles done
their work while Harry was concentrating on his descent? No. He
had to get down there and warn them. It was his fault that they
were there.

He released his grip on the crevice but held his body tight
against the wall. He wanted to move quickly, before the wind
started to howl again. He slid his body carefully into a crouching
position. His right cheek was covered in snow and probably frostbitten. He brought his knees forward and knelt on the little square
of granite.

He placed his hands on the side of the platform, so that he was
now pulled into a little ball. He lowered one leg, then the other,
putting all his weight on his arms and chest. He wanted to let
himself down until he could release his grip and drop gently into
the snow below. But he knew the moment he started that he didn't
have the strength. His arms gave way under the weight of his
body. He slipped off the precipice and spun downward. When he
landed, his left ankle folded under him. He bellowed and the pain
flashed through him.

He cursed, and the pain got worse. He fell forward, on his
hands and knees. The wind whipped around him. He ground his
teeth to keep from shouting again, but the pain clung tight to his
ankle and burned like a blinding light between his eyes.

He lay there for several minutes, trying to drive the pain out of
his head, hoping that the cold and shock would relieve it, and
knowing that if he stayed there, even for a short time, he would
freeze to death. When he decided that the pain had eased as much
as it would, he slid his hand carefully down his leg until he felt the

swelling around the top of his boot. He moved his hand a fraction more and felt the bone pushing out against his sock.

He had to get down, no matter what was left of his ankle. He picked up his skis, which he had dropped from above, and positioned them as crutches. He hobbled on them to the edge of the precipice, aimed his flashlight, and looked down.

From what he could see, the worst of the climb was over. He sat down on the edge of the rock, swung his legs out, dug the skis into the snow on the precipice two feet below, and stood carefully. He looked around, hobbled to the side of the next precipice, and repeated the process to the bottom of the cliff, where he slid down into a snowbank and felt bitter cold close around his testicles. At least they felt something, he thought.

The bitter gale had abated, and in spite of the pain, Harry thought he could hobble the final hundred yards to the cottage. He had to move fast, because off to his left, he could hear the snowmobiles. They were still moving away, but he knew that they would turn toward the water before long.

Harry dug the skis into the snow a few feet ahead of him, then swung his good leg forward. He did it again, and then a third time. As he began to move away from the quarry wall, the snow became deeper. Then, suddenly, the wind gusted again, cold and vicious. He put his head down and waited for it to recede. It did not. It blew hard, then harder. It screamed all around him, as though it had determined to keep him from reaching the cottage in time. Then it swept up the snow already on the ground and mixed it with the snow swirling in the air. It rolled the cloud of snow up the granite face and spun it back down onto Harry Miller, enveloping him in bitter, black cold.

He had lived on the island all of his life. He had seen the ocean when it towered ten feet above his boat. He had seen the sky when it was the color of death. But until now, he had known nothing of the island. Beneath the greens and blues of summer, when white sailboats dotted the thoroughfare, beneath the reds and browns of autumn, when the lobsters tasted sweetest, beneath the springtime yellow, when daffodils bloomed in island window boxes, at the center of it all spun the hellish black cloud that consumed him now.

And the wind would not retreat. It blew so violently that it sucked the air out of the center of the cloud. Then its claws sank deep in Harry Miller's chest and shook him viciously.

He fell to his knees. The pain in his chest was unlike anything he had ever felt. The claws of the wind were tearing him apart. He forgot the pain in his ankle. He fell forward in the blackness. The wind released its grip and subsided, but the pain would not.

And somewhere to his left, the snowmobiles were baying. They had turned toward the sea.

Harry had reached into his pocket, pulled out the flare gun, and loaded. He knew that he would never reach the cottage.

"You'd better not be fuckin' with us, Cal," shouted Len Haley.

"I took the wrong goddamn fork, that's all."

The four snowmobiles idled beside the cottage that Whiting had stumbled upon when he came out of the woods an hour earlier. The four drivers were coated white with snow.

"We'll just have to go back," shouted Bannister.

"Hey, look!" Johnny Mendoza pointed into the snow with his flashlight. There were ski tracks by the side of the cottage, where the snow had not reached to fill them.

At the base of the cliff, Harry Miller aimed the flare gun into the air and pulled the trigger.

"There it is again," shouted Whiting.

"And it's not lightning," said Darrow.

The world outside was suddenly illuminated in the dancing, flickering glare. The pines were shaking about in mad, wind-whipped spasms. The snow was swirling. The black ocean reflected little chips of light into the cottage.

Roger Darrow threw on his parka and grabbed his shotgun.

"Flare," shouted Haley. "Two o'clock."

Three of the men on the snowmobiles had seen flares before, hanging like giant phosphorous bugs above the burning jungle, flares glowing in hell. They were not surprised to see one now, streaking across the Easter's Haven sky and shattering against the granite cliff.

Rumrunner's Bulge was in darkness once more.

"Distance?" snapped Haley to Steiner.

"Five hundred and eighty meters," came the reply.

Haley looked at Bannister. "You get one more chance. Do we go straight through the woods or back out to the road?"

Cal tried to visualize the layout of the cottages on the waterfront. Then he told Haley to get out his map.

Another star shell burst above the water.

"Over here. Over . . ." Harry had fired another flare because he could not shout above the wind. In its fleeting light, he had seen Roger Darrow running toward him.

The wind was driving the flare across the sky and into the cliff. Harry's world went black once more. The wind gusted and the claws sank again into his chest.

"Harry!" Roger Darrow knelt beside him. He cradled Harry's head in his arms.

Harry felt warm breath on his cheek. "Watch out," Harry gasped. "Four snow—four snowmobiles, here to kill—" Harry felt the wind subsiding. "Listen . . ."

Darrow raised his head, and he heard them distant but distinct. One was moving to the west. One was straight ahead. And two were swinging away to the east.

A strange, strangled cry rose out of Harry Miller. Roger Darrow picked him up, threw him over his shoulder, and ran back to the house.

He kicked open the door and looked at Jeanne.

"I assume you know CPR."

She said, "Of course."

Darrow laid Harry down on the floor. "Then do it."

Harry was unconscious, and his face was turning blue.

Darrow looked at Miranda. "Four men are coming to kill these two and maybe us."

Miranda clutched her baby. "Oh, God."

Darrow took a rifle out of the closet and looked at Whiting. "Have you ever used a gun?"

Whiting shook his head.

"You've never used one either," Jeanne glanced up as she

pumped Harry's chest.

"I've learned." Darrow gave Whiting his shotgun and shouldered the rifle.

In the kitchen, the teakettle began to whistle.

"How do you fuel your stove?" asked Whiting.

"Propane gas," said Darrow.

"Is the tank outside?"

"Yeah."

"Wouldn't a bullet make it explode?"

"It might."

"Maybe we'd better get out of here."

Darrow thought for a moment, then he said to Miranda, "Wrap up the baby and take her to the shed." He turned to Whiting. "Turn on all the outside lights, then put these on." He took a yellow slicker and rubber bib overalls from the closet and flung them at Whiting. "You're going to get wet."

"I think this lobsterman's dead," said Jeanne. "I can't get a pulse."

"Don't give up," answered her husband.

"I never give up until it's absolutely hopeless."

She finished fifteen shots to his chest. She pushed his head back, held his nose, put her mouth on his, and gave him two breaths.

Darrow crouched down beside her. "Grab a blanket and your coat." He lifted Harry and threw him over his shoulder again.

Outside, a wide circle of light now glowed around the cottage.

At the west side of the cottage, Darrow kicked open the door to the shed, a small, dark space, about six by six, with fishing rods, garden tools, a lobster trap, a grappling hook, and a gaff hanging on the wall. Darrow laid Harry down on the floor, and Jeanne laid the blanket over him. Immediately, she found the xiphoid process bone, measured to the correct spot above the diaphragm, and began to pump Harry's blood through him.

For a moment, she and Roger were crouched together beside the body.

"I'm sorry," said Roger. He leaned forward and kissed her.

The sound of the snowmobiles was growing louder. Darrow stood. He looked at her, and his eyes filled with tears.

"Be careful," she said.

He turned and went out. She brought her mouth down onto

Miranda appeared with the baby in her arms. She sank into a corner and wrapped herself in the blankets.

They could hear the snowmobiles coming.

"I feel so helpless," said Miranda. "We should be doing something."

"Your baby needs you," answered Jeanne.

Miranda nodded. "And we can't lose Harry."

Jeanne continued to pump.

Darrow's last instruction to Whiting was "Try to get just one."

Then Darrow turned and ran up toward the rainhouse. Whiting went toward the water.

About fifteen feet from the back of the cottage, a V-shaped crevice had been cut into the island's granite lip. Whiting dropped himself into the notch, as Darrow had instructed. The crevice protected him completely on three sides. He could stand and fire the shotgun without exposing more than the top of his head. And a few feet behind him, the ocean smashed against the rocks. Its spray flew over him and its wash churned around his feet. His position was impregnable, unless a wave washed him away.

The cottage was just to his left, and beyond it he could see the shed where Jeanne Darrow and Miranda Blake huddled together. About twenty feet in front of Whiting, resting against the side of the cottage, was the propane tank and, beyond that, the clearing. Fifty feet above the clearing, in the trees and darkness, was the rainhouse wehre Roger Darrow crouched behind a three-foot wall and waited.

Whiting was in the crevice to draw fire, to shoot at anything that moved, and then duck. Or if the snowmobiles drove straight into the clearing, he and Darrow could have a cross fire. He hunkered down out of the wind and wrapped his hand around the stock of the shotgun. He was going to use it. He was going to survive. He had traveled three thousand miles to keep something of Roger Darrow alive. Now, he and Darrow were fighting for their lives together.

Roger Darrow was crouched behind the retaining wall in the rainhouse. He had a clear shot at anything that entered the circle of light around the cottage, and he could hear the four snowmo-

biles advancing through the storm. Two seemed to be moving
around to his right. Two were working on his left.

In the shed, Miranda Blake clung tight to her baby and counted the rhythm with Jeanne. Fifteen pumps. Two breaths. Fifteen pumps. Two breaths. It seemed to be working. Jeanne saw movement beneath Harry's eyelids, and she could feel a faint pulse.

Fifteen pumps. Two breaths.

Cal Bannister and Ken Steiner were speeding down Rumrunner's Road. Len Haley and Johnny Mendoza were cutting through the woods, close to the path that James Whiting and Jeanne Darrow had taken earlier.

Bannister had drawn the suicide assignment from Haley. While the other three moved in on foot to close off any escape routes, Cal was to drive his snowmobile into the clearing with three options: move through, reconnoiter, and draw fire; stop, knock on the door, and ask innocently if the flares were an alarm signal; or try to blow up the propane tank and flush them out of the cottage.

Bannister stopped at the beginning of the driveway, which branched off Rumrunner's Road and ran about two hundred feet to Knudsen's cottage. He sent Steiner on to the cul-de-sac at the end of the road, where two cottages overlooked the ocean.

He saw Steiner's snowmobile stop and the taillight go out. He looked at his watch. It would take Steiner five minutes to cut through the woods along the water's edge and appear by the side of Knudsen's cottage. After that, he would wait a few minutes more, to be sure that the others were in position. Then he would go in. His worry was Mendoza, a civilian who might not wait for the rest of the unit to take their places.

Roger Darrow had listened to the snowmobiles as, one by one, their engines stopped. Now, he heard only a single snowmobile idling off to his left.

At the water's edge, James Whiting crouched in his crevice

and waited. He had seen the beam of a headlight in his crevice and waited. He had seen the beam of a headlight shoot out over the water, then disappear. Now, he was looking down the rocky shorefront, expecting the driver to materialize from the shadows.

Roger Darrow shivered. The four inches of ice that covered the floor of the rainhouse were drawing all the heat out of his body. He looked behind him, into the darkness. It would be easy to disappear into the shadows, he thought.

He cocked the bolt-action rifle and looked through the scope.

A wave crashed high on the rocks and hit Whiting in the back. The ocean was rising, grabbing at him, trying to pull him out of his crevice. It came up around his knees, then receded. Another wave hit and the water rose again.

He looked to his right. As far as he could see into the woods beyond the light, nothing was moving. He looked to his left, toward the back of the house and the shed, and through the snow, he thought he saw something move.

He raised his head for a better view, and another wave slammed into the little crevice.

In the shd, Jeanne Darrow had stopped the CPR. She was cradling Harry Miller's head in her arms. His eyes were open and he was breathing on his own, but he seemed disoriented.

"It'll be all right, Mr. Miller. We'll have you out of here in a few minutes," she was saying.

The baby had started to cry. Miranda was opening her jacket to give it her breast.

A shadow passed in front of the shed window. Jeanne looked up. The shadow stopped. It turned and looked in.

"Oh, my God," whispered Jeanne.

The orange ski mask and the crimson blood stain. The creature had followed them from New York.

The shed window shattered.

Miranda screamed.

Glass flew.

A .22-caliber machine pistol thrust through the broken glass.
A wail of pain, terror, and helplessness rose out of Harry Miller.
Jeanne leaped up and pulled the grabbling hook from the wall.

Whiting saw the man at the shed window. He raised the shotgun, then he saw someone inside. He could not fire.
He vaulted out of the crevice and ran toward the shed.

Darrow saw Whiting bursting from the hole and disappearing behind the cottage. He cursed Whiting for leaving his gun behind. Then he saw the man by the shed, and he realized where Whiting was going.
Darrow raised his rifle scope to his eye and saw the orange ski mask. The creature had his arm inside the window and someone was wrestling with him. Darrow aimed and squeezed off one shot. High and to the left.
Jeanne had struck blindly with the grappling hook, tearing into the creature's arm and knocking the gun out of its hand. Now she was trying to pull back and strike again. But the creature held tight to her arm and the hook.
On the floor beneath Jeanne, Miranda was groping about for the pistol while clinging to her baby.

Roger Darrow held his eye to the scope and squeezed the trigger again. The bullet hit the corner of the shed and the wood splintered.

Whiting slipped on the rocks in front of the picture window. A wave crashed a few feet below him. Then he was up, running again, fifteen feet from the shed. He could see Jeanne's face on the other side of the window.
Then he felt a sharp, stinging pain in his right thigh and enough impact to knock him down. Two holes, front and back, had been torn in the yellow rain pants.
He heard a ricochet and saw an explosion of rock a few feet from his face. He looked back along the shorefront.

A man with a gun was rushing out of the woods near the crevice. It was Steiner. He dropped to one knee and fired at Whiting again. The bullet exploded in the rock a few inches from Whiting's head.

Darrow saw Steiner, who was now crouching in the open, holding the pistol with both hands and taking aim on James Whiting. He laid the cross hairs over Steiner's chest.

Whiting jumped up and tried to run toward the shed. As he moved, he glanced over his shoulder and saw Steiner's arm following him. Then it was flying upward, and Steiner was spinning crazily down the rocks and into the water.

Cal Bannister looked at his watch. It was time to move. He squeezed the throttle and the snowmobile shot up the driveway.

In the rainhouse, Roger Darrow slammed the bolt and drove another shell into the chamber. He felt the same sense of self-reliance he had known when he dropped his first deer and dressed it for Miranda. He swung the scope onto the shed again and saw the man in the ski mask stagger back, the grappling hook in his hand, as though someone inside had shot him. Then Whiting appeared from behind the cottage and leaped onto his back.

The snowmobile roared into the clearing. Darrow swung the scope into the rider, then remembered Harry Miller's instructions for hunting duck: Lead the target so that it flies into the bullet.

He squeezed off another round. The snow exploded in front of the snowmobile. He cursed.

Because of the noise of the machine beneath him, Cal Bannister did not hear the shots. He pulled up in front of the door, and a bullet shattered the windowpane beside his head. He dropped to his belly behind the snowmobile and looked around.

James Whiting gouged at the face beneath the ski mask, and the creature bellowed in agony.

Jeanne rushed out of the shed, holding the pistol that Miranda had given her. She had shot the creature once in the gut, but he was still standing.

He swung the grappling hook at her and knocked the pistol out of her hand. It went skittering down the rocks and into the water. Then he flipped himself forward and bucked Whiting off his back.

Whiting spun once and slammed hard onto the rocks. For a moment, he didn't know where he was. His ears were ringing. His mind was blank. His eyes were focused on the lattice work detail of the wooden lobster trap nailed to the side of the cottage.

The orange ski mask exploded into his consciousness.

He heard Jeanne shriek.

He saw the grappling hook lifting high into the air. Then it was hurtling downward, its prongs aimed at his throat.

He rolled away and the prongs chipped into the rock where his head had been. Sparks flew.

The hook rose into the air again.

Jeanne grabbed a shovel from the shed and flung it at the ski mask.

Cal Bannister shot out the light over the door. Then he blasted the floodlights at either corner of the house. The clearing in front of the cottage was in darkness now, although floodlights still illuminated the sides and the rear.

Someone in the rainhouse had him pinned. If he ran to his right, he would find no cover. He had to go to his left and dive behind the tool shed.

Darrow kept his rifle trained on the clearing in front of the cottage. He was concentrating on Bannister because he could no longer see Whiting and he didn't know where the fourth rider had gone. Hoping to hit the gas tank, he pushed another round into the chamber and fired at the snowmobile.

Len Haley was moving through the knee-deep snow in the darkness behind the rainhouse. He had heard the shots. Then, through the blowing snow, he had seen the muzzle flash of Darrow's rifle.

James Whiting and the man in the ski mask were stalking each other in a tight, threatening circle. The man in the ski mask held the grappling hook by its rope, and he was starting to swing it above his head like a lariat. Whiting had picked up the shovel and he held it so that the could knock the grappling hook away.

Both men were weak from blood loss and exhaustion.

A bullet tore through the padded seat of the snowmobile and smashed into the house.

Cal Bannister decided to move. He rose to his knees and fired three quick blasts toward the rainhouse. Then, in a low crouch, he ran and rolled to the side of the cottage. He jumped around the corner and flattened himself against the building. Behind him, he saw Mendoza and another man facing each other.

Then Jeanne Darrow looked out of the shed and startled him. He raised the shotgun. She screamed and dropped to the floor.

Roger Darrow cursed and rammed another round into the chamber. He had lost his target. He knew there was a fourth gunman, but he had to help them down at the shed. He slid five more bullets into the rifle and stood.

Len Haley had reached the rear of the rainhouse. He raised his gun.

The grappling hook flew at Whiting and dug into his left shoulder. He screamed.

Then the man in the ski mask pulled out a switchblade and came at Whiting. But he was not moving fast. He was gut-shot.

Whiting raised the shovel with his right hand and smashed it against the orange ski mask. The man fell backward. A black wave rose out of the thoroughfare and hit the rocks. The spray flew into Whiting's eyes. The salt stung. He wiped his eyes, and the man in the ski mask was gone.

Whiting pulled the grappling hook out of his arm and staggered back toward the shed. The pain was excruciating. At the
corner of the cottage, he fell to his knees and slumped forward
onto his forearms.

A shadow fell across the rock in front of him. Whiting looked
up at a pair of goggles, a Greenland parka, and the muzzle of a
twelve-gauge shotgun. He had no more strength to run or fight.

Roger Darrow swung his left leg over the retaining wall, and a
shot hit him in the back. It stood him up straight. A second shot
entered a few inches to the right, cutting into the aortic artery and
exiting through the stomach. But Roger Darrow did not go down.
He was strong, and the retaining wall helped hold him up.

Len Haley cautiously crossed the rainhouse floor. Darrow
turned. Haley saw Darrow's eyes and he knew that Darrow was
done. He lowered his pistol.

Roger Darrow placed a hand on the hole in his stomach and
swung his right leg over the wall. This hasn't happened, he was
saying to himself. This hasn't happened to me. This is someone
else.

He managed to stagger several feet before he stumbled into
the snow and fell forward, tumbling down the little wooded slope
into the clearing.

Whiting waited for the shotgun to explode in his face. Cal
Bannister slowly brought the muzzle past Whiting's ear and
leaned the gun against the house. He knelt down and propped
Whiting against the cottage.

The snow was still swirling, and Whiting was shivering from
blood loss and cold. Cal pulled off Whiting's yellow slicker and
looked at the arm. The flesh had been torn like a piece of venison.
Cal took off his belt and tied it as a tourniquet above the wound.
Then he took off his parka and wrapped it around Whiting.

"Roger!"

Jeanne Darrow saw her husband first. He was struggling
through the snow, trying to move toward the light at the shed. He

fell to his knees, then got up.

Jeanne rushed out to him.

Len Haley watched from the rainouse until he saw Cal Bannister appear in front of the shed and knew it was safe to go down. He leaped over the little wall and followed the trail of blood in the snow.

Miranda came out of the shed, still clutching her baby. She screamed and ran toward Darrow.

Cal Bannister looked in and saw Harry lying there, fighting for breath. He knelt beside the old man.

Harry turned his head away. "You'll have to shoot me," he rasped.

"No, Harry. I'm here to help you." Cal gathered the blanket around Harry's neck. "You're going to be all right."

The old man looked up at Cal. "What about the others?"

"They'll be all right."

Harry smiled.

Roger Darrow staggered. He did not feel the snow driving against his face, but he felt a bitter cold deep inside and a pain that rose and fell each time his heart pumped blood.

Jeanne reached him first, halfway across the clearing. She said his name. He look at her as though he did not recognize her.

She placed her hand on his and moved it inside. She felt the warm blood soaking into his parka. It was too dark to see the wound. "You'll be all right," she murmured. "You'll be all right."

Miranda called to him. His eyes shifted. Jeanne looked over her shoulder. Miranda was running out of the light, a shadow crying for Jeanne Darrow's husband.

Darrow managed to say Miranda's name in response. Then he pulled away from Jeanne and tried to walk toward the light. He took two steps and collapsed in the snow.

Jeanne knelt beside him and turned him over.

Darrow looked up at her. "Miranda?"

"Jeanne."

She thought she saw him smile. Then Miranda was beside them.

Roger looked at her. "Miranda?"

She answered and took his hand. Jeanne's eyes filled with tears. Miranda brought her face close to Darrow's. "I love you, Roger."   A spasm shook his body and he gulped for air. "Let me

—let me see the baby," he said.

The tears were rolling down Miranda's cheeks. She took the afghan from the baby's face and brought the child close to Darrow. "She loves you," Miranda was talking more loudly now because the wind was starting to swirl again. "She loves you, and I love you."

"We love you, Roger," said Jeanne.

Darrow turned his head. Another spasm gripped his body and he screamed in pain. Jeanne put her hands on his shoulders, but after a moment, the spasm stopped. Then the air rushed out of him in a single burst.

"Roger?" shouted Miranda. "Roger?"

Jeanne felt the tears coursing down her cheeks. The snow was turning Darrow's beard and eyebrows white. Miranda called his name again. Then a cry rose out of her and her body began to shake.

Haley walked past them, toward Cal Bannister, who was coming out of the shed.

"Is the other guy dead?" Haley asked.

Bannister shook his head. Haley gave him a dissatisfied look, then stepped around the corner of the cottage. Whiting looked up when he saw Haley approach with the pistol in his hand. Haley raised it to fire, then lowered it again.

"Answer me just one thing," Haley said. "Why did you throw me that chain?"

Whiting shook his head. He was too weak to speak or move. He closed his eyes and waited for the last sound he would hear.

Cal Bannister stepped around the corner of the cottage. "Lieutenant!" he called.

Haley turned.

Cal Bannister raised the shotgun and blew Len Haley into the darkness.

41

Roger Darrow's body was transported three days later to Saint Matthew's Island, where a burial service was held in the late afternoon. His coffin was placed on a little promontory that looked west across the Easter's Haven Thoroughfare. From there, a path wound through the woods and up to the little house where Roger Darrow and Miranda Blake had spent all but the last week of her pregnancy and the first week of her baby's life. It was the only house on the island.

The afternoon was bright and cold. A foot and a half of snow lay on the ground, and a space had been shoveled clear so that the mourners could stand by the coffin. After the service, Roger Darrow's body would be taken back to the tiny mausoleum at the Easter's Haven graveyard, where he would lay with the other casualties of winter until the earth thawed in the spring.

Miranda stood by the coffin and held baby Elizabeth in her arms. She wore her hair down around her face, as Roger Darrow had liked it, and she had dressed as he had always preferred her, in black turtleneck, gold hoop earings, jeans, boots, and down vest.

She had dressed him in his favorite clothes, a pair of comfortable jeans, a checkered wool shirt, and a cable-knit sweater.

Ellie Miller, wearing a black overcoat, stood on one side of Miranda. Jeanne Darrow, still wearing jeans and down parka, stood on the other side. James Whiting was next to Jeanne, his left arm wrapped in heavy bandages and sling, his right arm holding a crutch.

The Leans stood on the other side of the coffin, along with the Webb brothers, who knew Roger Darrow as Jim Carraway, the name he had taken after the explosion of the *Fog Lady*.

Beside them, Cal and Lanie Bannister stood with arms linked. From time to time, Cal's eyes shifted from the coffin to Ellie Miller. When she finally looked at him, he tried to convey his thanks with his eyes. She nodded, as though she understood, and looked back at the coffin.

On the morning after the storm, from his hospital bed, Harry Miller had said to Ellie, "He came here to get away from men like that lieutenant character. I've only ever known him to be a fair man, loyal to a fault. We should give him another chance."

Ellie had convinced the others—the Leans, Jeanne Darrow, James Whiting, and with some difficulty, Miranda Blake—that they should all stand behind Cal Bannister. He had done whatever he could to sever his link and make his peace with the past. He deserved a fresh chance at the future.

The only Hollywood people invited, Harriet Sears and Howard Rudermann, stood at the foot of the coffin, arm in arm, as though they were holding each other up.

No reporters had been permitted on Saint Matthew's Island, although four boatloads of photographers were ploughing back and forth in the choppy waters off the promontory, and a helicopter from a Boston television station buzzed the site several times.

The news media, however, had descended on Easter's Haven as soon as the blizzard broke and the story began to trickle down from Maine. Reporters had also descended on Vaughn Lawrence in Hollywood, John Meade in New York, the Reverend Billy Singer in Ohio, and an old character actor who for many years had exploited his resemblance to one of the most powerful men of the century.

The news media had been joined by the SEC, the FCC, and the FBI. The newly organized MacGregor/Lawrence Broadcasting System and its primary officers, John Meade and Vaughn Lawrence, within a day or so faced a variety of charges, including violation of antitrust laws and conspiracy to violate federal election laws.

Billy Singer told reporters that he had been deceived by John Meade and Vaughn Lawrence, and he was convincing enough that both the FBI and James Whiting believed him.

When reporters asked Ben Little to speak about his life as Andrew MacGregor, he declined. " 'Now my charms are all o'erthrown' " he said. " 'And what strength I have's my own,/Which is most faint . . . As you from crimes would pardoned be,/Let your

44 indulgence set me free.' "

On the morning that the story broke, before his name had become associated with it, Congressman Reuben Merrill appeared on the "Today" show and called for new legislation to govern the use of two-way interactive television broadcasting and polling. By that afternoon, spot polls were revealing that Reuben Merrill was no longer a serious candidate for the presidency, if, indeed, he ever had been. The following day, the FBI appeared at his office.

Meanwhile, former Wyoming Senator Thomas Sylbert hurried to Washington from the Caribbean. Acting like of offspring of an avenging angel and a wronged lover, he swooped into a press conference at the Madison Hotel, told the assembled media that he had been right about MacGregor Communications from the start, and announced that he was running for the presidency. In Last Vegas, he became a four-to-one underdog to win the nomination.

In Iowa, Lyle and Betty Guise cried again for Roger Darrow. Then Lyle called the Des Moines office of the Associated Press and said he would like to tell his part of the national story. The next day, a blizzard closed the Iowa airports and kept Lyle and Betty Guise from the funeral.

On Saint Matthew's Island, Reverend Forbison read from the Book of Genesis, verses 1 to ———, the Twenty-third Psalm, and, from Luke, verses ——— to ———, the Lilies of the Field. They were, explained Forbison, Roger Darrow's favorite readings.

Then Forbison asked if anyone had anything else to say.

After a moment of silence, Howard Rudermann raised his eyes and spoke. "If I should get a notion to jump into the ocean,/'Taint nobody's business if I do."

Jeanne recognized the opening lines of one of Roger Darrow's favorite songs. She smiled. Then Harriet smiled. And after a moment, Miranda smiled as well.

The Reverend Forbison stared for a moment, uncertain if Rudermann was mocking the ceremony or performing part of some Hollywood tribal rite. Then he smiled and thanked Rudermann for his comments.

The group recited the Lord's Prayer and sang, as far as they could, "Rock of Ages," which had been Reverend Forbison's suggestion. Then they covered the coffin in pine boughs that Miranda and Jeanne had cut on the island and went back through the woods to the house.

The island people walked together. Harriet walked between Jeanne and Miranda. Howard Rudermann dropped to the back of the group to accompany Whiting, who hobbled along on his crutch.

"Are you worried?" whispered Whiting after they had fallen behind by a few paces.

Rudermann shrugged. "I never knew enough to know what was happening. I had a lot of suspicions, but they had great taste in programming. I turned the last frame of 'A New Flag' last week."

Whiting stopped. His leg was stinging and his shoulder was throbbing. "That's all you care about, isn't it, Howard? Getting the film in the can."

The end of Rudermann's nose and the tips of his ears were red. The steam shooting from his nostrils made him look like an angry bull in an old Warner's cartoon. "How can you say that when I tried to warn you in New York?"

Whiting shook his head. "I never got the call, Howard. It wasn't enough. You worked with the people who killed your partner. Or did you know he was alive?"

Rudermann shook his head. "Only Harriet knew, and it was a terrible burden for her. All I knew was that Miranda lived here. I suspected something, but I couldn't afford to make waves."

"You told me to be careful because things weren't always the way they seemed, but you never bothered to find out the way things really were. If you had, Roger Darrow might still be alive."

"Damn you, Whiting," said Rudermann softly. "Damn you for asking me to be more than I am. I did the best that I could."

"You ignored the truth, Howard, because you were frightened."

"Yeah, well, Roger found out everything, and look what it got him."

"Until the end, Roger was running away, too. He wanted to lose himself somewhere between the past and the present, but every morning, when he walked out his front door, he looked across the thoroughfare and he saw that thing," Whiting gestured toward Easter's Haven.

The television antenna rose out of the pines like the structural steel framework of something new and unknown. The red lights flashed and blinked without pattern or pace.

"He couldn't escape that thing, Howard, even here, and he couldn't compromise with it, either."

"That's what it's all about," said Rudermann after a time. "Compromise."

Whiting shook his head. "Howard, I like you, but sometimes, you try to make things too easy on yourself."

The islanders had gone into the house. Miranda, Harriet, and Jeanne were standing on the porch. Looking down the path, they could see Whiting and Rudermann, the coffin beneath its pine boughs, and the sun turning red as it slipped toward the horizon.

It was getting colder.

"Shall we go in?" said Jeanne.

"In a minute," answered Miranda. "But first, there's something I want to give you." She pulled a video cassette from her inside pocket. "It's the last tape. It was shot the morning the *Fog Lady* exploded. It may help you to understand."

Jeanne took the cassette, weighed it in her hands, and shoved it into her pocket. Then she looked at Harriet. "Will it explain why my best friend lied to me?"

Harried looked down.

"When did you know?" asked Jeanne, trying to control her anger.

"The night of the funeral. Roger called me, suffering what he said was a fit of posthumous depression. I was so shocked I almost threw up."

"I know the feeling," said Jeanne coldly.

Harried started to reach out, then her hand stopped, as though she feared that Jeanne would reject her touch. "He told me what he'd done, and he said he wasn't sure he'd made the right decision."

"Which made me feel terrific," offered Miranda.

"He said his conscience wouldn't let him relax until he knew that there was someone to care for you and help you start a new life. Then he could start his."

Jeanne kept her eyes fixed on the horizon and the setting sun. "Why did you do it, Harriet?"

"Because I loved you, Jeanne." Harriet drew her teeth across her lower lip to keep from crying. "And I'd never stopped loving him."

"It would have been better for all of us if you'd told me the truth."

"No," said Harriet. "If you couldn't be happy together, I wanted you both to have the chance to be happy on your own. I thought I was doing the right thing."

"You weren't," said Jeanne softly.

Harriet put a hand on Jeanne's arm. "Maybe someday, you'll forgive me."

Jeanne turned to Harriet, and after a moment, she smiled. "It may seem hard to believe, but I've had people do worse to me in the last year."

Harriet threw her arms around Jeanne's shoulders and began to cry softly. Miranda put her free arm around Harriet, and the three women stood together until Whiting hobbled up the stairs.

"We're watching the sunset," said Miranda said to him.

Harriet wiped her eyes. "Yes. It's beautiful."

Whiting came to the end of the porch and stood beside Jeanne.

"Hurry up," Harriet shouted to Rudermann, who was still on the path below. "You'll miss the sunset."

"Don't let it start without me!" He ran to the end of the path and up the stairs.

The sun slipped away. The world was bathed for a time in deep red. The trees, the snow, the ocean itself seemed incandescent. The sun had filled them all day with light, and the glow remained after the sun had gone.

"Every night," said Miranda, "we watched the sunset from this spot. And after the winter solstice, Roger would remark every afternoon that the sun was setting a little further north."

Jeanne thrust her hands into her pockets. Her anger at Miranda had subsided. Pity and a sense of shared pain had replaced it, but she felt her resentment rising again. She struggled to put it to rest, then she sensed Whiting beside her. She slipped her hand into his.

"It was our favorite time of day," said Miranda dreamily.

"From the promontory," offered Rudermann, "he'll be able to watch the sunset forever. He'll always have the peace he found here with you in the last eight months."

Jeanne looked at Rudermann as though he had just slapped

her.

"You're wrong, Howard," said Miranda. "He told himself he was happy. He told me the same thing. But last week he said he was thinking of going off by himself to Europe. He was never satisfied."

Jeanne turned to Miranda. "I asked you something in the cabin the other night that you still haven't answered. Who's the father?"

Without hesitating, Miranda said, "Not Roger."

42

It was January, but in Los Angeles, it could have been July. The camellias in front of Jeanne Darrow's house were blooming. The lawn was green. The acacias and palms were covered in foliage.

After two weeks without ventilation, the house smelled stale and stuffy, as it had the first time she walked into the foyer.

Jeanne mixed a gin and tonic in the kitchen. Then she went into the study. She drew the drapes, turned on the television set, and inserted the video cassette into the player.

John Meade is sitting on the terrace beside the library at Brisbane Cottage. The sun is high and bright. His blond hair seems to shine. He wears a green Lacoste chirt and tennis shorts.

Roger Darrow sits beside him. He wears a sweat suit. He is perspiring and looks winded, as though he has just finished jogging.

Edgar Lean enters, carrying a tray with two glasses of orange juice, coffee, and croissants. Lean pours the coffee while the men make small talk about the beautiful weather, the island jogging trails, the tennis match they're planning for later in the afternoon.

"By the way," says Darrow. "Did you hear that bang this morning? It sounded like an explosion."

Meade nods. "A fishing boat."

"Anyone I know?"

Meade shakes his head, then settles back in his chair. "So," he begins. "My sister apparently has told you everything."

Darrow smiles that magnetic grin. "Why you failed to take over Lawrence/Sunshine, why you're merging with them, your political plans, and why Andrew MacGregor bears a striking resemblance to an old actor named Ben Little."

"Are you surprised?"

"I was surprised to find her here. I'd expected that she would

be in New York. I must say I suspected the political stuff."

Meade laughs. "Mr. MacGregor always had tremendous influence in Washington . . ."

"One of the reasons you couldn't let him die?"

"Yes, that and the fact that Miranda and I would lose control of the company if he died. But attempting to secure a national nomination for Reuben Merrill is a relatively recent development. It was my idea, but Vaughn Lawrence took to it immediately."

Meade sips his coffee. Darrow butters a croissant. A gentle breeze rustles in the pines on the bluff behind them.

"Once you think you have the power," says Meade, "you have to try to use it. Otherwise it slips away." He leans forward. "And right now, you're a very powerful man, because of your knowledge."

Darrow looks out at the water. "It's beautiful here."

"Do you intend to use the power?"

Darrow does not respond.

"To use it, you'll have to leave the island, tell the world what we've been doing, and you'll be destroying Miranda along with MacGregor Communications and Vaughn Lawrence."

Darrow stiffens in the chair.

"I have the sense that you'd like to stay here, especially after spending the night on Saint Matthew's Island."

Darrow looks out toward the thoroughfare.

"When you arrived here a few days ago," Meade continues, "you were not well. Already, life here has begun to heal you."

Darrow looks at the water for a long time, then says, "Everything back there just feels like it's coming apart. And when you get here, expecting to find a MacGregor to explain it all for you, you find that he doesn't even exist."

"Oh, he exists . . . somewhere," says Meade. "And his ideas exist. But when you realize that he isn't going to solve your problems and answer your questions, you can pull your life together and get on with it."

Roger Darrow stares at the camera. "This is the first place where I've had a sense of the order of things. Miranda and I sat outside last night and looked up at the Milky Way. We just lay together for hours and watched it pinwheeling across the sky. I haven't done that since I was a kid."

"You can't do it in L.A.," says Meade.

"We . . ." Darrow hesitates. "We made love out there."

Meade smiles, as though he is not surprised or offended.

"We looked at the stars a while longer, and she told me she's pregnant. She told me that the same stuff that made up the stars is inside her." He laughs and shakes his head. "She asked me to be the father."

Meade waits for a moment before speaking. "By day, you see the order of things. By night you see their majesty. And you have the love of a woman who's run away from the complexity and chaos, just like you."

"To find peace." says Darrow enviously.

"No. She'll find peace if you stay." Meade measures out a long pause. "And you'll find death if you leave here."

Darrow frowns.

"Vaughn Lawrence fears you," says Meade, "enough to kill you. Because he knows that MacGregor is dead, he has been able to force the merger of our two companies, on his terms. He does not want the world to know the truth. And you'll tell it if you leave here."

Meade sips his coffee and takes a bite of croissant. Then he carefully wipes the crumbs away from the corners of his mouth.

Darrow leans forward and bounces his legs up and down on the balls of his feet.

"Because of my position in this mess," says Meade, "I have no options but to agree with Lawrence. You however, may have one or two."

"Darrow looks up.

"The explosion you heard this morning?"

Darrow nods.

"It was the Fog Lady, Izzy Jackson's boat. Apparently a complete accident. But you were supposed to be on it."

Darrow's eyes bore into John Meade.

"Izzy Jackson has been taken to MacGregor Hospital and admitted as a John Doe."

"Why?"

"So that you can have the option of a new life. So that your knowledge will not leave this island and probably cause your death. So that my sister can have the man she loves."

"Izzy Jackson becomes Roger Darrow?"

Meade nods. "MacGregor owns the hospital. The county medi-

424 cal examiner owes his job to MacGregor. And the chief of surgery, Dr. Sanderson, would do anything to have his own medical program on cable."

Darrow does not respond, but the idea has caught him.

John Meade senses that Darrow is ready. He puts his hand on Darrow's arm. "You'll sense rhythms here that you'll find noplace else. They'll soothe you and bring you to the understanding of yourself that you've been trying to find for three thousand miles. You'll have the chance to find the simplicity in life again. Very few men ever do. You can cut yourself off from everything, tear out all the terminals that flash green and red in our heads, and live on your own. You've experienced everything else. Experience this, and maybe you'll find the answers that no one can give you, not me, not MacGregor, not anyone."

"Unless it's Miranda?"

Meade nods and smiles. "What about it?"

There is a long pause. Darrow looks across the thoroughare. He runs his hand across the stubble of the beard he had begun to grow. The wind rustles the trees.

"Say no, Roger. Say no." Jeanne's eyes were riveted to the screen. It was as if she thought she could change everything by changing the ending of the last tape.

"Say no," she repeated.

"All right," says Roger Darrow. "I'll do it."

"You fool, Roger," said Jeanne.
The tape ended. Static danced on the screen.

43

The next morning, Dr. Joseph Stanton pronounced James Whiting's kidney to be well and functioning, despite the beating it had taken. He warned Whiting that the transplant was nothing more than a holding action, and he could never again subject it to the kind of beating it had taken in the last few weeks. Whiting said that sometimes he thought most of his life was a holding action, a constant effort to hold body and soul together. He said he intended to sustain the effort, and he promised to take better care of the kidney.

On the ride home from the doctor's, through the familiar potholes of the Fenway and the Back Bay, James Whiting thought about Roger Darrow's holding action, fought on the ancient rocks of Maine. And he thought about his own. Roger Darrow had chosen a place where no compromise with the future could be made. For James Whiting, the compromise had been easy. Medical technology and the kidney of a man named Izzy Jackson had given James Whiting new life. But until he had taken Roger Darrow's last journey, he had forgotten how to live. He had embraced the future in a way that Roger Darrow never could. But until he had crossed Roger Darrow's America, he feared it as much.

And he thought about Jeanne Darrow. She had returned to Los Angeles to fight a small holding action of her own. She needed time to grieve, time to sit by herself and stare at her gardens, and after two weeks at his side, she needed time without Whiting. But she had promised, when they said good-bye, that early some morning, his telephone would ring, he would pick up the reciever, and she would be inviting herself to Boston.

It was ten-thirty when the taxi pulled up in front of Whiting's apartment. As he climbed out, he saw someone he recognized walking down the hill. He paid the cabdriver and hobbled over to the sidewalk.

"Good morning," he said.

"Hi," answered the young woman, and she kept walking.

"You don't recognize me, do you?" said Whiting.

She stopped and looked at him and smiled curiously.

"Your name is Carla Glynn, and you serenaded me just before Christmas."

"Oh, yes." Her smile became more familiar.

"And once before that . . . about eight months ago."

She remembered. She seemed to blush. She had brown hair, a beautiful smile, and in honor of the forty-degree temperature, she was not wearing a hat. She was also about eight months pregnant.

"When is the baby due?"

She patted the bulge beneath her overcoat. "About three weeks."

"Good. Congratulations."

For a few moments, they stood and looked at each other, as people do when they run out of small talk, and each waited uncomfortably for the other to speak.

"Well, I should be going," said Carla. "Take care of your injuries. I trust you didn't get them sneaking into some lady's bedroom."

"I wish I had." Whiting laughed.

She waved and started to leave.

"I hope your baby has a singing voice like her mother's," he said.

"As long as she's healthy."

"As long as she's healthy," he repeated to himself.

He watched her move carefully but gracefully down the hill and did not take his eyes from her until she had reached Charles Street and disappeared around the corner.

He started to go into the apartment, but he realized that something was different. He looked at the sidewalk across the street, then glanced at his watch.

On the day he left for Los Angeles, the sun at noon barely scraped across the rooftops of the houses on Beacon Hill. Now, at midmorning, its rays reached the snowbank on the other side of the street. The snow was melting, and the water was washing down the hill.

Whiting stood on the sidewalk for a time, looking up at the

brightness, feeling the warmth of the sun on the side of his face. Then he heard the muffled sound of a telephone ringing inside the building. It might have been in Dave Douglas's apartment, or it might have been Jeanne Darrow calling him from Los Angeles. He turned and hobbled up the stairs.

Eight weeks of winter remained, but the days were getting longer.

About the Author

WILLIAM MARTIN, a native of Boston, was graduated from Harvard College in 1972. He received his MFA from the University of Southern California, where he was awarded the Hal Wallis Screen Writing Fellowship in 1976.

In 1980, he published his first novel, *Back Bay,* which fast became a best seller, remaining on the *New York Times* best-seller list for a total of fifteen weeks. *Back Bay* was also an alternate selection of the Book of the Month Club and a best seller in paperback with Pocket Books.

William Martin lives in Boston, Massachusetts, with his wife, Christine, and their sons, Billy and Danny.